Witches & warriors & wise women

Other Books You Might Like,
Available from Prospective Press...

Off the Beaten Path 1
Eight Tales of the Paranormal
AN ANTHOLOGY

Off the Beaten Path 2
Eight More Tales of the Paranormal
AN ANTHOLOGY

Off the Beaten Path 3
Eight More Tales of the Paranormal
AN ANTHOLOGY

The Legacies of Arnan series
Draigon Weather • Wing Wind • Long Light • Storm Forge
PAIGE L. CHRISTIE

Amber Witch
REBECCA WYNICK

Sweet Divinity
MEGAN PREWITT KOON

The Would-be Virgin
And Other Tales
SUSAN SURMAN

West Palm Gig
SUSAN SURMAN

Afternoon Sun
SUSAN SURMAN

Prospective Press Presents™

Volume One

Witches
&warriors
wise women

Prospective Press
Winston-Salem

PROSPECTIVE PRESS LLC

1959 Peace Haven Rd #246, Winston-Salem, NC 27106
www.prospectivepress.com

Published in the United States of America by Prospective Press LLC

 TRADEMARK

WITCHES, WARRIORS, AND WISE WOMEN
CONCRETE DREAMS, VOLUME 1

ISBN 978-1-943419-23-4

Printed in the United States of America

Trade Paperback Edition
First Prospective Press printing, June, 2020

The text of this book is typeset in Alegreya
Accent text is typeset in AquilineTwo

Contents

*Welcome
to your
Dreams*

Foreword

Yellow streetlamps slice the damp shadows of a canyon built of asphalt, concrete, glass, and steel. A distant siren wails in counterpoint to the bright pings of the night's last streetcar or the quiet chimes announcing the last crosstown bus. The door to a cellar club opens, shooting a pale gray cloud of cigarette smoke and a blast of raucous music into the dark. The door thuds shut. The faint squelch of a determined tread tramping through the puddles left by a recent rain replaces the frantic gaiety of brass, strings, and drums.

A lone figure crosses a band of sulfurous light. A tan trench coat is belted tight around the figure's waist. A fedora angles over one eye.

This is an iconic image of the modern city: a solitary hero emerging from a low place to battle the demons of the post-industrial dark. If you believe the twentieth-century books and movies that imprinted this vision into our minds, that hero is always male, specifically a white man of a certain class—a paladin of the old European school, his armor only slightly rusted from all that rain.

Come on. This is the twenty-first century. We admitted women hold up half the sky years ago, and we're finally acknowledging what was always there in the primary sources behind our history books. The urban world has always been diverse. Its texture, energy, and achievements are the direct result of people of all ages, races, and gender identities meeting, sharing, and sometimes coming to blows as they strive to better the world for themselves and those they love.

The purpose of the Concrete Dreams series is to celebrate that diversity through urban fantasy anthologies featuring less-heard voices and overlooked heroes. This, the first volume, brings women to the fore with stories of witches solving murders and righting wrongs, warriors battling evil, and wise women finding the truth and settling scores.

It also speaks to the concrete dreams that make up our vision of the modern city itself. Our notion of the city, of towns, villages—of any community people have made for themselves—isn't that of an inert object or an interchangeable set piece. Each community is as much a character in these stories as the people acting upon its stage.

Travel with us now to the Chicago of Jody Lynn Nye's "Seeing the Pattern," where a college-age member of the city's Sandmen's Guild must track a serial rapist through the dreams of his victims. Gail Martin lands us in a "Heap of Trouble" in Charleston, South Carolina, where a clairvoyant antiques dealer and her weaver mage colleague tackle a plague of ghosts tied to the dark history of one of the city's stately homes. J. D. Blackrose's "Poisoned by Sugar" shifts the scene to Cleveland, where a witch fights to save her coffee shop and her freedom from a charge of murder. While in Tucson, Arizona, the guardian of the Jersey Devil and her charge battle to keep a mystically powerful gem from falling into the wrong hands in Paige L. Christie's "A Devil to Help."

Urban fantasy doesn't only exist in the here and now, however. Darin Kennedy's "God Willing and the Creek Don't Rise" tells a tale of Dry Creek, Nevada, on the cusp of the twentieth century, where a witch and a marshal fight to save the souls of a town that doesn't really want her help. Soul saving is a more personal affair for the magical warrior of Nicole Givens Kurtz's "Destroying Angel," who seeks to reclaim her own soul in the frozen north of an entirely different era's arctic camp.

Personal salvation also lies at the heart of "Rowena's Curse," Rebecca Wynick's tale of the penance of crows in present day Asheville, North Carolina. But cities and towns don't always represent salvation. In Alexandra Christian's "Unbroken" the world beyond her characters' mountain hollow is a whited sepulcher, where moonshine and dark magic provide the only hope of justice for a young woman's untimely death. The legacy of cities proves even more complex in Michele Tracy Berger's tale of "Cemetery Sisters," where ghostly sisters from the 1920s threaten the life of a high school senior in a post-apocalyptic near-future town not far from "an old city called Tulsa."

Sometimes the urban landscape is a dream of the life we'll never really live. But as evidenced by the Hamblin, Tennessee, setting of Janet Walden West's "Stalking Horse," concrete dreams and concrete reality can be one and the same. When that happens, be careful of your friends, because the villain isn't always the one you expect.

Neither is the hero. So cinch your belt and tip that fedora lower. Hear the click of high-heeled boots over pavements damp with evening rain. Witches, warriors, and wise women can wear trench coats with the best. Join them now as they traverse the dark and light of the cities that live in our concrete dreams.

—Jean Marie Ward
May, 2020

Seeing the Pattern

Jody Lynn Nye

Teni Nickaboine yawned, throwing her arms up over her head on her bolster bed in the small dorm room in Northwestern University's Chapin Hall. She grinned at her roommate, a dark-skinned African-American girl with a long, slim neck and flat-ironed black hair who was still perched over a textbook at the built-in desk at the end of her bed.

"I've got to be up at five. Can you throw some sand on me, Ayosha?"

Ayosha Gilbert glanced up from her Psychology 101 textbook and grinned back.

"Oh, you," she said. "I'd think you going swimming for two hours and running five miles would tire you out enough to sleep for a month!" But she tucked a spiral-bound notebook into the text to keep her page and reached into the neck of her neat, royal blue blouse. The soft silver pouch that emerged was the size of a regulation softball, but it was never visible until Ayosha needed it. She shook her head at the wondering expression on her roommate's face. You'd think that after a month of seeing it Keni would have gotten used to it! Well, maybe it would take a while longer. She wasn't used to magic—real magic—in her life, and Ayosha was.

A major in clinical psychology from southern Georgia, Ayosha had been a member of the Sandmen's Guild since she was fourteen years old. She'd been brought into the Sandmen by an old friend of her adoptive family, Lucille Barstow, the chapter's guildmistress. Aunt Lucy insisted that she had a natural affinity for creating dreams and steering dreamers to a happy place. Like Aunt Lucy, Ayosha was a lucid dreamer, had great small motor control, and endless empathy for her fellow human beings. Lucy had taken the young girl under her wing and brought her into the guild. Ayosha had to absorb lots of rules, such as keeping the confidence of those whose nocturnal visions she observed, and not to tweak those fantasies without need. She was still nervous about her place in the Chicago guild. There always seemed to be rules she was breaking, but she tried hard.

Learning to go out at night to help clients with their dreams had also helped Ayosha get over her early fear of the dark, a not inconsiderable benefit. She also slept very well when she did get a few hours of shut-eye, useful now that she was in college, with a ton of homework and a growing social life on top of her Sandman duties.

Since the sand renewed itself when exposed to moonlight, it was nothing to use a few grains to help out a friend. She'd asked Keni not to tell anyone about her side job. So far, Keni had kept her word. She kept trying to get Ayosha to join team sports, but Ayosha preferred to keep her hair and nails nice. The two of them got along very well, although they had little else in common.

With thumb and forefinger, Ayosha extracted a good pinch of sand and flung it in Keni's direction. The twinkling grains flew exactly as far as they were supposed to, and settled down on the girl's long, athletic body, shedding a placid orange-pink light over her narrow face and long dark hair. Keni sighed blissfully, and her eyes drifted shut. Ayosha smiled. As soon as a misty vision rose above Keni's head, Ayosha picked up her coat and slipped out of the room and down the stairs to the street.

October in Chicago felt so much colder than Atlanta. Wind swept in over the massive lake to the east. Ayosha huddled down until the upturned collar of her new winter coat covered her ears. A few cars rumbled by, their headlamps twin searchlights that washed her with light, then vanished into the darkness. She could hear her bootheels click on the damp pavement. Snow wasn't due for a few weeks, but she fancied she could smell it on the air.

Though it was after ten, she was due to meet her fellow Sandmen at the Block Museum, on Arts Circle Drive. A group of Tibetan monks were doing a demonstration of creating a mandala with sand. Her guildmaster, Mr. Wendell Pinkwater, had arranged for a private talk by the abbot after museum hours. The curator of the Block, while not a Sandman, belonged to the House Brownies, another service guild. Ayosha was curious to meet not only the monks, but him, too. Mr. Pinkwater and most of the guild officers thought the other magical unions, like Fairy Godmothers, Guardian Angels, and Tooth Fairies, and especially the Djinn, Djinni and Efreets' Guild, skated on their fairy-tale reputations, so she was never encouraged to meet or hang out with them. As a newcomer, Ayosha didn't want to make waves, so she didn't reach out. She had far too much going on in her life as it was.

The grand building stood in darkness except for a couple of lights on the corners, and one small bulb burning through the window above the grand main entrance. Mr. Pinkwater met her at the door and ushered her inside with his usual fussiness. He was the palest white person Ayosha had ever met, with lank white hair and ice-blue eyes. His skinny frame loomed over her as he guided her to the big open gallery.

"You're the last," he said, clicking his tongue. "Hurry. Khen Rinpoche Jamyang has already started."

The rest of the guild members stood around the perimeter of the floor, staring with avid eyes at the scatter of yellow-robed, brown-skinned men with shaved heads and bare feet. The monks held objects like funnels which they tapped with a metal tool. From these, they poured controlled streams of black sand into what would obviously become an amazingly intricate pattern over sixteen feet across. As the sand touched the floor, wisps of colored light rose from it. She caught a glimpse of a vivid red flower here, a blue-feathered bird in flight there, an echoing canyon filled with golden light that made her gasp with wonder.

"Is their sand like ours?" she whispered to Penny Nayland, an older white woman with short red curly hair who volunteered as the guild secretary. "Is it magic?"

"Not quite," Penny whispered back. "It doesn't come that way. It's regular sand. The monks imbue it with their visions." She gestured toward a short stocky man in a yellow robe and a hat shaped like a rooster's comb. He turned to look at them. Embarrassed, Ayosha fell silent. The abbot gave her a beatific smile, as if delighted to see her, and continued in his soft voice.

"...We clear the space in which we pray or do other devotions. A cluttered room makes for a cluttered mind and soul. This space was already very clean," he added, with an approving glance toward the small, tawny-skinned, dark-haired man standing well back beside the door, Mr. Harper the House Brownie. "We make it our own. Once it is fresh and open, we can begin. We state our good intentions, asking the forces of goodness to bless this site. There are certain asanas we do that are in preparation for creating a mandala. We played sacred music earlier today with many of the university students in attendance. All during our work, we pray, reciting mantras that clear our minds and allow the purest of intentions to inform our work.

"We outline the pattern of the mandala first, and meditate upon it. Then, we begin to introduce the colors and details. In Tibet, mandalas are usually created on tables, small, small." The abbot held his hands about a yard apart. "This work is large as a gift to the city and the university, in thanks for your support of our people and our religion. But," he smiled again, "once it is finished, we destroy it. Nothing is permanent. But it existed for a time, teaching us to take joy in the ephemeral nature of the universe."

"Too deep for me," rumbled the voice of Trevor Stuart, a big light-skinned black youth who was on the Wildcat football team. He was three years ahead of Ayosha, and a popular man on campus. She would never have known him if not for the Sandmen.

"All nature is deep," the abbot said, with a twinkle in his deep brown eyes. "As you gaze into the lotus, you realize there is layer upon layer of reality, drawing you ever inward toward Nirvana." The group laughed as Trevor hit the side of his own head with the heel of his hand.

"What happens if they make a mistake?" Ginny Long asked. The thin, white-haired Asian woman was a worrywart, but a gifted Sandman.

"Ah. The impermanence of it means we can be at peace with a mistake. It exists, it exists no longer, it has always existed. Like dreams. Have you never felt as though you are living something you dreamed long ago?"

They all nodded. Ayosha frowned. His words sounded strangely familiar. She realized she *had* dreamed this moment, years ago, when she was little in southern Georgia. Monks, their voices droning, painting pictures on the floor, colors floating all over the place. She had never mentioned it to anyone, because her mama said talking about oneself was the height of conceit. She looked around the room, trying to recall all the details. What the monks here were doing was a thing of beauty, but she had a sensation of dread, as if a door was about to open and something bad jump out of it.

Her mind was dragged back to the presence by the sound of applause. The abbot smiled at them, then went over to pick up one of the little funnels and filled it with black sand from a wide brass bowl on the floor. Their audience was at an end.

Mr. Pinkwater cleared his throat.

"Thank you, Khen Rinpoche. We must be going." He fixed his pale eyes on the rest of the Sandmen. "You all have your ongoing assignments. Of course, you will notify board members if you take on additional clients or are unable to assist people you have been helping. Good dreams to all."

"Good dreams." The members echoed his words before filing out into the night. Penny smiled at Ayosha and slipped between the buildings into the darkness. Ayosha kept walking, away from the grand campus, down Central Avenue toward the women's shelter. She had known more than a few single mothers back in Georgia, but the poor souls here had suffered abuse at the hands of partners or parents, and been made homeless, through bad relationships or bad luck. She felt it was her responsibility to use her talent to give them a few pleasant visions that would live in their memories in their waking hours. It was the least she could do.

Cold as the night was, it didn't feel lonely. Ayosha could see the images of dreams through the walls of the residential buildings as she passed them. Most nighttime visions consisted of scrambled symbols from dreamers' daytime activities, so she saw brief flashes of people inside an El car staring out the window or down at their phones, the radiant faces of children laughing, plates of food, television screens, a few squirm-inducing images of sex, glints of sunlight off shop windows, office desks, and so on. One caught her eye: a monster with huge teeth growing larger and larger in the dreamer's mind. She could sense the dread. Automatically, she turned toward that building, but the monster changed to a slamming car door and vanished. Another Sandman must have seen the same image and gone to counteract it. With longtime clients who had issues they had to work through, Sandmen sometimes let nightmares happen, introducing palliative elements to help handle the terror. Ayosha enjoyed the challenge of making dreams balance. She loved it when she could provide happy dreams to people who needed them the most.

The shelter had a Guardian Angel on duty at the desk. Golnar Patel, a hawk-faced woman of sixty with wings of silver in her sleek ebony hair, fixed her big, dark eyes on Ayosha when she entered the lobby, and gave her a brief nod. To Ayosha, the unfashionable, baggy, dark green cardigan sweater the woman wore might as well have been solid steel armor. It was her doing that made the acoustic tiles of the ceiling and the painted paneling of the walls feel like thick, impenetrable stone that no enemy could breach. Ayosha wondered why her guildmaster didn't trust the Angels even though their job was to protect the vulnerable. She settled down in one of the squeaky, yellow naugahyde chairs near the desk, and stretched out her senses.

The shelter had thirty beds, not enough for the area's need. All of the women had at least one child with her; some had three or four, some sharing the mother's bed while infants and toddlers slept in cribs or on mattresses on the floor. Ayosha read the visions she saw arising throughout the facility, and tweaked an image here or there to make them less frightening. The rules for Sandmen were stricter here than for other clients. She was forbidden to learn their names, for their protection and hers, though sometimes she heard them spoken in the women's dreams. She could, however, identify people she had helped before. Their style and most frequent images left lasting impressions. Ayosha could also see the faces of their children, and sometimes that of their abusers. Her life as an adopted daughter of a blue-collar rural family hadn't been ideal, but no one had ever beaten or threatened her. Instead of names, she gave these clients nicknames.

Laughing Santa had fallen asleep by then. This woman, whom Ayosha thought was also African-American, had taken her kids to the shopping mall so they could sit on Santa's lap and tell him what they wanted for Christmas. The Santa was a plump, elderly white man with a real, full, pure white beard and mustache, and such kind blue eyes Ayosha liked him immediately. In the woman's dreams, her two children, about five and seven years old, dressed in snowsuits and knitted caps, started to tell him their wishes. He laughed, deep and hearty, from the depths of his belly, a really jolly laugh. The dream was a comfort to this woman. Ayosha could never hear those giggled requests, but it didn't matter as long as the children were smiling and safe on Santa's lap. Sending a few grains of sand her way, Ayosha added happy Christmas music she had listened to on an album owned by her mother, and dancing elves with brown skin and big brown eyes, just like the children's.

She squeezed her eyes tightly, leaving Laughing Santa alone with her fantasy, and reached out to the next dreamer. One after another, she added encouraging messages and positive images.

The flash of a knife caught the light. Ayosha gasped as the next dreamer felt the pain of a sharp silver blade gashing her shoulder. Blood fountained up in a geyser, splattering the walls and ceiling of a gray-walled apartment. She had an impression of intense blue eyes fixed on her. She heard the whimpering of the woman, who stumbled away from the knife and the eyes, pushing aside endless pieces of furniture with desperate hands. Loud panting and the clash of metal pursued her until she came to a door. The dreamer flung herself through it and shoved the door closed, but hundreds of knives showed around the edges of the wood. With a thud, the point of a blade plunged through the panel near the sleeper's hand.

Ayosha felt her heart turn over. This woman's images, though harrowing, were unfamiliar. She must be new to the shelter.

In the dream, the door rattled threateningly, thrusting again and again against her weight. Unconsciously, Ayosha leaned forward to keep it shut. The woman's strength was failing. Soon, the door would be flung open, and all the knives would plunge into her. Ayosha could feel her desperation.

Ayosha took a good pinch of sand into her palm and blew it in the direction of the vision. As the orange grains twinkled their way into the peeling beige wall, she concentrated on changing the image. The next time the door bulged inward, the woman's strength was quadrupled. She pushed the door so hard, all the knives broke off like icicles and tinkled to the floor. The door itself turned to a steel bank vault. The panting and howling faded away.

You're safe now, Ayosha thought at her. The woman would not be able to hear her words, but they translated into images of security and comfort. The door shed a thick, light-blue quilt that fell over the trembling hands. They gathered the comforter close. It gave off the sensation of peace as it curled around the woman in the dream. She sensed the dreamer relax, possibly for the first time in months or years. *You're safe here. Sleep.*

"She lost an eye to the bastard," Golnar said. Ayosha jumped at the voice. She glanced up. "He got out on bail. She's terrified he'll find her. He won't." That last was said so positively that Ayosha gulped. Golnar went back to her vigil, but the fierce gaze that swept over Ayosha had a touch of benevolence now.

The frightened woman behind the wall relaxed at last into the usual, non-menacing images of REM sleep. Ayosha took a moment to pull herself together before tackling the rest of the sleepers in the shelter, filling their drowsing minds with encouragement and positive visions. She always wished she could do more. She rose from the creaking vinyl and zipped up her parka.

"Thanks," Golnar said, terse as always.

"God bless them," Ayosha said, and meant it. But for divine grace she could have been living in one of these places, too. She had no idea why her birth mother had given her up, but it might have been because of a violent partner.

§

Because of the demonstration at the museum, her rounds ended late. Ayosha's ears and nose were numb with cold by the time she got back to the residential college.

LeMar Stafford, the RA on duty, was also a member of the Guardian Angels. He gave her a collegial nod, as one professional to another, and aimed his eyes up to the clock. Four AM Ayosha felt the cold gather in the pit of her stomach. Keni would be up in an hour, and Ayosha had an eight AM class. She'd have to use a good dose of sand on herself to try and catch up a whole night in three hours or less.

It wasn't always enough.

"Ms. Gilbert, are you with us?" asked Dr. Ackerman, the Psych 101 professor. Ayosha's head shot up. She realized she had been staring out the window without seeing anything. The other students giggled. The short, stout woman regarded her with kindly exasperation. "Please explain in your own words why an intelligent person would continue to work for a boss who has continually belittled them and held them back from advancement."

Ayosha grabbed for every fact she could remember about fear of change, Stockholm syndrome, social pressure, inertia, and reduced self-worth, and blurted something that sounded a whole lot better in her head than it did coming out. Ackerman seemed pleased anyhow, and moved on to the next student.

She slogged through the rest of her day. It was a privilege to attend Northwestern University, one of the greatest colleges in the United States, but she couldn't skate on anything. Not only were the classes challenging, but NU had a lot of mandatory activities, like the Wildcat Welcome that had taken up the entire first week of the year. The Welcome had introduced her to the faculty and support staff, as well as helping her to meet the rest of the students in her year. She had been invited to participate in numerous discussion groups and societies which she didn't feel comfortable refusing, but on top of her Sandman duties it was a lot. How Keni did it all *and* competed on the swim team baffled her. Ayosha managed to get a small but refreshing catnap in a library carrel that enabled her to make it through her last class. Finally, she returned to her room and dumped her books and shoulder bag on her desk.

"Hey, Ayosha," Keni said. Ayosha turned to greet her, and stopped with her mouth open. Her roommate was not alone. On her bed, she was curled up against the side of a young man. They were both reading with the Biology 101 textbook that stood open on his chest.

"I'm so sorry!" Ayosha exclaimed. She scooped up her bag. "I should leave."

"No, it's okay," Keni said, with a grin. The couple unwound, and the youth sat up with his finger holding his place in the book. "This is Chuck, my boyfriend. We both come from Hayward. His family lives three houses down from mine."

The young man shook Ayosha's hand. Like a lot of swimmers, his wood-brown hair was clipped short. He had a firm, dry grip, and hazel eyes that stared maybe a little too intently into hers. Ayosha didn't know what to make of him, but she sensed she would never date him herself. He had a...wrong feel. She couldn't put a finger on it.

He put on a smug expression. "So, you're from Georgia? Are you a cracker?"

She tried to keep her dander from rising, but she knew by the alarmed expression on roommate's face that her eyes were flashing fury.

"Crackers are white," Ayosha said, deliberately keeping her voice dead level. "You're from Wisconsin. Are you a cheesehead?"

He frowned at her, obviously not expecting a retort. "They don't keep cheeseheads on the reservation."

"Then maybe we both ought to keep away from insults, Chuck," she said, forcing calm into her voice. That had just escalated to ugly. She was ashamed of herself for snapping, but something about him put her on edge.

Keni looked worried. Automatically, she stepped in between the two of them.

"I think Chuck's a little cranky because he's overtired," she said, her voice a little too high and nervous, not at all like the confident athlete Ayosha had come to know over the past month. "He's having trouble sleeping, too. Could you, uh, help him?"

Ayosha hesitated. She was too overloaded with the clients she was already caring for, including the new one she had acquired the night before. Still, she rued her sharp response to him, and wanted to keep Keni happy. She must be able to help him somehow. Her hand went to the hidden bag at her throat.

"Maybe I could give you something," she said at last.

"Drugs?" He gave her a scornful look. "I'm on the swim team, like Keni. If I test positive for any controlled substance, I'm off. I'm not going to lose my scholarship!"

"No, not drugs," Ayosha assured him, already regretting making the offer. "Just a help. Non-narcotic, not addictive."

"A herbal remedy? Organic?"

"Well, sort of," she said, at a loss to explain Sandman sand to a complete stranger she didn't really trust. As far as her experience went, it was made of moonlight. Whether she could consider that organic, she wasn't sure. She gestured toward the door. "I'll...I'll get it for you."

She didn't want him to see the source, so she found an empty envelope in her drawer and took it into a bathroom stall with her. The pouch came out of her collar without a problem, but the sand resisted going into the envelope. The glowing orange grains sifted through the paper and drifted toward the tiled floor. Ayosha had to move her feet to keep them from landing on her. She didn't want to fall asleep in the stall.

Oh, come on, she coaxed it. *It's for a good cause. He might be kind of fratchety, but I wouldn't be much nicer if I was short on sleep. He's Keni's boyfriend. Just a few nights' worth, please and thank you.*

The next pinch stayed in the envelope. She added four more, in case he didn't catch up on his rest right away. Tucking away the pouch, she returned to the room and offered the sealed envelope to Chuck.

"It's a kind of powder," she explained. "Just sprinkle a pinch over your head when you go to bed."

He didn't seem to trust her any more than she trusted him. He took the envelope with the same expression he would have if someone offered him dog mess.

"What if it doesn't help?"

"If it doesn't help, go to the medical center," Ayosha said. The uneasy sensation overwhelmed her. She grabbed her purse and slung it over her shoulder. "Look, I'll come back later. Y'all have a good evening."

"Ayosha, it's okay. Don't go!" Keni called, but the door swung shut between them.

§

She didn't see her roommate much over the next few days. When she wasn't in class or hanging out with the others in the residential college common room or around the campus, she went to the Block Museum to watch progress on the monks' mandala with her colleagues from the guild. Sandmen had an affinity for sand, Penny pointed out. They saw things going on in the construction that no one else could have understood. Ayosha loved seeing the design coming together a bit at a time.

The yellow-robed men hummed as they worked, a strong nasal sound that filled the room with a powerful aura that even people who didn't work with magic could feel. The painting on the floor took more form daily. Now the monks added blue and yellow sands to the outline, working from the center outward. Although the image didn't have any obvious symbols of Chicago, it felt like all the good things about the city. Ayosha liked the "get things done" attitude of the people up there, the friendliness to strangers, the civic pride in the architecture, the gardens, and the culture, and a little bit of a chip on the shoulder for being considered a "Second City," as though Chicago were some kind of afterthought after New York. Overall, she sensed the enormous wave of peace that grew within the circular pattern. It would be an amazing work of art when it was finished, but when the monks destroyed it and released its power, the gift of magic would spread a mantle of peace over the city. Mr. Pinkwater had stressed that it had to be directed at just the right moment, or that much magic could wreak havoc. She could well understand that. The mandala contained more power than she ever thought she would wield in a lifetime as a Sandman.

The abbot, always smiling, answered endless questions from the onlookers, who included numerous Sandmen Ayosha knew. Ginny, as always, fretted about the fact that the unfinished mandala was affecting her dreams.

"Is this a permanent change?" the thin woman asked the abbot.

He smiled. "Nothing is permanent. The magic strikes like the lightning. It has its effect, then it moves on, leaving us to consider the changes it wrought."

"But it makes me so *uneasy!*" Ginny complained.

The guildmaster fixed a searching gaze on her. "The effect may spread out to the rest of the Sandmen throughout the city. Please report any other unusual dreams or visions to the guild."

Ayosha thought about mentioning her memory to them, but decided not to. After all, it had been several years; how could it have a connection to the present? And she had been reading up on déjà vu for her Psychology 101 class. Sometimes people imagined they had been in a certain situation before. It was a function of the brain that seemed to race ahead, leaving an impression of recalling a memory that was only nanoseconds old.

The tone of the monks' chanting changed as one of the younger men brought out another broad bowl, this one filled with scarlet sand. As it was added to the design, Ayosha saw more vivid, vital pictures rise from the unfinished pattern, people dancing, animals running, musicians playing, though she couldn't hear any of the music.

Penny, the guild secretary, sidled through the crowd to her.

"Ayosha, I wanted to ask: have you heard about the female student who was attacked on your campus two nights ago? She told the police she didn't remember a thing, but when she came to, she was covered with bruises, and she had obviously been assaulted."

Ayosha was horrified. "No! Poor thing."

"Can we assign her to you?" the older woman asked.

"Well...certainly, you can." Ayosha hesitated. Her nightly sessions at the shelter had been pretty hard since she started helping Knife Lady. The dreams always began with the flash of the blade and the glare of those brilliant blue eyes. It took a double pinch of sand to steer the woman into a more positive dream, but Golnar said she was starting to relax in the shelter.

Penny picked up on her reluctance immediately.

"We're running you into the ground, aren't we? Never mind. You're so eager to say yes that we keep piling assignments on you. I'll put her on Wendell's roster. He's good at finding tiny clues and flashes of insight in dreams. He might be able to pick out what few impressions are in her subconscious mind. They might not help her identify her attacker, but I hope we can help her start to heal."

"You can give her to me. It's all right!" Ayosha said, alarmed that they might think she wasn't able to handle the job.

"No, dear." Penny patted her arm. "You're a sweetie for offering, but you're here to get a good, solid college education. We appreciate that you stepped in for that young woman at the shelter."

The guild secretary took one look over her shoulder at the growing mandala, and slipped away. Ayosha still had a few minutes before she had to run off for her math class. She enjoyed the feeling of the new red magic. It felt like fire. It warmed, but she could see easily how it could burn instead. She wondered how long it took these monks to learn how to keep it under control.

As though he could read her mind, the abbot glanced up from his labors and grinned at her. She returned a tentative smile, then gathered up her bookbag and purse to leave. A hand grabbed her arm. She shrieked, and everyone turned to look at her. She shook her arm loose, ready to run, then recognized the man.

"Chuck!" She looked around. "Is Keni here?"

"No!" The athlete glared down at her. "I wanted to talk to you alone. What was that you gave me?"

"Just something that helps me sleep." Ayosha forced herself to stay calm.

"It knocked me flat out! Is it drugs?"

Over her shoulder, she saw Wendell Pinkwater move closer, his ice-white brows drawn down. She gave a little shake of her head, and he withdrew.

"No!" she assured Chuck. "It's all natural." *About as natural as it could be,* she thought. *Or maybe* super*natural.* At the thought, a little smile quirked the corner of her lips. "I promise, it's not bad or habit-forming. No narcotics or anything."

"Well, all right," he said. The tense expression melted away. "I could use a few more doses. It worked like...magic."

"Well, certainly," Ayosha said, relieved. She glanced around. Several Sandmen were still in the big chamber, but too many strangers could see her. "Let me get some for you. I'll leave it with Keni, all right?"

"Yeah. Thanks." Chuck spun on his heel and left without another word. Ayosha almost gawked as he left. Her mama would have said he lacked any social graces, but maybe he felt awkward asking a favor of someone he hardly knew. She made a mental note to fill another little envelope for him later on.

Pinkwater bustled up to her with a frown of concern. "Is he another new client?"

"My roommate's boyfriend," Ayosha admitted. "I gave him a little sand because he said he was having trouble sleeping. Just a few doses." Guilt twisted her stomach. "Am I in trouble for that?"

He pursed his lips. Drawing away from Ayosha, he beckoned a couple of the other guild officers over and had a low-pitched talk with them. Treasurer Garrett Likusarian gave Ayosha a disapproving look, but Penny sent her a reassuring nod and smile. Ayosha fidgeted, waiting to learn her fate.

Pinkwater returned. "It's not unheard of for Sandmen to allow clients to self-medicate," he said, looking as though he was making an enormous concession, "but it should be rare, and given only to people you think are trustworthy."

Ayosha immediately felt guilty. She didn't really trust Chuck, but she hated him to go without the help she could give.

"I'll remember that," she promised.

$

Word of the student's assault spread all over in the next few hours. The news reports on television and online left her name out, but everyone on Northwestern's campus learned it from a friend of a friend of a friend. The student was released from the hospital, but didn't return to her dorm. Ayosha hoped Mr. Pinkwater could find her and help her. She had her hands full with her classes and the people whose dreams she was already trying to guide.

Warnings went up on every bulletin board and university web page to be aware of one's surroundings. No one in the group Ayosha met with to have lunch could talk about anything else.

"But how long before they catch him?" Cheri Malkin complained, flicking a perfectly manicured hand palm up. "I don't want to stay in my dorm like a *nun*."

Despite their uneasiness, the others laughed. Ayosha loved the mental picture of fashionable, confident, *Jewish* Cheri in a blinged-up habit and a Bible on her iPad.

"I'm *in* her residence hall," Nita Velasquez said, wrinkling her nose. "We're all tiptoeing around, worrying we're going to be next."

"Is the guy stupid enough to pick on another woman in the same dorm?" one of the others asked.

"Is he stupid enough to do it again?" Cheri asked.

The answer, unfortunately, was yes. Two days later, another woman was knocked unconscious and attacked, this time not far from Ayosha's residential college. The university intranet lit up with warnings not to go out alone, especially at night.

Chuck had come to visit Keni that evening. The three of them sat on the beds for a while making small talk. Ayosha finally felt so uncomfortable being an obvious third wheel that she picked up her purse.

"Well, I have to do something," she said, with a cheerful smile. "I'll be gone a couple of hours, so don't wait up for me."

Keni sprang up. "No, don't! What about the mugger?"

Ayosha shook her head. "I'll be all right. I'll keep my eyes open."

Keni knew about her duties. Ayosha saw her struggle for a moment with having a cozy evening with her boyfriend or doing the decent thing by protecting her friend.

"Chuck, will you go with her?" Keni asked.

"No!" Both Ayosha and Chuck protested at once.

"I don't need his help, thank you very much," Ayosha added.

Keni put on her "stubborn" face and threw her back dramatically against the door. "Then you're not going. The guy is getting more violent! You could get killed!"

"I'll be fine!"

"I'll take you," Chuck said, suddenly. "It's okay, Keni. I'll be back. Maybe she can get someone to walk her back later."

"Okay," Keni said. "That's a good idea." She sent a questioning look toward Ayosha, who nodded reassuringly.

The two of them went out into a blustery night. Tiny snowflakes stung their faces. Ayosha tucked her scarf around her nose and mouth. It killed her to have to wear a hat, but it was a choice between her carefully styled hair and frostbite. Chuck, like Keni, hardly seemed to notice the cold. He stumped along beside her in his thin jacket with no hat.

They walked in uncomfortable silence for a while. As they came close to the edge of campus, she wondered if she could ditch him before she had to turn onto the street where the shelter lay. He seemed to have a desperate need to say something, so she stopped under the next street light.

"What's bothering you, Chuck? I know you didn't want to come out with me. What's on your mind?"

He stared away, over her head.

"Look, I'm sorry. Could you give me some more of that glow powder?"

Ayosha goggled at him, but he wouldn't meet her eyes. "Again? It's only been a couple of days! That was enough for the rest of the week."

"My roommate took it," Chuck said, furiously. "How about it? I need it!" His voice echoed off the front of the brick and stone buildings on either side of them. "Please!"

"Why don't you tell him to stop taking your possessions?"

"He's my best friend," Chuck said, as if that explained everything. Maybe it did. He fidgeted, shifting his shoulders. "Come on, help me out. Please?"

Ayosha had a horrible feeling well up in the pit of her stomach. Those victims had no memory of their assault. Someone using Sandman sand who didn't know what they were doing would just knock themselves or someone else out. She peered up at the tall youth, saw the unease in his eyes. Could Chuck...? No! How horrible to think such a thing! But, what if...?

"It's funny that neither woman who was attacked could remember what happened to her, bless their hearts," Ayosha said, resuming her walk. Chuck didn't reply. He just glared at the sidewalk ahead of him. She reached the corner and touched his arm. "I'll give you some more, later on. You have to let me go on alone from here."

Chuck's eyebrows went up.

"Why? Keni told me to stay with you."

Ayosha shook her head. "Because I can't let you see where I'm going. I volunteer at the women's shelter. I don't want to hurt your feelings, but they don't want men finding out where it is. They've suffered horrible things. Thank you for coming all this way that you did."

Chuck put on a mulish expression. "How do you know I won't follow you?"

"I have to trust you. Keni believes in you." *Besides,* she thought as she left him under the streetlight, *I can make sure you don't remember where we went.* But she was ashamed of herself for even considering using her sand for ill purposes. The guild might even throw her out.

To her relief, he was gone when she looked back.

With an eye out for trouble, she hurried through the biting wind to the shelter. The moment she stepped through the door, she relaxed, thanks to the security spell laid on it by the Guardian Angel.

The more Ayosha thought about it, the victims hadn't been choked unconscious, nor had they borne any trace of drugs like rohypnol—what knocked them out had to have been something like Sandman sand. She couldn't believe that any of her fellow Sandmen would ever do such a thing. Their mission was sacred. The guild went back millennia in ancient Greece, supposedly from beings called the Oneiroi. So, the attacker had to have access to sand or another means of rendering his victims unconscious without leaving a trace. Ayosha worried that she might have had something to do with it.

She put the worry in the back of her mind, and concentrated on her clients.

The nightmares of the women in the shelter grew worse over the next week. A third girl was assaulted, putting everyone on edge. The report was repeated over and over again on the news, and reporters were everywhere, asking for information and getting sound bites for their broadcasts. Ayosha kept going back to see the monks working on the mandala. She couldn't wait for it to be finished. The city needed peace, as soon as possible.

She couldn't get rid of the uneasy feeling that Chuck gave her, leaving whenever he visited the dorm room. As soon as he appeared at the door, she grabbed for her coat and purse, no matter what time of night it was. She worried that he had been lying about running out of sand.

Keni finally confronted her when she came back late one night.

"Have you got a problem with Chuck? Did he say something to offend you?"

"Keni..." Ayosha hesitated and swallowed. There was no easy way to broach a subject like that, but she had to. "Look, is it possible that Chuck might know something about the attacks on those women?"

Her roommate backed off in horror. "No! No way! He's a good guy. Why would you ask me something like that?"

"I'm really sorry. I hate to even ask, but does he have an alibi for the attacks?"

Keni's face flushed red with anger. "He doesn't need one!"

"Are you sure?" Ayosha asked, keeping her voice gentle. "I hate to push. I've given him a lot of Sandman sand. He could have done it."

"It doesn't have to be him," Keni said, challenge lighting a fire in her eyes. She crossed her arms. "Maybe it's his roommate. Chuck keeps saying he's taking the sand you give him."

"Well, I will just go and talk to him myself." Ayosha shouldered her purse and marched out of the room.

§

With only a few days to go before Halloween, the dorms and fraternities were decorated with ghosts, giant spiders, and green-faced witches. Ayosha had the uneasy feeling that someone was following her, but any time she looked around, the only eyes on her were those of plastic skeletons or weird pumpkins. She kept her hand on the pouch at her throat. If someone tried to jump her, she could throw a pinch of sand on him, and run for help. She glanced around. The bare trees on the easement looked like skeletal hands in the pale yellow light from the street lamps. Perhaps she ought to have asked Keni to come with her.

She found the residence hall where Chuck lived, and went to the reception desk. She didn't really like the idea of confronting him. Keni liked him. She wouldn't have kept seeing him if he ever showed signs of being violent, but Ayosha had to learn the truth.

"Can I talk to Chuck Tanner?" she asked the resident adviser on duty.

"Sure," the RA said, pushing the visitor's book toward her. "He's in 309."

She signed in and put the sticker he gave her on her coat. The RA aimed a thumb toward the elevator.

This dorm had a different feel than hers. It looked messier, and smelled very different, with heavy overtones of body spray and sweat. More men than women lived there; their dreams differed so much from the women at the shelter that it felt like changing channels. Ayosha saw a lot more sports symbols, some sex, and a wide variety of humiliation dreams. One was so intense that she started to reach for her pouch, then saw dreams changing, one after another. A drift of orange light came through a wall right in front of her and traveled into a closed door. She smiled to herself. *Trevor.* It felt good to know he was close by. The dreams of the young man in the dorm room turned from the dreaded math test in a cramped classroom to a lively game of Frisbee on the lake shore.

She knocked hard on the door of room 309 and raised her voice. "Chuck? It's Ayosha. Can I talk to you?"

No answer. She banged again with the heel of her hand. She couldn't hear anything beyond it. In a way, she was relieved not to have to face him, although sooner or later she would have to anyhow. It would haunt her forever if she was a party to attacks on her fellow woman students.

She tried one more time, then went back to the elevator. She'd have to confess to the guild officials what she thought was going on. Mr. Pinkwater would be upset. He might even call Aunt Lucy and tell her. Ayosha hated to have Aunt Lucy disappointed in her after the whole North Georgia guild had supported her college dreams.

At the RA desk, she pulled off the sticker and handed it back.

"Did you get what you needed?" he asked.

"No, he wasn't there."

"Do you want to leave a message?"

Ayosha thought about it for a moment. What could she say that wouldn't sound weird on paper.

"No, thanks," she said. "I'll probably see him tomorrow."

The outer door opened, letting in a gust of cold air. The young man looked up.

"Hey, there's Thomas Raymond, his roommate! Hey, Thomas, do you know where Chuck is?"

The student coming in the door pulled off his woolen hat, releasing a shock of long, floppy, light-brown hair.

"I don't know. Last time I saw him was around dinnertime."

"Well, this girl is looking for him," the RA said, helpfully. Thomas turned a smile to her.

"Hi. Can I help?"

"Yes, I..." Her words died on her tongue. He was good-looking, very good-looking, and he had wide blue eyes, the bluest eyes she had ever seen. To her horror, she realized she knew those eyes. They haunted the dreams of a poor young woman she had never met face to face. She had seen those eyes too many times in nightmare after nightmare. Chuck's roommate was Knife Lady's assailant! Ayosha backed up a pace.

He *had* been stealing Chuck's sand, and using it to disable his victims. He was the campus attacker!

She had to go. She had to find someone and tell them.

"What's the matter?" Thomas asked, but he'd have to be blind not to see the open terror on her face. His brows drew down. "Come with me. We'll wait for Chuck together." He reached for her arm.

"No. No! Keep your hands off me." Ayosha said, backing away. She stumbled toward the door. Thomas followed.

"Hey, where are you going?"

Panic choked her as she rushed out. She ran to the right, off the sidewalk and around the side of the residence hall, letting the bushes close ranks behind her. Shouting and running footsteps told her he had come out of the building in pursuit of her. He must not be allowed to catch her.

The frigid night air almost blinded her. A good gasp of it woke her up and brought her to her senses. She and Thomas had never seen each other before. He knew she wasn't one of his victims. She bet he was afraid she had witnessed one of his crimes. In a way, she had. He must need to find out what she knew. She must not let him catch her.

She had been a fool! If she had just stood there and talked calmly to him, she could have found out more about him, and quietly reported him to Golnar. Now, she couldn't go back to the shelter at all.

Nor, she realized with sinking heart, could she return to her dorm. She had left her name on the sign-in sheet. Anyone could look at it and find her name in the university register. Thomas could also ask Chuck who she was.

She was a stranger in Evanston. She knew of few safe havens. Maybe she could hide with one of the members of the Sandmen guild. Almost all of them lived at least a couple of miles away. Trevor Stuart was in the dorm she had just fled. Where could she find her fellows and get help?

The museum. All of them had been hanging out there in almost all their spare time. The mandala was getting toward finished. Maybe the power of good that was welling up in it would be able to stop him finding her until she could figure out what to do. Gathering her courage, she started making her way toward the Block. It would be tough to do without letting herself be seen on the streets or sidewalks, but she had to.

Her cell phone rang. She scrabbled through her purse for it. The small screen almost blinded her in the dark, but her eyes adapted swiftly. Keni.

"Hey, where are you?" her roommate asked. "Thomas, Chuck's roommate, just turned up looking for you. He said he had to talk to you."

"I'm...busy," Ayosha said, hoping she didn't sound too breathless. She kept her voice down so the people in the building she was running behind couldn't hear her. "You didn't tell him where I was, did you?"

Keni hesitated. "Well...I said it before I thought. I told you like to hang out at the Block Museum because of the Tibetan monks. I'm really sorry. Are you okay?"

"Is he there?" Ayosha demanded.

"No, he left a few minutes ago. Can I help?"

The young Sandman couldn't choke out a single word. She hit the END button and stuffed the phone back into her purse.

She had to beat him there. The museum had only two doors, and the main entrance would be locked by now. It didn't matter. She had to take her chances. Despite the cold, her ungloved hand rested on the pouch at her throat. If Thomas managed to find her, she would throw the contents all over him and take the consequences from the guildmaster.

Her heeled boots were weighted down with a lot of mud from the gardens and lawns by the time she emerged on the street near the museum.

Not a single car ran on Art Circle Drive. Ayosha kept out of the light cast by streetlamps as she hurried toward the rear door of the building. She hoped Mr. Harper was still there. If not, she heard that anyone making a mess in a House Brownie's domain would make him appear out of nowhere. She had enough mud caking her heeled boots from the lawns and gardens to make a streak all the way around the mandala.

The rapid smack of footsteps made her glance in the direction of the sound. The blue-eyed man had spotted her! He came pelting across the wet pavement. Was that a knife in his hand?

She started running toward the building. *Oh, please, God,* she prayed, *let the door be unlocked!*

God was in the mood to grant miracles that night, because the cold metal handle pulled outward without trouble. Ayosha plunged into the yellow light and dashed down the hallway.

She heard the monks intoning their meditative chant through their noses. She started to cry out for help, but just couldn't bring herself to interrupt the sound. The rapidly thawing mud on her shoes made her slip. She caught herself on the handle of the door to the main display room just in time to keep from falling flat on the floor.

Her ankle twisted on the slick marble tiles. Pain shot up her leg. On hands and knees, she crawled inside and helped herself up.

Dismayed, she realized that only the monks were there. Khen Rinpoche Jamyang gave her a mild look and went back to drawing in a few finishing touches with bright green sand. Ayosha could feel the tremendous amount of power in the chamber roiling around like the beginning of a thunderstorm. She limped toward the monks, feeling as though she were swimming against a massive tide of magic.

"Help me," she said. "Please. There's a man. He has attacked innocent people. He wants to hurt me."

"He will not harm you," the abbot said in his gentle voice. "He harms only his own karma."

"He has a knife!" Ayosha said, her voice rising with every syllable. "Please, you have got to do something!"

"We are doing something, and nothing." The abbot spoke in a calming singsong.

"There you are!"

Thomas Raymond almost glided over the smooth floor. He looked as benevolent as a saint, his blue eyes nearly glowing with benevolence. He held out a hand to her.

"I don't know why you ran away from me, Ayosha," he said, his voice lilting and gentle. "I wish you had told me who you were! Chuck said you were the one who gave him the wonderful gift to help him sleep. He was nice enough to let me use it, too."

Ayosha held her chin up in defiance.

"He said you took it without his permission," she said, trying to sound calm even though her insides were twisting with fear.

"Maybe," Thomas said, a little smile playing around his lips. "But he couldn't keep a fantastic thing like that all to himself. It's like magic. It *is* magic, isn't it? I never tried anything like it. You have to share it with me."

"So you can attack people?" Ayosha was shocked at being so forward, but she was glad to see his face go blank. "I know what you did.

You have hurt at least four women! That's going to have to stop right now."

"I don't know what you're talking about." Thomas shook his head. "I just want your sand to help me sleep. You can do that, can't you? Give me a big bag of it, and you'll never see me again."

"I'm never going to give you any," Ayosha said.

"You're wrong," he said, edging toward her. His eyes locked on hers. She couldn't look away. "You'll give me whatever I want, or I'll just take it."

He stood between her and the door. The monks ignored them. Even if he attacked her, she doubted they would step in to help. She prayed for Mr. Pinkwater or any of the others to come and help her.

"Where do you get it?" he asked. He reached out and trailed his fingers over the back of her hand. She jerked her hand away. He grinned. "If you send me to the source, I won't have to bother you anymore. All I want is your magic sand." His fingers traveled upward and brushed her cheekbone. She flinched backward. "You're so pretty. You could belong to me, too." His other hand pulled back the fold of his jacket. A big hunting knife in a sheath was tucked into the waistband of his pants. "You decide: pleasure, or pain. The choice is yours, Ayosha. Come with me. I can make you happy. All you have to do is give me what I want."

All *she* could think of was the terror in Knife Lady's dream. Those eyes, and that knife. He had the weapon on him! If she could disarm him, she could bring the weapon to the police, but he was bigger and stronger. If she reached for her pouch now, he would take it away from her. It could be replaced, but he would still have enough sand to knock out a hundred women.

The monks' humming changed key. They must be close to finishing the mandala. She felt the power of it thrumming through her like a giant speaker at a concert. There was so much magic there—why couldn't she use any of it to strike down this monster?

A thought struck her as forcefully as the magic at her back. She could take him down, if she dared. The City of Chicago wouldn't have its gift, but at least they'd be rid of a criminal who preyed on the weak.

"You want magic sand?" she asked, forcing a smile to her lips. She tossed her hair and let her head drop back to meet his eyes. "It's right here." She took his hand and turned him to look.

He gave her a puzzled frown. "The picture on the floor? It's just a work of art."

"It's more than that," she said, hoping she sounded convincing. She had only one chance. "You had my sand in your hands. You know what magic feels like. Can't you sense the power in this room? There's more magic here than you will ever see in your whole life. Look!"

He stared, those blue eyes glowing greedily.

"This is where you get the magic? I want it. Fill up a bag for me."

"Oh, you can have more than that," Ayosha said. She begged forgiveness from whatever deity that the monks prayed to, threw her arms around Thomas, and toppled them both over onto the edge of the mandala.

At once, Ayosha felt she was drowning in images and sounds more vivid than anything she had ever seen by day. The power of the sand painting exploded around them. The massive storehouse of magic that the monks imbued it with shot through her like electricity. Her body sunfished, flopping on the floor like a fresh catch while dreams tried to overpower her consciousness. She fought to gain control as she had been taught, but it was hard. Giant ants chewed on her limbs, each bite as painful as acid. She pulled a red blanket away from her face to gasp for breath. Thousands of bright brass keys unlocked nerves all over her body. She found herself in an aquarium already crowded with a shark and a beluga whale. Then, she floated out among the stars, freezing in the void. Earth was far away. She crawled toward a point of light.

I am here, she told herself firmly. *I am in Evanston, Illinois. I am not asleep!*

With the utmost resolution, she pried her eyes open and rose unsteadily on her injured ankle. The monks stood at a distance from her, watching with reproachful eyes.

At her feet, Thomas tossed and writhed like a snake with its head cut off. Those blue eyes were wide open with fear. His knife had fallen out of his belt and skidded a dozen feet away, landing in the ruins of a lotus blossom made of pink and red sand.

"Serves you right," she said to him. She limped off the ruined mandala and retrieved her phone from her purse. She had a couple of calls to make.

§

Mr. Pinkwater and a dozen others arrived in the museum within a short time. The guildmaster tut-tutted over her injured foot. Other Sandmen pulled Thomas up from the floor. His eyes were closed. Ayosha was glad not to see the fierce blue gaze any longer.

"I'm so sorry about the painting," Ayosha said over and over again. "It's the only thing I could think of to do."

"It's all right," Penny Nayland reassured her. "You had to."

"Are the monks going to try and repair it?" She couldn't guess how. Thomas's and her struggles had wiped out a good eighth of the big circle. The sands where she had fallen were a blur of mixed colors.

"No," Mr. Pinkwater said. "It's already broken. They're finished with it."

So they seemed to be. Under the abbot's direction, the yellow-robed men were packing away their brass bowls and funnels in humble cloth bags. They no longer hummed or chanted.

"So there won't be a presentation for the mayor," Ayosha said, sadly. "I'm so sorry."

"Don't be," the guildmaster said, pursing his lips. You helped to catch a dangerous criminal."

"But no police officer is going to listen to me if I tell them I know he's guilty because I saw someone's dreams!"

"No police officer," Penny said. "There are other forms of justice."

A door banged open somewhere out of sight, and Ayosha felt a cold wind rush into the room. Golnar entered in its wake, looking nothing like the middle-aged woman who sat at the desk of a shelter for battered women. From the shoulders of her plain cardigan sprang huge, luminescent white-feathered wings. Her face glowed with the same fierce light. The monks stopped their packing and bowed to her.

"Where is he?" she demanded in a voice that sounded like the knell of doom.

Pinkwater rose, an unusual expression of respect on his face. He pointed to Thomas Raymond. Golnar advanced upon the prone man. Ayosha struggled to her feet, suddenly regretting having called her.

"What are you going to do with him?"

The Guardian Angel gave her a sad smile.

"Deliver him to the authorities. He will not escape his fate. Don't look like that. Did you think I was going to kill him?"

"Maybe?" Ayosha said. "The Bible says 'an eye for an eye.' I thought maybe…"

"That's not justice." Golnar shook her head. She knelt and lifted the man as though he weighed less than Ayosha's purse. No one stood in her way as she carried him out of the room.

Ayosha surveyed the ruined mandala. So much work, wasted!

"I wish I could do something to make this better."

"You can help," Pinkwater said, his face kindly. "You know our affinity for sand—of all kinds. Watch the others."

Her fellow Sandmen spread out around the circle. From their own pouches they took pinches and blew it over the gigantic colored image.

Like little eddies on the lake, the sands began to move. Grains quivered of their own volition, then rolled or scurried or bounced in all directions. The undamaged part of the mandala glowed, the colors intense and vivid. Each particle of sand seemed to know where it ought to go. The black grains crawled like ants, reforming the lines that Ayosha had disturbed. The rest of the brilliant dust waited until the outlines were complete, and nestled into them. Once a section was restored, it caught fire from the rest. Image after image filled in, composing itself until almost the entire pattern was complete and alive with power. Only a small section remained undone. Small heaps of red and yellow bubbled, waiting.

Ayosha suddenly realized that the monks had gathered beside them and resumed their deep-throated chanting. She caught Khen Rinpoche's eyes, and he beamed at her.

"Go on," he said. "Breaking is remaking. It is your turn."

She glanced up at Mr. Pinkwater. He nodded.

"With good intentions, remember," he said in caution. "We are privileged to be part of this gift."

Hardly daring to believe she was a part of such a marvelous whole, Ayosha reached into the pouch at her throat. The twinkling orange grains danced on her palm.

Let nothing but good come from this wonderful thing, she thought. With a gentle breath, she sent them flying. They settled on the remaining portions of sand, which eagerly took their places in the mandala. Now complete, the gigantic artwork filled with energy, until it was more powerful than it had been when she had entered the room. The other Sandmen smiled at her, and she smiled back. The gift to Chicago was intact once again, Knife Lady and the other victims would get to put their attacker away, and she felt more than ever like a part of the magical community.

"It's like a dream," she said, with a smile, "only I get to be awake for this one."

Heap of Trouble
Gail Z. Martin

"More glowing orbs." Teag Logan sat back from his laptop computer. "I haven't seen this many reports of spirit lights outside of the Old Jail in...come to think of it, never." His dark hair, cut skater-boy long in front, hid his face as he stared at his screen.

"Can you find any connections?" I asked, leaning against the counter and sipping a cup of coffee.

Teag shook his head. "Other than that they're all happening in Charleston, and in the older sections of the city? No. At least, not yet," he amended. "I'm working on it."

I came back to the kitchen table, where my laptop was open, displaying a search screen. Teag had stopped by my house after work, and we'd ordered a pizza for dinner. "The appearances are getting more aggressive," I replied. "At least, according to what the tourists are posting on the rating sites. People are getting chased by bobbing lights, tour groups scattered by dive-bombing orbs, and more than one driver claims that 'glowing balls of lights' caused accidents.

We've got to figure out what's going on before someone gets hurt."

I'm Cassidy Kincaide, owner of Trifles and Folly, an antiques and curios shop in historic, haunted Charleston, South Carolina. Teag Logan is my assistant store manager, best friend, and sometime bodyguard. Taking responsibility for stopping ghostly harassment might seem strange for people who run an antiques store, but Trifles and Folly isn't your average shop. I'm a psychometric, meaning I can read the history or magic of objects by touching them. Teag has Weaver magic, so he can weave magic into fabric and weave data into information, making him a hell of a hacker. My business partner, Sorren, is a nearly 600-year-old vampire who co-founded the store with my ancestor 350 years ago. We're part of the Alliance, a secret coalition of mortals and immortals who get cursed and haunted objects off the market and protect the world from supernatural threats. When we succeed, no one notices. When we fail, the destruction usually gets chalked up to a natural disaster.

Tonight, Teag and I were holed up at my house, trying to figure out what had Charleston's ghosts in an uproar. "Have we missed a practitioner moving into the area?" I asked.

Teag shrugged. "I would have thought that Rowan or Donnelly would notice a powerful new witch in town." He referenced two of our friends who frequently brought their talents in magic and necromancy to help with the threats we fought against—the forces of darkness and things that go bump in the night.

"Someone could have brought in a powerful relic," Teag said.

"Maybe. But again, if it were just someone mucking around with magic or powerful objects, Rowan and Donnelly would have picked up on it."

"What I don't get is why it started all of a sudden." Teag reached for his half-empty glass of sweet tea. "Like someone flipped a switch."

"And it's not just at one location." I looked at the map where we had already marked all of the reported incidents we could find with red dots. Other than covering the Historic District and the antebellum houses South of Broad, the marks included museums, private homes, public parks, restaurants, shops, tourist attractions, members-only clubs, and—frequently enough to be dangerous—the middle of streets.

"Nothing about this looks like a normal haunting," Teag said, shaking his head. And that right there summed up my life. We could use the term "normal haunting," and it made perfect sense.

"We'd know if there'd been some sort of massacre," I said, only partly in jest.

Charleston is a beautiful city built on a bloody history. The Spanish, French, English, and Americans all fought over the land and its harbor, and before the Civil War, the port was the busiest slave market in the United States. Back in the day, sailors and soldiers brawled, pirates raised hell, cutpurses stalked the dark alleys, and spoiled young rich boys challenged each other to duels. Yellow fever epidemics claimed tens of thousands of lives. Add a jail that in its day housed everything from serial killers to prisoners of war, often under abysmal conditions, and it's easy to see why Charleston is one of the most haunted cities in North America. But nothing in the history—published or secret—suggested that there had ever been a mass killing in the area where the orbs were terrorizing people.

"Some of the newest reports talk about ghostly faces in windows or candles that move from window to window in empty buildings," Teag said. Restaurants, hotels, and shops may thrive on ratings sites to drive customers to their businesses, but the comments are a gold mine for tracking paranormal activity. Tourists either think they've seen a clever show, or get scared out of their wits, and either way, they can't wait to tell everyone on the internet.

"So whatever's causing it is getting stronger, or affecting more spirits." I looked back at my computer, wishing it would just spit out the answer.

"What worries me are the reports of seeing people who look solid and then they just vanish into thin air." Teag ran a hand through his dark hair. "Or the ones who report a 'feeling of dread' that made them turn around and leave. It takes a lot of juice for a ghost to manifest that strongly. They weren't doing it a month ago, so what changed?"

"I asked Kell what he and his team have run into." My boyfriend, Kell Winston, heads up SPOOK, Southern Paranormal Outlook and Outreach Klub. They're experienced ghost hunters, and legit when it comes to documenting haunts. "He confirmed an uptick in activity that seemed to come out of nowhere."

"Looks like we need to go for a walk again," Teag said.

I glanced at the time. "It's already eight. Don't you want to spend the evening with Anthony?" I asked, mentioning Teag's long-time partner.

"Yes, I'd like to spend the evening with him, but his firm's been tied up with that big case that's been in the news, so he's been working all hours." Anthony is a lawyer at his family's law firm, a powerhouse in the Southeast.

"Kell's busy with a project, so he won't be stopping by either," I said in commiseration. Kell is a freelance video producer when he's not busy with SPOOK, and work is usually feast or famine.

"You know, the track record for big increases in spectral activity is pretty grim," Teag said. "It's never been for a good reason."

We had fended off several rather dire situations that all caught our attention because of ghosts behaving badly. It takes a lot of power to upset spirits over a large area, and often there's malicious intent behind it. So we knew to tread carefully.

"No time like the present," I said, standing and gathering what we would need to stay safe while we did some recon. I grabbed the backpack I keep stocked and ready to go, and double checked the supplies. Plenty of salt, a large bottle of holy water, a coil of rope infused with colloidal silver, and several iron knives would provide a good baseline of protection against ghosts, along with the silver, agate, and onyx jewelry both Teag and I wore. Since we weren't sure what we might be going up against, we made sure to conceal both silver and steel knives in sheathes beneath our jackets. I had a few more tricks up my sleeve, and I knew Teag would be equally well prepared.

I patted my little Maltese dog, Baxter, and told him we'd be back soon. He gave me a skeptical glare, then trotted off to finish his kibble. Teag and I headed out to my car and drove down to the Historic District, with both of us keeping an eye out for anything strange.

"Shit!" I jammed on the brakes as a flash of light bobbed in front of the windshield, then braced myself in case anyone behind me couldn't stop. Fortunately, no crash came. "Did you see that orb?" I asked Teag breathlessly. He looked a little pale and wide-eyed himself.

"Yeah. When we get back, I'll look to see if there've been more accidents than usual in this area. I bet there have been, even if the drivers didn't tell the cops about the orbs."

I could just imagine trying to explain to a police officer that a ghostly light made me wreck my car. Even if a driver had reacted to a spooky glowing ball, most people wouldn't mention it.

We found a parking space—a minor miracle given how quickly the curb spots fill up in the residential areas—and went for a stroll. Normally, walking in Charleston's historic neighborhoods is one of my favorite things. There are so many beautiful homes and gorgeous gardens. Tonight, I felt on edge, waiting for an attack.

I could see the tension in the way Teag moved. He's an experienced mixed martial arts competitor, and it shows in the way he carries himself. Teag is tall and lanky, but although he looks lean, I've been in enough fights beside him to know it's all whipcord strong muscle. While I can hold my own in a fight, I'm more likely to rely on magic than clever footwork.

The hot, humid evening felt sultry even for Charleston. I pushed a strand of strawberry blonde hair behind my ear, sure that with my pale coloring I was already flushed from the temperature. We had walked a block before I realized what seemed strange.

"There should be more people out walking."

Teag nodded. "Yeah. Usually, you're dodging people out with their dogs, or just stretching their legs after dinner." Charleston is a walking town, both for tourists and for those of us lucky enough to live here. So the lack of pedestrians seemed odd, maybe even ominous.

I'd driven us to the edge of the area where the sightings were concentrated. We wouldn't be able to cover all the territory tonight, but we could certainly walk toward the center of the disturbances and see what happened.

"I'm pretty sure we're being watched," Teag said, dropping his voice.

My intuition told me the same thing, although I didn't see anyone on the sidewalk or peering out through the windows. The night felt too quiet, the air too still.

As we walked, the temperature grew colder, although in Charleston's sub-tropical climate it was far too early in the year for the weather to cool off. The back of my neck prickled, and the hair on my arms stood up as if the air was charged with static electricity. I let my wand fall from inside my sleeve into my hand, the handle of an old wooden spoon from which my touch magic could pull deep emotional resonance to harness power. Teag shifted, and I saw him palm an iron knife in one hand and a silver blade in the other.

"There!" I hissed, pointing toward the shadows where a live oak tree hung over a wrought iron fence. The gray form of a woman in an old-fashioned dress was clearly visible, looking solid enough that someone might not have taken her to be a ghost at first glance if they weren't expecting haunts. Off to the left, a blue-white spirit orb materialized out of nowhere, bobbing at chest level near the door to a home on the other side of the street. I felt gooseflesh rise, although moments before I'd been sweating.

"Look!" Teag pointed toward a historic home with darkened windows. I could make out a ghostly image framed by one of the casements, something that should have vanished in the blink of an eye, but didn't.

"Over there."

Teag followed my nod toward a home on the opposite side of the street where a candle flame inexplicably hovered inside a dark upstairs window.

The sense of being watched grew even stronger, an oppressive weight that carried with it a sense of dread. I'm not a medium, and I have no special ability to speak with the dead. Yet my touch magic can often pick up on the emotional resonance a spirit leaves behind on objects, giving me a second-hand insight into the temper of the ghosts.

"I don't think they mean to hurt anyone, not directly," I said slowly as I tried to make sense of the impressions my gift gave me. "They're disoriented, frightened, and angry, but not with us. It's like they're frustrated, and that's making them lash out the only way they can."

"How do we find out who's calling them?" Teag asked, as smaller orbs danced around us like fireflies. If the residents in the nearby homes saw the dancing lights, they chose not to show themselves. Maybe they were hiding behind drawn curtains and closed shutters, hoping that whatever roused the spirits of the dead would soon send them to their final rest.

"I think we need to pull Alicia into this." Alicia Peters, another ally of ours, is a gifted medium. "I can sense the ghosts' mood, but I'm not getting images that are clear enough to get an idea of what's going on."

"It would help to know what got them riled up all of a sudden," Teag said. "Something changed, and until we figure out what, we're all in danger."

Teag and I stood back to back on the sidewalk, as the orbs dove and rose, and a fog of spirits gathered all around us. I didn't want to antagonize the ghosts since they hadn't yet done anything truly hostile. They had shown themselves, perhaps their only way to communicate.

"We aren't here to hurt you," I said in a low, steady voice like I was talking to a spooked horse. "We might be able to help. Please don't harm anyone. We'll figure this out."

For an instant, the lights grew brighter, the wind picked up, and the ghosts looked nearly solid. In the next breath, they vanished, leaving us alone on a balmy summer evening.

"I think they might have heard you," Teag said. "Now let's hope we can keep our side of the bargain."

§

The next morning, Alicia called me before I had a chance to call her.

"Cassidy, something weird is up with the ghosts. I keep hearing 'let us go,' and then I get images of some really weird glowing bottles and an old-fashioned Victrola record player. Does that mean anything to you?"

I was out walking Baxter around the little garden in back of my house, and my stomach growled because I hadn't eaten breakfast yet. "No. At least, not yet. Was there any other context? Do you get anything out of it?"

"Except for a feeling of being trapped and an overwhelming sense of anger, no," Alicia replied. "Except..."

"Yeah?"

"I had a few other impressions, but nothing to back them up. I don't think that the ghosts I sensed are the ones causing the freaky haunted stuff people are talking about. The regular ghosts feel...disturbed. Upset. They might be warning us. I also think that the ghosts that went with the bottle vision had been dead for a long while. And they weren't nice spirits. We need to be careful. There may be a reason someone felt they had to keep these ghosts locked up, and setting them free might not be a good idea."

"Unfortunately, if they're causing problems, they're not as locked up as they used to be," I said. "So whatever's kept them in check this long is failing, and we need to find out where they are and how to keep them from hurting anyone."

"I'll keep listening for what I hear from any of the spirits who feel like communicating," Alicia assured me. "And I'll let you know what I find out. Yell if you need me."

I went back inside, finished my breakfast and coffee, and got Baxter settled for the day. Before I had even pulled out into traffic, my phone rang again. This time it was Valerie, a local tour guide who is also a good friend.

"Hey, Cassidy, what's going on with the ghosts? My customers like to be mildly spooked, not scared out of their wits." Valerie was one of the best ghost-tour guides in the city. The normal ghosts didn't make her bat an eye, so this was more confirmation that what we had going on was something that was anything but "normal," even for Charleston.

"I don't know yet, but I'm planning to find out. What have you seen?"

"Zippy orbs all over the place, ghosts sightings where we don't usually see any, and so many cold spots, I started expecting snow."

I told her what Teag and I saw on our walk, and what Alicia had reported. "I'll let you know if I hear what's causing it," I said. "And if anything changes, call me."

Teag and our assistant, Maggie, were already at the shop when I got there. Teag greeted me with an official-looking envelope in hand. "I figured you'd want to see this. No idea what it is, but it looks important."

I frowned as I read the return address, a local law firm. When I tore the envelope open and read the contents, I had to re-read the letter to make sure I hadn't imagined it.

"What?" Teag asked.

"Trouble?" Maggie echoed.

I looked up at them, utterly confused. "Someone I've never heard of just willed their house and all the contents to Trifles and Folly."

While Maggie and I handled customers in the front of the store, Teag went to the break room to research our mysterious benefactor. I also texted Sorren, my vampire boss, because this was the kind of thing he'd want to know about. After that, we were busy enough with customers that I didn't come up for air until the pizza delivery guy arrived and I realized Teag had called in an order. Maggie and I took turns going back to the kitchen to take a break and eat.

"Find anything?" I asked as I took a bite of pizza.

"Irene Sacripant, the person whose name is on the deed and the will, lived in the house for thirty years." Teag leaned back in his chair. "The problem is, there's no record at all of her existing before then. No birth or marriage certificates, no hits on the genealogy websites, nothing."

Teag is a super hacker, so if he can't find someone, there's nothing to find. I glanced toward the door to the front, to make sure no one was close enough to hear.

"Think she's one of 'our' kind?" Meaning witch, vampire, shifter, or some other supernatural creature.

"Yeah, I think it's likely. And thirty years ago, it was easier to disappear and invent a new identity than it is today. I've got a call in to Rowan and Donnelly and a few others, to see if they know her. But there has to be a reason she left the house to Trifles and Folly."

"That's a first. I've never had anyone bring the estate sale to us before."

"I'm really curious," Teag said. "When can we get access to the house?"

"According to the letter, I need to go in and sign some papers. Maybe I can see if I can do that this afternoon, but the letter sounded like it was all wrapped up with a bow." I tossed my paper plate in the trash. "We need to be smart about this. I have a feeling Irene didn't pick us out of all the antique shops in Charleston because she wanted to sell off the family silver."

"You think she's got something supernatural in there?"

"Don't you?"

Teag pushed his hair behind one ear. "Well, yeah. I just wanted to see if you thought the same thing." He stretched his arms and cracked his knuckles. "If you're okay with running the front a while longer, I'd like to keep digging. I've got a feeling that Irene was hiding her real identity, maybe hiding from someone. The house is up on the Ashley River, kinda remote."

"Maggie and I can cover the store," I told him. "It could be that Irene didn't have any heirs, and knew we'd take good care of her belongings. But my gut tells me that she picked us because of our 'special skills.' I think we just inherited a heap of trouble."

Teag researched for a while, then came up front to cover for me while I went to see the lawyer, and a late afternoon surge of customers kept us from any meaningful conversation until after we closed. Maggie—who knows the scoop about what we really do—made us promise to call her if we needed anything, and headed home.

"Did everything go okay?" Teag asked as we locked up.

I nodded. "It's all signed, sealed, and official. Although, there was one thing that was a little off. The lawyer said that Irene's will was adamant that I be given a detailed floor plan of the house."

"Sounds to me like there's something she wanted you to find."

"Sorren said he'll stop by my place after dark. Is Anthony still working late?"

"Yeah. He's been dragging in around ten, so as long as I'm home before then, he'll never notice. At least, not until the case is over."

"I've got stuff in the fridge for dinner, and we can see if we can dig out any of Irene's secrets while we wait for Sorren," I said. Teag agreed and followed me in his car back to my place. Baxter yipped and danced when Teag followed me in, then chased me into the kitchen for his dinner after he got his snuggles. Teag and I chatted about the customers and local gossip while we made supper and ate, waiting to get back to the Irene problem until after the dishes were done.

"She wasn't much of a joiner," Teag said. "Which is unusual for Charleston. Especially thirty years ago. But I think I've turned up a photo."

I leaned over his shoulder. The grainy picture was from a newspaper article, and from Irene's expression, she wasn't pleased to be captured on film. "If that's really Irene, at least the photograph rules out her being one of the kinds of creatures who won't show up on camera."

"Well, that's something," Teag said grudgingly. "I'm going to try to run it through facial recognition software. The resolution isn't great, and we'd be trying to match to a photo from before 'Irene' showed up here which assumes those pictures would have been digitized, but I'll give it a go."

I spread the floor plan out on the table, and both Teag and I bent closer for a better look. "It's a big house, but I don't see anything unusual in the drawings," I said, trying to figure out what had been so important to Irene. "And given where it's located, there's definitely no basement."

"No hidden rooms, secret passageways—at least nothing marked."

"Maybe that's the point," I replied, straightening. "Maybe she wanted us to find where the house has been altered."

Teag raised an eyebrow. "Clever. The plans alone don't give anything away, but she's counting on us going through the house."

I nodded. "The more I think about it, the more I doubt what Irene wanted us to deal with is going to be out in the open. Or at least, I don't think the big problem will be just sitting in plain view."

As soon as the sun set, I heard a knock on the door. I'd been expecting Sorren, but the way Baxter immediately sat with a goofy grin on his face confirmed it. Apparently, vampire glamor works on dogs, and my dog was utterly bespelled.

"Hello, Cassidy. I take it Teag is here, too?" Sorren asked as he stepped into the hallway. Sorren looks like he's in his late twenties, although he's centuries older. With his blond hair in a trendy cut, gray eyes the color of a storm at sea, and dressed in a concert t-shirt and artfully ripped jeans, he looked like a grad student. Back in the day, he was the best jewel thief in Antwerp, before he was turned. Now he spends his time hunting down dangerous magical objects, moving among the many stores like ours he's established all over the world.

"In here!" Teag called from the kitchen.

Sorren followed me back to where Teag was still at work on his computer. Sorren listened intently as I filled him in, both on the odd inheritance and everything we had learned about Irene Sacripant.

"I don't recognize that name," Sorren said, frowning. I can't imagine sifting through six centuries of memories when I sometimes can't recall the name of someone I met last week. "But the photograph seems familiar, though I don't think from Charleston. Interesting."

"We don't know where she was before she moved here—or who she was," Teag said. "The facial identification software is still looking, but it's a slog when it comes to old photos."

"I'd like to send Rowan and Alicia over to the house to get a feel for it—from the outside," I said. "Nice to know what might be waiting for us." I'd run into magical traps and aggressive ghosts too many times to walk in blind.

"I'll go with you when you enter the house," Sorren said, not making it a choice. "I agree that whoever this Irene was, she sought out Trifles and Folly because she expected there to be supernatural problems with her legacy. It would have been nice if she had given us a clue."

It's not uncommon for us to run into haunted objects and cursed heirlooms. A few real estate agents know to call me if they run into spooky problems with houses that come on the market after an owner's death. And more than once, we've had to deal with collectors who acquired problem objects that had some seriously bad mojo attached to them. I shuddered to think what kind of trouble might be waiting for us in that old house.

"Do you know if Donnelly has noticed any issues with the local ghosts?" I asked. "Because I'm hearing things from Alicia and Valerie."

"Archibald has been away handling an issue," Sorren replied. "He's only just returned. I'll check in with him and meet you at the Sacripant house."

§

Teag and I drove out to the old house. "Rowan said she didn't pick up any magical traps around the outside of the house. She couldn't guarantee that the inside was safe, but she said that the power she sensed didn't feel like a threat, even though it was very strong," I said.

"And Alicia picked up on ghosts, around the house and in it, and she was worried about them being dangerous," Teag added. "So... maybe magic, definitely angry spooks. Totally our kind of thing."

I had Rowan on speed dial in case something went wrong, but she would have offered to go with us if she was worried about magic. In Alicia's case, if there were dangerous ghosts around, I wanted the medium as far away as possible because her gift could make her vulnerable. Teag and I came prepared, although I hoped that tonight's trip wouldn't turn into a fight.

We pulled up to the house at twilight. The Sacripant place was probably at least a hundred years old, a two-story white clapboard house with deep porches on both levels. It must have been grand once, but it had fallen into disrepair, with peeling paint, an overgrown lawn, and missing shingles. Large live oak trees formed a corridor along the driveway, old enough that their gnarled limbs dipped to the ground and rose back up again, and their upper branches hung heavy with Spanish moss. This close to the river at dusk, fireflies rose like fairy lights from the grass, and bullfrogs croaked. I could smell the salt marsh and beneath that, the wet-leaf smell of mold and decay.

"You're sure we haven't been pranked?" Teag wondered aloud. "Because that looks like something right out of a horror movie."

"Perfect place to meet a vampire then, isn't?" I replied. Despite my attempt at humor, I agreed the place looked creepy, exactly like Hollywood's idea of a haunted house.

"It's a big place for her to live all alone," Teag said as we got out of the car. Neither of us wanted to go closer until Sorren was with us. Teag glanced from side to side. "And there aren't any neighbors close."

"The obituary said she was in her eighties." I wondered about the woman who had lived here. None of Teag's picture-matching programs had worked, but I figured that was due to how bad Irene's single photo had been. That didn't give us much to work from. Maybe we'd find a better one in the house, or with luck, the answers to Irene's mysterious past.

"I trust you came prepared." Sorren came up from behind us soundlessly, and I managed to merely flinch instead of jump. Moving soundlessly is one of the perks of his Dark Gift, along with enhanced strength, healing, heightened senses, and of course, near immortality.

"Of course," I replied as Teag nodded, and I hefted my backpack full of salt, holy water, and silver, in addition to the weapons and protective charms we wore. Sorren didn't look heavily armed, but his abilities were lethal on their own, and I saw two iron blades in sheathes on his belt.

I hadn't needed my wand when we had confronted the ghosts downtown, but I felt better feeling its comforting weight in my hand as we walked toward the house. I jangled the old dog collar I wore wrapped around my left wrist, and the ghost of Bo, my old golden retriever, appeared next to me, my spirit animal and protector. Silver bracelets and an agate necklace helped to ward off supernatural threats.

Teag carried an iron blade in his right hand and had a second blade ready in a sheath on his hip. A hand-loomed belt woven with protective magic wrapped around his waist, and I knew that the knots dangling from it stored extra power, like batteries for him to draw on. He wore amulets of his own, a hamsa and an *agimat*, and an earring of black onyx. We both had loose salt and iron shavings in our pockets. We knew the drill. It was showtime.

"I've called Archibald. He'll meet us here as soon as he can," Sorren told us. It says something about my life that I take comfort in having a powerful necromancer along for the ride.

The night felt darker as we reached the steps to the porch. Although the place was badly in need of maintenance and minor repairs, for its age, it didn't look at risk for collapsing on our heads. That was a plus. I hesitated on the steps, listening to my magic. When there's a strong resonance, I can pick up on it through the soles of my shoes, and the impressions already beginning to creep into my consciousness were disquieting.

"Cassidy?" Teag asked, hanging back.

I nodded to let him know I was okay. "There's bad stuff in there. Nothing we didn't already know." As Teag opened the door and invited Sorren inside—it's a vampire thing—I concentrated on the input from my psychometry, hoping for something more helpful than just "trouble."

"There's a lot of negative psychic energy," I said, trying to put feelings into words. "It's seeped into the house itself, so whatever's causing it isn't new. But I think that losing Irene made it worse." I shook myself out of concentrating so hard, so I could pay attention to my surroundings.

"Can it contaminate us?" Sorren asked.

I shook my head. "It's not a sickness. More of a deep rot."

"How did we not notice this place, with that kind of energy?" Teag asked.

"If Cassidy's right, it hasn't always been...transmitting...like this," Sorren said. "Perhaps Irene was the key to keeping the energy in check, and now that she's gone, whatever was bound is working its way free."

That thought chilled me, but I felt certain Sorren was correct. I stood in the old house's entranceway and looked around. Teag had turned on the lights, but they barely made a dent in the gloom. Either Irene had used very weak lightbulbs, or the house had a darkness that light itself couldn't dispel.

Long ago, the house had been grand. Now, the inside looked as worn and shabby as the exterior. A layer of dust lay over everything, and heavy cobwebs in the corners and on the chandeliers made me suspect they predated Irene's death. I had feared that she might be a hoarder—one more reason to leave everything to the store to sort through—but as we moved slowly from room to room, I realized that given her age, the house was surprisingly uncluttered.

"No mirrors," Teag noted as we moved from the parlor to the dining room. "That's odd."

A surge of vertigo hit me so hard I stumbled. Teag swayed on his feet as well. Only Sorren seemed unaffected. "Did you feel that?" I asked, a little breathless.

"Yeah, but I don't know where it came from," Teag said. "It felt... weird...like getting a head rush on a roller coaster."

"I felt nothing," Sorren said, frowning. "Interesting."

I walked into the library. High bookshelves filled with leather-bound tomes and a worn, comfortable chair beneath a floor lamp gave me an idea of how Irene spent her evenings. On the far side of the room sat a leather couch that looked comfortable and well-used. A writing desk with tidy stationary and pens sat against one wall. Tucked into the corner on a mahogany stand was a very fancy, old-fashioned Victrola, albeit one that appeared to be custom-made. I hadn't noticed any portraits or photographs in the more public rooms, but here I spotted several framed black and white photographs and yellowed newspaper clippings.

I looked at the shelves, noting that each one held a variety of silver-plated knick-knacks nestled among the books. Fine white dust covered everything, even thicker on the shelves than elsewhere. I saw chunks of onyx and agate, minerals known for their protective properties, used as bookends. Bundles of dried plants tied with ribbon were nestled on shelves, on the mantle, and on the windowsills. The room held the faint odor of sage, and I saw an abalone shell filled with ashes that I guessed was used for frequent smudging. Sigils that I recognized as wardings against evil had been drawn on the windows with soap.

"Irene must have been afraid something was going to get in," I said, noting the abundance of precautions.

"But we haven't seen any markings or protective objects in the other rooms," Teag pointed out. "Maybe she made the library her fortress."

My attention went back to the photographs. "I think I've got something," I called out. I leaned over for a better look, hesitant to touch anything and activate my magic unless I had to. More than once, a strong reading has knocked me flat on my ass, and we still didn't know what we were up against.

The woman in the photograph was a much younger version of the matron in the picture Teag found online. Irene sat primly in a long black gown at a table surrounded by six other people, all of whom were holding hands. The newspaper clipping's headline read, "Chicago Welcomes Famed Medium."

"She was a medium," I reported as Teag and Sorren joined me. Teag lifted the framed article to read it in better light.

"That's Irene," he said, "but this says her name is Catherine Jenkins." He set the frame back on the bookshelf and reached for his phone, doing a quick search.

"That's interesting...Catherine Jenkins shows up quite a bit. She was a medium who appeared to have real talent, and she traveled all over, often hosted by the rich and famous. Even some of the infamous—a few reputed mobsters were big fans of her Vegas appearances. Oh..."

"What?" I prompted.

"According to this article, she vanished without a trace thirty years ago. She wasn't married and didn't have children. Some of the theories said that the Mob put out a hit on her for knowing too much, and others said she might have committed suicide."

But we knew better. Catherine—Irene—had pulled a disappearing act worthy of Houdini, and lived out the rest of her life in seclusion. "Why would a medium choose to live in a haunted house?" I asked. I didn't have any special talent to see ghosts, but my psychometry picked up on plenty of ghostly energy. Even if I didn't see them, I knew they were all around us, some stronger than others, watching and waiting. And as Alicia warned, I had the distinct impression that not all the ghosts were friendly.

Sorren had moved to the desk and withdrew a folder, wiping off a layer of dust. The vibrant red of the cardstock seemed out of place among the faded memorabilia of Irene's exile. "I have the feeling Irene wanted us to find this," he said. "Since it's quite a bit newer than anything else here." He flipped open the cover, revealing more articles and a slim journal. Sorren set the journal aside and leafed quickly through the clippings.

"It would appear that Catherine Jenkins attracted a questionable clientele in the years just before her vanishing act," Sorren said. "Mobsters, politicians of ill repute, and very rich men with sordid reputations apparently wanted her to plum the secrets of the afterlife for them. She was investigated for her connections, especially when some of her clients disappeared. None of the charges stuck, but that's not very forgiving company."

I looked at the photograph of Catherine at the séance table. "Do you think she was coerced into doing readings for crooks and wanted out?"

"Maybe," Teag said, moving to stand beside Sorren. He picked up the journal and turned the pages. I looked over his shoulder, but at this distance, I couldn't make out the cursive script in faded ink.

"If I'm reading this right, I think Catherine took notes on the sessions she had with her more infamous clients," Teag said. "Just from the ones I've read, it looks like they wanted her to contact other dead criminals to find out where they hid their stash, or get information that they could use for their own benefit."

"Let me see what I can pick up," I said. Teag pulled out the desk chair, and I sat since I didn't want to find myself suddenly on the floor from a particularly strong reading. Teag and Sorren stayed close, protecting me since I was vulnerable in a trance.

I laid my hand flat on the journal, and immediately, I saw the room through Irene's eyes. Everything looked fresher, newer. Opened curtains let the sunshine in, and the dust and cobwebs were gone. The library looked comfortable and lived-in, but I could feel the uneasiness of the woman who had made it her hermitage.

Irene was afraid. I picked up on the fear clearly, though the reason was less clear. She felt guilt over the way she had been forced to use her gift, and she loathed the men who had coerced her into being a part of their crimes. And yet, I had the oddest feeling she wasn't afraid of being found, or that she feared arrest. No, her fear ran deeper than that. She didn't fear death. Irene Sacripant feared the dead.

I came back to myself with a gasp, and Teag gently took the journal from me. He pulled a sports drink from his backpack and pressed it into my hand. I gulped it down, needing the sugar and wanting a moment to compose myself and order my thoughts. Bo's ghost, my spectral protector, bumped against me, reminding me of his presence and protection.

"She was afraid of the spirits doing...something," I told them. "But I'm not sure whose ghost she was worried about, or what she thought they'd do. Maybe she thought that the ghosts the mobsters made her contact were angry at being disturbed."

"I'd like to read that journal more closely," Teag said. "There were some odd phrases about 'preserving souls' and 'cheating the scales' that don't make a lot of sense."

Sorren shook his head. "I think we're missing something here. The story doesn't add up. Let's have a look upstairs, and then see if we can find anywhere that the blueprints you talked about don't match the current rooms."

The second floor held bedrooms and bathrooms. All but one appeared to have been long disused. Some of the rooms weren't even furnished, and the bedchamber that had been Irene's was oddly devoid of personal possessions beyond clothing.

"It looks like she spent most of her time downstairs," I said. "In the library, I'd guess."

"That room does appear to have been her focus," Sorren replied, in a tone that made me wonder what he was thinking.

Another wave of vertigo almost dropped me to my knees. For a few seconds, everything around me looked blurry, and I had the oddest sense that it was reality itself and not my eyesight that was affected. This time, I swore that the house shook beneath my feet like we were having a private earthquake. Beside me, Bo's ghost growled and bared his teeth.

"Did you—" I asked Teag, who nodded with a sick expression as if he wanted to puke. My stomach was fine, but my head had started pounding. Once again, Sorren missed out on the excitement, and I figured it was no accident that the undead guy wasn't being affected.

"Let's finish what we came to do so we can leave," Sorren said, and I knew his response was from worry for our safety.

Teag unfurled the blueprints, and Sorren paced off each room upstairs, comparing the dimensions to those on the drawing. All of them matched exactly. Sorren found the access to the unfinished attic, but a quick examination revealed nothing hidden or even stored among the rafters.

He repeated the process downstairs, starting in the parlor. The front room, dining room, and kitchen all matched the blueprints. But in the library, Sorren's measurements didn't add up. He paced the walls again, and once more the numbers were off.

"We're missing a couple of feet along that wall," Teag said, pointing to the back of the library.

We all walked over to take a closer look. I squatted to look at the floor. "I think there's a salt line here."

Teag and Sorren ran their hands along the shelves and the supports, pressing their fingers into crevices, checking to see if any decorative carvings might activate a hidden latch.

I hung back, readying salt and holy water in case we were attacked. "It's gotten colder in here," I noted. "And it feels like we're being watched."

"I think...yes. There," Sorren murmured, and we heard the snick of a hidden latch. Part of the bookshelves swung forward like a door.

Inside the secret compartment were more shelves, but instead of books, these held rows of glass jars and odd wax cylinders. The jars were each topped with a strange collection of copper wires which both fastened the stopper securely and extended down into the containers themselves. More disturbing were the odd flashes of green and blue that flickered intermittently like a slow heartbeat.

"What the hell?" Teag said.

I moved closer, still keeping weapons at the ready. Inside the hidden room, a thick layer of salt lay on the floor, which Sorren and Teag were careful not to disturb. Suddenly, the abundance of silver, onyx, and agate decorations on the shelves made a lot more sense.

"Those are Leyden jars," Sorren said. "Bastardized, to be sure, but the spiritualists of the eighteen-hundreds thought the soul to be mostly electrical, and the jars could store electricity somewhat like a battery.

"Those rolls. They're Edison cylinders," I said in a hushed voice. "That Victrola wasn't created as a music player; it was originally meant to record the voices of the dead."

"So you're saying that Irene recorded the confessions of the dead, and trapped their souls?" Teag asked, aghast.

It all clicked into place. Catherine's hatred of her criminal patrons, their unexplained deaths, and her dramatic disappearance, as well as Irene's voluntary exile and the numerous warnings. Hell, it even gave me a good idea about what was up with all the ghosts downtown, if they were afraid Catherine's bottled criminals might stage a jailbreak and descend on the city. All the orbs and manifestations were good spirits trying to warn us in the only way they knew how.

"She got her revenge," I replied. "Whether or not she killed the men who forced her to work for them, I think she stole their souls. Maybe she wanted to punish them or thought they might cause harm from beyond the grave. But that's why she went into hiding. She was their prison guard."

"And once she died, without her magic to help keep the souls contained, they've started to 'leak,'" Teag added, taking a step back reflexively.

"I'm not entirely certain about her motives, but I think we have discovered why Irene left the house—and its contents—to the shop," Sorren said in agreement.

"No mirrors," I said, suddenly making the connections. "Stories say ghosts can hide in reflective surfaces or travel between mirrors. That's why there aren't any."

"So we've basically got a toxic waste dump of damned souls," Teag said. "And we get to be the supernatural hazmat crew."

I felt a chill against the back of my neck, but not from the ghosts in the hidden chamber. The air behind me stirred, and I had the overwhelming sense that someone stood behind me. "Where did Irene die?"

"No idea," Teag replied. "Why?"

"I'm betting she passed away right here," I said. "And I don't think she ever left."

The door to the hallway slammed behind us, and the wooden slatted shutters closed by themselves as the lights flickered wildly. The temperature plummeted as if we were in a walk-in freezer, so cold I could see my breath. The house shuddered, hard enough this time to rattle the objects on the bookshelves and make the chandelier swing.

Vertigo hit me hard, making me reel, and I caught myself with a hand on the edge of the writing table. The room...wavered. It shimmered like heat rising off asphalt, its dimensions skewing until it looked as if it were trying to fold in on itself.

Teag had gone pale, looking as if his knees might buckle. Sorren drew both his iron blades, alert for an attack.

"Look!" As my vision cleared, I could see what had caught his attention. A red pinprick of light glowed almost too brightly to look at, right in the center of the wall behind the Leyden soul jars.

Irene's ghost took shape, standing between us and the shelves, and I could not tell whether her intent was to protect us from the trapped souls or to keep the glowing jars safe from our interference. Bo lowered his head and growled, baring his teeth

My teeth chattered, and gooseflesh rose on my arms. The air felt charged with twisted energy; perhaps the tainted magic used to imprison the souls or force their unwilling confessions. Irene did not attack, but she did nothing to lessen the assault to our senses. Behind her, the red light grew from a speck to a larger dot.

"You willed the house to us." I thought perhaps Irene didn't recognize us and thought that we were come to steal or harm her unholy collection. "We're here because you summoned us."

Teag moved behind me and grabbed the journal. He paged to the end, and then looked up at Irene's determined ghost. "It's not just the evil spirits you trapped, is it?" he asked. "There's something else here we need to figure out before we try to deal with the jars, and you want us to figure it out." Irene nodded.

The house shuddered again, sending a fine white cascade down the bookshelves. *Salt*, I thought. *Not all dust. She lined the shelves with salt. But did she mean to keep the souls inside, or keep something else out?*

Another tremor, this one hard enough to rattle the glass dangles on the chandelier. Behind Irene's ghost, the *pop-pop-pop* of shattering bottles sounded like gunfire as three of the Leyden jars exploded, freeing the spirits housed inside. I didn't need to be a medium to feel the shift in the room and know that the ghosts who had freed themselves were malevolent and hungry.

Three glowing red orbs from the broken jars dove at us as Bo snarled and jumped to intercept. I didn't know what would happen if those orbs hit us, but I doubted it would be good. Teag deflected one with a slash of an iron blade, which made it veer and dimmed its light for a second. Sorren's quick reflexes kept him out of the way of the dive-bombing balls of energy, and he struck again and again with his iron knives, forcing the spirit lights to draw back or lose some of their glow. I couldn't spare much attention for Irene, but I wasn't sure whether her ghost was trying to block the orbs or us. The orbs blinked in and out as we tried to hold off the attack and Bo continued to lunge and snap at them.

My martial arts experience wasn't as extensive as Teag's, and I didn't have Sorren's speed. I leveled my wand at those that came my way, and pulled on its strong emotional resonance, sending a blast of cold power that swept the balls of light out of its path, and rattled the bookshelf behind them. I angled my shot, so I didn't break any more of the bottles, and after I hit the orbs a few times, they drew back, giving me space.

The orbs obviously disliked contact with iron as much as they reacted to the force of my magic, and whether being struck hurt them or drained energy, it didn't matter so long as it kept them clear of us. Our defense hadn't gotten rid of them, but they were considerably dimmer than when we started, and I wondered if they could recharge, or if we might win if we could outlast them.

"Cassidy, the light!" Teag said, and I saw that the fiery red light had grown to at least the size of a quarter. "What is that?"

"Nothing good," Sorren replied.

The room shuddered, but this time it felt different. Even Sorren jolted with the tremor, and in the next heartbeat, the door to the hallway crashed open, splintering with the force that broke through the power holding it shut.

Archibald Donnelly framed in the doorway, and behind him, Father Anne Burgett. Donnelly was a big man with a shock of white hair and the kind of bushy sideburns and mustache that went out of style with the Civil War. Put a pith helmet on him, and he'd look like one of those English colonels from the height of the British Empire. Father Anne, a highly unorthodox Episcopalian priest, couldn't be overlooked with her short, spiked black hair, clerical collar over a black t-shirt, and steel-toed Doc Marten boots.

"Watch out!" I shouted to warn them. "Irene trapped souls and they're getting loose!"

Donnelly gestured and spoke a word of power. A golden glow sprang up between where we stood and the wall of jars, keeping the orbs—for now—on the other side along with the slowly growing red light.

"She's not their jailer. She was helping them cheat death," Donnelly replied, anger sparking in his eyes. His gaze fell slightly behind me, where a cloud of mist coalesced into the figure of the woman in the photographs. "Aren't you, Catherine?"

He didn't wait for the spirit to answer. "The criminals were afraid of having to pay the consequences for their actions. They feared eternal judgment, going to hell. And so they bribed Catherine to 'bank' their souls, putting off the inevitable. She *was* their guardian—and their protector."

"So you can just send them on, right?" I asked. I'd seen Donnelly go up against some scary-powerful entities. A few bottled ghosts seemed tame in comparison.

"Unfortunately, these aren't just any souls. They've grown stronger and even more vengeful by being contained," Donnelly replied, glowering at Irene's ghost. "For a medium to use the gift to do such a thing is forbidden in every tradition. The reckoning they've cheated has grown impatient."

"You mean hell's coming to get them?" Teag asked, horror making his voice sharp.

"That's exactly what I mean. Without Irene's magic to hold the wardings in place, the containment spells are weakened. They've been degrading since her death. And when they fail, a hell-mouth is going to open to lay claim to the souls that belong to it."

Holy shit. We were on the brink of a supernatural Chernobyl.

"So she willed the house to us to clean up her mess?" I asked, feeling a lot less charitable toward Catherine/Irene's ghost.

"That's my guess," Sorren said. "It wouldn't be the first time we've ended up picking up the pieces after someone else made an unholy bargain."

"We've got one chance," Father Anne said, stepping up to stand beside Donnelly. "When Archibald drops the barrier, I'm going to chant Last Rites while he keeps the hell-mouth from opening completely. All of you need to keep the spirits off us—they're going to fight as hard as they can to keep from being destroyed. But be careful—you don't want to get sucked into the maw yourselves."

No indeed.

"Ready?" Donnelly rumbled. "Now!"

The scrim of glowing power vanished. The orbs had regained their energy, and they launched a furious attack, ignoring us to dive at Donnelly and Father Anne, recognizing that they had the magic to send them on.

The glowing red hell-mouth had grown larger, at least the size of a baseball, and blindingly bright. How much larger did it have to get, I wondered, before it could pull us all into its infernal blaze?

I didn't want to find out, so I gathered my magic and used the cold force of power that blasted from my wand to sweep the orbs away from the priest and the necromancer. Bo dodged and lunged, planting himself squarely in front of Father Anne and Donnelly. I was on their right, with Teag on their left. Sorren moved fast enough to blur, wherever he was needed.

The room shuddered once more, knocking the silver statues from the shelves and sending picture frames crashing to the floor. The crystal chandelier overhead vibrated hard enough that its pendants clattered like wind chimes. The rest of the Leyden bottles exploded, sending shards of glass flying as the terrified souls imprisoned inside fled the judgment seeking them.

The air smelled of sulfur and ash, but still freezing cold. Maybe my imagination got the best of me, but I could swear I heard distant screams coming from the direction of that infernal, blood-red light. Father Anne shouted the Last Rites defiantly, while Donnelly wove magic to recapture the dozens of soul-orbs that careened through the room. Irene's ghost had grown stronger, gray but looking almost solid, and I realized that she had gained enough energy from our magic to call to her power.

"Push when I say," I heard an unfamiliar woman's voice whisper in my ear as a chill ran down my spine.

The ghost orbs dimmed, whether because of necromancy or the Last Rites, and Irene raised her arms, standing only a few feet from the hell-mouth. She threw back her head and shouted something I could not hear, but the ghosts took heed, gathering around her.

Now.

I mustered my courage, reached for my magic, and *pushed* with all my power, sending a blast from my wand with all the energy I could summon.

The blast shoved Irene and the orbs that clustered all around her directly at the glowing hell-mouth. Donnelly shouted, and threw up his glistening barrier as soon as my burst ended, as Father Anne called out the final words of the Last Rites at the top of her voice. Bo huddled next to me, his spirit safe on this side of the energy curtain.

The hell-mouth widened, and I had to look away because it was like gazing into the sun. But I glimpsed Irene, silhouetted against the crimson fire, shoving the orbs into the inferno, and then, with a scream, being drawn inside herself. The maw flared, and I threw up my arm to shield my eyes. Wails and shrieks filled the air, deafeningly loud.

Then, suddenly, all went dark and quiet.

I lowered my arm and opened my eyes. The far wall held no glowing bottles, wax cylinders, or pulsing orbs. Everything was gone, and in its place was a blackened scorch mark where the hell-mouth had been. Irene and the souls she had helped to cheat fate were gone.

"Was that really...Hell?" Teag asked, in a voice just above a whisper.

Donnelly shrugged. "It was what they expected, feared, and thought they deserved. It is real enough for them." His unruly white hair looked like it had stood on end, and the outlay of power showed in his eyes.

"Expectations are powerful things," Father Anne replied, her voice raw from shouting. "But where they've gone, they won't trouble anyone, ever again."

"What would have happened, if you and Irene hadn't forced the souls through?" I asked, not sure I wanted to know the answer.

"The hell-mouth would have taken them, and everything else it could pull into itself," Donnelly answered. "And without my magic and Father Anne's litany, there's no saying whether it would have sealed back shut."

"Thank you all," Sorren said. Donnelly inclined his head in acknowledgment, while Father Anne just shrugged as if it were all in a day's work. Sorren looked to Teag and me. "I believe we've removed the danger that caused Irene to will us the house. But tomorrow, I'll meet you here at dusk, and we'll check everything over again to make sure. If there are any other tainted objects, we'll handle them, and the rest can be appraised."

I looked around the room. Other than the disarray near the bookshelves and the burn on the wall, you'd never know we faced down a soul-fueled nuclear meltdown. No one outside the house would ever know how close the world had come to catastrophe. But we knew, and even if that knowledge didn't change the world, it changed us.

We saw things we couldn't un-see, knew things we couldn't forget, and would dream of what could never be expunged. It wasn't the magic that kept us sane and functioning, it was each other, and the small network of allies and loved ones who believed in us. In what we did, anything could happen, and every day could be the last, so I'd learned to find comfort in the small things that grounded me.

"I'd really like dinner and a drink," I said. "Anyone care to join me?"

Stalking Horse

Janet Walden-West

*M*y new-ish partner was on a roll, more reckless than the caffeine-hyped morning drivers blowing by us. "We need to cultivate a better quality of cases."

"Our cases are fine."

"*Really*, Samantha. We need more Rodeo Drive instead of rodeos. Mud masks instead of—mud. Filet mignon instead of Burger King."

"There was steak involved last time."

"That—that was a bull demon, not steak!"

"You bit it. Same difference."

Rachel's eyes turned the color of swamp gas, a bilious green, visible even through her sunglasses. "We will never speak of that again."

Turnabout was fair play, even with an irritated Kelpie. "Oh, like you haven't put me in some hellish situations."

"A makeup counter is hardly hellish."

My voice rose over the whine of our tires. "It was Sephora on Black Friday. Someone stabbed me."

"With an eyebrow pencil. So dramatic." She rolled her eyes, back to plain human green, and flopped against the passenger seat, as dramatic as she'd just accused me of acting.

Not that bouncing off the cushy, heated leather seats was much of a statement. Heated steering wheel, too. Rachel's ride, which she'd insisted we use in place of my more serviceable truck.

Her lifestyle bore little resemblance to mine. To my old lifestyle, anyway. There was something to be said for sleeping in motel rooms instead of my truck.

"Thank you for facing down the shopping hordes for me," Rachel said. "You were very brave." A smile curved her lips.

"I suppose it wasn't *the* worst experience I've ever had."

She swiveled in her seat, facing me. Sincerity replaced her teasing. "Everything is better if you have someone to share with. I owe Andrea for pairing us on that wisp hunt."

I wasn't sure what to do with the serious turn in our conversations. Supernaturals took the owing of favors with a life and death fanaticism. Rachel had only agreed to that hunt, one she'd never have touched otherwise, especially working with a human like me, to discharge her debt to Andrea. Saying she owed Andrea again meant Rachel put herself back under a *geas*. She thought I was worth another binding promise.

I was glad, too. Although I was still adjusting to a lot more than a higher class ride. "That's a lot. To promise."

Rachel nibbled at her lip, a true oddity, because she never risked lipstick on her teeth. "Having someone that I can be real with, someone I can trust implicitly, is close to priceless."

Oh.

The silence dragged on long enough that Rachel frowned. "Anyway. Back to discussing more fitting jobs. Look." She held up her phone, although navigating Atlanta traffic during rush hour didn't leave me time to check her screen. She waved it, sending sun glare bouncing off the screen and into my eyes. "This case is ideal."

"Let me guess—a mysterious haunting at a day spa." I grabbed for a lighter topic.

"Poltergeists might be less homicidal if they engaged in a good detox and hot stone massage occasionally. But no. Do you remember the unsolved string of murders earlier this year that garnered all the media coverage?"

My amusement died a swift death. I flexed my jaw, unclenching muscles, and got out, "Hard not to."

The murders had been brutal—women disappearing then the bodies turning up days later. What was left of them, at any rate. The deaths were strung out all around the country, initially making it difficult for authorities to connect them as the work of the same killer. Especially since forensic evidence had been scarce and contradictory.

The weird evidence made sense if the culprit wasn't human. My old partner had sworn that was the case.

Her belief had gotten her killed.

Oblivious, Rachel continued, more animated by the second, fingers flicking and the sparkle of her iridescent gel manicure and stacked rings punctuating her enthusiasm. "This case is ideal. The human authorities had no leads and no evidence, which I always found intriguing. However, if the killer is supernatural, that explains everything. According to Brookie, that is exactly the situation."

I'd followed the killer's trail as far as Lexington, then it had gone cold. For months. No bodies, no leads. Like I'd dreamed it all—except for the fresh grave in Zara's family plot. I breathed, and concentrated on details. "Brookie?"

"Yes, she's a business woman I know."

I glanced away from the Escalades and Hummers taking the Gwinnett County speed limit as only a loose suggestion and glared at Rachel. "Bullshit. What kind of business owner has details on murders?"

Rachel glared back. "She is a witch. A very accomplished one, with a well-regarded practice supplying charms, spells, and other high-quality necessities to the magical community."

"A witch." My lip curled on its own accord. "Now that's a trust-worthy source."

Rachel looked at me over the top of her sunglasses, her expression severe. Reminding me that while she appeared to be a late twenty-something fashionista, she'd watched Edinburgh undergo the Industrial Revolution. "I've known her since she was a child, and I do trust her."

Whereas she'd only known me for a few months. I flushed at the verbal knuckle-rapping, and made a *go-on* gesture.

"A certain buyer has come to her attention. This person request-ed a relatively complex set of charms. Charms that act as magical scrubbers, clearing away things like blood, DNA, and other markers."

My heart rate picked up. Exactly the kind of thing to sanitize a murder scene and body and baffle CSI teams across America.

"This buyer seemed satisfied enough with her work that he came back for more. But by that time Brookie was suspicious. The request was very specific, suggesting this person had prior knowledge of exactly what they wanted. Few witches are capable of that level of intricacy." Rachel's voice dropped, an eerie resonance lapping un-derneath her words, like speaking while on open water. "Brookie's mentor was one such witch. She died under mysterious circumstanc-es four months ago. From the state of her shop, everyone thought it was a break-in. Now though..." Rachel spun her phone in a circle on her knee, auburn brows furrowed.

I'd already figured out her tells. "What aren't you telling me?"

"I cross-referenced Brookie's sale and outstanding crimes. The newest murder fits. When I asked, she got me sell dates from her mentor's invoices. They match the other murders."

The green and white overpass signs and high-rises hazed red in my vision, tinted by my spurt of outrage. There was only one reason to supply a track-erasing charm to supernaturals. "She sold—repeat-edly—to a murderer. She enabled those crimes."

Rachel turned away, staring out her side window. "She had no way of knowing."

"Charms that scrub away blood and DNA? Come on."

"Supernaturals have to eat, too. The charms could have been for anything. We can't always leave traces of dead elk in national parks or stray cattle on ranches, either. Nor can hunters on cases that turn bloody."

Rachel was the only supernatural I knew of that hunted, so that excuse wasn't flying. "What I'm hearing is that nobody cared about the death of us expendable humans. It didn't matter until it was a fellow supernatural."

A new distance gaped between us, more akin to the depth and width of the Grand Canyon than the few inches of console space that physically separated us.

"Brookie isn't supplying the buyer any longer." Rachel's voice dropped to a near-whisper. "But before she knew, she sold him the second set of charms. They were drop-shipped to a post office box near Knoxville a few days ago."

Despite the heated seat, my blood chilled.

I whipped the SUV over, ignoring the squealing tires and blaring horns, taking the off-ramp, heading for I-75 and Tennessee.

One more charm was out there. One more woman was on a killer's radar.

§

"Legitimate business, my ass." I slammed the door on the post office. Tried, anyway, my anger frustrated by the door's slow-release mechanism. "What legit company sells to a person they've never met, who use a series of untraceable wire transfers, and an anonymous post office box?"

The postmaster hadn't known anything, even when I caved and allowed Rachel to compel him, using her equal parts useful and terrifying psychic ability on him, the same amped up power of suggestion that let Kelpies draw unwary humans to them, then to a watery death.

"It's the age of online business. Anonymity is the whole point." As we stepped onto the main street, Rachel dodged a couple who looked like they'd escaped a Ralph Lauren ad.

Not that *main* meant much here. The address had led us to a tiny, rural burb well outside bustling Knox County. My frustration mounted as I crossed the downtown, all of its four blocks. Post office, cutesy shops, a couple of equally cutesy restaurants, a supposedly historically significant depot, and a tiny police station-library-city hall combo. No room to hide and nothing here that suggested a serial killer's haunt.

Mountains ringed the town, casting deep shadows as the short winter day drew to a close. "This can't be right. No serious predator is gonna pick a fishbowl of a town as its hunting ground. There sure as hell isn't any anonymity here. No way to blend in when everybody already knows everybody, and has their nose in each other's business. A stranger would stand out like a twenty-foot billboard."

Two steps, and I finally realized I was talking to myself. I spun, nerves on edge. Rachel stood stock still in the middle of the faux-cobbled street. Her slow, intense gaze tracked over the gentrified brick-and-beam shops and the Friday shoppers flowing in and out of stores.

Despite my turtleneck and vest, my skin pebbled, nothing to do with the November weather and coming darkness. I rubbed up and down my arms, banishing the chills. The people giving us irritated looks and skirting around the two chicks blocking the flow of traffic didn't understand what they walked by, but my body recognized danger.

Rachel watched the passers-by the way a well-fed leopard watched herds on the savannah. Content for the moment, but cataloging and storing information for the next hunt. Identifying the old and the weak.

"Ooh, but you're not seeing what I am," she said, her voice barely a breath.

A horn blared, a driver irritated as another car swooped in and stole one of the few parking spaces. Rachel seemed to shake herself, and was once again my travel mate, the person more concerned with sheet thread count than hunting strategy.

She caught up to me and grabbed my arm, Kelpie strength showing, hauling me to a wrought iron table outside a little bakery. The enticing sweetness of vanilla and fresh bread floated out as a customer exited. "Look around," she said, abandoning my arm and rooting through her purse.

"I am. Small town. Insular. Nosy people. Missing people will be noticed a.s.a.p." I rubbed circulation back into my arm.

She smacked the table, the dull thump reverberating like a muffled gong. "I'll give you small. But look. I'm sure you're accustomed to being the least best-dressed in a crowd, but I'm not. And I have competition today. Why is that?"

I let the mostly accurate snark go and sat. I took a minute to people watch. The couple outside the post office hadn't been a fluke. Almost everyone that drifted past was more North Face and Urban Outfitters than Wranglers and RealTree. Their outerwear was meant for show, not working around barns and tractors.

There was a dearth of muddy work trucks, but plenty of Kias and Priuses.

A man hopped out of one—the car that had cut the other car off moments earlier. The driver hadn't gone more than a few steps before he was stopped by a trio of women. One held out something to him, a book or notebook. We were too far away to hear the conversation, but the body language broadcast just fine. The guy signed whatever it was and handed the paper back, but his hand lingered on the woman's a beat too long. When one of her companions spoke, he transferred his attention, not even trying for subtle.

Seemingly pleased by what he saw, he put an arm around the speaker's waist, and drew her into his side. Way too possessive and intimate for someone that'd been a stranger a minute before, even if he was some kind of celebrity.

"Here." Rachel's command jerked my attention back. She'd dug out a tablet that she flipped around to face me.

I shook off second-hand discomfort from catching the handsy-guy interaction, scooting closer, and stared at an idealized country farmhouse and acres of trees, fog-wreathed ridges, and wine glasses scrolling down the screen. A logo in the corner glinted, tasteful cranberry and gold—*Gooseberry Farm. A full event experience.*

"Bed and breakfast. Full service spa." Despite myself, I snorted, because, of course, and kept reading. "Guided meditation hikes, yoga, HIIT classes, and horseback rides. A concert hall—whoa, with real CMA headliners. Winery and brewery. Holy crap—fox hunting? People still do that?" I stared at the red and white clad equestrians and sleek hounds on the slide show.

"This isn't some mom and pop B&B. This is an elite, lucrative operation." Rachel tapped the table again, accenting her point. "It's funding this town. Hamblin is small, but it's based on tourism and Gooseberry Farm."

Tourism. A revolving door of strangers who came, shopped, stayed a few days, and left. No one would notice if anyone they just met wasn't here the next day. "The perfect hunting ground," I said.

I sat back and watched the crowd again, thinking like our killer. The profile Zara had put together, the files on the victims and their photos and stats. At least half the people visiting were women under thirty, in groups and alone. A perfect fit for our killer. It should've felt promising. Instead, my stomach clenched hard enough it felt like it banged against my spine. There were too many potential targets and only two of us.

Our killer had picked up his package the day before. He'd been here long enough—or done his homework from afar in advance—to have narrowed his options. He'd probably found a safe home base. We'd just rolled in and were starting from scratch.

A light touch on my elbow jerked me back to the present.

Rachel tilted her head, hair falling and creating a curtain, giving us the illusion of privacy. Voice low, she said, "We will figure this out in time."

I didn't know if it was enhanced Kelpie sense of smell or centuries of insight that let her read me so easily. Easily enough that it felt intrusive. Whatever she saw on my face, she lifted her hand away.

But the interruption had cleared away my panic induced stasis. Right. When in doubt, get to the heart of the problem, then work outward. I switched my attention to the mountains. "Gooseberry is the reason this town is thriving, and the reason our guy is here."

"Hello, ladies," a deep, booming, masculine voice said.

A shadow fell over us and we both jumped. My hand went from the table to inside my vest, reaching for the compact Glock out of habit. A whiff of brackish water came off Rachel, momentarily obscuring her usual Hermès perfume, giving away her startlement.

The guy I'd spied on the street made himself at home, butting between us. He gave us a mega-watt smile, one that brought out his dimples. Despite the weather, he had on a thin sweater, one snug enough to make out the six-pack abs underneath. A vee of brown skin only a little lighter than mine peeked from the neck of his shirt.

Rachel recovered first. "Can I help you?"

"I could not help but see that you're considering Gooseberry." The name came out on a soft roll of R's, giving away his roots, not exactly Spanish but somewhere southern European. He drew Rachel's tablet closer.

"It is the only civilized place I've seen here." Rachel slipped into her dilettante mode, giving a shudder.

"Very true. You must visit." He tapped at her keyboard, then pointed at the screen.

Hairs stood up on my neck, but I leaned in. A video clip played— our inappropriate stalker in an outdoor kitchen. He had on an apron. And not much else, lots more golden skin and that six-pack visible as he did something with spices and a steak. His accent was more pronounced, sexing up his lecture. Much as I hated cooking, grilling suddenly got hella more interesting.

The guy—Chef Tomás Martins, according to the heading—smiled again. "I am here only for the week. My classes are full, but you come anyway. They are a magical experience. Tell the concierge I said you are special guests. Perhaps we'll even have time for a private lesson."

With that, he pressed a card into my hand, winked, and strode away.

My skin tingled and when I glanced down, I'd crushed the card, its edges cutting into my palm. *Magical experience* His rabid interest in the women earlier, and the offer of a private lesson for us made sense if he was a killer shopping for his next victim.

Zara's killer might've been standing right. Beside. Me. "I need to get inside Gooseberry Farm."

Rachel reached into her purse again and came out with her wallet. "Getting into a luxury resort? You're playing my song."

§

Some clichés stayed relevant because they were true. Like money talks.

With a dazzling smile, Rachel accepted her glossy black credit card back from the manager at the reception desk. "Thank you for being so accommodating. Sometimes a girl just has to get away on the spur of the moment, yes?"

"Of course. "I've already added you to Tomás' class," the man said. "Please don't hesitate to let us know how we can make your stay more enjoyable."

Amazing how an open credit limit garnered that response. As well as having already heavily tipped the valet, bellboy, anyone else available to throw cash at, and pre-booking the inclusive spa day. She hadn't had to stoop to supernatural suggestion to slide us right in, no eyebrows raised.

I tuned the chit-chat out, mapping out rooms, exits, and the feel of the place as we followed the bellboy and our luggage through the first level of the sorta rustic-sorta magazine spread central house, outside around a paved stone path that climbed a hill to our cottage. A cottage with a name—Cloud's View. The lodge's version of the Presidential suite. The cottage came with a complimentary golf cart. Because this place was ridiculous, featuring not just the renovated main house, but smaller cottages, spas, restaurant, brewery, barns, riding trails, hiking trails, bike paths...

As the guy wrestled our luggage cart through the front door, I eased past and grabbed my largest bag, the one containing things civilians ought not accidentally see. Struggling under the weight of Rachel's bags, the bellhop never noticed.

"Would you like these in the master suite, ma'am?" He'd already pointed the cart that way.

"Here is fine." She discreetly handed him a large bill, a distraction from the oddity of a society princess willing to unload her own luggage.

As the door clicked closed on the bellhop, Rachel grabbed all of our bags, lifting them like they weighed nothing.

Reminded once again that my partner wasn't human, I followed her to the suite. Despite the cottage's size, there was only the one lavish bedroom.

We'd shared rooms before, but not a bed. The situation simply... hadn't come up.

Oblivious, Rachel was unzipping bags and talking. "From what little I was able to put together on the drive, I can't isolate a pattern in the murders. The victims are all different looks and body types and there's no connecting hobby or job."

All of which I already knew. Guilt stabbed at me. Rachel hadn't given me any reason to doubt her—not on the hunt where we'd first met where she'd literally pulled my ass out of the fire—or on the half dozen since. Zara and I had never kept information from each other, even when we were just newbies. Hunter partnerships were built on a basis of trust. Even supernatural-human partnerships.

I had no excuse not to level with Rachel. I pulled out my laptop—loaded with Zara's notes—and played with whether we were partners enough to share this.

"You need to shower," Rachel said.

The laptop I'd unpacked slipped and I grabbed before it hit the reclaimed barn wood floors. "Excuse me?"

"You smell of Kelpie." Pink tinted Rachel's fair cheeks. "We've been in close enough proximity that you've picked up a hint of my scent. Another supernatural will detect it immediately. That could lead to a bit of an unfortunate territorial dispute over resources, as well as alerting them to our presence."

Resources. As in human prey.

Rachel swore she didn't feed on humans. The hunter conclave wouldn't have allowed her to keep breathing if she did—never killing a human was our Golden Rule, and that applied to all of us, human or otherwise. Rachel had convinced everyone that her fortune came from exploiting wealthy people who enjoyed attractive, cultured companions. When she wasn't hanging out at Cannes, she used her resources hunting, policing her own kind.

But the fact that we were having this conversation was a reminder that she wasn't human. That she'd lived for centuries, seen things I couldn't understand. That there was a similar barrier between her and humanity, no matter her hobbies or how she dressed.

She didn't prey on humans now. But that wasn't a guarantee that she hadn't once upon a time. There were too many things we didn't know about each other.

I did know that lying to her was probably unforgivable. I sure as hell wouldn't stay with, or work with, anybody who lied to me.

I also knew I couldn't go after Zara's killer with a creature that might've done awful things to people, no matter how far in the past those misdeeds were. Yeah, I owed Rachel. I owed Zara's memory more.

Grabbing my shower kit and bag, I headed for the bathroom. And kept my mouth shut, the desire to share gone.

§

I scrubbed and exfoliated Kelpie pheromones off, while Rachel kept up a running commentary of the farm's evening offerings.

I raised my voice enough to be heard through the cracked-open door. "What theoretically looks most popular with singles?"

Keys *click-clacked.* "For my money, were I a vacationing hottie— the wine tasting tour, the evening horseback ride under the stars, and of course, the hands-on cooking demo with Tomás. Emphasis on hands-on."

"Cooking? Seriously?"

Her put-upon sigh carried clearly. "You've seen him. So, yes."

More keystrokes followed. "The wine tasting is out. It's a tiny, curated group. Not the best scenario for luring a vic away."

I let the last of my guilt, and my new partnership, wash down the drain with my shampoo bubbles. "You should take the horseback ride. I'll take hottie chef."

The central heating whirred on, the only sound as I cut the water and grabbed my hair dryer. I flipped it on, buying time. Hiding from the inevitable.

When I finished, Rachel's voice came from a foot away, like she was facing me with only the bathroom door between us.

"Am I wrong in thinking Tomás is our primary suspect? He's attractive and has a magnetic personality, which attracts women. I.e., a pool to screen for potential victims. He travels, which accounts for the fact that the murders were spread all over the country. I haven't had time to check them all, but I wouldn't be surprised if the murders correspond with his teaching gigs. We are both already enrolled in his session tonight."

I pulled on every bit of training I'd ever had, keeping my tone matter-of-fact. "No lie, he looks good for these crimes at first glance. However, we're going in with only superficial details and assumptions. Everyone visiting here has the financial means to travel widely. You also saw the same thing I did when we checked in—this place doesn't lack for male guests. Don't you think it's prudent to do our due diligence, check out the possibilities?" I held my breath, hoping I hadn't oversold and made Rachel more suspicious.

She finally answered. "I suppose that's true. But why should I take the ride? Staying together feels smarter. We can check other possibilities if Tomás doesn't pan out."

"You and your Kelpie BO." I'd already discovered it was difficult for other supernaturals to pick up Rachel's scent outdoors. "Tomás didn't have a chance in town, as breezy as it was and no more time than he spent near you. But in a hot, enclosed kitchen? Feels risky. You outdoors with natural horses will confuse any supernatural though. Plus, a horseback thing sounds like something that'd attract straight men. We don't have time to spare. We have to maximize our resources and find this guy, fast." That was pure truth.

Rachel's sigh carried. "I loathe hard deadlines. So much stress." Zipping and rustling almost drowned her out as she added, "There's a dress code, even for classes. Come here and I'll get you ready."

I stepped out and had the satisfaction of seeing Rachel legit speechless. One of her myriad makeup bags dangled from her hand like she'd forgotten she held it. Ditto the slinky jumpsuit in her other hand.

Keeping Rachel off balance enough not to reconsider my flimsy excuses, I did a pirouette, my skirt flaring around my knees in a rippling red and gold wave, showing off my legs. "Think this will do?"

Rachel snapped her mouth closed. "Where did you—is that a BCBG dress?" Her eyes narrowed. "You never mentioned any familiarity with fashion, much less this year's designs."

"You know what they say about assuming. Ass and u." I hadn't actually chosen it. Zara had.

"Can you fight in that?" Rachel's brow arched.

I threw one of her quotes back at her. "You'd be surprised at what I can do in heels."

These weren't heel-heels, but cute, square-heeled ankle boots. Complete with enough shaft for a small, folded blade hooked and hidden inside. The corset-style top of the dress had a few mods, too, including a garrote wire threaded in the bodice framing, and narrow, shallow pouch-pockets in the folded seaming, containing a mix of silver dust, iron fillings, and blessed Cyprus shavings. An all-purpose mixture created to be blown or dusted in the face to temporarily freeze Weres, vamps, Fae, and anything demonic long enough for me to put a more permanent stop to the threat.

I stopped in front of the mirror set into a brocade vanity in the corner. I clasped a gold chain around my neck and bent, making sure the locket strung from it didn't swing too far out.

"That doesn't match."

Using my thumbnail, I flicked the square locket open, exposing the crystal inside. The clear gem colored crimson, and heated. "It's hard to find stylish magic-alert jewelry. This'll warn me when I'm near our killer."

Rachel made an interested noise. "So that's how hunters identify human-passing supernaturals."

The charms were an open secret in hunter circles. Despite her profession, that nobody had clued Rachel in was telling. None of her human hunter contacts were willing to let her in on the secret.

I snapped the locket closed and held it away from my neck, the metal already uncomfortably hot in her presence. It heated further as she glided closer.

"Be still." She caught my chin in warm fingers.

I froze as she stopped nearly nose to nose with me. She dusted a glimmering powder over my cheeks and chin. Her fluffy makeup brush dipped lower, swirling over my chest, highlighting my cleavage. "There. Perfect."

She let go and stepped away.

I remembered how to breathe and skirted her, and my unreliable feelings.

Rachel grabbed a black case, one of mine, and upended it on the bed. She grabbed the tiny stud earrings that'd been inside and thrust one set at me. They were magically enhanced, one an earbud, the other a mic, so we could stay in contact. We—I—had them made after a Werebear picked up the feedback from the electronic kind, and got the jump on me. Rachel and I had used them weeks earlier on a job.

I took them without touching her.

Rachel sat on the bed, putting her pair in, faint lines creasing her forehead, watching me as I threaded mine into my ear lobes.

I avoided meeting her eyes. Not chancing letting her see the lie in mine. "Let's ride."

"Is that some racist Kelpie remark?" Rachel's eyes crinkled in amusement, the same teasing we'd accidentally fallen into before our first hunt, a joke that had become our pre-hunt ritual.

"You should get to the stables."

"I'll alert you before jumping in, of course." She failed at hiding the hurt at my ignoring her teasing. "You do the same. Be careful. You do look like the perfect bait."

I shouldered past her and strode into the darkness. After tonight, things like new bonding rites and the possibility of sharing a bed would be as dead as Zara's murderer.

§

Inside the kitchen that more closely resembled a television set than a commercial space, I smiled and admired diced condiments and spotless prep counters, holding an untouched glass of wine for show. The cooking demo was at capacity, and ninety-nine percent of the crowd was female.

I'd scouted around the edges for the last fifteen minutes, listening for anything useful as the group got to know each other, with no luck. My gut said the killer was here tonight. I knew in my bones it was Tomás, but Rachel might be listening, so I had to go through the motions.

I gave in and inserted myself into a conversation with the only two men in the group, getting a glare from the brunette woman I cut off, leaning in front of her so that the locket swung closer to the youngest man.

He was only a little over my height, every blond hair in place, and brave enough to wear a light cream cashmere sweater to a kitchen event. My acrobatics all but put his face in my cleavage. "Oh, did you say you were from Texas, too? The Houston area? Maybe we're neighbors."

He wrinkled his nose, and backed off half a step. "Austin, actually, and only temporarily." He turned back to the brunette, dismissing me.

Since the locket stayed inert against my breastbone, I returned the favor. I scanned and found my last suspect on the far edge of the group. When I turned to the older guy, he gave me a far more welcoming return smile, gaze dipping to my highlight-powder enhanced chest before settling on my face. The lecher-level was high with this one.

Silver sprinkled among his black curls, but his shirt stretched across wide shoulders and a broad chest. Possibly in preparation for the hands-on cooking portion, he had his sleeves rolled up, revealing forearms corded with muscle.

Completely practical. Plenty fit enough to kidnap and dismember a woman, too.

He took my evaluation as interest, and his smile grew. Wide and hungry. Square jawed, with a well-tended five o'clock stubble, he was the kind of rugged that appealed to lots of women. He cut around a knot of attendees, moving my way.

A flicker of uncertainty sparked in my gut. I angled to meet him, the fake recon turning real.

"Hello, hello." Tomás' accented voice filled the spacious kitchen, interrupting my progress. The crowd homed in on our host like magnets to their opposite, cutting off my view of my new suspect.

Tomás held his arms wide—he had on a shirt, instead of the bare chest and apron I half expected, although the tee was tight enough to outline his abs like a second skin—and beckoned us in. He didn't bother introducing himself, attitude saying plainly that he was confident we all already knew, and were there solely because of him. "Please, everyone. I apologize, but we are running late. I had unexpected personal business to take care of. Sometimes pleasure comes before business, yes?"

He waved again. "Come, have a seat. I'll tell you about the magic we'll make tonight. Then you can join me." He winked. "I'll choose my most enthusiastic student as my personal sous chef."

Another *magic* reference and a personal one-on-one? Sounded like the perfect setup to select and isolate a target afterward.

"He's confident."

I twitched at Rachel's voice in my ear, then scowled as a tall woman beat me to the center seat along the counter, the spot closest to the chef. Coincidentally, the one beside the older guy as well.

I lifted my glass, pretending to sip as camouflage. "You have lousy timing."

"Am I distracting you from the pretty boy? Lie and tell me he isn't as yummy as I remember, because I'm already not in a good mood."

"Why?" I paused in jockeying for a spot.

"Everyone here is distressingly human, although less distressingly, also female. The scenery is lovely, but the ride is a bust as far as suspects. This was a waste of time."

My gaze jumped from the chef to the curly haired guy. Mine wasn't a bust. Everything in me was telling me the killer was in this room. "Tomás is arrogant, but that's all I can say. I'm not getting a vibe," I lied.

More truthfully, I added, "The charm hasn't alerted."

Rachel swore, switching from English to Gaelic before winding down. "Still. I'll fake a reason to return to the stable. We aren't far away. Then I'll join you."

"Don't bother. I don't need you—I'm writing this off and leaving soon." I quashed the pang of loss. I couldn't waste energy thinking about this being our last conversation. I had obligations to fulfill, no matter what it cost me.

Her tone sharpened. "Fine. I'll return and circulate through the main house, and we can compare notes after."

I worked my way to the last empty seat. Away from the action and detection range of my charm, but conveniently located near the mise en place, all the neatly arranged ingredients the chef needed for whatever he was preparing tonight. With everyone's attention on Tomás, I pulled out the ear studs and dropped both into the ramekin of salt. I held my palm over the dish, muffling the twin pops as the salt nullified the magic, turning the set from coms linking me to Rachel to plain, inert jewelry.

§

"Let's get started," Tomás announced with another exuberant wave, the exertion pulling the shirt tight over his chest.

I'd never admit it to Rachel, but when an enthusiastic blond side-swiped me in her rush to get closer, I teetered on my heels, losing a precious second regaining my balance. Women closed around the chef and his cooking station like a prison wall snapping closed, leaving me on the outside, a row away.

A hand caught my elbow. Helping me regain my footing, but not letting go after. I looked over my shoulder. Right into dark eyes and that ravenous smile.

"Enthusiastic crowd," the guy said. "It's a little more than I bargained for."

"You don't like competition?"

"Not especially." His gaze swept me from head to toe, or at least, leg to breasts. "You don't seem like the type to play second fiddle, either."

I twisted in his grip to face him and leaned in, heart tapping out my anticipation against my breastbone. Half my attention fixed on the square of metal against my throat, the other half assessing my target. His hand was warm and lightly callused, and when I checked him out through my lashes, making eye contact, there was no pull to his gaze. Not a vamp or Fae, then.

I inhaled, and only caught notes of synthetic musk and leather from his cologne, none of the grave dirt-and-rot tang of a ghoul or necromancer.

Which only left a Were creature. Were anythings were easily capable of dismembering a human.

All I had to do was pretend to fall for his charms, get him outside, anywhere on the secluded acreage, and puff the silver-laced mixture on him. It would give me time to grab the bag I'd hidden in our room, the one with more than basic hunter supplies. Then this murderous asshole and I could spend some quality time together, with him in silver chains.

He—it—took my attention as approval. His grip tightened, close to painful, fingers digging in. He reeled me in, my breasts crushed against his chest. Pressing us together from chest to thighs. Way too high-handed, even if our flirting had been real and I had been interested in getting to know him better.

The necklace stayed an inert lump, its only warmth coming from my body heat.

I rose to my tiptoes as if I meant to go in for a kiss, letting the charm brush against the swatch of skin visible at his collar.

Nothing.

I kept the contact for another heartbeat, but it didn't change the results. My necklace stayed a chunk of boring jewelry. He was human. "Son of a—look. Never mind."

He stiffened. He also kept the contact, even as I dropped flat on my heels and tried to pull away.

My temper spiked on a hit of frustration. I snaked my hand down between us, grabbed and twisted. "This was a mistake, and you need to back off."

He paled at the pressure on the family jewels and turned loose of me like I was coated in acid. "Jesus. All you had to do was say you'd changed your mind, you crazy—"

I turned my back on his complaints. Tomás was it. He had to be.

§

The hands-on portion of the class began, the participants' excitement rising, feeding mine.

I should have included Rachel in this class. Her technique for plowing through frenzied shoppers fighting for the last limited edition gift set would've come in handy. I grunted as I took an elbow to the gut from the tall chick in front of me, who wasn't giving up her prime spot at the chef's side. The woman at his other side hadn't been any kinder, ruthlessly crushing my toes under her sharp heels when I'd angled in.

The bland guy from Austin glared at me as I got between him and Killer Heels, the same woman he'd been talking to earlier. I made an apologetic face at him. His night probably wasn't going to get any better, judging by the way the woman hung on the chef's every word and ignored him.

The smoke of charring steak filling the air, I prowled the kitchen. The gleam of metal pulled me to the back of the kitchen. A leather case was unrolled on one prep counter, knives spread neatly like diamonds on a jeweler's display cloth.

I trailed my fingers over the display, metal slick and cold. High-quality steel. The edges razor sharp, as well-honed as anything in my special bag. A chrome kitchen torch sat off to the side, compact but powerful.

The block of machinery taking up a whole prep table turned out to be an industrial meat slicer. A smaller blade and grater combo, maybe meant for vegetables, nestled underneath. Both had safety guards to protect users from slicing off fingers. Safety features weren't ever infallible, though.

One of the on-site restaurant's selling points was that they butchered their own locally sourced meats. Another minute of searching, and I found a rack holding heavy kitchen snips, a mallet, and a tool that couldn't be disguised as anything but a hacksaw.

Spur of the moment, I altered my plan. There was a certain irony in using Tomás' knives, and his profession's tools, against him. I'd memorized the wounds on all of his victims. With enough time, I could recreate each slice, burn, and crushed joint.

The chatter from the group behind me crested. I turned as Tomás diced and passed out amuse-bouche sized pieces of the completed dish. I accepted mine second-hand, passed back by another guest, not even giving me the iffy chance to touch the chef's fingers for a possible charm hit. That was okay. I knew all I needed to. The charm would only confirm facts.

I relaxed on a stool, biting into beef still red and warm in the center, enjoying the heat from the chimichurri as the group thinned out slowly, those really only there for the culinary experience drifting away. Those more interested in the celebrity aspect hung on longer, inventing questions that our chef finally resorted to answering in bored monosyllables. Either he didn't like anyone here as a victim—or he already had one stashed. His "personal business" that had made him late for a sold-out class. I'd relish getting the location of his would-be victim out of Tomás even more than I relished the perfectly seared bit of steak.

Finally, only the hardcore remained—Killer Heels and her hopeless admirer. As she touched the chef's hand, I barged in, physically pressing her out of my way, speaking to him. "Wow, that was amazing. I barely saw anything though. You mentioned something about private lessons. Something intimate where I could catch up?"

He glanced at me and interest brightened his bored face. "On occasion, yes." He held out his hand and I took it. He leaned in and I forced my muscles to stay relaxed and kept the star-struck expression going. Lowering his voice, he asked, "The tall, lovely gentleman you were with earlier—do you share?"

I glanced in the direction his chin tipped. To the guy I'd all but temporarily neutered. Then down to the charm, still dead as a doornail. Around my shock, I mumbled, "Umm, you'd have to take that up with him. Feel free."

He squeezed my fingers and abandoned me to my confusion, striding to the guy. Whatever was said, Tomás shrugged and left alone. I caught a glimpse of Killer Heels and the older guy, heads close together, maybe comparing notes on being rejected, making their way outside.

Alone, I slumped against the counter, the stone a cold line along my hips. I'd been wrong. Wrong and arrogant. My radar was...fucked. I'd wanted revenge so bad that I'd convinced myself the killer was here, then that Tomás was him.

I'd failed another woman, whoever the real killer was torturing while I ate Kobe beef. I failed Zara. Again.

"Getting turned down—no, getting cock blocked—sucks, doesn't it?"

I jumped at the venomous tone, and glanced over my shoulder. Mister Only-Temporarily-from-Austin glared at me, cheeks flushed.

"Making wrong choices sucks." I shrugged and turned away.

"Bitches like you, always turning down us good guys. You deserve everything I'm going to do to you, the same as all those others."

Hairs stood up on my arms and I shoved off the counter, whirling. Too late.

Austin lunged, locking a hand around my wrist, hauling me half over the counter edge, knocking air from my lungs.

The charm had been wrong. Whatever he was, he'd found some way to mask his supernatural powers from detection. Bracing my knee on the prep stand, I leaned back hard, knee bruising and shoulder burning, fighting his weight. I shoved my free hand into the folds of the corset. Came out with the handful of dust and threw it into his face.

He sneezed. Let go, swiping his nose. Not freezing. "What the hell is it with this stuff? Some new self-defense trend?"

Human. He was *human*.

"Stupid trick didn't work for that bitch in Memphis either."

At his smug comment, I fought past my shock and focused. Right at the barrel of a gun he'd pulled, pointed at my forehead, like an endless hallway to the underworld. Austin held it steady, despite his red-rimmed, teary eyes.

"You're *human*." Rage surged through me like a tsunami. At his pride and smugness. That this weak little worm was the one responsible for so much pain. That it hadn't been a magical battle of wills with a necromancer or an honest hand-to-hand fight with a raging Werewolf that ended the fastest, smartest hunter I'd ever known—but a fucking preventable *mistake*.

"You didn't set off her charm. That's how you took her out." Unlike every other vic, she'd only been shot and left to bleed out. Now I knew why.

I lunged around the table.

His eyes widened at my charge. The gun barked. Stone chips showered me, nicking and biting, his shot going wide.

I caught his gun hand between both of mine. Trapping it. I twisted it toward him in a sharp snap. Taking the gun as his wrist gave a pop. He cried out and shoved.

My stupid heel skidded, twisting under me. I threw my arms out, fighting not to fall, and the gun fell. Austin scrambled past, cradling his arm. Aiming for the back door. A yard past it, the wooded hiking trail started. If he hit the trees, I'd lose him.

I caught my balance, knee screaming. Bolted after him, grabbing a knife from the chef's displayed case on my right.

His hand closed on the doorknob.

I locked my fist in his collar, jerking him to a stop and crashing against his back. Whipped the knife around, blade laying across his throat.

He finally froze. "Don't kill me."

"Later." I let go of his collar and hauled his good arm around behind his back, cranking until his shoulder threatened to give. Soaking up his harsh gasp, hungry for more of his pain. "I have something fun in mind for you first. Move."

I headed him out the back door. Prepared to break the only real law hunters and humans agreed on.

§

I drew icy air and the bite of evergreens into my lungs. Frosted grass crunched under our boots. "Where were you taking her?"

When Austin didn't answer except to shiver, I gave him a tooth-rattling shake.

"Wh—what?" He squeaked out.

"Do not fuck with me. You have this down to a science—you weren't randomly grabbing a vic and torturing her in the first available alley. Where were you planning on taking that woman?" I cranked harder on his shoulder, savoring the creak of the joint tested to its limit.

He gasped. "The rear of the property. North side."

I pointed him away from the last of civilization, short grass giving way to little more than a deer track. The path circled behind our cottage, heading deeper into the area not reclaimed for guest use.

The few tree and underbrush ended at an ice-rimmed stream. A low mist hung, water a few degrees warmer than the air. A tiny stone bridge led over it, to the hulking outline of a barn.

I shoved Austin into action, our feet thudding on weathered boards and echoing off the water like a fading heartbeat.

Unlike the rest of the fieldstone barn, the doors were recent additions. Well-oiled, one gave under my push. Light pooled over the stones, a modern lantern sitting in the corner. The bright silver-blue halogen illuminated a scene out of a B horror movie.

The old barn now served as the resort's catch-all, broken farm implements and furniture stacked across the back wall. From the dust and grit, this was a rarely used dumping ground.

The gleaming metal shackles hanging down from a thick timber beam, and the expensive generator and electric saw were a jarring note against the aged wood and stone.

Closing the door, I cut off the outside world. I nudged at the pile on the floor in front of me with a boot toe, and a cheap propane torch fell over with a metallic rattle, scattering duct tape, zip ties, razor blades, and needle-nose pliers crusted in dark gunk. Plus an amber bottle of tablets and a foil packet of plastic vials with snap off ends, both with the label from a Mexican pharmacy.

I dragged him to the center of the room. The cuff on the end of the chain fit tight around his good wrist, nearly cutting off circulation. "Custom made for smaller wrists, huh?"

"We can work something out." The guy licked his lips, eyes shrewd even now. "You aren't a cop. You can borrow whatever you want here. Use my site. That guy that blew you off earlier—"

His offer died on a shriek. I jerked the cuff as tight as possible around his broken wrist, and stood back, watching him writhe, until I got bored.

Pawing through his cache, I spun the torch in a wobbly circle. I didn't usually enjoy fire. Flames were unpredictable, which made it too easy to exceed the damage you intended to inflict.

I was okay with playing those odds tonight.

The soft clink of the chains stilled—it didn't take him long to grasp that moving only increased the pain. His panting breaths came out as fog against the unheated air. At last, he brought himself under control. Despite his bloodless face and the deep pain-lines etched around his lips, he got out, "I have contacts. More sites. *Better* sites, with all the amenities, not primitive like this. I've never worked with anyone, but you're promising. We can work together. Expand to couples."

The stout doors crashed open like they'd been hit by C4, wood splintering and falling in a soft rain.

"She already has a partner." Rachel blew through like a super model storming the runway. She hadn't changed clothes, still in the blood red riding jacket.

"Samantha Vasquez, do I look ditchable to you?" Rachel planted herself in front of me, arms crossed.

"I told you. I don't need you." It tasted like a lie on my tongue. I needed her. But I needed this more.

Rachel didn't buy it, eyes narrowing to pissed slits. A moldy green rolled over the clear emerald, her temper rising.

She opened her hand. My ruined earbuds sat in her palm. "You're shedding blind rage like Weres shed fur. I caught your scent before I even arrived back at the stables."

"Go away. I'm busy." I pointed the torch at Austin.

Rachel spun, and was on the guy in a blur.

He jerked hard, terror overcoming common sense in a harsh clank of chains. Rachel grabbed his chin, his skin whitening under her grip. She leaned close, nose inches from his skin, inhaling along his neck and jaw.

She swore and shoved him away like she'd smelled something foul, spinning to face me. Hers was horrified. "Bloody fucking hell, Sam. He's a human."

"He's a murderer."

Rachel froze, that eerie thing she could do where only her eyes gave away that she was anything other than a statue. Still and lifeless as a log floating in a pond. Or an alligator hidden under the water, camouflaged but for its eyes.

Mist rose around her, like the fog over the stream outside, hazing her. Her eyes glowed brighter, like cheap neon.

"Stop. Wait." Austin charged to the end of his chains, leaning hard enough toward Rachel that he was on tiptoes, arms stretched behind him to their limits, broken one swollen grotesquely already. "This is a misunderstanding, okay? I didn't know you thi—uh, people—were hunting here. Honest mistake."

Rachel turned on one polished heel, molasses slow. The swamp mist swirled faster around her, a living cloak. Underneath, something dark and gleaming, like a wet pelt, shone in patches where there should only be Scottish-pale skin and expensive wool jacket.

Instead of pissing himself in terror, excitement brought color to Austin's cheeks, and he talked faster. "I had no idea this was your territory. This trip was a last minute favor for another sales representative, and I had a spur-of-the-moment itch. I admit I didn't do my usual homework. You can understand, right? No harm, no foul. Like I told your friend, you can use my setup as an apology gift."

I turned the valve on the tank, and the propane gave a soft hiss. Rooting with my toe again turned up a lighter, and I squatted and scooped it up.

"We've got no beef here. I only kill humans, not supernaturals. Same as you guys," he babbled, gaze now fixed on my torch.

The lighter wheel rasped against my thumb and the gas caught with a soft *whoosh*.

Rachel smiled at him, her teeth suddenly squarer and whiter than human. "Then pray tell, how do you explain the death of Evelynn Goodwife?"

His throat worked and some of the color drained from his face. "That was a one off. The witch sold to me, then had the nerve to threaten to turn me in to the police. That was pure business—I did what anybody would when double-crossed on an honest deal."

I stood. "Can I get on with killing him now?"

Rachel's hands curled in, glossy pelt sprouting along her elegant fingers, manicured nails morphing to serrated claws. Her voice rolled, echoing like a foghorn over water. "He's loathsome, but nonetheless still human. I'll not touch him, and neither can you."

My jaw ached, but I ground out, "Do what you want. Put my bags outside. I'll grab them after I'm done here."

Rachel whipped around, shock readable even under her morphing features, big eyes going even wider and more equine. "You can't mean that."

"Get out."

She moved in that inhuman blur.

Placing herself between me and my prey. The heavy, wet stink of peaty bogs and dead fish rose, snuffing out the last trace of perfume and horse. Her voice belled. "This isn't you. Make me understand why you would sacrifice our partnership, and your life, over this."

My grip tightened, the torch weirdly cold in my hand. "He killed…" I hadn't said her name aloud, not even when I stood on her parent's porch and told them she was gone. "He killed Zara. My partner. He's the one, and he's not walking out of here."

Rachel gave one slow blink. The swamp rot stench died out. She bent her head, almost a bow. "You should have told me."

"I wasn't sure—"

The echo was gone, and something like weariness rode her voice when she spoke again. "You weren't sure whether you could trust me. Still."

We both already knew the answer. "He's mine." A hot wash of possessiveness fought its way up my throat, nearly choking me.

"Your touching him is out of the question."

No one was robbing me of revenge.

Fire really was the worst way to die. It worked on everything—humans, animals, water demons. The flame turned from blue to white. I took a step. Into Rachel's personal space.

She squeezed her eyes closed. When they opened, they were plain green. Pretty, but only human. So was the emotion in their depths. Her cloaking fog swirled down like it was sucked into the ground, vanishing. Leaving only an average height red head with better than average clothes.

"Sam…" She faltered. "You can't do this. Trust me. This is to save you, not him. I don't give one hot damn about him."

My hand started sweating, the tank slipping. "You don't get it."

"I do. But once you cross one line, no matter how valid your reason, it becomes easier to cross the next line. Eventually, there are no lines left. That's why hunters don't allow what you're doing. Rationalizing that he's a monster instead of human is no different than rationalizing humans are food."

"You're leaving anyway, so what does it matter?"

"You're operating on grief, revenge, and self-destructive decisions. You lost your friend and partner. I've lost many over the years.

Please don't take my new one." She held out her hand. Perilously close to the flame, the smell of singing hair and skin enough to wake my gag reflex.

Suddenly, I just wanted this to be over. "I'll—I won't linger. I'll slit his throat and I'm done."

She shook her head. "Rule one is that supernaturals answer to hunter law while humans answer to human laws. Every hunter out there will be after you if you violate that oath."

I'd quit worrying about luxuries like morality and futures when Zara died.

I thought I had.

"If you're set on this course, I can do this for you." Rachel beckoned for the torch. "I've made mistakes. I'm trying to make reparations. But no one will be shocked I cracked and did this. They'll assume you had nothing to do with executing a human."

"Why? I lied to you. Didn't trust you. Kinda threatened you." Dampness traced lines down my face.

"I forgive you." The same sincerity I'd seen days ago, before I betrayed her trust, shone from her. "I'm mad at you, but I do forgive you."

I gave the tank valve a savage twist, killing the flame, and set the damn torch down. Then scrubbed both hands over my face, swiping at tears and snot. Rachel had my back, even when I couldn't see it. I couldn't sacrifice my new partner for my old one's memory. "He's human. He gets human law."

She searched her pocket and came out with what I very much suspected was a pocket square, handing the snowy linen to me to ugly-cry in.

Chains rattled behind us. "Listen you bitc—"

Rachel backhanded the guy, the love tap stunning him into silence, not looking away from me.

I blew my nose and sniffled. "Where do you stand on compelling humans against their will?"

A hint of mist floated across her eyes. "I have no moral qualms there."

We turned to our prisoner. His head wobbled, her handprint still vivid against his skin, but he had enough self-preservation left to backpedal in a vain attempt at evading his fate.

I stepped behind him, one arm around his throat, knotting fingers of my other hand in his hair. Forcing him to meet Rachel's glowing green gaze.

§

Under our dining table's cover, I flexed my bruised knee. The resort restaurant also had a dresscode, and heels really did suck. Tomás—who was damn accomplished even if he was a publicity hound—paused beside us. "Are you exquisite ladies enjoying your meal?"

Rachel gave him a dazzling smile and answered in Portuguese.

I kept most of my attention on her tablet screen, and the local news coverage. Austin's—AKA The Traveling Salesman Killer's—photo dominated the corner of the screen, local and national law enforcement taking up the rest, along with every news outlet in the US. I tapped the volume higher, in time to hear the lead FBI agent lean into the microphone. "Our suspect has cooperated fully after turning himself in, his conscience demanding he confess. He is in the process of giving us a complete list of his victims as well as details and locations. The evidence appears incontestable. We'll be asking for the maximum penalty—"

Rachel flicked the tablet closed, a freshly lacquered nail resting on the case. "One does not shovel in a four-star meal, especially a chef's seasonal tasting menu, while watching television. We are going to have to work on your learning to enjoy the finer things in life."

Maybe there were still lessons I could learn.

"I am working on it." I lifted my wine glass in toast, and across the cozy farmhouse table, Rachel matched me, our glasses clinking.

Cemetery Sisters

Michele Tracy Berger

The cemetery never scared Welcome Sparks, even as a child. Cutting through it to get home provided the quickest route and allowed unrivaled use of her imagination. She would make up stories about people, looking for the oldest headstones. Most days after school, before it got dark, she'd pick an interesting gravestone, settle in and strike up a conversation. She'd share things that didn't sit right in her mind.

She might say, "Ana Sterling of 1950, if you were here, I'd show you around Thistleview. Not that there's very much to see. In your day, I bet you use to go into that old city called Tulsa, not too far from here. It's not there anymore now, Ana."

Or, "One day the preacher's wife slapped me for not wearing a slip. After service, she asked me to come in the back to talk to her and before I knew it, she had her beefy hand on me. The preacher's wife said, 'Welcome, can't you see your breasts are falling out that dress? Do you want to end up like your mother?'"

Mama never said I had to wear a slip, Ana. I don't even have a slip. I stopped going to church after that. The preacher's wife doesn't bother me anymore. She doesn't even speak to me at all. She just looks right through me as if I'm some piece of old cobweb. Were slips big in your day, Ana? I bet they were. People had money back then from what I've read. They went places that needed slips."

On this day seventeen year-old Welcome made her way through the forested part of the cemetery, where the red cedars were thickest and some of the oldest headstones lay. She paused and sniffed, noticing the coolness in this part of the cemetery. She then heard words sung by a female voice:

My funny valentine
Sweet comic valentine
You make me smile with my heart

Goosebumps pebbled her pale skin and she hunched into her ragged coat. The phrases repeated, and Welcome looked toward the nearest stand of trees. She darted behind one and then another, thinking that she had been followed by some of her stupid classmates.

After a few minutes of frantic searching and finding no singers—she knew no one in town that sounded as good as that voice—with every vein straining in her face, she listened.

Another female voice rang out, this one deeper in tone:

We're trying to come throu...
Come to us!

The moment seared her like when she waited for the once a month afternoon train. On most days, Welcome dreamed of getting on the train to leave town. She imagined holding a bag of butterscotch candies in one hand and an old suitcase in the other. Wherever Welcome stood or sat, she sensed the trains, every part of her alert and yearning.

Pricks of excitement and danger bit into her, making her hop from foot to foot. She couldn't make herself stand still. Nothing she had heard so far in her life sounded as good as these voices. They made her feel as if her favorite butterscotch candies were melting on her tongue. No, it were as if she floated in warm butterscotch candy. She ran up and down the stretch of the cemetery. Welcome overturned rocks, peeked behind headstones, climbed a small tree and searched for the origin of those voices until she could barely see in front of her.

Exhausted, she remembered her responsibilities. *Mama will wonder where dinner is.*

"Please, whatever you are come to me," she said at last, the frustration catching in her throat. On the rest of the walk home as the sun sank, a feeling of utter sadness swept over Welcome.

Maybe everyone in town is right. I'm going crazy, like Mama.

§

The next morning, she let herself believe that the voices were real. She had heard something; she couldn't be crazy. Yet.

As she approached the thicket on her way to school, she observed and listened. She concentrated on every robin that flew by, every thrush that skittered through the fallen leaves, and noticed now how this part of the cemetery made her feel as if she walked through a cool mist, despite the warmth of the sun. She gaped at the way the light weaved in and out through the red cedars' conical branches. When she knew she could tarry no longer, she forced herself to move and touched her right hand to every tree as if to leave a sign for something that perhaps waited for her.

§

Mrs. Dori Gavey jolted Welcome's attention when she said, "Welcome, I think that you are very talented. You are my best student and the only one that I want to talk with about life outside Thistleview."

Welcome stared at her teacher with the warm smile trying to understand why she was asked to stay behind. The day had dragged on as it often did for Welcome in school. She sat watching and waiting, looking at the clock every few minutes, willing the hours to pass. The only time that she felt awake enough to say or do anything meaning-ful was in Mrs. Gavey's 'design and implementation' class; known as 'dimps' among students. Tall, shapely, red-haired Mrs. Gavey came to Thistleview about the time Welcome began the sixth grade. She was the only person Welcome knew who had come, in recent years, to Thistleview to stay. Mrs. Gavey's hire was the last attempt by the town to provide students with classes about cities in case someone wanted to go 'out there,' which increasingly no sensible Thistleview resident desired. Welcome often felt sorry for her as no one seemed much interested in Gavey's specialty subjects of building, design, or city history. Most of the girls begged out of it and decided to go to the domestic arts classes instead, but Welcome enjoyed learning about urban design, architecture, mechanical drafting, and how the great old cities were constructed and what they were like many de-cades ago. They sounded like made up places—Hong Kong, Oakland, Venice, Brisbane—but through Gavey's lectures, Welcome imagined herself traveling to them. However, today even the talented teacher's lecture on 'Cityscape Leisure Activities Prior to the Great Separation' felt remote.

"Let me get to the point," Mrs. Gavey said, sitting back down at her desk and motioning for Welcome to pull up a chair.

"I want you to apply to a college. I think there are several that would accept you, especially in New Orlando. Has anyone talked with you about your future, Welcome?"

Cities! New Orlando! Of course, she had heard of it, but no one in Thistleview talked openly about cities. One didn't talk of much in Thistleview, period. They had everything they needed here.

"No, Ma'am," Welcome said, her mind spinning from the men-tion of New Orlando. New Orlando wasn't even one of the places the trains from Thistleview traveled to!

"Well, it's time that someone did as you're graduating soon. I've taken the liberty of reaching out to a few contacts outside of here about travel permits. I should have more to share in about a week. We'll start making a plan then."

Welcome nodded as Mrs. Gavey walked her to the door. She couldn't stop smiling.

Welcome scratched the name New Orlando over and over again in her mind as she walked home. *To ride the train out of Thistleview!*

That night, she lay on her stomach with a map made from hemp showing the towns like Thistleview that were part of the Great Separation, which had sprouted up about fifty years ago—the towns that had separated themselves from the remaining, functioning cities after the virus and war. Connected to the rest of the country by a rail system, these towns advocated for self-sufficiency and a way of life that was simple and traditional.

What a wide world there was outside of Thistleview! She could go anyplace, if she could just make herself get on that train.

$

Day after day, color and definition leaked out of her world. She still could find no voice and no music. She *had* imagined it all!

"Welcome, come here," her mother screeched.

Welcome rose from her bed to see what her mother wanted. Her mother sat in the bathtub with several candles lit. Her cup of amber liquid was still full which told Welcome that she had only been soaking for a short time.

"My back needs a scrub," her mother said, closing her eyes and pointing.

Welcome avoided as much as she could her looking at her mother's pale naked body. She, however, could see her mother's breasts well in the candle light. They looked fallen to her, and not just flat as she'd seen of long-ago primitive women in ancient magazines in the Knowledge Centers. Fallen, as if all the life that lived inside her mother had given way.

At least she's not lifting and playing with them, like she usually does. Mama doesn't know she's crazy. She hears voices, talks to them. Maybe that's the way it will be for me. At least I won't lift my dress in public. I'm reminding myself right now to not do that to myself. Maybe I'll be a funny old crazy woman.

She grabbed the old and worn loofah, picked off the moldy spots, and began. While she scrubbed her mother's ruddy colored back dotted with moles, she occupied herself by counting how many ants crawled around one claw foot of the tub.

"I'm thinking of your daddy tonight," her mother said.

"Yeah," Welcome said, trying not to show undue curiosity, which would require more scrubbing, but hearing anything about her father was always of interest.

"He brought me to this house and said, 'Welcome home, you're mine.' And we lived just fine. And I fixed him eggs, and Spam when we could get it, almost burned, 'cause that's the way he liked it," she said. Her mother grunted as if the memory poked at her now. She continued, slightly above a whisper, "He'd go away with a crew and scavenge in the worst of the old cities, make his money and come back to me. No matter what people in town said about me, he never cared. He never cared. He didn't even care that I started to hear the voices soon after being with him."

Welcome's attention drifted, she already knew this much about her father.

"But one day, he got dressed as fine as I'd ever seen him. Nice black pants, a red shirt and black jacket and I said to him, 'You up and put your clothes on. You leaving and can't say goodbye?' He looked so strange that day. I remember looking at his lips, they looked like they puffed up to make a kiss and then like he bit into something sour. Those lips! His lips always looked swollen, like someone had punched him. You got those swollen type lips, too."

Her mother absentmindedly picked at the skin on her arms and looked up at Welcome. "Your father said, 'Why say goodbye, when welcome is so much nicer?'"

"He left like he was going to take a walk right into town, like he was going to see someone. You were due soon. I didn't even ask him to get me anything; I wasn't having no cravings for nothing except to get you out of me. You were tearing me up with all that kicking and moving. I thought I was birthing a banshee," she said, her dry laugh cutting the air.

"He never came back. You were born three days later, and I named you Welcome."

Welcome shook her head; her father couldn't have left. It couldn't be true. Her mother was making it up. As she made up most things.

She felt punched. "You told me he died traveling to salvage." Welcome let the heavy, dirty sponge drop into the water.

"You're growing up now. I thought you might want a taste of the truth."

Her mother drew her knees up to her large chest. "Go and boil me some water for tea."

As Welcome got up to leave, she held on to the door with her back to her mother. Mama, I'm sorry that he did that to you. But, I don't understand. You named me Welcome because that's the last thing he said?"

"Don't be sorry and no!" her mother said, splashing a hand in the water, "Your dad was a fool. I named...I named you Welcome so I can look at you and think of something good and inviting and so that you can never say goodbye to me. Never."

Welcome closed the door, feeling as she was a toy that her mother picked up and played with on occasion. *Mama never makes any sense.*

Later that night, Welcome dreamed that her father was a gray-haired giant who lived in the biggest ditch at the end of the world. He owned pretty things and ate them one by one, with a large fork and knife, and wore red and black shoes.

§

After several weeks of exploring every perimeter of the cemetery, yet still not hearing anything, Welcome wanted to up her odds at finding the mysterious melodic voices, especially that first voice she heard. She took matters in her own hands.

She knew she would need to see Mr. Applegate, the caretaker of the cemetery. She knew Mr. Applegate to be a solitary widower, and that he was son of Lily Applegate, buried in the cemetery. She saw him in town from time to time and thought he always smelled good for someone who worked at the cemetery.

The wind blew hard as she made her way round to his house at the northwest edge of the cemetery. As she walked along, huddled in her thin coat she looked down and saw a trapped water bubble under the ice. She squatted so that she could get a better look at it. It is waiting for something to turn it into the rigid structure that it will be if the cold continues, or if a warm turn of the weather has its way it will stay water and merge into other puddles, she thought. *That is me, that trapped little pancake size of water. What will become of me? Will I thaw or will I freeze?*

Holding this question inside, she knocked on the blue door of Mr. Applegate's house. Another knock brought her face to face with Mr. Applegate. His brown face had a slack appearance as if he were about to smile, relaxed his muscles, but then decided against it. He looked twice her mother's age in the face, but Welcome saw how his chest bulged under his beige long sleeved shirt and how his muscled arms hung down, relaxed.

He looked around her and then fixed his lopsided face on her.

"Welcome, you with anyone?"

"No, Mr. Applegate, I've come by myself to see you."

He paused for a moment and then opened the door wide. "Come in."

Grateful to be asked in, she rubbed her hands against her arms, stamped her feet, and took in the dark house and the framed pictures on the wall of him and his deceased wife, Wilhelmina. For a moment, her mind conjured up the best piece of lemon meringue pie that she had ever tasted. His wife had made it for a church event when Welcome was very young. Her tongue oozed saliva responding to the memory of it. Her mother never baked and everything in town was rationed, including sugar.

They stood in the hallway looking at each other.

"Something wrong with your mother?" he asked.

"No," she said casting her eyes down. "She's fine."

"Take your coat? Get you something to drink? The cold made me not want to get out of bed today," he said, attempting at a smile through tobacco stained teeth.

"No, I can't stay long. I wanted to know if I could help you tend to the cemetery after school on some days."

"For pay?" He belched and then put his hand to his mouth, "Excuse me."

She shrugged, "I guess." She shifted some to not look directly at him. Her mother had showed her how to lean to one side and look slightly past men's shoulders. Her mother made her get up and practice all sorts of things at night after hearing her voices. Sometimes the voices told her useful things like what plants to grow in the garden to use on burns or cuts or teas to make when Welcome was sick. Looking slightly away helped right now though because Welcome's heart raced, and her head pounded with such force, she could barely think. And, what would she do if he said no? She needed to know she wasn't crazy. Finding the voices would help.

"Not much extra work right now as it's winter," he said.

She saw him taking her in, her thick hair, unnaturally and prematurely gray in the very front and the rest jet black. Her mama always said, 'Thick, gray and black hair like some wild raccoon.' Her head dropped slightly and the expression on her face seemed to give him pause.

"But, I could use a bit of help around here every now and again, especially when it gets warmer. Your mother says it's all right?"

"Yes." The lie fell from her lips before she could even think about it. *Mama don't need to know everything about my life. Won't matter to her if I'm crazy or not long as I make her dinner and take care of her.*

"I guess you're pretty strong—you're bigger than me when you stand up straight," he said, then laughed.

She smiled though she wasn't sure if she should. Welcome pretended not to notice how he looked at her, stared now in a different way, a way that made her feel like she should flatten and roll herself out thin, like a piece of dough, and slide backwards under the bottom of his door. Like he knew there rested a wild energy in her that could get stirred up. Maybe it comes from being with so many dead people; maybe he's forgotten what it's like to be around girls, she thought.

With her round face and unusually long eyelashes, Welcome knew that she was growing into an attractive, if not beautiful young woman. Boys no longer called her 'gray slime' even if they didn't ask her out. She was five feet, eleven inches in bare feet, and three inches taller in the hand me down heels her mother made her wear from time to time and that Welcome chose this day. Before leaving school she made sure to go to the bathroom and wash her face, removing all ink stains, around her mouth, from chewing on her old pen.

"So, I can come by when the weather gets better?" Welcome asked, pressing.

The question broke the staring spell and he nodded, "Sure can. You want something warm to drink before you leave?"

"No, Mama's probably wondering where I am. Thank you very much and I'll be around soon."

§

On her rounds, that spring, Welcome discovered that the cemetery was a busy place. There was always a dead body to help dig a grave for, flowers to place at headstones and cleanup after the kids who loitered about on weekends. She was honest and returned wallets, lost keys, and other small items that occasionally turned up near the graves. She mowed and watered the grass and helped Mr. Applegate trim trees.

Through the lengthening of light she waited for the voices to return. She whistled to keep occupied, continuing to make up stories about the deceased. To test her own limits, she used the headstones as hurdles when she knew Mr. Applegate wasn't around. She'd spring up and unfurl her long legs and let mud splatter onto her face. Running around breathless, she'd collapse on the ground.

"Did you like that?" she said to no one in particular. "Here let me try again."

"Talk to me someone or something," she whispered into the night before locking the front gate up, feeling loneliness webbing inside of her.

$

One day at the cemetery, while contemplating if she should take some flowers home to cheer up her mother, she heard her name spoken clear as a bell.

"Welcome, over here. Look up."

Directly across from her the faint impression of a young woman sat high up in a tree. She waved.

"We did it! I should know to trust you, Millicent," the woman in the tree said, a trill of breathiness evident.

Welcome dropped the flowers and stiffened. It was one thing to hear voices and another thing to see what? An apparition? A hallucination? Now that the moment arrived, Welcome didn't know what to do.

A second voice, deeper than the first and familiar sounding said, "Yes, you should. But I'm afraid that we're scaring her half to death."

"Sister, will you hush, she's looking at us. She's so pretty."

Welcome stared. The woman in the tree, became more visible now. She sat with her legs crossed, dressed in brown, high-waisted trousers and a white linen shirt. Black peep-toe heels graced her feet. The young woman looked to Welcome to be in her mid-twenties. There were no lines on her heart-shaped face. She held Welcome's gaze with a wide open smile that made Welcome feel special and blush in a way she never had before. And, then in a moment the woman disappeared, everything except her delicate hands with slim tapered fingers.

"Oh, goodness, I thought I had it right," the second voice said.

Welcome stared as the hands kept gesturing about. "Well, this is most distressing" the tree woman said. "I'm here, but I'm not here."

In a moment a second figure appeared right next to where the other one had been sitting. She looked like the first figure except her hair was darker than chestnut brown and not as wavy as the other woman and she had a prominent mole under the nose. She wore a blue button-down dress, with distinctive shoulder pads, that came to her knees and a pair of loafers.

This second figure said, "Please Welcome, do come close. We've been trying to come through for such a long time."

Welcome knew that she couldn't be intoxicated. Welcome had never had a full drink in her young life. On one long ago Christmas she appeased her mother by sipping some hideous concoction that her mother put before her. "Drinking always makes me feel better," she had said to Welcome. "I can drown out the voices that way."

Maybe I should run. But, in the moment Welcome reviewed all the fun things that had happened in her life, without her causing them. After taking that depressingly small tally, she pulled herself up to her full, impressive height, wiped around the edges of her mouth, and stepped toward the tree.

§

Welcome could not tell anyone about her new acquaintances. She looked over her shoulder as she approached what the sisters called 'The Grove" the area of the forest that they appeared. She'd meet them after school. A week in and she couldn't remember a more special time in her life.

They were the Pontey sisters, Grace and Millicent, born and raised in this area during the 1910s, almost 110 years before the Great Separation. They told her scraps of their memories: making a roast duck with crabapple stuffing, sewing buttons on a coat, playing with porcelain dolls when they were girls, and listening to records. Grace, the younger sister, was her favorite. She was the singer. Her face was dimpled, clear-skinned, and when she came through she smelled like lemons. Welcome guessed correctly in that when Grace died, she was in early twenties. Her laugh sounded like a tinny tinkling bell. She was shy and quiet, not like Millicent, older at least by ten years. And, Grace called her dumpling from time to time. Grace was getting good at materializing, but sometimes she'd get confused and only her slender hands showed, wildly gesticulating. Sometimes she could not maintain her image and said that it was too tiring, and just talked instead of materializing.

Sharp-faced Millicent asked questions and without warning might chafe at something Welcome said, her mood souring.

"The living don't understand anything. They don't take advantage of what they got right under their noses," Millicent said one cold spring afternoon.

"Don't say that. What do I have here?" Welcome said.

"You feel the sun on your face right? When your mother fries fish or bakes something good, it stays in your nose—right?" Millicent asked, coarsely.

"My mama don't fry fish and her baking will make you sick."

Millicent tutted. "Dead is dead. Bad cooking one can live with."

"Millicent! There's no need for rudeness," Grace said.

Millicent disappeared then.

A silence tightened like a cord between Welcome and Grace.

"I don't think that she likes me," Welcome said standing up and stretching her legs.

"My sister often takes getting used to," Grace said and then cocked her head. "To be fair, she's not been herself lately."

"What do you do when you're not here with me?"

"We think about our lives. Regrets, choices, losses. We argue. We mourn. Millicent roams and experiments with her abilities."

They waited for Millicent to return but after a bit, Grace said with a wink, "More time for us."

After singing a song for her, they explored the creatures of the Grove—the moles, foxes, and birds, and Grace showed her how to see the glow around animals. "If you are very calm, you can see the light that is around all living beings. And, if you know what you are doing, you can ride that light."

"What does that mean?"

Before Grace could answer Millicent appeared then and with a grin that showed all her teeth.

"Did you miss me?" she said, her grin growing wider.

Before Welcome could answer, Millicent waved her hand, "Forgive me. We should not talk of sad times and the past; it is a joy that we can be together." And then floating close to Welcome, she looked into her eyes and said. "Tell us everything about you, Welcome."

An icy tremor twisted Welcome's insides as she tried not to notice how Millicent's super wide, uneven-teeth-pressed-tightly-together grin unnerved her.

$

Despite her reservations about Millicent, Welcome always wanted to know more about their lives. They had been raised in a family with plenty, one of the wealthier families in the town.

"What did it feel like to be free? Have money?" Welcome said.

"I wasn't free, Welcome," Grace said. "Yes, we had money and nice things, but our father dictated much of our lives."

"Yes, he was a bore, wasn't he?" Millicent said.

Grace nodded. "You made it fun though, sister. Millicent always begged father for more parties and when I was married, she came over and cheered me up."

Welcome paid attention. This was the first time Grace had mentioned a husband. And, the thought of parties made Welcome swoon inside. Parties were rare in Thistleview.

"I married young, as my father wanted. My husband was a doctor." Grace shook her head and Welcome could feel a deep anger ripple through the ghost. Grace's presence faded some, but she kept talking. "Although he was supposed to be devoted to healing, he was cruel and small-minded. He tried to dictate everything I did." Grace shook her head, a frown clouding her face. "Oh, in those days, that was the way it was." She smiled at her sister who was looking up at the sky.

"What did you do all day? Did you work?"

"We were healers, in a way," Grace said.

"Nurses," Millicent corrected.

"Healing was a talent," Grace said, her face brightening.

And as Grace opened her mouth to say more, Millicent waved a hand, "Hush, you always talk too much, dead or alive."

Welcome jolted back. Grace's shimmery smile instantly disappeared. A look that Welcome couldn't read passed between them.

Millicent's pinched face spat though she possessed no saliva. "The men then were small-minded and cruel and most women were sheep-like, scared of their own shadow. Not much has changed."

"That's not true," Welcome said, feeling heat rise in her face. "Mr. Applegate is kind and Mrs. Gavey is the smartest person in the town."

"My sister is right, I do talk too much," Grace said with a wave of a hand. "What is in the past needs to stay there, right sister?"

Grace is the peacemaker between them. Welcome noticed with interest that although Millicent changed the subject to talk about her favorite music from when they were young, she never answered Grace's question.

They sat that way in silence for a few moments.

§

Her mother spooned out the sticky casserole. "Sorry about the edges, they're always so hard for me."

Welcome nodded. *Be grateful as Mama hardly ever cooks.* She looked down at the gray and white almost square shape on her plate. Her mama really did try. She did. She dragged her fork through the block of casserole and steeled herself. Mrs. Gavey had kept her promise and talked with Welcome at length about her prospects, the risks and challenges of leaving Thistleview. Their conversation had settled into Welcome and had made her even more aware about what it meant to leave. In her small room at night as she was going to sleep, she would imagine that the train was coming for her. For a few moments, the roar of the train became her second pulse, her life dependent on its metallic vigor. The approach of it vibrated the small pile of books and the old wooden hamper in her room. Welcome would imagine every object near her, animate with possibility, as if the rusty clock on the wall and the makeshift bed also yearned for their own adventures. She'd twitch, bite into her pillow and yelp as she felt the imaginary train arrive full blast past her house. After the shaking, she'd shrink, knowing that she still lived in the same squat house; her mother's light snoring next door lulling her back to sleep. She'd awake in the morning, disappointed that her ghost train hadn't taken her away.

It's time for me to say something.

Welcome took a deep breath and said, "Mama, Mrs. Gavey, said that I was good at studying the old cities and building things. You know, with my hands. That I might be able to go to college. She said she would help me apply for the special requests needed."

Her mother's eyes fixed on Welcome, but she said nothing. Welcome continued talking, her words spilling out in a rush. "Daddy was good at building things."

Her mother nodded. "Yes, he could put his hands upon something and change it. Like that table," she said pointing.

They both turned to look at the old oak table topped with a vase of dying flowers.

"But, girls don't know how to make things but trouble."

"Girls can build things!" Welcome felt the heat rising in her face.

"You're not going anywhere. You are going to stay right here and take care of me when I become old," her mother yelled, her eyes narrowing with defiance.

Welcome flinched then steadied her gaze. "When is that Mama? When will you get old?"

"Well, I'm already old."

Her mother shrugged and leaned both elbows on the table looking into her daughter's face. Welcome noticed that, for a moment, her mother's blue eyes looked clear, clearer than the sky. Her mother dipped her head. "Some days I can't tell where I am, what the past is and where now begins."

"I know, mama," Welcome said. She could see how the anger had fled her mother's face, leaving a slack expression and a trembling mouth. Her mother started crying softly and rubbing her arms.

Watching her mother, all of Welcome's plans faded away. She got up and hugged her. Her mother's body went limp, and she slid out of the chair into her daughter's arms. They landed on the floor. Welcome rocked her, noticing how small her mother's body felt. In her ears, she whispered, "I'll stay, I'll stay."

§

Welcome found the sisters' talents pretty amazing. Millicent was always eager to show off. They could conjure an item from memory, and it would appear for a few moments. And, as Grace had said, they had the ability to ride a creature's light and even subtly control its actions.

Welcome loved the birds that made their home in the forest of the cemetery. She delighted in seeing the thrushes circle around and the talkative iridescent grackles. On this day, they watched a grackle come close.

Millicent went silent and Welcome noticed the bird's bodily glow change from a low to a brighter light, which she was used to seeing from Grace's lessons. The bird went about its activities pecking at the ground, looking for worms in the moist earth.

The bird stopped and let out a shrill cry unlike any of its usual whistles and croaks. Welcome turned to Millicent whose face tightened and gaze was locked onto the bird.

Grace's eyes widened and she leaned forward. "You have become quite advanced, sister."

Millicent ignored them, but a self-satisfied and spine-chilling grin spread across her face that made Welcome shiver.

The grackle shot into the air and Welcome caught her breath. She put her hand to her eyes as she followed the bird's rapid ascent.

"Millicent, that's enough, don't you think?" Grace said.

"I'm trying to get my spirit in," she said, Welcome noted a sharpness in her voice.

Up and up the bird flew. Welcome felt the hairs on her arms rise and she watched with puzzlement as a blue light formed and bubbled around Millicent. *That's new.* Welcome exhaled with relief as finally the bird descended. But something was wrong with the bird. It zigged and zagged through the sky. As it returned toward them, the bird's high-pitched cry blasted Welcome's ears.

"Oh, stop it, whatever you are doing. You're hurting it!" Welcome said.

"I'm almost in," Millicent said, her voice throaty and rough.

The bird came nearer, flying through the sisters and around Welcome's head. Its black eyes had a wild look and blood trickled from its mouth. Welcome could no longer see the bird's natural glow, instead it looked as if it had been coated with thick blue paint. Finally, the bird's distress ended, and it fell to the ground with a sickening thud. Welcome rushed over. She picked up the bird.

Dead.

"What did you do?" Welcome wailed, cradling the dead bird.

Millicent frowned. "Tried to join into its body."

"That's not right, inserting yourself in." Welcome said, screwing up her face. Her stomach clenched. She didn't understand what Millicent was doing, she just knew it was cruel, wrong and unnatural.

Millicent's blue image grew brighter and the look on her face was distant and impassive, her thin lips pursed. "What would you know about right and wrong? Do you know how long it has taken me to perfect that kind of experience? The grackle was going to die someday, and today it died being part of a greater thing."

Welcome had not seen this unfeeling side of Millicent.

"She's right," Grace said quietly. "It's not becoming of our creed. You went too far."

Millicent disappeared abruptly.

"Come back, Millicent. Explain what you did," Welcome said. "I want to understand." She turned to face Grace. "Your creed? What did you mean by that?"

"Please do not press me, Millicent is already upset," Grace said, frowning.

How does Millicent act when she is upset? Welcome wondered.

"Keep your secrets then, I'm going home," Welcome said. She left to bury the sacrificial bird.

§

For a few days, Welcome avoided The Grove, but she missed Grace. She felt even more alone at school as she had told Mrs. Gavey that she wasn't interested anymore in college and leaving Thistleview. It hurt her to turn away from Mrs. Gavey but she knew she couldn't ever leave her mother.

When Welcome arrived in the Grove at the usual time, she was surprised to only find Millicent.

"Where's Grace?"

"She's away...resting." Millicent said.

This had never been the pattern of their visits, but Welcome was so troubled by the sinking feeling of being stuck forever in the town, she sat down and put her hands on her head.

"Something troubles you?" Millicent asked.

Welcome looked up, frowning. "You're not going to hurt another bird, are you?"

"No, I know how that bothered you. I'm sorry. Let's get your mind off of whatever it is bothering you. Want to play a game?"

Welcome was starting to feel lightheaded. She looked at Millicent for a long moment. "Maybe I should go, or we should call Grace."

"This game involves you and Grace, but really, it's a favor," Millicent said.

Welcome cocked her head. Her stomach roiled. *I should leave.*

Millicent came closer and Welcome could see the faintest outline of a bluish haze around the ghost. "She needs your help, Welcome. She's not doing well and there's something I want to try, and I need you."

Welcome wondered how ghosts couldn't feel well but she figured this was a question for Grace later. "I'll do anything to help her," Welcome said, sitting up with attention.

"Yes, I figured that you'd want to help. You're such a good girl," Millicent said softly, a human coo.

"Get settled against that headstone there. This won't hurt at all. It will feel like going to sleep."

Welcome did as she was told, and she could already feel her eyes drooping.

"I want you to think about Grace," Millicent said.

It felt to Welcome as if she were drifting far away, but when she opened her eyes, Millicent floated near her.

"Close your eyes and concentrate on Grace. Wouldn't it be nice if you could get closer to her? Wouldn't you like that?"

Welcome blushed. It was if Millicent read her mind and knew about the way Welcome fantasized about the train. Her entire body relaxed. And, then she noticed a warmth creeping across her skin. She didn't have the energy to open her eyes. Was Millicent touching her? Weren't ghosts supposed to be cold? This was a delicious warmth, not a coldness.

"I guess," Welcome finally answered, her mind fighting off drowsiness.

Strange symbols and geometric shapes appeared in her mind's eye. She saw a brilliant pulsing blue light. And, then nothingness.

After several moments Welcome thought she heard her name being called through a long hallway. She wanted to rush toward it, but she was stuck somehow, pinned down. Why was it that she couldn't move? The blue light was all around her, forcing her back. She felt a slamming against her head. She strained toward the voice that called her name. She knew that voice!

"Grace! Grace, where are you?"

"Follow my voice," Grace said.

With mental strain, she peeled herself away from the blue light that clung to her, the blue that threatened to ingest her. She dashed toward Grace's voice.

"Hurry!" Grace said.

She found a door where Grace stood and Welcome reached her hand out.

§

When Welcome opened her eyes, it was dark. She sat on the ground. How did she get here, near Mr. Applegate's house? Her head hurt. "Grace?" Welcome called.

"Welcome," Grace called slightly above a whisper. Welcome strained to see in the dark. She then saw Grace's hands. Something was wrong, Welcome could feel it.

"You're back here?" Welcome said, shaking off grogginess. "Are you better? Did I help?"

"Go home!" Grace croaked.

"I was with Millicent trying to help her, for you."

"Oh, Welcome, she..."

"What's happened to you?"

At that moment, Millicent appeared. "You did well, Welcome, thank you."

"Millicent, what did you think you were doing?"

"Shut up, Grace, you're scaring Welcome."

Grace let out a wail and Welcome covered her ears.

"Go home now, Welcome," Millicent ordered.

"Grace, are you all right?"

"I need to talk to Millicent," Grace said, her voice faint.

And then they were both gone and Welcome was left with a sinking feeling and a temple-splitting headache.

§

Welcome entered a small building near her school. The interior was decorated like a lodge with mounted animal heads against multiple walls. She hated having to come here, to talk with the Custodians of Knowledge. She walked to the back of the room where the ancient, frail and never smiling Custodian Lawson sat.

"Custodian Lawson, I 'm looking for information about the Pontey sisters...er...if there's anything about them."

Yesterday's encounter with them made Welcome curious about who they were as living people. She was going to have to lie to the Custodians, which she didn't like, and sweat pooled in her armpits.

He coughed but did not move from his gargoyle-like position.

"Come again?" he said with a slow move of lips and raspy voice.

"It's for a class project. We need to find out information about people who lived before, before the Great Separation," Welcome said, her voice rising.

At that moment, a man with silver and black hair close to her mother's age emerged from another room.

"Hi, Custodian Lawson III," Welcome said, and dipped her head, a sign of respect. He was the one that came to their school to talk about the responsibility of knowledge and how the Custodians of Knowledge helped keep order. He had taken over for his father who had died suddenly of a heart attack. Mrs. Gavey never looked happy when he came to visit her class.

"It's always Troy for a pretty girl like you, Welcome," he said with a wink. Welcome exhaled and told herself to relax. He was the nicest of the three Custodians.

She repeated what she had told his grandfather.

Custodian Lawson III nodded and walked over to where his grandfather sat. "Grandpop didn't you know something of the Pontey sisters? I remember you talking about them when I was a boy. Something you heard from when you were young?"

The gargoyle like man stared back "Come, again?" He coughed and Welcome noticed the thickness of his cataracts.

"Oh Grandpop", Custodian Lawson III grumbled. "I'll go in the back and check."

"Thanks," Welcome said.

And under his breath Welcome heard Custodian Lawson III mumble, "What am I going to do with you in a few years?"

It took what seemed like forever and Welcome walked around the room to avoid Custodian Lawson's stare. She picked her nails to avoid looking at him.

He then, softly, mouthed the name Pontey, as if grinding it between his teeth.

Custodian Lawson III returned and brought out a number of boxes. He motioned for her to approach the long table, perpendicular to the large desk where his grandfather sat.

As they unfolded the old papers and yellowing materials, Welcome grew increasingly alarmed. Her insides burned. Her eyes took in that every paper screamed headlines about the 'Murdering Sisters'. Black and white photos of them reflected an accuracy as they looked now.

"God, Grandpop, now it is all coming back to me. These women went on a killing spree, right? Two upstanding men died by their hands; says here that they killed themselves," he said pointing to an article.

Blood pounded in Welcome's ears. Welcome could feel herself swoon and placed both hands on the table for support.

Custodian Lawson III eyed her suspiciously, "You look like the world is coming to an end."

"I'm okay," she managed say.

Hastily bundling up all the papers and placing them back in the boxes, he added, "You don't want to do a history project on them. They're not upstanding ladies. Hey, what about Mrs. Colby? Now there's a woman."

The preacher's wife? Welcome wanted to stamp her feet and say not if you sent me to hell right now, "Thank you, I'll ask my teacher about it."

"Witches!" the gargoyle croaked so loud it felt as if the sound would burst her eardrums.

The sudden outburst startled both of them. Custodian Lawson III said, "What, granddad?"

His old dry lips repeated, "Witches. They were witches."

Welcome got out of there as fast as her feet would take her.

§

As soon as she was out of sight from the Custodians of Knowledge building, she ran straight to the Grove. She didn't care about missing classes.

"Sisters!" She yelled, her voice thick and strong, surprising herself. She called several times.

Grace appeared first, as always. "What, what is it?"

"The Guardians, they said," Welcome dropped to her knees, the words choking in her throat. "I saw, I saw the papers. You killed them."

Millicent appeared where she liked to perch on an old gravestone, her eyes glittered.

"I told you she would find out. We should have said something," Grace said, her eyes dull and almost colorless. "Lying always makes things worse."

"Let her think what she wants. She's a big girl. Right, Welcome?"

"It is true that we killed those men, but it didn't happen the way that you think," Grace finally said.

"What's wrong with you?" Welcome said, momentarily forgetting the shock of her discovery.

"I don't know. I don't feel like myself," Grace said.

I can't trust anyone. Everything tasted bitter in her mouth. Her secret friends were not friends. They had done something terrible in their day.

Welcome's heart raced and her mouth narrowed to a slit, in a low voice she said, "I must be mad to have believed you. You are evil and I am evil and probably crazy."

Welcome felt her head swim and as she turned away, she heard Millicent say, "She's too angry to listen now, Grace."

§

Welcome had avoided the cemetery for days now, using the more traditional path to school. Coming up the path to her home, fear shot through her. Custodian of Knowledge Lawson III. was walking up to her worn porch.

"Custodian Lawson III?".

When he turned, she saw no kindness in his eyes.

She nodded to him. "My mother is probably asleep right now."

"I'm not here to see her, Welcome."

"Oh?" Welcome said. She stopped at the base of the porch.

"I asked Mrs. Knox about your special assignment."

Welcome almost choked. She had not thought that he would investigate. *How could I be so stupid? Custodians always wanted to know everyone's business.* She should have asked Mrs. Gavey to cover for her. Would she have done that?

Welcome's hard-earned bag of candies slipped out of her hand, opened and the sweets scattered in the dirt. She made a move to retrieve them and he stepped down two steps. She froze as she took in his hardened face.

"Lying is a sin, don't you know that by now, Welcome? Where'd you find out about the Pontey sisters? My father said they're not buried in the cemetery."

She was truly dumbfounded. When she had asked the sisters about were their headstones were, they had said that time had eroded their modest headstones and since their family line had died with them there was no one to do upkeep. Welcome had wondered about that explanation but didn't pay it too much mind. She never liked to press them about their deaths, figuring they didn't much want to remember.

"I just make up stories about people in the cemetery. It keeps me busy while I'm there. Pontey is an unusual name," she said, hoping the lie came out smooth.

He walked down the steps slowly, his voice lowering, "Maybe you shouldn't be working in the cemetery. You don't want to end up like your mama, all alone and crazy, now do you?"

She was about to defend her mother when the door burst open.

"Her Mama ain't alone and she ain't crazy, at least not today."

They both jumped as if shocked with a live current of electricity. Mrs. Sparks stood there in a disheveled housecoat and ripped maroon stockings. "What are you doing this side of town, Lawson?"

He curled his lip. Welcome knew that they had gone to school together long ago and there was no love lost between them.

"Oh hello, Lila. I was following up on some information for Welcome as she came for a visit a few days ago. Everything is settled now. I'll be going now."

Her mother's mouth quirked, and she charged at him. "That's the shittiest lie that you ever put your sorry mouth to. Get off this land... get out of herrrrrrrrrrrrrrrrrrrrrrrrrrrrrrrrrrrrrrrrrrrrrrrrrrrrre."

Caught off guard, Custodian Lawson III flinched and ran down the steps.

Welcome's mother darted inside the house and in a flash brandished a meat cleaver.

"Lila, stop it! I'm leaving," he yelled. No need to get crazy."

Once he had gotten into his old car and taken off, Welcome allowed herself a full breath. Welcome felt protected, but she saw the hateful look that he gave both of them as he drove off. He was not done with her yet.

Her mother stood looking at her daughter, a wheezing sound blowing from her lips every few seconds, "What trouble have you gotten yourself into, Welcome?"

"I made a mistake trusting someone," Welcome said and turned so her mother wouldn't see the tears forming into her eyes.

"Story of my life," her mother said, following Welcome and closing the door behind her.

Her mother didn't ask her any more about it, and that made Welcome grateful and sad at the same time.

§

For a few days Welcome tried something she hadn't attempted in a long time—to make herself interested in the other kids around her. Although they drew away from her, she observantly followed behind some of the girls and tried to show interest in their incessant chatter about boys and graduation. They wanted nothing to do with her and instead of feeling rebuffed, a relief passed through her. She wasn't like them and wasn't interested in them.

She found herself sighing when she reached the crossroads between the shortcut to her house through the cemetery or the regular route. She didn't want to let Mr. Applegate down. But the bigger pull to the cemetery was the empty inside of her. She missed Grace, despite everything. And, she was worried about her. She felt a flush heat her face and creep across her chest. She was angry with herself for wanting to go back, they had lied to her. Welcome walked toward the cemetery. She would be responsible. Yes. She would go and do the job and ignore the Grove. It was possible to do. She would not give in to checking up on Grace.

After her tasks were done, she edged by the Grove, but didn't call out to them.

As she turned, Grace appeared in front of her. "Oh, Welcome!

My dear, my dear, oh how I have missed you!" her voice tinkled. Her words flowed faster, "I know you are still angry with us and I understand. But, I must have a few moments with you. Oh, I must!"

Welcome was secretly happy to see Grace, but she made the sternest face she could muster. She folded her arms in front of her. "Five minutes, Grace."

Grace's face brightened and she nodded. "I can't bear for you to think we were murderers. Our aunt taught us the healing arts. Some people have a talent for that life and way of being. My sister and I practiced it, in a gentle and safe way."

"Witchcraft?" Welcome said trying to hide her interest.

"Some would call us witches, though that was not what we called ourselves. It's what the men in our town said about us. Remember I said we were healers? We were. One day, my husband, the doctor, caught me helping one of his patients, and asked what I was doing. I had created a powerful salve and with proper spell work, it was very effective. He hated it, labeled it unscientific. So, Millicent and I went to nursing school to give ourselves some legitimacy. My husband hated that, too. Under the guise of being nurses, we created healing sachets and salves. People in town started coming to us and some women wanted to know our secrets. We showed the women what we knew and formed a secret group. The power of my sister and me grew, and my husband and his friends in town became envious."

Looking into her eyes, Welcome could feel the truth of Grace's words.

"There were eight of us in the group and over a year, they killed us. All of us."

Welcome's eyes bulged.

"One by one. Some were made to look like accidents, some just disappeared. They very carefully covered up their tracks."

Chills raked across Welcome's arms.

"It took Millicent and me time to put the pieces together. My husband was a coward and never did the actual killing, but planned them. His fellow partner was the one that came into the house and found me as I was packing to leave. Thank God, Millicent happened upon us as she got a sense of what was to happen. He was strangling me, Welcome."

Welcome shook her head and instinctively hugged herself as she listened to Grace's story.

"I looked into his hate-filled eyes while I struggled. And, then Millicent was there and clubbed him with a heavy lamp and pounded him until he was good and dead. Another one of my husband's cronies came to check if the deed was done and we took him by surprise. We ran after that and hid out in the forest and tried to leave, but we had no car and not much money of our own. My husband organized a group of men to find us which they did. They killed us and threw us in one of the ditches, on the land near your house.

Welcome walked to her and felt herself tremble. "What a horrible and cruel thing they did to you and Millicent. I can't imagine how afraid you were."

"Oh, it is so good to talk about it, to reveal it to someone else," Grace said. "There is something else, the more important thing. Welcome, you must leave here at once."

"Why?"

"Millicent is planning something, and you are to be part of it."

"What would she want with me?" Welcome said.

Do you remember that day when you woke up and Millicent and I were arguing?"

"Yes, of course. You seemed ready to tear at each other, but we never talked about it."

"She wants to become flesh again. That day, she put a marker on you."

Welcome raised her eyebrows and Grace as if in anticipation of her question rushed on. "She has created a connection between you and her. It is called impregnation of spirit. Something we were studying when we were younger. Like what she did with the bird. She is planning something terrible I fear."

Grace bowed her head. "She was always the more talented one. I've never been the strong one between us, and I regret that now. She's been draining my essence for years. Feeding off of me you might say."

Welcome's head swam as she listened to Grace's revelation. Panic tightened in her throat and she looked into the ghost's eyes, "I can't leave my mother."

"It's the only way, Welcome. You must, you must. You must leave and never look back. Or else, she will be able to move in your body and bind your will to her own. Once she controls your body, she can take control of other's bodies."

Something went cold inside of Welcome, "Was contacting me all part of her plan? Did you ever really want to get to know me?"

Grace's eyes grew soft. "You must believe me, Welcome, meeting you has been the very best thing. I thought you were the loveliest person I had ever met. I thought us lucky to have you. I have been here with my sister for a long time. She does not want to go toward the light and my love for her has blocked my chance of moving on. Her hateful heart will keep her here. I have hoped for years it would be different. If only it were different. I was lonely, Welcome. You changed that and for that I am eternally grateful."

They heard the call of a thrush and Welcome drank in Grace's words and the feelings behind them. "I don't want to leave you," she said, choking out the words.

"There's not much more left of me. I have made my choices and I know that I will find peace soon. You have your whole life to live. You will always be my funny Valentine."

Welcome looked up in the darkening sky, racking her brain about what she could do to help Grace and herself. The train would not arrive in town for another week. One piece of Grace's story came back to her.

"You said that you were buried near the ditches by my house?"

"Yes," Grace nodded.

"I was always teased about where my house is. They thought my father was crazy buying a house so far from town, so close to the cemetery and too close to the train tracks."

Welcome had often pondered the position of her house. The railroad tracks sat kitty-cornered to the road that led to her house. The edge of the town's large cemetery sat less than a stone's throw from the road behind her house. Parallel to the tracks laid six half-finished ditches; the smallest one right near the edge of the train track. During a grander and more ambitious moment in Thistleview's history, when her mother still talked to people and they didn't come away scratching their heads, Mr. Brooke, head of town services, initiated a plan to bring better plumbing to the house. She knew that her mother did something to scare the workers off and then soon after that the town ran out of money for those kinds of repairs. The dug up, moist earth beckoned to her and sometimes on sunny days and when her mother lay in her bed, wide-eyed, talking to voices who "knocked" that day, Welcome wrapped in an old natty comforter walked the short distance and jumped into one of the depressions, rooting herself into the earth, feeling held by it.

"Grace, I've got an idea. I think my mother can help me."

§

Welcome sprinted to her house. "Mama, mama," she called as she open the front door.

Her mother was slumped on the old beat up couch. She bolted up, "Jesus Christ, you are about to split my ear drums. What's wrong with you?"

"Everything, but I think you can help me. You have to help me."

Mrs. Sparks narrowed her eyes. "What are you talking about? I need my sleep."

At that moment, Welcome noticed a blue light penetrating the door. Her mind felt as if it was being slammed against a table. She shook off the feeling and focused.

"Mama, we have got to go out back, now!"

She grabbed her mother's hand and pulled her from the couch. She ran with her mother through the small house. "It's the voices, Mama."

Welcome tore open the screen door and dragged her mother down the short flight of steps.

"I'm the crazy one!" her mother yelped. "What's happened to my daughter?"

Welcome grabbed her mother's face. "Mama, you've always heard voices since we've lived here?"

They stood nearest the smallest ditch and Welcome could feel the heat from the ground snake its way up into her shoes.

"Yes, yes," Mrs. Sparks murmured. "Telling me their troubles and dreams. Terrible noise."

Pinpricks of fright dotted Welcome's consciousness as she looked back at the house, now encased in dark blue light. *Millicent must have been practicing all this time to leave the graveyard.*

"Together we have to call on them. A bad woman, a hurt woman is after me from the other side."

"You gone crazy, too," her mother said, voice gone raspy.

"No, I haven't. Please you've got to focus. We have to ask them to help us. They have been trying to get your attention all my life!"

"Who?"

"The women who were healers. They all died here. Take my hands, Mama."

The woman did as she was told and clasped her daughter's hands.

Welcome could hear them already, whisperings coming from the earth.

"Call to them, Mama!"

"I don't know how. I'm crazy."

"You are not, crazy, Mama! You are a healer; you just haven't been trained."

"What? Those voices always talking a mish mash," her mother said, eyebrows raised, eyes questioning, disbelieving.

Welcome stomped her foot. There's no time to make her understand. She pointed as Millicent's cobalt form detached itself from the house and floated toward them. Her mother's eyes grew big. "Look! That spirit is coming for me. She's going to make me do bad things."

Her mother drew herself up, "The hell she ain't!" Her mother locked on to her daughter's hands. "What do I do?"

"Concentrate and call to the voices. Ask them to come through. They have wanted to for a long time!"

Welcome saw as her mother's face struggled to comprehend her daughter's words.

"Come through you tormenting voices," her mother shouted without hesitation. "Come through, I need you."

Mrs. Sparks rocked back and forth, keeping her eyes shut. Mother and daughter had both sunk to the ground, shivering and holding each other.

Welcome heard her mother calling out names that she had never heard before: Jesse, Edith, Ruth, Susan, Delilah, and Patricia.

Welcome strained as Millicent was almost upon them. *No more time!*

Welcome gulped in a breath and joining in with her mother screamed, "Healers of Thistleview, come and claim your own. She has lost her way. She has broken and will continue to break the covenant of your ways. Bring her back into the earth and let her rest."

A shadowy female figure rose from the earth and Mrs. Sparks grabbed hold of Welcome. Mother and daughter instinctively drew back.

"You've got to take her away, you can't let her hurt my daughter, not my daughter. You been talking to me all these years. Please, please, please," Welcome's mother babbled. Millicent's laugh boomed. "They are too late. This, Welcome is too late."

"Our sister wants revenge for what has happened," the apparition said.

"I know, but all those people are gone and dead and all she has done has been to pervert the very things that made you good while you were alive," Welcome replied.

"I have promised you a way to be free," Millicent's shadow said.

"She has hurt her sister, Grace," Welcome said.

"Grace is weak," Millicent said and Welcome could hear the irritation in the ghost's tone.

"She wants to be flesh for her own amusement. She does not belong here in this time," Welcome said.

Welcome could feel other forms take shape around them. Soon mother and daughter were encircled by female spirits and for a moment mother and daughter felt all the fear and pain that they had suffered at the end.

Her mother wailed and fell away from Welcome. "Too much!"

Baring her teeth through the psychic connection, Welcome continued to address them, shouting though her throat felt raw.

"You have kept my mother's company long enough. You have fed on her but never gave her enough of yourself to make her see you! You have used her for all these years, but have never taught much of anything that is useful. You have made her think that she is crazy. Is that the way of your kind?"

Her mother lay on the ground, her body curled into a tight ball, shaking and panting.

And, finally, there was Grace hovering above them, only a bare shimmer of her face visible.

Welcome rose. She pointed at all the forms gathered. "You must take your sister and keep her on your side. I promise that if you take Millicent away, my mother and I will honor you. We will honor your deaths. We will receive your teachings. We will share your teachings and help heal others. You will live through us."

All went silent and then the dead women gathered together. First, they collectively breathed in and Grace's form disappeared. And, then with their gravelly voices they chanted, and Millicent's swirling blue energy grew fainter and fainter though her screams were of such a pitch that both mother and daughter fell on their backs covering their ears.

§

"That's it, Mama," Welcome said. She'd been encouraging her mother's efforts with the rabbit.

The rabbit, a few yards away, startled at Welcome's voice.

Her mother flopped onto the blanket they had spread a few hours before and wiped the sweat away from her brow. "There's nothing like feeling a creature's energy."

Welcome nodded. She patted her mother's shoulder, a feeling of gratitude washing over her. It had been a good day. Not all of them were. The healers had warned Welcome that her mother's progress would be slow. She had a lot of healing to do. But, that was fine by Welcome. Each day her mother got stronger. They laughed more and talked in ways they hadn't ever before. She would stay here with her mother for a while, building something new.

Welcome heard the knock at the screen door. Her mother bolted up, her gaze unfocused.

A"Are you sure about this?"

Welcome squeezed her mother's hand and nodded. "There is strength in numbers."

"Can we trust her?"

"Yes," Welcome said. "She can choose."

As she walked through the house to answer the door, she felt the rightness of her decision like a hum inside her. She would gather some women here. They would honor the healers and learn from them. They would help her and each other. *They might help see Grace again, too.*

Smiling, she opened the door and greeted Mrs. Gavey.

Destroying Angel

Nicole Givens Kurtz

"*O*ut! I want out of here!" Valek, he once renowned for slaughter and soul snatching, roared, his voice filling the tiny dome-shaped house.

His dark eyes flickered between Manola's full-fledged smirk and the key she held high in the air. He lacked a body, and therefore a mouth, but his telepathic link to her remained as strong as the first day he'd seduced her, folding her will into his, making her a weapon. A link she wished her magic held enough strength to sever.

Valek's soul flitted around its spherical prison. Despite the cloudiness his actions caused, somehow his burning scarlet eyes, brimming with anger, remained.

"Patience. Rushed work is shoddy work twice done." Manola cupped the key and placed it into her cloak's pocket.

With an annoyed sigh, she walked away from the orb, which pulsed in time to Valek's angry outbursts. She pulled the cloak over her head and placed her hand on the cold door handle. Crisp air shot through their fragile building's cracks and crevices. Their hasty escape from the Minister Knights to this place on Earth, with its horrid cold, had been the result of Valek's complete lack of patience. This planet crawled with humans, but Manola hadn't been human for some time. Her soul had been stolen ages ago by Valek.

And now, the tables had turned.

She'd kept his soul, now hostage, in its own glass orb. The soul, snatched in the battle with the Minister Knights, saved him from death. Thinking back on it now, her rash decisions left her in a worse situation than when she'd started. They'd managed to escape the Minister Knights with their lives, but only just.

Damn those meddling slugs. Manola knuckles ached and she realized she held the door handle in a death grip. She relaxed her hand and rubbed it along the skimpy, poorly lined, leather pantsuit. It wouldn't protect her from the icy temperatures. But, it didn't matter. She could not feel the cold; the only feeling that remained within her sought freedom from the walking corpse she'd become. She wasn't alive nor was she dead—but she existed in a sort of strange stasis.

If she could get her hands on her locked-up soul, the piece of her that Valek still retained, then she could be entirely human once again—if she could locate the right sorceress to commence the reunion of body and soul.

So many *ifs.*

Time. Manola had nothing but time.

Truth be told, she wasn't sure she wanted to be among the living again.

Not yet.

"Where do you think you're going?" Valek yelled from behind her.

She glanced over her shoulder at the small, grapefruit-sized sphere as it glowed in furious, emerald-colored illuminated flashes. Valek's soul swirled around in irritation. The rickety desk shook with his outrage.

"It has been long enough, witch! Free me. Now!"

Manola rolled her eyes in disgust. She'd complete the reanimation when she found a suitable host. This little deserted patch of land the Circle of Onasis had sent them to wasn't much more than a village near the Arctic Circle. Not very populated. She'd been spying and watching the villagers for weeks, but she wasn't about to explain this to Valek. With her annoyance keyed to explode, she stalked back to the desk, wrenched open the velvet lined drawer, and placed the orb inside.

"Manola! Answer me!" Valek screamed.

Using her booted foot, she slid the drawer closed with a soft click, thus silencing her lord and master.

For now.

The three-room shell of a house once belonged to fur traders. She took out a tiny knapsack and noted, not for the first time, how much smaller the amount of currency had become. Valek, once the wealthiest businessman of his kind, had descended into poverty. And she along with him.

That would not do. Not at all.

Groaning, she slipped a coin from the bag and tossed it into the air—catching it, almost without looking, as it fell. Valek would know how to make more money...more profit. She smiled. He had few other talents. If he had been standing in the room, she would not have even thought such a thing.

Valek, back in flesh—although good—wasn't all soft, round edges.

A little over two years had passed since her encounter with the Minister Knights of Souls and throughout that time, she had planned—reflected. She'd crept around the shadows and pits of this hunk of land—seeking and spying. The only ones who came here were those whose businesses dealt in blood, flesh, or both.

Now that the time to implement her plan approached, she could feel it energizing her and making her flesh almost glow with excitement.

With this burning in her core, she turned the door's handle and stepped into the cold.

Revenge would be sweet and swift.

§

Nestled along the eastern ridge, *The Tradesman* spat out customers and harbored criminals. Inside the metallic-domed bar, a large open-mouthed hearth burned. Hot flames popped and crackled, startling some of the already tightly wound patrons. Some folks said it was wood. Others said it was bodies that supplied the heat.

None of it mattered to Manola. Tucked into the darkened corner, she watched from the cluster of shadows, her hood casting her face in gloom. Not many new people came here. Still, Manola was here for only one purpose.

She saw everyone in the bar, whores and lechers, fallen warriors and the ill. But it was Ganger who drew her attention. His greed spoke to her. He was exactly what she needed.

Competing with the fire's noise were the sounds that came from Ganger the gutless. He sat astride a barstool and bellowed his complaints to the others as a familiar argument reared its ugly head.

"These are not my people." Ganger signaled the barkeep for another warm ale. Spit raced down his chin, and he wiped it away with his arm.

"They are, you lying danker beast!" Another trader swept Ganger's drink to the floor, where it crashed and splashed all over the incoming woman's boots.

No matter. *The Tradesman* always overcharged and over watered. A greasy grin smeared across Manola's face. She made her way to the bar, keeping her face hidden in her hood's shadow. She took the seat closest to Granger, and gagged. Manola wanted to spit out the very scent of Ganger from her nostrils and her mouth. Disgusting pig of a man. The irony—Ganger, a beefy man, who had more warrior days behind him than in front, had an appetite for women, drink, and finely prepared food. Why he stayed in the village, Manola didn't know. With information culled from her spies, she'd discerned that his stay had increased his appetite...for everything.

Hoards of women had been sold and bartered through *The Tradesman* in the time she'd been left on this horrid strip of land.

The trades*man*.

None of them had been male.

Manola listened in to the on-going conversation."Those. Aren't. My. People. These dirty sacks of skin aren't my kin." Ganger sent spittle at his accuser across the bar's polished stone. He rose with his fists balled up and his belly rumbling in fury.

Manola narrowed her eyes. *Liar. Liar.* The people shackled outside the bar's warmth were *his* people—their black skin shining, their eyes large and luminous, and their lips trembling in shades of blue. They all bore his mark. The trader, who had wanted to sell a few of his older women to Ganger, moved away from the bar, cursing under his breath.

"Lousy, cheap bastard," he said, tossing the comment over his shoulder.

Ganger didn't want poorly equipped females from his dismal and decrepit homeland. Females with large, saggy breasts didn't vie for the same currency as those with natural, unenhanced pairs. Elusive and difficult to find, women without the gigantic, artificially reworked bosoms earned a respectable price on the market. Manola knew this, and so did Ganger.

Pushing her hood back, she arched her back, being sure to reveal her tightly coiled body. She knew what lured men's attention, and Ganger's in particular.

The barkeep slammed another mug on the bar in front of Granger. Ale sloshed over the side and onto the counter. Ganger didn't notice, for his attention had been snared. Manola tossed back scarlet hair and crossed her long legs. She picked up his ale.

Ganger turned on his stool to face her. "Beautiful evening."

Manola gave him a small smile.

He drank in her fitted bodysuit, her long legs, and on up to her suit's V cut—as if offering an invitation to peek under it. His gaze came to rest on her bosom.

"You'll fetch a ready price on the market," Ganger said, his greasy smile wide. "You looking for work? Eh?"

Manola sipped more of his ale. Goddesss, it was horrid, bitter stuff.

"Are you deaf, woman? Mute? Or both?" Ganger adjusted his girth to face her. "Aye, you, heed my words. The ale is gonna cost you a pretty coin."

His beard twitched. He was not one who readily accepted refusals of any kind, least of all from women. Manola knew this, but she held her breath against his rancid exhalations as he leaned closer to her.

"You want something ma'am?" The bartender interrupted Granger's open mouth. She wore her hair tied back, and a no-nonsense authority on her face. "He bothering you?"

"Anaïs, mind your own damn business." Granger glared. "You know the consequence of meddling in mine. Don't you?"

She ignored him and kept her eyes on Manola. "Did you want your own drink? We got in a new shipment of wine, red, I think."

How a person like Anaïs Noa managed to work in a place like *The Tradesman* had everything to do with the area's dire economic opportunities, but Manola had problems of her own.

Ones she wasn't going to add to Anaïs's own list of woes.

"Thank you. I'm fine."

Anaïs nodded, and pushed on down the bar. She tossed another look over at Manola, before helping another patron.

"Now, I know you can talk. So you were ignoring me." Granger raised his hand, reading himself to stand and drag her out by her hair and into his cages. Manola smiled at him and placed her full attention on him. She nodded her head as if to affirm his suspicions.

Other than Anaïs, no one bothered to stop him or pay them much attention. This bar was like thousands of others. It thrived on profit and discretion.

"Yes, I heed your words. A fine evening it is," she whispered seductively in Ganger's direction.

He paused and lowered his arm.

"You are a beautiful angel."

She met his gaze with an unwavering look. "A destroying one."

"I doubt that. Sexy little minx like you." He laughed, and all his fleshy bulges quaked.

She did not smile or giggle at his compliment.

"You ain't from here. Are you?" An alarm tingled across his body.

"No one is." Manola drank ale and then sighed, but kept her bolted-on smile. *Best wrap this up quick and dirty.*

Ganger stroked his beard. "You drank my ale. You either pay the barkeep or me. After all, this is *The Tradesman.*"

"Oh?" She leaned back on the barstool. "I thought you bought me that ale."

"Pay or trade."

"Gimme a minute."

"Only a minute." Granger replied. "Then I decide."

She stood and walked back toward the restrooms.

Ganger settled on the stool half a heartbeat.

Manola vanished into the restroom stall and dug out the small stash of ash-colored leaves. She snapped her fingers. A small flame erupted in the palm of her hand. She put them leaves in the flame, watching them burn. After a few seconds, she cupped her other hand over the fire, putting it out. Next, she used a small bottle to scoop up the ashes. Once she corked the bottle, she whispered to the contents, "You're on in five."

She washed her hands in the sink's icy water, dried them on her hair, and headed back out to the bar.

Manola reclaimed the stool beside him. "I'm back."

Not wanting the opportunity to pass, Ganger adjusted his belt. "Join me in a private room so we can settle up." It was not a request, but a command.

Manola nodded and, before leaving her stool, finished his drink, guzzling down the liquid's last bitter bits. She slapped down a silver coin on the counter, nodded in Anaïs's direction, and started for the door.

"Follow me," she said to Ganger.

Ganger scowled. "You paid."

"You decided to trade." She waited for him at the door.

From the look on Ganger's face, she could see that he could hardly believe his good fortune.

"Yeah." He wiped the saliva spilling down his chin. "Angel, I'll follow you anywhere."

Manola gestured to the outside darkness. "I pick the place."

"Once I'm done, she will still fetch a fair price," Ganger said under his breath.Once they pushed through the door, the wind lay still, and the glow of lanterns bobbed in the air like floating stars. Manola wanted this over as fast as possible. Granger stank, and the putrid odor didn't begin to cover the awfulness of the man.

The two hurried through the worn cobblestone streets that snaked from the sagging downtown district up through the sorrowful cluster of brothels, just a little way from the bar. Manola had to stop often to make sure Ganger followed. His girth slowed him, and his wheezing was a shawl around him. Dulled by drink and lust, Ganger had been hooked, and now she had to reel him in.

They came to a halt in front an abandoned house. A sole window faced the road. The inside lay in pitch blackness, and the noise of nocturnal animals as they hunted and prowled punched holes into the otherwise quiet night.

Ganger shook his head as if in a daze.

Manola unlocked the door and pushed it open. "Are you ready for the time of your life, great warrior?"

He patted his belly. "So, my reputation extended to whatever crap country you crawled out from!" He stroked his beard in pride. "I knew you were different."

She approached him and draped her arm across his shoulders. "Oh, yes. Warrior. Business man. Peddler of flesh."

Something inside him pinched in worry. He shoved it aside, as Manola unzipped her jumpsuit, and peeled it off in slow, seductive movements. She'd been rendered to this base level of entrapment so many times in her long life, it no longer registered.

As her full form came into view, Ganger's throat went dry. "So perfect…"

Had Ganger not been so focused on landing her in his bed and taking her for himself, he would have noted the tone of her voice and fled. Being as he was, he did not. Sweaty and out of breath, Ganger could only nod.

Manola kept the smile on.

"You like? It's all natural. No implants. No enhancement." She tossed her hair back over her smooth shoulders and peered at him. She walked back and forth, modeling her angelic form with grace and a touch of desire.

For perhaps the first time, Ganger's skin prickled at her laughter and he was afraid. He swiftly squashed it, for this was only a woman. Once his passion was spent, he would be done with her. Perhaps her own life would end just at the point he exploded within her.

With that last thought, he stepped inside.

§

Manola snared the former warrior. If anyone came seeking Ganger, no one would remember what she looked like because her magic had allowed him to see exactly what he wanted—his desire.

"Are you comfortable?" she asked, patting the bed beside her.

"Aye!" He reached for her. "Gimme those delicious delights!"

She sidestepped his advanced. "Don't be in such a hurry."

"Now, wretched woman!" Ganger tried to grab her again.

She shook him off and as bewilderment appeared on his face—how could a woman dislodge him so—he slumped back against the rear wall. "Aye, you playing hard to get."

She picked up her purse and removed her fan. She unfolded it before turning back to face Granger.

"You like?" She gestured a hand over her nude body. In the other, she held a fan, an ornate black one decorated with wings.

"Perfect." Ganger wiped his mouth. A thin layer of sweat beaded above his upper lip. "Come here. Now! Stop your teasing."

She stood up, whirled around him, and with one hand slammed him back against the room's wall. The entire place shook.

"I told you to wait." The undercurrent of power coursed through her voice. This piece of pathetic DNA had it coming. "You know, Ganger. Your hunger for women will one day kill you."

With his mouth ajar, and confusion filtering over his features, tiny insects scoured over his bugling belly. They raced down Manola's arm, rising through her pores. His eyes fluttered beneath closed lids and his breathing came in shallow breaths. A thin trail of blood slipped over his porky cheeks and down toward his slacked mouth.

Manola raised the fan and placed it against his throat. Scores of insects poured from its tips. They burrowed into him. The more he screamed, the wider his mouth, the more that entered. Soon his shouts were muffled until only silence remained. He struggled against her, but she was stronger.

After a few moments, exhausted, Manola lowered the now empty fan, and went to stand by the fireplace. A fire heated the bottom of a round, black cauldron. She dumped in the ash from its bottle. Next, she stumbled over to the desk drawer and took out the sphere with Valek's soul.

"It's about time!" The joy in his tone was clear as a bell in her mind. He swirled around and around as if celebrating his upcoming release.

She put it back on the table. Her body ached. Wrestling Granger took more energy and strength than she'd prepared for. Conjuring always took a toll, even though she couldn't die. Her reanimated corpse took magic to maintain, and when she used those powers, it drew from the same well. The black magic fan summoned the insects and that always took energy.

Manola added the ingredients to the cauldron. It had taken time to accumulate the necessary solution and parts to create the soul transferring mixture, but she had robbed, traded favors, and performed certain acts to get them all.

Even murder.

The moment was upon her, but she could not feel the exhilaration.

Inside the cauldron was a clear liquid, bubbling hot with anticipation. This would free Valek's soul, and once out of the sphere, it would fly—freely into the mixture. Once a part of the mixture, Manola would feed it to Ganger. He hadn't died—not yet. The insects' slowly and methodically consumed him—not a quick death. She needed Ganger unconscious. If he'd been awake, well, Valek would have to wrestle Ganger's own essence for control of the body.

Valek promised to give her back her soul.

She expected a double-cross, but she had wishes of her own. Manola leaned over the cauldron and whispered,

"Captured, held in the arms of Zel,
the body's very essence is the meld,
that binds together flesh and soul,
Come, Valek, to your new home!"

The orb on the table broke open and Valek's soul, a silky gray wisp, flew from its prison and into the cauldron, where the liquid instantly cooled. She scooped the liquid into a goblet. She would force the liquid into Ganger until none remained.

She took it to Ganger and opened his mouth. Startled, he moaned, but he lacked strength to do more than shift a little this way and that. His eyes flashed open.

"Drink. Drink for life." Manola said in cooing tones.

Dizzy and befuddled, Ganger did as she asked. Even as she forced him, his eyes remained trained on her exposed chest. So enamored by her physical attributes, he never suspected her deceit.

Few did.

Save Valek, whose pretty package had been her own undoing.

§

Sometime after midnight, the cauldron lay empty and the fire had burned down to embers. Valek glanced up at Manola from his spot near the fireplace. His thin lips snatched back in a sneer so sinister that she stepped away from him in fear. When her back touched the wall, she forced herself to meet his eyes.

His skin stank of ale and old sweat, as if the body had suddenly quit without telling the brain—rusty and worn out.

"This is the *best* you could do?" he yelled, his eyes glinting in the candle's light. "This—this—heap of a body! Rubbish that should have been spared the suffering of living and put out of its misery!"

The menacing in the words would frighten the skin off an animal, but it was Valek's words out of Ganger's mouth that forced a soft giggle to ripple up from Manola. She swallowed it, because now that Valek was back in flesh, he was as dangerous as ever.

"Yes, my lord," she managed to say, stepping back a few more paces from the arc of Granger's sword in Valek's fist. His wrath knew no limits or excuses. "This village has few men of excellent sculpting come along this path. I've waited for months, Valek. Forgive me..."

In his Ganger suit, Valek held up the blubbery, hairy arms and dropped them. He turned this way and that, trying to look at his new body.

"This will not do!" he said.

She agreed. Upon performing the ceremony, Valek's soul sought out the body of Ganger, whose soul still resided somewhere deep within the resonance of his mind. The insects would slowly devour Granger's soul until he didn't exist. Valek would have to command the body. He didn't have much choice; Manola did not have the spheres to call his soul out of Ganger's body again.

For now, Valek was stuck.

"...sluggish, slow, heavy, and terribly wide," Valek was saying, his hands on his overlapping stomach. "This will not do!"

Yes, she was getting that point.

"My Lord, we could, uh, we could return to the castle. There, I can mix a remedy that will transform this, uh, body, into something more to your liking."

Ganger's eyes ignited as they connected with hers. He stepped toward her, naked and covered with brushy black hair. "You could have done that all along! Why keep me caged in that sphere for all this time!"

Without warning his hand shot out and snatched her up by her throat. She laughed, because she could not die, but it stung, nonetheless.

She managed to explain. "Only. On. Existing. Bodies."

Valek dropped her to the floor. "Curse this awful flesh. It smells."

She rubbed her throat. *Bastard!*

"This is why I selected that body. It is without usefulness—save one. It will transport you back to your castle so that you may be refined."

Valek nodded. He seemed distracted and she wondered if the soul of Ganger had risen to try to reclaim his body.

It would make no difference.

Valek's will and soul would win. Now free from its confines, it would not be easily caged or extinguished again. The rage would make sure of that.

She did not call to him, for a distraction might be the only edge Ganger's soul needed to expel Valek. Instead, she sat down in the blackened corner, feeling the icy floor against her legs and waited. Patience was a virtue and she had been very patient.

Valek spun around, breathing heavily, for he had exhausted Ganger's endurance.

"I want this body refined, Manola." His mouth became a slash of fury. "Gather our belongings. I want to go to that bar where you found this heap and gather more to our cause!"

Manola nodded again, her attention diverted to the chore of collecting her belongings and her own thoughts of revenge. Though she didn't have a soul, she still had wants. She sighed. How would it be to be able to touch and feel again? To taste food? To feel the softness of the leather she wore, or the points of Valek's whip? Now only a numbing existence remained. After eons of doing evil, vile things, she longed to be human again.

"Did you not hear me?" he said over his shoulder.

Manola nodded as she went about picking up her items, for she had brought nothing of Valek's. There had not been time, but she had been crafty enough to get Valek's soul before he died.

When she'd gathered their small items, she stopped. She needed Valek to help her get her soul back, now that she'd helped him. Of course Valek could end up keeping his word, but now that she'd placed him back in flesh, he neither wanted it nor mentioned it.

How many more years would she have to exist in the void between living and death?

I can wait no longer.

"Valek." She dusted off the floor's debris.

"What is it?" he said, whirling around. So out of sorts with the body that he nearly tripped and fell.

She didn't answer with words, but instead used her body language to communicate her interest. The hiss of the jumpsuit's zipper fractured the silence.

Valek quirked an eyebrow. "Put your clothes on. You are not worthy."

"No?" Manola frowned. She continued to remove the suit from her body. "I didn't get the chance to fulfill my promise to Ganger, but even after finding you a host body. I am unworthy? What about returning my soul?"

"I care not! Your soul will wait until I am ready, Manol! There are much more important things now. I want to crush the Minister Knights for what they have taken from me!" Valek pounded his fist onto the fireplace's mantel.

More important than her soul? Manola kept her face blank, but his words were a dagger through her heart. Two years she'd worked to put him back into flesh. Decades spent in his service, as his lover, as his victim, and as his nursemaid. Inside her, a crack fissured. Hot, angry rage hissed out.

"But you're wearing him so well, my lord." Manola pushed her power of persuasion into the words.

Her magic never worked on Valek—too much narcissism to burrow through—but it had worked on the *other* inside him. Granger, she would be able to reach. So she spoke to him. He lacked the mental strength to overtake Valek, but all she needed was an opportunity.

After several, short minutes, Valek turned to face her. His gaze had been pinned to her nudity, and, with hands outward, he stalked toward her, ready to finally taste the fruit he'd been denied before.

"Perfect," he slurred. They were Ganger's words, but in Valek's voice. A shiver raced down her back, but she had to act.

Manola grabbed the miniature daggers she kept in her boots and lunged at Valek. One landed in his thigh. The heavyset former warrior stumbled, but lumbered forward, undeterred. She whirled out of his greedy hands and stabbed him in the side of his throat with the other dagger. At once, blood sprayed.

Manola leapt back, out of the blood's warm arc, but it sprayed across her face, for she hadn't moved in time. She wiped it from her skin and grinned.

"You will pay for this!" Ganger coughed out blood. "You. Will..."

"I have already paid." She spat out the words.

Valek's words came in Ganger's voice and thus, they didn't pack the same level of warning or danger. Pain etched itself across his face, twisting it in agony. He managed to yank the dagger from his throat, which just created more of a mess.

Manola didn't wait. She snatched up her few belongings she'd just packed for Valek and disappeared into the cold night.

Poisoned by Sugar

J. D. Blackrose

The bell's usual pleasant ting rang a discordant note and I gritted my teeth, knowing that the bell earmarked that particular tone for one very special individual. My assistant, Molly, flashed a nervous glance at our visitor, raised her eyebrows at me, and cleared the path to the cash register. I'd already told her that she didn't have to deal with him. Magic Beans was my shop, so that meant my customer, my problem, my nausea.

"Hello, Arthur," I said, hoping the churn in my stomach would ease up. I grabbed two antacids from the bottle under the cash register and chewed them down.

"Aren't you going to wash your hands, now that you've touched your mouth?" Arthur Dreck was a high school math teacher, loathed by his students. But more importantly he was the head witch of the local coven. He could turn me into a newt with a glance or sour all the creamer in the shop with a word.

Worse, he could ban me from performing any kind of magic in

the Greater Cleveland area, and though my power was quite low, limited to runes, I valued my ability to use them to help people. The coven didn't consider me powerful enough to have me as a member, but I could heal small hurts, reduce pain, and I had a touch of metalmancy, which meant I could fix machinery. So, whether I liked it or not, I had to suck up to Arthur Dreck.

"Of course, Arthur. One moment, please." I tucked a strand of my brown hair behind my ear as I turned on the tap, perspiration already dripping down the center of my back. The espresso machines and regular coffee brewers heated the counter and cash register space with a little too much fervor, and despite my careful planning when I built the place, I burned my inner forearm and bicep because I was a tad too short to reach everything and stood on my toes to access the upper shelves. This caused me to lean into the hot equipment, and zippo! A burn. Luckily, I could heal some of them myself, and a nice aloe/arnica cream from the local witches' apothecary did the rest.

I wiped my brow with the back of my forearm, glad I never wore makeup, which would be smeared down my face by now.

"Did you just touch your skin again? Cleanliness is next to Goddessliness, Quinn. I'd like my tea without your germs, if you please."

I doused my hands in hand sanitizer and gloved up, counting to ten. I had no idea why he came here if he disliked me so intensely. My special blend of tea was delicious though, and I supposed he liked the atmosphere. Magic Beans was cozy, with warm wood flooring and a wide-open conversation area, along with nooks and crannies where a customer could seek privacy. The best thing was the smell. A mixture of fresh-brewed coffee, chocolate, and cinnamon—every person who walked through the door stopped to take a deep whiff.

In fact, a customer entered at that moment, and I watched as she inhaled. Her shoulders relaxed on the exhale and she smiled. "Smells fabulous in here," she said to the room. She looked at me. "Whatever you're making, I'll have three." She took her place in the queue.

I grinned at her, and then turned back to Arthur.

"Besides your tea, is there anything else I can get for you?" I scooped the blend he liked into a tea infuser and let it steep.

"A scone, please, and not that one. I want the middle one. No, not that one, that one," he said, pointing. "No, Quinn! The fourth from the back, second column, two from the front. Really, why is this so hard?"

In his agitation, Arthur dropped his newspaper and bent to retrieve it. His wide rear end brushed against the woman behind him in line, who was already tapping her toes.

"A little personal space, please, Madame!" Arthur bumped the woman with his hip and removed cash from his money clip to pay for the scone and tea. "Sugar, please, Quinn."

"There is sugar on the self-service kiosk, Arthur."

"I pay for service, missy, and you know it. Three sugars, please."

I dumped three teaspoons of sugar into the tea, wondering how on earth he could drink it that sweet, placed his scone on a plate, and handed both to him with a wan smile.

"Bring it out to my table, please. My hands are full, as you can clearly see." He demonstrated how encumbered he was by holding up his paper in one hand while clutching his slim fountain pen in the other.

Sashaying to his favorite chair, he snapped his newspaper open, and made a show of uncapping his pen. I placed the scone and tea in front of him. "Enjoy," I managed, biting my tongue.

"The scone is chilly. I shall have to wait until it comes to room temperature, and by then my tea will be cold. I expect a free refill for this outrage."

"Sure, Arthur. Whatever."

I kept my eye on him as I made my way back to the counter. He looked at his watch and huffed and puffed, as if he were waiting for someone. My chiming wall clock told me we were deeper into the morning than I had realized. It was almost eleven.

A new customer was a harried mom with a baby in a stroller. She ordered a large mocha, and a muffin for the two-year old.

I told her, "I'll bring the mocha out to you in a moment. Why don't you take a seat near the window? There's good light and space for the stroller." The mom gave me a tired smile of appreciation.

I made the mocha personally, while Molly took the next customer. I made it extra chocolaty, and rotated my body a fraction as I grabbed the whipped cream so no one could see me draw three runes with my finger on the cup. The white symbols for peace, calm, and rest melted into the drink, just as they were supposed to. I walked the coffee over to the mom.

"No sleep?" I asked as I handed her the cup.

"None. My husband says I should take the night shift since I can 'nap when the babies nap' during the day, but he doesn't understand that's when I get everything done. I'm exhausted."

"I'm sure the coffee will help."

She picked up the baby to nurse and gulped the hot brew. "It would have to be magic to do that."

I winked at her. "You never know."

I continued serving customers. "Do you want whip? Extra caramel? Earl Grey or Lady Grey? Yes, the muffins were made fresh this morning." I didn't notice time passing until my clock chimed noon. The mom was gone, and I hoped I got to see her tomorrow to find out if she felt any better.

"Hey, Quinn?" asked Molly.

"Yeah?"

Molly blew her bangs off her forehead, and rubbed her hands together, one foot tapping. Her hair was red and frizzy and always in her way. I thought it was adorable. She hated it.

"The fridge is on the fritz. Can you do that thingamabob that you do to get it rolling again?"

My metalmancy came in handy since I was constantly fixing things that died at inopportune moments in the shop. Molly knew I was a bit like her mom and that I used runes and minor spells, but she didn't know any details. She just knew I could fix things.

"Just a loose coil in the back. Help me pull it away from the wall—"

A heavy thunk made us turn, but it was the scream that made me run.

Customers were moving chairs out of the way and I couldn't see what was going on. I elbowed my way through.

Arthur Dreck lay on the floor, not breathing. His face was blue, his tongue protruding, and there was absolutely no question that he was dead. My heart did a little leap of joy, which I squashed down as I dropped to my knees. Hiding my hand with the other one, I drew a rune of healing on his chest and leaned in to listen for a heartbeat.

Silence. Not a lub-dub. Not a wheeze.

I tried to clear his airway, but his tongue was so swollen that it blocked his mouth, no matter how I tried to create space. Another customer knelt to help me, but also failed. Panicked, I called the police as several other people tried to revive him. One person thumped on his chest in a fast rhythm, singing The Bee Gees' "Stayin' Alive," to get the beat.

The remains of Arthur's tea and scone sat on the table, only half-eaten. His newspaper floated to the floor and his pen rolled to join it. Molly absently picked the pen up and put it back on the table, her eyes never leaving the body on the floor. She was green, and her eyes were wide with shock.

"Did anyone see what happened?" I asked, looking around for anyone to shed some light.

"He gasped, grabbed his throat, and keeled over," said Xavier, a regular who didn't drink coffee, but came in every morning for hot chocolate. Xavier's dreads swung as he shook his head and muttered. "Couldn't happen to a nicer person."

"Hey. Respect for the dead, son," said an older man, Isaiah—who drank his coffee black—as he bent to look at Arthur.

Xavier held his hands up in mock surrender.

"Geez, Arthur, had to go out with fanfare, didn't you?" said Isaiah, raising his head to gaze at the rest of us. "Did he choke?"

I had no idea what happened, but I did know one thing. The head witch of the local coven, whose members didn't hold me in high regard, had just died on my coffee shop floor, and that coven was going to be looking for answers.

My fears were realized a moment later when cute, pixie-haired Violet Wayland marched through the door, took one look at Arthur on the floor, sucked in a shocked breath, and stuck her finger right in my face.

I'd had an unpleasant relationship with the vile Violet Wayland. She'd been one to pull wings off flies when no one was looking. She once charmed my hair neon pink as a practical joke, and when I'd confronted her about it, it hadn't gone well.

We were in high school, and I shook like a leaf but called her out after school.

"Violet!"

She'd turned in a delicate pirouette, and her posse, including that stuck-up Jennifer Blackstream girl, gathered around her. Jennifer had no power but always wore that pointed witchy Halloween black hat that made me roll my eyes. I couldn't stand her either. I ignored her and soldiered on.

"This isn't funny, Violet. Turn my hair back!" I lifted my chin and stepped toward her, hoping she didn't do something worse. No one gathered around me.

"Or what, Quinny? Change it back yourself. If you can."

"You know I can't, Violet. It's your spell. Fix it."

She turned her back on me. "Your problem," she said as she sauntered away.

I stood there, seething, trying to figure out what to do. People pointed and whispered behind their hands, and my humiliation grew.

The next day, I decided to do what only I could do, and the best time was lunch.

"Violet, I want to apologize for making such a fuss yesterday. I'm getting used to the pink. I think it might be my color."

"Whatever," she rolled her eyes and turned to her friends.

"Shake? Let's have a truce." I held out my hand. She threw me a look that told me I wasn't worth her time, but flung her hand into the air and gave mine a limp shake. I took that split second to transfer a rune from my hand to hers.

At the end of lunch, Violet fell over the bench of the cafeteria table. A giant laugh spread across the room as the bitch queen hit the ground. Furious, she pulled herself together and stalked from the room, banging her shoulder on the doorjamb as she did so.

Her whole day was a series of accidents. She broke her pencil. She stepped on a football player's foot, and worst, she stumbled backwards into a teacher, knocking him to the ground, where he dropped his graded test papers. They scattered everywhere and enterprising youth slipped a few copies into their pockets. When the teacher realized, he had to negate the test and every student had to take it again.

That went over well.

But, that's what happens when you mess with a rune witch. You get...clumsy.

Problem was, though I felt better, I'd pissed her off, and Violet lived only two ways, to my mind. Pissed on and pissed off.

Bad blood ever since.

Now, in my café, Violet looked like she'd stepped out of an Indonesian anime cartoon. Her purple-streaked hair reflected her name and framed a heart-shaped face, snub nose, and almond-shaped brown eyes, and her tan skin practically glowed. In fact, it *was* glowing, literally, and I wondered what magic she used to make that happen.

"What did you do to him?" she demanded, her voice so strident that Molly startled and fled to the safety of the serving counter.

"Calm down, Violet. I don't know what happened to Arthur. Was he sick?"

"No, he wasn't sick," she said and sneered. "He was readying to retire, and was about to give me more responsibility. Now, you've ruined everything."

"Whatever," I said, repeating what she'd said to me years ago.

I ignored Violet and put the *Closed* sign on the door while we waited for the police, who showed up two minutes after I called, ambulance in tow. The medics hurried in with a stretcher, but it was obvious to them that Arthur wasn't coming back to us.

"This the guy?"

"Yes. His name is Arthur Dreck."

"The math teacher?"

"Yes," I answered. "You knew him?"

The medic gathered her hair and tied it into a quick pony tail. "My cousin had him for geometry in tenth grade. She needed post-traumatic stress disorder treatment after that. We even got her a golden retriever therapy dog."

I swallowed, holding back my comments.

A finger tapped my shoulder and I turned to see who it was.

The first thing I saw were blue eyes—amazing ocean-blue eyes—with blond eyelashes that framed them perfectly.

The man in uniform was Detective Brian Garett, if his name tag was to be believed, but I skimmed that part. I focused on the snug pants that cradled him just right, the biceps bulging underneath his short-sleeved shirt, and the easy-going smile that lit his face.

The easy-going part snapped away as he said to me, "This the vic?"

"Vic?"

"Victim."

"I don't think he was a victim of anything, other than maybe a heart attack. He was sitting here by himself and fell to the floor dead." I pointed. "Xavier saw the whole thing."

Xavier gave a small wave.

Detective Garett said, "I'll get to you in a moment, Xavier, and you as well, sir," pointing to Isaiah. "I need to interview all of you."

"You're acting like a crime was committed, detective," I said, a bit of steel to my voice. I didn't like his tone.

"I don't know what happened. Could be natural causes, but I need to consider all the possibilities. Tongue protrusion is often a sign of poisoning."

"Poisoning!" I took a deep breath and let it out long and slow. "No one is poisoned in my café." I straightened, my shoulders stiff, and walked away, hoping that he wouldn't notice that my hands were twitching with the need to hex him.

He called after me. "You the owner, Quinn Sojourner?"

"Yes."

"Good. I want to talk to you last." He turned to poor Molly, her normally white freckled-skin even paler than usual. "You work here, too?" Molly nodded. He moved closer to her and I changed direction and followed, rushing to place my arm around her.

"I'm not going to bite her, Ms. Sojourner."

"Could have fooled me, detective."

Garett rolled his eyes and sighed. He flicked a ball point pen in his right hand and held a notepad in his left.

"What's your name?

"Molly. Molly Gaffney."

"Spell it."

Molly spelled her last name. Her body was trembling.

"Age?"

"Seventeen."

"How long have you worked here?"

"Six months, but I've known Quinn longer. She's a friend of my family."

Garett turned to me. "Friend how?"

My skin flamed hot, I was so furious. "I know her mother." I avoided mentioning that her mother was a witch. Molly didn't have any power whatsoever, nor did her brother. Her father was a normal, so it didn't surprise me that the magic had ended in that family.

"Did you see Mr. Dreck fall?"

"No. I was fixing coffee for someone else."

"Did you make Mr. Dreck's order?"

Molly's voice trembled. "No. Quinn did. Mr. Dreck wasn't a nice man and she said I didn't have to deal with him."

"Is that true? Interesting."

I was miffed and I didn't care how sexy the detective was, he was an arrogant asshole. Frightening my employees! Insinuating I'd kill someone! Of all the nerve. I nudged Molly away from him and told her to clean up as we'd be closing early for the day.

I stomped through the kitchen and slammed coffee mugs, muttering to myself the entire time.

I grumbled all the way to the storage room where I sorted boxes and labeled items with color coded tags. I was aggravated. When I'm aggravated, I organize. A cool breeze on my neck made me whirl around, ready to give Detective Garett a piece of my mind.

"Why did you kill me?" demanded Arthur Dreck.

I stared in horror at Arthur's ghost. "Are you serious? I didn't kill you! And also, don't haunt this place. We don't want you. The truth is, I didn't want you here alive, you mean old coot, and I don't want you haunting me now."

The ghost shrugged. "Too bad. I can't leave, smarty pants, because I was murdered and can't leave until the murderer is apprehended and punished."

"Oh, you insufferable pest! I can't believe this. You made my life miserable and now you're making your death miserable for me, too."

Arthur straightened his tie. "I did nothing of the sort."

I placed both hands on my hips. "You were cruel to me every single time you stepped in this store, and you voted to keep me out of the local coven, you overblown creep. If that isn't making me miserable, what was?"

Arthur sniffed. "Your powers are too weak to be of help to the coven, Quinn, so yes, I voted you out. My job is...was...to take care of the coven, but I don't expect someone of your limited intelligence to understand the greater good. It still doesn't explain why you killed me."

"I didn't kill anybody. Now, go away."

"Well, I'm glad you didn't kill anybody, Ms. Sojourner, but I hadn't accused you, yet." Garett's voice came through the storage room's door.

"Scat!" I whispered at Arthur's ghost, making a shooing motion.

The detective sounded peeved. "I will not 'scat,' Ms. Sojourner. I have questions that need to be answered."

"I'm sorry detective. I wasn't talking to you." I opened the door and the detective looked around.

"Then who were you speaking to?" he asked.

"A cat. A stray cat. Nothing more. Let's go into the main room to talk." I sent a sharp look to Arthur's ghost, who followed us through the door.

Arthur's body was gone by the time I arrived in the main room, and Arthur's ghost stared out the window watching the ambulance drive away. He marched back to where I stood with Detective Garett, his eyes aflame with anger.

"I'm looking forward to watching you get caught and punished," he said at me.

"Oh, shut up."

Garett said, "There's no need to be rude. I haven't even asked a question yet."

I shook my head. "Detective, my name is Quinn, and I'm afraid we've gotten off on the wrong foot. Let me get you some coffee and we can talk."

"I'll pass on the coffee, thanks, given I'm not sure what was in Mr. Dreck's."

"He had tea."

Officer Garett took notes on a small pad. "What kind of tea?"

"A special blend I make. He's had it dozens of times."

Garett's eyebrow rose. "A special blend you make? What's in this blend?"

"It's a green tea with a touch of chamomile and hibiscus."

"I'll need that tea." He motioned to a gloved cop who had joined us while I was in the back. Molly showed him the tea canister and the policeman placed it into an evidence bag, along with my entire canister of sugar.

"You can't honestly believe I killed Arthur?"

"I don't believe anything or anyone. I believe evidence."

I stared over Garett's shoulder to see Violet on her phone, gesturing wildly, while Arthur jumped up and down in front of her, trying to get her attention. When that didn't work, he moved over to Xavier, who didn't see him either, and then to Isiah, who rolled his shoulders as if he'd gotten a chill, but that was all.

Garett snapped his fingers in front of my face. "Quinn. Ms. Sojourner. Are you paying any attention?"

"Yes, I am, but it has been a trying morning."

"I understand. Don't leave town. I'll be in touch."

"Not going anywhere. I live right across the street."

"I know," he shot back as he stepped out the door. The bell's cheerful ring at his departure did nothing to improve my mood and I scowled at it. It tinkled a jaunty tune at my ire.

My customers were discussing various theories about what killed Arthur.

Violet paced, her face reddening as she carved a path in my floor. She stopped to point to me.

"This is your fault, Quinn."

"I repeat. No, no, it's not."

Violet got right in my face. Her face was tight, eyes squinted, and her lips were pressed together. "Don't you know what you've done?"

I grabbed her elbow and pulled her outside, closing the door after us. I dragged her to the back, where the parking lot was empty. "Violet, what's going on? You know I didn't do anything."

"He died here. You are responsible!" Violet lifted her arm, pointed it right at me, and shook her hand like she was splattering paint. A burst of searing heat went through me. I staggered back against the wall.

"What are you doing? Are you crazy? What the hell are you doing?" My pulse skyrocketed from a normal eighty beats a minute to a million-and-a-half in point two seconds.

She threw another burst of heat and I dodged to the left, just avoiding it. My right arm was singed, but I didn't take any major damage. I tried to juke to the right, but she followed. I tried to slip to the left, but again, she was right with me.

"I spoke to the coven," Violet said, circling her hands in a rotating motion, circling me like a shark.

"Yeah, I'm sure they were sad to hear about Arthur, but why are you attacking me?"

I had no idea what to do and my mind buzzed with static. Violet was strong enough to qualify as a battle mage. Me? I made plants grow and fixed refrigerators.

I rolled on the blacktop, shredding my back against the loose pebbles, but managed to come up behind her. She had to spin to find me, which gave me time to throw my body into hers and knock her to the ground. When in doubt, blunt force would have to do.

I popped back up, panting and terrified at this unexpected assault. I ran toward the store entrance, but she released a fire ball and caught me on the backs of my legs. My legs flamed in pain and I fell to my knees, crying out.

"We agree that you killed our coven leader, and the coven elected me your judge and executioner."

"Stop this, Violet. Stop this! Witches don't kill innocent people, especially not other witches. Arthur had a heart attack or something. Stop this madness." I crawled, pulling with my hands to get away from her.

Arthur poked his head out of the brick wall and looked at me and Violet. "Violet! What are you doing? You can't kill her! Wait for the law to do that." His eyes were wide and he brought his hands through, scrambling to get out.

"Quinn, I can't leave. I'm anchored to the store. Watch out, roll left!"

I did as he advised, and another fireball scorched the ground where I'd been. I traced a quick rune of healing on my legs and the pain lessened. I scrambled to my feet and ran, fleeing for the front of the building, betting she wouldn't attack me with witnesses.

I couldn't understand why she would go this far, or how this situation had deteriorated so fast. Since when did the coven hand out death decrees? I flung my body at the café door, jumped inside and locked it. Violet stood on the other side, nostrils flaring. After a more curse words and a lot fist shaking, she stomped to her car and left.

"What the hell was that all about?" demanded Arthur.

"Why was that woman so incensed?" asked Xavier. "Are you all right?"

I was glad they hadn't seen the attack itself, just Violet's angry visage. "Violet thinks I murdered Arthur." I pressed my hands together so they couldn't see them shaking.

"That's ridiculous. We were all here. Despite what Detective Garett said, Arthur died of natural causes," said Xavier, as he gathered his things to leave. "Stay in touch. I'll see you tomorrow. We believe in you. Don't worry. It will be fine." He unlocked the door, slipped out, the doorbell ringing gently. I quickly locked it behind him.

Arthur huffed. "All fine except that I'm dead! I don't consider that to be fine."

Isaiah cocked his head. "Did you hear someone talking?"

"No."

"I must be imagining things." The old man shook his head and left.

I whirled on Arthur, pointing a finger at his transparent face. "What's happening? You know more than you're saying."

Arthur drew himself up, offended, but I pursued him as he floated toward the back of the shop.

"Leave me alone. I've had a bewildering day."

"Fine. But we will talk tomorrow. I want to know why the coven endorsed my murder. Until a few hours ago, you were their leader, so get ready to tell me everything. Violet seems to think she was getting a promotion, more responsibility. She told me I'd ruined that. You *will* explain that nonsense to me."

He faded away.

Before I left, I fixed the fridge. The coils were going bad, but with a rune that meant "whole," I got them working again. The corrosion flaked away and the metal was shiny and solid. Useful little rune, that was.

Still unsteady, I left the shop and fled to my apartment, glancing right and left the whole time, glad the streets were busy.

$

I eyeballed the street outside my condo complex, searching for Violet or any other member of the coven. I didn't see anyone, but it didn't mean they weren't there. I hadn't slept all night, tossing and turning, thinking about the events of the past day and how everything got so topsy-turvy.

At first, I was certain the autopsy report would show a medical reason for Arthur's death, but I was plagued by the obvious question. If Arthur had died of natural causes, why was his ghost haunting my store? I was determined to get answers.

But first, I had to make it to my shop without getting fried, or soaked, since it was raining. I wove a rune with my right hand for luck, held its gossamer strands in my fingers, and dashed across the street. I made it to my door, joining Molly, who was already huddled under the eaves. She didn't look well—pale, drawn, and she'd been chewing her bottom lip again.

I unlocked the door. "Your lip is bleeding."

"I know." Her voice was a whisper.

"It's going to be okay, Molly. Try to put yesterday out of your mind."

"He died, Quinn. Died."

"People have a way of doing that, for all sorts of reasons. Come on, go inside."

I gestured Molly through and dropped my rune, happy I'd made it.

Only to get hit in the back full-on by a blast of wind that threw me into the door. I crashed into it, breaking the glass, which cut my nose. Blood dripped from my forehead down my cheek.

Molly screeched and leaped for me, but I slammed the door shut and wouldn't let her out. It was too dangerous. I scanned the area for my quarry and saw her, Violet, across the street readying a second attack.

"What the fuck?" I said, my anger growing. I used a tunneling spell for my voice so it went across only to Violet. I couldn't hold it long.

"Violet. This must stop! I can't believe the coven approved outright murder!"

In answer, Violet bared her teeth and launched another wind attack. The force of the assault knocked me off my feet and I tumbled down the sidewalk. A passerby helped me up, but I didn't even look at him.

I might be a weak witch, but I was a witch, and I would fight back.

I wiped blood from my face and held it in my palm, using it to fuel a spell that I normally wouldn't have been able to do over a distance, praying it would work. Violet stepped into the street, heading my way, so it was important I act fast.

I grabbed the metal of the street light and cranked it hard, searing the metal at the base, where it fell in front of Violet's foot just as she stepped off the sidewalk. I added a little juju and the lightbulb sparked in her face.

Traffic came to an abrupt halt, brakes squealing. I used what energy I had left to pull a car by the bumper so it wouldn't blindside another. After that I was dizzy, thirsty, and my vision wavered. Even with the blood, that kind of magical effort was more than I should have been able to do.

Molly was by my side, pulling me into the cafe, and shoving me into a chair. She dabbed at my cuts with witch hazel, while I sat there, stunned, and watched the traffic snarl. Violet was gone, and the police wove their way through the mayhem, sirens blaring.

The streetlamp was a twisted wreck of metal, and I wondered out loud how I did that.

"I helped you," said Arthur, sinking to the floor, a little more transparent than before, his voice fainter. "I was able to share a little of my power with you. I don't have much as a ghost. It is diminished, but there was enough to give you a boost."

"Thank you. I couldn't have done that without you, even using my blood." I waved Molly away. "Molly, I'm fine. A few cuts aren't going to kill me. Could you call the glass guy? Number is in the address book under G."

Molly sniffled and her eyes were red. "I was afraid you'd die, too."

"Sorry to disappoint," I said with a grin.

"Disappoint!" Molly threw her arms around me. "I don't want anything to happen to you."

"I know, hon. See what you can do about the glass company, okay?" She nodded and hustled off.

"Thanks for the assist."

"You're welcome," the ghost said. His voice was low and throaty.

"You going to tell me what's going on now?"

Arthur sighed and floated in front of me, crossing his legs like a genie.

"It's something I should have taken care of before I died, but..." He looked out the window at the debris and disarray. "I thought I had more time."

"Exactly what should you have taken care of?"

The ghost cast his eyes down, unwilling to look at me. "Violet. I knew she was getting out of control, but I'd hoped she'd come to her senses."

"Go on."

"Violet was one of my most promising pupils. Her power is a swirling molten mass of force waiting to be tapped. I believed I could get her to focus it in a positive manner."

"I'm taking you didn't."

Arthur scoffed. "Don't be dense, you dolt. Of course I didn't, or she wouldn't have tried to smear you on the sidewalk."

"Ah, there's the Arthur I know. Flattery will get you nowhere."

He dismissed my statement with a wave of his hand. "I don't have time to waste with obvious or self-referential remarks." He considered that for a moment. "Well, given the circumstances, maybe I do, but I still don't like them."

"Okay, Professor Not-So-Obvious, what are you saying?"

The ghost shifted in the air and his chest moved as he took the phantom version of a deep breath. "Violet became interested in spells that border on the gray area."

"She was dabbling in black magic."

"She expressed an interest."

"Arthur, did you tell anyone about this?"

He looked away from me again. "No."

"What kind of spell was she researching?"

He floated, silent.

"Arthur?"

"She wanted to know how to siphon magical energy from another witch. She posed it as a battle tactic originally, and I thought it was an interesting strategy for modern combat, one that could actually reduce harm, particularly collateral damage."

"You mean people, humans, innocents."

"Yes."

"Arthur, now that you're dead, who takes over coven leadership?"

"The coven members will vote. My guess is Mrs. Whippley."

I pulled out my cell phone. "Do you know her number?"

He recited it from memory.

"Hello? My name is Quinn Sojourner. I am trying to reach Adele Whippley please?"

A male voice responded. "Are you a friend?"

"I'm the owner of Magic Beans."

"Where Arthur Dreck died?" The man's voice grew in volume.

"Yes."

"You need to kill my mother, too?" The man was yelling now.

"I didn't kill anyone! I'm worried about her and would like a few moments of her time."

I heard a muffled voice in the background.

"Fine," the man said. "She wants to talk to you, but be quick about it. She's not well."

A woman got on the phone. Her reedy voice was hard to hear.

"Quinn?"

"Yes, ma'am."

"What happened to Arthur?"

"I don't know, and he doesn't know either."

Silence.

"What I mean, Mrs. Whippley, is that Arthur's ghost is with me."

"Oh, that's good. Tell him I said hi."

"She says hi, Arthur."

"Please send her my regards."

"He sends his regards."

"That sounds like Arthur. Listen, Quinn my dear, I don't know what's wrong in the coven, but it is something serious. Stay away, for your safety."

"So, the coven didn't release a death warrant for me?"

"Heavens! Why would you say something like that?"

"Because Violet Wayland attacked me twice now, blaming me for Arthur's death. She said the coven approved it."

"Of course we didn't. Listen...you have..." Her voice faded and all I could hear were hacking coughs.

Her son got back on the phone. "Don't call again."

Bam! He disconnected.

"Arthur, I think Violet stole Mrs. Whippley's power."

The ghost hung his head. "We have to stop her."

I paced, chewing up distance with my feet, clomping back and forth with frustration. "Exactly how do you think we are going to do that? You're anchored here. I've got a tenth of the power Violet does. I can't do this on my own."

"I can help," came a tiny voice.

"Molly?"

The girl stared at the ground, but gave a short nod.

"What are you talking about?"

Molly's tears splashed to the ground in giant drops. "Arthur!" she cried, staring right at the ghost. "I killed you. I'm so sorry. She said if I played a joke on you that she'd teach me magic. It was supposed to make you loopy, like you were drunk, not kill you."

"You can see him?" I asked, my brow furrowed, struggling to understand. "You performed magic?"

"When you put the sugar in Arthur's coffee, I performed a gewrixle spell with sugar I had in a baggie in my pocket." Her whole body shuddered. "Here." She pulled a small Ziploc bag out of her back pocket. It contained about three spoons of sugar.

"How is this possible? You don't have any magic."

The girl stamped her foot. "Yes, I do! It's small, but it's there. I can feel it, and Violet said she could feel it, too. She taught me the gewrixle spell."

"A gewrixle spell is sophisticated magic. It transfers like for like. You magically switched the sugar, after I put it in Arthur's mug?"

Molly dropped to the floor, wailing. "I'm so sorry! I didn't know you'd die, Arthur. Please believe me."

The bell tinkled a joyous, happy sound, and my clock chimed the hour even though it was ten minutes early. I gave my clock a hard stare. It sneezed and chimed again.

"Bless you," said Detective Garett.

How could I explain that my clock sneezed, not me? I couldn't, so I said, "Thank you."

"Young lady, are you okay? You've been crying," Garett peered at Molly in concern.

"I'm fine, thank you. Allergies." Molly scampered behind the counter, hiding her face from the perceptive detective.

"What can I do for you, Garett?" My voice was brusque. I'd been through an ordeal with the attack and the bomb Molly dropped. I didn't have the patience for a detective hell-bent on accusing me of murder.

"Mr. Dreck's tea might have been poisoned. Our toxicologist believes the poison was in the sugar."

"Yeah, sure." I plopped into a chair and flapped my arm in front of my face in a 'whatever' motion.

"Yeah, sure?" He glared at me, and I swear Detective Cutie-Patootie Buns was ready to pull out his handcuffs right there. I closed my eyes and let that thought percolate for a moment. It was a nice thought, in a totally inappropriate way.

"I was being sarcastic."

"Not something to be sarcastic about, Ms. Sojourner." He removed his jacket, which was soaking wet, and hung it on the back of a chair at a high-top.

"Let me get you a towel." I hauled myself up and retrieved a towel from the back, avoiding Molly's eyes. Arthur had disappeared.

"Thanks," Garett said. He towel-dried his hair and I took the moment to admire his biceps.

"I'm sure your toxicologist is wrong. My sugar is not poisoned, and frankly, I've had a hard morning, and don't want to deal with false accusations."

"You had something to do with the streetlamp out there?"

I pinched the bridge of my nose. "No. I was simply outside when it fell. I got knocked over by the wind also." I gestured to the cuts on my face.

"Oh. Sorry. Are you okay?" His face reddened, embarrassed that he hadn't noticed.

"Yeah, I'm fine, thanks."

"Can I get a cup of coffee?"

"You're not afraid of the poisoned sugar?"

"Well, here's the thing," he said, following me to the counter. "The sugar in Mr. Dreck's tea might have been poisoned, but the sugar in your canister wasn't, and eyewitnesses swear you scooped the sugar from that canister."

I handed him a coffee, one sugar, one cream. "I did indeed, so obviously the poisoned sugar theory is incorrect." I made air quotes around 'poisoned sugar theory.' "Did anyone check his heart, his lungs? Look for a stroke, perhaps?"

"His family has requested no autopsy, so without other evidence, we're calling toxicology inconclusive and ruling the death natural causes."

"Good. I'm glad to hear that. Not glad Arthur died, but glad the whole murder thing has been cleared up."

Garett sucked down what was left of his coffee. "Not cleared up. Cleared for now. I'll be hanging around to keep an eye on you."

My clock jingled a gleeful little two-tone chime and the bell on the door rang without anyone opening it. I'm glad my mechanical friends were so happy at Garett's statement, but I wasn't.

"I know a good clockmaker if you want your wall clock fixed," Garett said. "Those old clocks are special."

I leaned my elbows on the table and rested my forehead in my hands. "You have no idea."

§

Customers lined up, all wanting to talk about the downed street lamp, and several noticed the cuts on my face. I gave everyone the same story about the wind and falling down. They murmured appropriate words of commiseration or solace, and we went on through the day. All the while I watched Molly like a hawk and wondered where Arthur was.

We stayed open late and my bell rang a quiet note that told me it was tired when we finally closed. My clock must have been, too, because it was running five minutes slow. Dusk led to night, the traffic slowed to almost nothing, and the hustle and bustle of the day faded. The lamp post had been removed and the street was darker than usual.

I, however, was just getting started. I clapped my hands twice.

"Family meeting! Molly, Arthur! Get out here. Time to pow-wow."

Molly slunk in, head bowed and dropped into a chair. I grabbed another chair, turned it backward, and sat on it facing her. Arthur appeared, hovering over a third chair like he wanted to sit on it, but knew he'd go right through.

"Molly, take me through your discussions with Violet, and tell the truth, sweetheart, because your actions resulted in someone's death, whether you meant it to or not. So 'fess up, every detail."

Molly squirmed in her seat but answered, her voice calm. "No one believed that I had magic, because it took so long to manifest. I knew Violet from school. She was the older, cooler girl with the exotic face, gorgeous hair, and petite build. I knew she was a powerful witch, and I thought she might understand what it was like to be underestimated."

I rolled my hand to indicate she should continue.

"She was nice to me and said she would teach me, even though she wasn't supposed to, like it was a big, exciting secret. We met a few times and she helped me learn the gewrixle spell. I asked her to teach me runes, like you use, and she got offended, so I didn't pursue it."

"Those aren't her specialty. Too delicate. She's big on raw power," said Arthur.

"She taught me a levitation spell, and how to turn on a light. Small things, but I felt great being able to do them and couldn't wait to show my mother she was wrong."

She grew silent moment and took a deep breath before she continued.

"One day she asked me to help her play a trick on Arthur. She made it sound like she wanted to tease you because you were such a stick-in-the-mud—no offense—and she asked me to switch the sugar. She told me it would make you dizzy and a little drunk, and she was supposed to meet you here anyway, so she'd make sure you got home. It was supposed to be funny. She wanted to take some selfies with you and post them on Facebook in the coven's forum."

Arthur's ghost gained color, turning a light pink.

"She's smart," I said. "She made sure she wasn't here when you performed the spell, so no one would suspect she had anything to do with it."

Arthur floated right and left; watching him made me dizzy. His color melted from light pink back to white, but now he was encircled by a corona of red. "She wants power. She knew she couldn't siphon it from me because I would notice the spell encroaching. So, she decided to kill me and drain the rest of the coven."

"Why does she want to kill me?" I asked, rapidly assessing and dismissing theories as fast as they occurred to me.

My bell tolled a jarring, jangling, sour note, one I had never heard before and it wouldn't stop, a relentless warning that danger approached.

"Take cover!" I screamed as I pushed Molly to the floor, shoving chairs and tables in front of us.

The door exploded inward, shards of the remaining glass flew everywhere. A fireball flared over our heads, hit the coffee brewers, and melted them into slag.

Violet's body, as tiny as it was, eclipsed whatever light was still on the street, and the shop was plunged into darkness. My mangled door lay on the ground, and chairs and tables, blown to smithereens, were scattered everywhere. The force of her blast leveled my serving counter, razing it to the ground. Some pieces were no larger than matchsticks.

I couldn't see all the damage from my position on the floor, but I knew it the second it happened. I experienced a solid, aching punch in the gut as the shop died, my clock succumbed, and my bell tolled its last. That bitch killed everything I had built, spelled, and loved.

I rose to my feet, wiping splinters from my hair. "Violet! I accuse you of murder, wanton destruction of property, as well as my attempted murder. What do you say?"

"Piss off, weenie-witch. I knew as soon as I walked in the day Arthur bit it that you would figure out the real trick. I mean Molly, that stupid cow, fell for everything I said—hook, line, and sinker—but when I saw her face that day, I knew eventually the jig would be up and you'd know the truth."

"You admit to Arthur's murder?"

"And I admit to yours, preemptively."

"I don't plan on dying that easily."

"Oh, you are going to die in a terrible fire, my dear. But first, you need to bleed a bit so I can siphon off what little power you have."

Violet swept her arm down in a low arc, hooked a pointy shard of glass, and hurled it at me. I ducked and shoved Molly away, pushing her toward the still standing self-serve kiosk with its sugar and plastic utensils, curdled cream and stirrers. With Violet focused on me, I hoped that Molly could stay safe tucked into that corner.

Violet charged again, but got snagged within Arthur's form. He'd found a way to become dense, like a figure made of spider webs, and she screamed as she tore at the silk.

"What the hell is this?"

"Arthur. He's not at all happy with you."

For one moment, Violet was shocked into silence. "His ghost is here? I'm stuck in his ghost?"

"Yup, and you are going to stay there while I call a few other coven members. I can't believe you've drained all of them. Besides, Mrs. Whippley wants her strength back."

My cell phone was still intact, and I dialed Mrs. Whippley's number again, hoping her son wouldn't answer. Arthur squeezed and held Violet fast. She was stuck in mid-air, and to the naked, human eye, it looked like she was caught mid-leap by a quick photographer. Arthur's eyes glowed red and it was creepy as hell.

Mrs. Whippley's number rang twice before she picked up, but then Molly screamed, and I dropped the phone. Arthur shouted, "I can't hold her!"

Violet held a knife in her hand, one she'd materialized out of thin air. She hacked away at the remaining gossamer threads that was Arthur's ghost and her prison. With each slash, she destroyed a bit more of him, his spirit disappearing with every cut. I stared at the destruction, my hand to my mouth, unable to do anything to stop her.

As soon as her right arm was free, Violet launched the knife toward my head. Her throw was precise and well-aimed. I could no more dodge it than dodge my own shadow. I had time to close my eyes, and that was all.

Bonk!

A plastic knife hit me on the forehead and fell uselessly to the ground. Surprised, but unable to focus on that particular miracle, I held up my hands as Violet attacked, tracing a protective rune in front of my body. She hit it square on and bounced back, her face an angry snarl, her body vibrating with stolen power.

Arthur's remnants reached out to stop her, but he was too weak. Violet readied a fireball and I knew that was the end.

Until her own knife plowed through her neck, severing her carotid, and she dropped to the ground. A light flicked on, a gentle glow that calmed my nerves.

"Mrs. Whippley?"

The old lady wiped her hands together, as if ridding them of something distasteful. "Thought she'd stolen all my power, did she? Crazy bitch. Good work on the gewrixle spell Molly, dear. I'm sure Quinn appreciated being hit with a plastic knife more than the sharp, pointy one."

I gawked at the two of them. "Molly exchanged the knife midair?"

Molly stood, dusting off her pants. "Sure did. Violet taught me that spell a little too well."

Mrs. Whippley tightened her apron and shifted in her slippers. "Excuse the way I look. I was making cookies when you called, and I teleported right away."

I gawked some more. "You can teleport?"

"Of course, dear," she said, pushing her bun back into place. "I'll teach you sometime. And Molly, it's time to begin proper lessons."

"Mrs. Whippley, your voice was weak on the phone. Your son told us not to call back. We assumed you'd lost your power."

"I had a cold, dear."

§

"Ms. Sojourner? Can you fix this chainsaw? The bar was damaged and the chain fell off. It's not safe to use."

My contractors had discovered that I could fix anything with a wheel, a gear, or a pulley, although they didn't know how. I took the chainsaw to the back, talked to it, and got it back on track.

My bell lay on a shelf, dented, but recovering. My clock was also mending, but it would be some time before either chimed again. I'd done all I could, and now the magic had to do its thing. Poor things almost didn't survive.

I was about to return to the front and give the contractor his chainsaw back when I saw him.

"Arthur! You're back! I thought Violet destroyed you."

The ghost held his chin high. "She tried to, but she forgot who she was dealing with."

"It's good to see you, but you can move on now. Your murder is solved."

Arthur peered at my bell and clock. "It's interesting around here."

"Does this mean you're...staying?"

"Yes, Quinn, it does. You always chill the scones incorrectly and someone needs to supervise."

His afterlife was going to be the death of me.

I jumped as the bell gave a little ting-ting.

"Ah, for whom does the bell toll?" Arthur intoned.

"I don't need you here. You can leave."

"I'm sorry to hear that, Quinn. I was going to ask you out for lunch." Detective Garett stood in the storeroom doorway.

"I was talking to the cat." I glared at my new shop ghost, grabbed the chainsaw, and marched past Garett into what would be my new shop, my bell tinkling merrily behind me.

God Willing and the Creek Don't Rise

Darin Kennedy

The desert horizon at daybreak routinely ranks among the most beautiful things I have the privilege of seeing on a regular basis. This particular day, the palette of colors the goddess has chosen to announce the coming morn strikes my eyes as full and robust as any sunrise I can recall in my twenty-five years. The deep gouge in the land that used to hold a raging river heads due east and disappears into the rising ball of warmth and light, the layers of rock within like some old-timey painting that would hang in one of those fancy museums back east.

The entire vista is so poignantly sublime, its beauty brings tears.

If only the entire scene weren't upside down.

The hemp cord that encircles my bare ankle bites into my flesh with a thousand little fibrous teeth as I dangle from the corner eave of this flyspeck of a town's excuse for a jail.

"Can't put a woman in the pen with a man," the deputy, a man named Vasquez, had whispered loud enough for me to hear as he slid the rope around my ankle.

"Wouldn't look right," the other man agreed.

"We'll just leave her out here till the sheriff gets back." The deputy tightened the loop of rope around my ankle and hauled me up into the air. *"Won't be but a couple of hours."*

A couple of hours. I'm going to wipe that shit-eating smirk off his leathered face.

Still, a far better thing to be hung by one foot than a noose around the neck, I suppose.

Five months till the twentieth century begins and here we are acting like it's three centuries ago in Salem, Massachusetts. Will people never learn not to fear what they don't or simply can't understand?

"Hello?" comes a quiet voice from the shadows of the overhanging roof.

"Yes?" I answer. "Is someone there?"

A girl, no more than thirteen years of age with tawny skin and thick brown curls, materializes from the shadows and slips quietly to my side.

"Who are you?" she asks, studying the rope encircling my ankle, her Latin accent thick yet easy to understand. "Why have they done this to you?"

"My name is Rhiannon," I grumble. "As for why they've done this, you'd have to ask Deputy Vasquez."

"Vasquez?" Her voice drops to a whisper. "But..."

Voices. Approaching from around the corner. The girl's eyes go wide with fear I don't quite understand. In a blink, she's gone.

And that leaves me at the mercy of the lawmen of this town. I shouldn't be surprised. They did say they'd come for me at first light. I'm guessing they went and told the sheriff who it was they had strung up at the jail, which is ironic because Bill's the main reason I'm stuck in this flyspeck of a crossroads a hundred miles from my bed, my home, my life.

Not that I'd ever tell him that.

In any case, the man may never understand exactly who or what I am, but at least he keeps his promises. I could have summoned sufficient wind or even a bit of fire to free myself, I suppose, but destroying the town jail wasn't exactly the calling card with which I hoped to announce my return to his corner of the world.

Around the corner they come. Sheriff William Blatt and his posse. Bill and I have crossed paths more than once since I moved out west. Not the worst man I've ever met by any stretch. In fact, we were friendly for a while after that thing in Five Pines last year.

A bit more than friendly, truth be told. That's what you get when you mix a close call with death and way too much whiskey. Here's hoping some warm feelings still stir somewhere inside that barrel of a chest. If there's one thing I remember about Bill, though, it's that he understands a lawman is just that. And if you want to survive out here, the law must come before the man.

As if the laws of man apply in a situation like this.

From my inverted vantage point a foot above the ground, my curly locks dangle and mix with dirt and gravel and equine excrement as Bill and his dozen or so no doubt fully deputized boys gather round me in a half circle. I bring my chin up to my chest and do my best to shoot invisible daggers at Sheriff Blatt, but he deflects my icy stare with the same smarmy smile that once could make my heart skip a beat.

"Cut her down, Vasquez." Bill slips his mount a hunk of turnip and takes a step in my direction, his boots somehow retaining a high luster despite the dust that covers everything in this godforsaken place. "Me and Rhiannon here need to have a little pow wow."

Bill's second, a tall Mexican and the man who strung me up in the first place, pulls a machete from a leather sheath at his side. He makes short work of the rope holding me aloft while another of Bill's posse, a rangy man sporting a handlebar mustache, holds me off the ground so my skull doesn't hit with the full force of one of Sir Isaac Newton's apples. I'd like to think he was doing me a kindness, but I can't help but notice that both his hands somehow find their way to my backside as he lowers me to the ground.

He and I are gonna have words before this is over.

I extricate myself from Vasquez and Handlebar's not so tender ministrations and pull myself to my feet. After brushing the dust from my worn jeans, I pull a shock of curly brown hair from my eyes and lock gazes with Bill. This time, he looks back.

I've seen determination in those eyes. Laughter. Kindness. Ardor. Lust.

Maybe even a hint of something more.

But today? Nothing but cold fatigue.

"Bill."

"Rhiannon."

"After Five Pines, I expected a bit more...hospitality."

Bill lowers his eyes. "Five Pines was a long time ago."

"That's funny, Bill." I crouch and rub at my blistered ankle as ten thousand invisible ants begin to crawl across my foot. "I remember like it was yesterday."

"I've been told I'm hard to forget." He retrieves my boots from the trough at the far corner of the building and deposits them by my side. "What are you doing here, Rhiannon?"

"Dry Creek seems like a nice place." I fix him with an angry glare, the ice in my eyes replaced by fire. "Didn't want to see it burn."

Handlebar steps to Bill's side. "Is that a threat, Miss?"

"Nope." I slide a boot onto the foot that doesn't feel like a hunk of dead meat covered in maggots. "Just a guarantee."

Vasquez cocks his head to one side. "*Diablos*, Sheriff." His accent is thick, like the girl's. "She was speaking of *devils*."

"She always speaks of devils, Vasquez." Bill shakes his head sadly. "Only *diablos* around here, though, are the ones between her ears."

"That's bullshit, Bill." I yank on my other boot and jump to my feet, the sensation along my sole like I stepped on a pile of loose nails just struck by lightning. "And you know it better than anyone."

"I have no idea what you're—"

"Don't you dare try to play this off, Bill. You know exactly what I'm talking about." I note the faux confusion on his face and let out a frustrated grunt. "Not two years gone, I saved your ass, remember? Pulled that hell-mutt off you before it could take a chomp out of that stubby neck of yours. Where I come from, you yank a critter with fangs the size of knitting needles off a man's chest just before it rips out his windpipe, you earn a little courtesy." I step forward until I'm nose to nose with the man and try not to remember the last time we were this close. "And that particular pup's mistress? You may have chalked up her charms as simple tricks from yet another 'lady of the evening'..." I shift my gaze to Handlebar. "But if you had had the first idea how accurate that description truly is, your knees would have been knocking loud enough to be heard in the next town."

Bill clears his throat. "I suppose you're going to tell me she was some sort of demon sent to feast upon my soul."

"Not necessarily." I crack my neck. "She might have stopped at just your heart."

"That's enough." Handlebar puts an ill-advised finger in my face. "Like any of us are going to listen to all this cockamamie talk about ghosts and goblins."

"That's my life you're talking about." That's when I notice it. The crucifix at his chest. Well worn. A tool of the trade. And around the neck of the guy whose hands were just on my ass. "Careful, *Padre*."

He steps back. "Bill?"

Bill raises a hand. "Don't let her shake you, Graham. She just spotted your cross."

Handlebar's hand goes to his neck and pushes the crucifix back inside his shirt. "Mind your business, witch."

I allow a wicked smile to part my lips and raise a mocking eyebrow. "And here I didn't think you believed in 'ghosts and goblins.'"

"What a person believes they can do can be dangerous, regardless of what they might actually be capable of." His eyes narrow at me. "Sometimes even more so."

"What I believe is that if you and this little posse of Sheriff Blatt's don't let me do what I came here to do, then each and every person in this town will be dead by sunset."

Bill, Vasquez, and Father Graham all take the statement in stride, but my words raise a hubbub among the rest of the posse. Out here on the frontier, a lot of things go bump in the night; some natural, others not so much.

No matter how big and bad a man might be with a six-shooter at his side, the darkness makes us all children again.

"All right," Bill cuts in, doing his best to assume some control. "Look, Rhiannon. I'm sorry about my boys stringing you up, but as I understand it, you were all but foaming at the mouth raving mad when they found you by the well."

"I was divining by the only legitimate source of water in this fly-speck of a town." I cut my eyes in the direction of Dry Creek's resident priest. "You know, communing with a higher power?"

"God is the only higher power we need in these parts, Miss Rhiannon," Father Graham mutters, his lips barely moving beneath his handlebar mustache. "We don't need your kind of help around here."

"If your God is all you've got, Padre, then you'd better start praying for every last soul in this town right now 'cause your asses are nothing but grass before the reaper's scythe."

Bill's eyes bulge with vexation. "Enough with all the crazy talk, Rhiannon. You seem to have returned to your senses. Now why don't you stop with the riddles and tell us what you think is coming for us?"

"Not what, Bill." I close one eye and study him with the other. "Who."

Bill's face pales a shade. "Who, then?"

"His name..." I throw a dramatic pause, and the entire posse leans in as if I'm about to reveal one of the secrets of the universe, "... is Solomon."

"Solomon," Vasquez whispers. *"El rey de la Biblia."*

"Not even close." I glance in the priest's direction. "Though it's not outside the realm of possibility the two met at some point."

"This Solomon person," Bill asks, "what makes him so dangerous that the entire town needs to fear for their lives?"

"He may have a name," I say, "but I never said Solomon was a man."

Father Graham watches me with a raised eyebrow, as if unsure whether to scoff or listen. "If this Solomon is not a man, then what is he?"

"Evil." I crack my knuckles, and then the vertebrae in my neck. "And I don't mean 'knock over a bank for some paper with dead presidents and Indian chiefs printed on the front' evil. I'm talking the real thing." I stab a finger in the priest's chest. "The kind *you* preach about from the pulpit and yet pray in your heart of hearts isn't real. The kind that led Eve to eat the apple, Cain to murder Abel, and Herod to murder the first born of an entire nation. He Who Waits for the Sunset. The Hunger that Hides in the Darkness. He Who Cannot Be Sated. Solomon has gone by all of these names and more...for centuries. The story is always the same." My eyes drift back to Bill. "He will eat the soul of every man, woman, and child in this town for lunch and still be hungry when dinnertime rolls around."

"Stop." Bill steps over and steadies one of the men in his posse who was already looking a bit on the anemic side. All my talk of death and demons sent the blood rushing from his face and he looks like a stiff wind would send him ass over eyeballs.

"Sorry, Bill." My hand finds its way to my hip. "Just answering the good priest's question as thoroughly as I know how."

"I know what you're trying to do." He cocks his head to one side. "You're trying to send my entire posse of deputies into hysterics."

I suck in a quick breath through my nose. "I can scare them a little now so they can prepare themselves, or they can shit their pants and die in a few hours when Solomon rises to feast upon your little town."

"Listen to her." Vasquez points in my direction, his finger shaking. "*Mi familia...*"

Bill stares sidelong at Vasquez for a long moment and then gives me a quick up and down. "All right, Rhiannon. You may be playing us all for fools, but I'm listening. What's it going to take to defend Dry Creek from this Solomon creature you say is coming?"

My lips spread in a wide smile as I head for the door to this building that serves as both sheriff's office and jail. "I thought you'd never ask."

§

The gathered menfolk of the town number around two hundred. Bill has ordered all the women and children to lock themselves in their homes or storm cellars, like mere wooden doors will hold back a force of nature like Solomon. They may as well stack up a deck of playing cards to block a cyclone.

Most of the men are armed with revolvers or rifles, but an unfortunate few have shown up with little more than shovels or pitchforks to defend themselves. Dry Creek may be the next to last stop on the way to a silver mine, but the money from Sterlington sure hasn't helped out the people around here all that much.

Not that all the firepower in the world would guarantee victory this day.

A few younger men, some who don't appear old enough yet to need a razor, stand interspersed with the crowd. Most hold their heads high, proving the fine line between bravery and foolhardiness, though a few look like they might wet their pants at any moment.

Truth be told, those are the ones with a far better handle on what's about to happen.

"All right, Rhiannon." Bill rests a hand on the revolver at his side. "I've gathered every able-bodied man in this town and we're here to listen to what you've got to say."

"For all the good it will do us." Father Graham says it just loud enough that the gathered crowd can all hear his little jab.

"I've got news for you, Padre." I offer an apologetic shrug. "If everything I've heard about Solomon is true, then he's likely coming for you first."

The color rises in the priest's cheeks, but he's wise enough to hold his tongue this time.

"Enough squabbling, Graham." Bill's gaze leaps from priest to me. "You too, Rhiannon."

"Fine with me." I scan the crowd with glaring eyes. Not one of the men meets my angry gaze. "Tell your posse to keep quiet. If they listen, some of them might live to see tomorrow."

"Some?" comes a tremulous voice from the back.

"Look, all of you, this town is about to face an evil that has walked the earth longer than any of us can imagine. Some say he's a fallen angel from before the Garden. Some say he's a spirit of the earth awakened when man first murdered man. Most agree that his chosen name is a reference to the famed king of the Bible, the wisest of the wise. I've heard his name whispered on the winds of every corner of this great land for months and for some reason, the whispers have all led me to this town, this day."

"So," Bill asks, "you've never even seen this 'Solomon' thing that you've got everybody changing their long johns over. How will you even know when or if he's here?"

"Oh, I'll know." I circle the crowd of ten score men and boys. "We'll all know." I cross my arms and head to the front of the gathered mass of men. "I realize that me calling myself a witch would lead anyone in this town with half a brain to believe I'd welcome this monster's arrival. That I'd join with him and lead him hand-in-hand right into the heart of town to let him have his way with your women and children before feasting on the lot of you..."

At my words, one of the younger men at the center of the crowd goes down like the proverbial sack of potatoes. Bill mutters something about "locked knees," but I suspect the fall had a lot more to do with the thought of being filleted alive by an arch-demon from hell than any blood pooling in the legs.

"Trust that when I tell you I want nothing more than to stop this monster and save this town from whatever is to come, I am being sincere." I allow my gaze to dance from one set of eyes to another, to the young and the old, the brave and the terrified. "Will you stand with me?"

A dense quiet overtakes the crowd. I'm tempted to pull the hair-pin from my bun, let it fall to the ground, and see if the old saying has any merit.

"All of you, listen." Bill pulls over the proverbial soapbox and stands by me before the men of his little town. "I have no idea what's coming, but if everything Rhiannon here says is true, it will all be over by tomorrow morning, one way or another. If you'll give her and me the next few hours, hopefully we can put this unpleasantness behind us.

A gentle murmur works its way through the crowd and one by one the men and boys step forward, ten score men united by just a few words from the man with the star over his heart.

Bill always was pretty...persuasive.

"Wait." Father Graham steps forward and spins on one heel to scan the crowd. "Where's Wilbur Driscoll and his boy, Jim? We need every man and boy in town together on this."

"Wilbur and Jim left out early this morning," comes a voice from the opposite side of the mob. "They're out at the mine."

"A mine?" I ask. "You're mining here?"

"This place has always been a mining town." Bill raises a hand in an effort to calm me, for all the good it does. "Wasn't always Dry Creek, you know?"

"Tell me."

"This place used to be Silverton, that is till they found a way big-ger vein of silver ore a few miles north of here. Most everyone moved that direction, built a new town on a more hospitable section of land, dammed up the river..." He glances in the direction of the empty river bed a hundred feet or so away. "Now, they're Silverton and we're—"

"Dry Creek." I study the men. "And these men and families."

"They're the ones who stayed. Many of them work at the new mine but didn't want to leave. And some, like Wilbur, have kept up the search closer to home." Bill pulls in a deep breath. "If Wilbur is right and he's truly found a vein of silver, it could really turn this town around." At his words, a hopeful murmur runs through the mob.

"With all due respect, Sheriff, I'm trying to stop a demon spawned in hell below from strolling into your town and eating every last soul alive. Are you sure that now is the best time for people to be digging holes?"

"Well..." Bill's hands find their way to his pockets as his chin drops. "Wilbur's not exactly going to be *digging*."

"Then what is he—"

I nearly jump out of my skin, along with every man and boy that calls Dry Creek home, as the sound of a distant explosion buffets our ears like a dozen thunderbolts at once.

The color drains from Bill's face. "Wilbur's spent months preparing. The dynamite came on the train two days ago." He looks east at the plume of smoke and dust and ash forming above the tree line, all color draining from his cheeks. "That's it, isn't it? That's what brings this 'Solomon' down on us."

Before I can answer, a jet of green flame erupts from within the cloud of smoke in the distance and splits the sky as keenly as a hot poker through fresh snow.

"Ready your men," I murmur as my mind sets to working. "And send someone to tell the women and children to stay quiet regardless of whatever they may see or hear."

Only Bill's wide eyes betray his forced calm. "And what are you going to do?"

I stride in the direction of the local general store. "I'm going to try not to die."

§

The Driscoll mine sits just shy of a mile outside of town. Bill, Vasquez, Father Graham, and I, along with a half dozen of Bill's best men, are less than an eighth of a mile out when all ten galloping horses stop dead in their tracks and rear. Despite the bucking beasts of burden, all but one of us remain mounted, at least for the moment. I use everything my mother taught me about the spirit that lies at the heart of beasts to calm my mare as well as the horses close enough for me to influence. Still, when all is said and done, only three of the horses will move another inch toward the Driscoll mine: Bill's, Vasquez's, and mine.

"Vasquez," Bill shouts, motioning to a young man with freckles and red hair, the boy's horse already halfway back to Dry Creek, "take Adam with you." He shoots a barbed glance in the direction of Dry Creek's holy man. "Graham, you hop on behind Rhiannon."

"Like hell I will." Graham covers his own mouth as if truly shocked the words passed his own lips. "I mean—"

"Padre," I intone in my most conciliatory tone, "what likely awaits us at the mine is evil beyond anything either of us have ever faced. We may not like each other an awful lot, but for the moment, we have a common enemy." I swallow back both my pride and the bile percolating at the back of my throat. "As much as it pains me to say so, I could really use your help."

"Are you quite certain?" His eyes narrow at me. "All I have to offer is my belief in a God you think is powerless to help us survive this day."

I squint right back at him. "A power ripped from hell itself is coming for us all. At the moment, I'll take any assistance I can get."

"If you're willing to work with me, then I suppose I'm willing to work with you, Miss Rhiannon." A new conviction fills his features. "God help us all."

Graham climbs up behind me and wraps his arms around my waist, far more careful with both his hands and his words than at our first meeting.

Perhaps I've misjudged this man of the cloth.

"I will say," comes a gruff whisper in my right ear, "that I certainly hope you've got something approximating a plan in that pretty head of yours."

And perhaps not.

"That makes both of us," I answer.

Bill takes off on his gray stallion. Vasquez and the Adam kid follow atop a jet black horse and I give my mare a gentle thigh squeeze to signal her to follow the tiny caravan. Graham clings to me, clearly not used to riding bareback behind the saddle, especially not behind a woman.

"Careful," I mutter across my shoulder at the priest. "Might burn your hands on the witch if you hold on too tightly."

"Just ride," he answers, though his grip doesn't diminish a bit.

The last leg of our journey boasts only half our original group, the five of us atop three horses and the remainder of the party retreating with the horses back toward town.

Bill's jaw is set, his expression imperturbable as always. Vasquez eyes every tree as if he expects a mountain lion to leap down as he rounds each curve in the road. Adam keeps up a brave façade, I recognize dread when I see it. I shoot him a confident smile and he answers with an anemic grin just as Bill pulls his horse between mine and Vasquez's.

"You sure you've got everything you need?" he asks. "Like you said, we may only get one chance at this."

"Salt, a trio of iron rail spikes, gunpowder." I pull the wineskin full of water from my waist and pass it back to Father Graham. "Hey, Padre, can you say some words over this in case we need some holy water?"

"Don't scoff." Graham lets go one hand and accepts the wineskin. "That being said...I don't really have anything else to do back here *but* pray."

Holding tight to my waist with his remaining hand, Father Graham drops into a singsong murmuring that can only be some form of blessing. Good to know he seems to be taking this whole thing seriously. I wasn't kidding when I said I was going to need his help.

"Holy shit." Even more surprising than the good father's words is the sight that prompted the borderline blasphemy to fall from his lips and interrupt his prayer.

Directly ahead of us, standing in the center of the road, a man holds a boy's limp and bloodied form in his arms.

"That's Wilbur Driscoll," Graham mutters as I rein in our mare. "And...his boy."

"Maybe." I sniff the air, attuning all my senses to the matter at hand in an effort to confirm my worst suspicions. "Maybe not."

It's all there. The not quite correct hue to the skin. The faint hint of brimstone. The shuffling footfalls of one not quite accustomed to a new body.

By the goddess, sometimes I hate being right.

"That thing may wear the form of Wilbur Driscoll, Padre, but that's not who stands before us."

Bill stops his horse dead in its tracks. Vasquez and Adam pull up on one side and I coax our mare forward to join them on the other. As I draw close, I note how the two men somehow manage to keep any emotion from their face. The eighteen-year-old behind Vasquez, on the other hand, appears for all the world like he's about to let go his bladder.

"Gentlemen." The old man in the road, his head not resting quite straight atop his neck and shoulders, ignores my presence and chooses to address Bill, no doubt a deliberate choice. "Thank you for coming for me." His gaze drops to the flaccid form resting in his arms. "There's been an accident."

"I'm sorry to hear that, Wilbur." Bill studies the man and it's obvious his lawman's instincts are picking up on the same cues my particular senses made plain. "What happened? Is Jimmy all right?"

I'm uncertain if Bill heard what I told Graham about this "Wilbur Driscoll" that stands askew in the road not fifty feet ahead, but his hand rests on the grip of his six-shooter, suggesting he understands all too well that's not his friend looking back at him with a devilish half-grin.

While Bill deals with him, I focus on keeping our trio of horses calm, endeavoring to conserve my energies as I have a sneaking suspicion the next hour—assuming we last that long—is going to take everything I've got and more.

"Your boy," Vasquez asks, "is he still breathing?"

"I can't tell." The thing speaking with Wilbur Driscoll's lips, tongue, and vocal cords doesn't even try to sound concerned. "One of you mind coming and checking on him?"

"Set him down, Wilbur." Graham takes a leap of faith and dismounts from our horse. "I'll come take a look."

"Padre..." I whisper. "That thing isn't who it says—"

"Quiet." Graham shoots me a silencing glance. "Let me handle this." Before I can stop him, he's closed the distance between us and Driscoll by half. "You never answered Bill, Wilbur. What happened to Jimmy?"

"The mine. The dynamite. The rocks." The thing calling itself Wilbur Driscoll studies each of the men in turn, continuing to make a point of not addressing me or even acknowledging my presence. "It was all over so fast."

"Put him down, Wilbur." Graham stops midstep and raises a hand before him. "And step away so I can have some room to work."

"Step away?" Driscoll's smile goes slightly wider. "And why ever would I do that?"

"You're not Wilbur Driscoll and we all know it." Bill draws his revolver and levels it at the fiend wearing his friend's flesh and bones. "Graham, get away from that thing."

Less than ten feet separate Graham and the man who should be grieving rather than appearing as if he's about to burst into laughter.

"Put Jimmy down." Graham gestures to the dusty road. "If he's dead, there's nothing more you can do to him. If he's still alive, then we can help him."

"But what if I get hungry later?" Driscoll's visible flesh—his face, his arms, his hands—goes a shade darker, his skin adopting a blue hue. "I had the foresight to bring a snack to avoid any unpleasantness, but if you'd rather I feast upon you five and your—"

The crack of Bill's revolver sends gooseflesh up my arms even as it sends Driscoll's head flying backward, a spurt of dark blood flying from an inch above his right eye. The boy drops in a heap at his feet as his father's occupied shell of a body falls backward like a felled tree. I shudder as Wilbur Driscoll's skull bounces off the dust-covered road like a child's rubber ball.

Such a fall would knock any man senseless or worse, assuming of course they survived a point-blank gunshot to the head.

Unfortunately, what we're facing isn't a man.

Not anymore.

Graham hesitates for all of half a second before rushing forward to grab Jimmy up from the dusty road.

That's when all hell breaks loose.

One second, Driscoll lies still as a corpse on the ground; the next, he's on Graham like a rabid animal. He claws at the priest's face, but the miner's worn nails do little damage.

His canines, on the other hand, work all too well.

"Help!" Graham screams as Driscoll takes a hunk out of his shoulder, not quite close enough to the neck to hit any of the major vessels, thank the goddess. "Get this monster off me!"

"Stay," I mutter to the horse as I dismount, the satchel at my side heavy with the various implements I brought to fight this monster.

"A woman?" Driscoll looks up from his perch atop Graham's chest as if noticing me for the first time. Torn flesh hangs from his teeth and thick crimson runs down his chin. "This is the best you have to send against me, Sheriff?"

"I am no mere woman, something you'd know if you bothered to look past the surface." I return his sardonic grin. "A lesson you could stand to learn, *Solomon*."

His entire body stiffens at the use of his true name. Good. I've hit a nerve.

"Who are you, woman, to speak my name so openly?" He leaps to his feet and takes a step in my direction. "On second thought, never mind. I'd planned to save you for dessert, but if you insist on stepping to the front of the line, I will happily allow you to be my first course." He surveys each of the men in turn. "More than enough meat for later."

Graham stumbles to his feet and staggers for our horse. Lucky for him I have the demon's full attention, at least for the moment.

"Listen." Bill clears his throat. "I'm not sure what you are or what you've done to this man who I count among my closest friends..." He stares down the barrel of his six-shooter from his perch atop his horse. "But trust that I understand I talk with someone else now and will not hesitate to finish you if you—"

Solomon's form becomes a blur as he rushes in our direction. Bill's horse, strikingly brave till that moment, rears in fear and sends its rider to the dried mud that serves as road in a place like Dry Creek. Before Bill can so match as catch his breath, the monster dodges his horse's flailing hooves and rips Vasquez from his own skittish stallion. Blood flies as the monster wearing their mutual friend's form rips out the deputy's throat with his teeth and breaks the man's neck with his bare hands.

His skin shifting darker another shade, Solomon looks up from Vasquez's bloody form and stares hungrily at Bill.

"Your turn, Sheriff."

"No." I hurl one of the iron railroad spikes at Solomon, sending a silent prayer to the goddess that it finds its mark. End over end it flips before impaling the monster's torso with a satisfying thunk.

"Arrh!" Solomon's attention returns to me with a vengeance. "Cold iron, eh, woman? You came prepared."

"I'm just getting started." I pull the sack of salt from my satchel and spin, surrounding myself with an unbroken circle of the white powder. "Now." I bring my hands together before me, my head tilting to one side as I study this husk of a man formerly known as Wilbur Driscoll. "However shall I bind you?"

"Of course." He pulls the iron rail spike from between his ribs and lets it fall to the ground. "Witch." The word leaves Solomon's borrowed lips as a spittle-laden curse, but one with a modicum of respect. At least we're beginning to understand each other.

Graham runs for me. His shoulder oozes blood but if all goes well, he'll live.

Wait. His right leg has taken a hit too. He can barely lift it from the ground, and with each step, the toe of his boot leaves behind a shallow trench in the dirt road.

"Stay back!" I shout as he draws close. "Padre!"

"Help me." With his good foot, Father Graham steps across my circle of salt, his opposite foot disrupting a moment later the only thing keeping Solomon from doing to me what he just did to Vasquez. "Please, help me."

"Yes, witch." In a blink, Solomon rushes from Bill's side and, with a mocking flourish, steps across the interruption in the salt circle. "Help him." Before I can so much as inhale to speak a word, he has Graham and I by our throats.

"Now, the only question." He lifts both of us off our feet with no more effort than if he were comparing a pair of cooking geese at Christmas. "Which of you wants to watch as I snuff the light from the other's eyes?"

"Eyes..." Graham croaks as he pulls the wineskin before him and sprays its contents directly into Solomon's face.

With a scream quite literally ripped from hell, Solomon drops the both of us and claws at his face with the Wilbur Driscoll's rough miner's hands.

"Burns..." he grunts between clenched teeth. "It *burns!*" His skin darkens another few shades toward black, leaving Wilbur Driscoll's husk the color of ash.

Not wasting a second, I grab Graham's sleeve and pull him with me as I sprint for our horse. A blast from Bill's shotgun sends Solomon to ground again, though I don't count on that buying us more than a few seconds.

"Bill, get your ass back on that horse and head for town as fast as you can." I push Graham at our mare and will the beautiful animal to remain still with every ounce of mental energy I can spare. "Now, Sheriff."

For once, William Blatt skips the part where he asks me the whys and wherefores of what I'm asking and instead complies with a quick nod. As he leaps back onto his horse, my eyes shoot to the youngest of our entourage, the all-but-forgotten young man left atop Vasquez's, his eyes wide with confusion and terror and rage.

"That thing..." he mutters. "It's coming for us all." His breathing goes ragged even as his face goes beet red. "My mother. My sister. You can't have them, you monster."

He's working himself up, no doubt, to do something brave.

One man's courage, however, is another man's foolishness.

"Adam Skipper," Father Graham says as the boy pulls himself forward onto Vasquez's saddle. "I know what you're thinking, but—"

"That thing is blinded, Father." Adam tugs at the reins and points his horse directly at Solomon. "I can slow it down while you three get back to prepare the town." His eyes narrow at the dark form clawing at a face that once boasted Wilbur Driscoll's handsome features. "Promise me you'll keep my family safe."

"Don't do this, Adam." Bill turns his horse in the direction of Dry Creek and motions for the boy to follow. "Come with us."

"Yes, Adam. Come. With. Us." I focus my thoughts on both boy and horse in an effort to shift either of their minds, if but an inch. I needn't have bothered. He's made up his mind and his horse is too skittish to influence with anything other than leather and steel.

"Go, Bill." I direct him up the road back toward Dry Creek. "We'll be right behind you."

Bill hesitates but a moment longer and then spurs his horse into action. I shoot Adam one last look before bringing my own horse around.

"No one else needs to die today." Somewhere between lofty goal and empty promise, the words feel like a lie even as they pass my lips. "Come back to town with us."

"Keep them safe." With that his only answer, Adam whips the horse with both reins and digs his spurs into the beast's flanks, sending the terrified animal hurtling at the temporarily blinded Solomon like a bull rushing a Spanish matador. At the last instant, the horse dodges to one side and the boy shoots out one boot, catching Solomon square in the chest and sending the man-turned-monster sprawling. Their first pass a success, the boy brings the horse around and launches into a second run at the demon in our midst.

This time, however, Solomon is ready.

Catching the boy's foot in one outstretched hand, he rips the young man from his mare and hurls him into a boulder just off the side of the road. A sickening crunch fills the air as the boy's leg snaps against the jagged hunk of rock. He howls in pain, clutching his shin where a razor sharp shaft of bone protrudes from an ugly tear in his flesh just below his knee.

"My God," Father Graham utters from behind me. "Adam..."

I've seen injuries like this before. He'll be lucky if he keeps that leg. Luckier still if he walks another day in his life. And that's all assuming he even survives the day.

That's when a horrible realization strikes me.

Solomon now has a horse.

"Go!" I shout to our mount, willing the horse away with voice and heels and reins and thought. "Or he'll do the same to all of us."

§

Dry Creek is but a few minutes by road at this speed, yet time seems to stretch out with each curve in the road. More than once, the sound of hoofbeats to our rear prompts a glance across my shoulder as we rush back to Bill's little corner of the west, but when I look back, all I see is our own trail of dust with no sign of Solomon.

Regardless, my taunts and Graham's holy water assault all but guarantee Solomon's pursuit, not to mention the scores of souls ripe for the reaping in Dry Creek.

"One thing I'll tell you, Padre." I reach back and give the priest's knee a friendly swat. "I don't know what else you've got going on between those ears of yours, but you must truly be a man of faith for the water to have hurt Solomon like that."

He lets out a pained sigh. "I hate to disappoint you, but that wasn't your water I sprayed in his face." He pulls my wineskin up from an inner pocket of his long coat.

"But...what, then?"

"There are times for faith and miracles, Miss Rhiannon, and there are times to let a little whiskey do its work."

"You brought an entire wineskin of whiskey?" I shout over the din of galloping hooves.

"You said we were off to fight the Devil himself, so I came prepared." He lets out a bitter laugh. "A little liquid courage can go a long way."

"Never were truer words spoken." At the continued echo of hoof-beats from behind, I spur our horse forward. "I might even argue that in your time of need, your God truly did provide."

Graham doesn't say another word, the admission of the truth about his "holy" assault on Solomon costing him quite a bit of face before a woman he no doubt pictured tied to a stake above a pyre less than an hour ago.

Pride is one of the seven deadly sins, however, and I am strangely happy to have helped the good Father shed a bit of his.

As we round another corner, we finally catch up to Bill, his horse nursing a mild limp as it continues up the road.

"We're almost back," he shouts as we pull up alongside him. "You think the gathered men of my town can stop this...thing that has taken over Wilbur's body?"

I consider my words carefully, as I've seen the men and women of this world overcome worse odds.

There was that ghostly business in Charleston, SC. Can't believe we all rallied behind a vampyre of all things to stop that madness.

And that village in northern Mexico that somehow drove the resident bat demon taking their children back to its dark cave.

This is different, though.

Ghosts are already dead and Camazotz is more creature than god. Solomon, no matter what form he currently wears, is intelligent, evil, immortal.

"They'll have to," I answer. "They have no other choice."

"Oh, I know they'll fight." Bill continues to force along his injured horse. "I just want to know it's possible for them to win."

I consider the question. All we have is hope, and I refuse to dash Bill's on the rocks of despair.

"Truth be told, Bill, anything is possible."

"God willing," Graham grumbles "and the creek don't rise."

Wait. The creek.

"Come on, boys." A faint smile finds its way to my face. "I've got an idea."

§

We arrive at the edge of town having hastily discussed my bones of a plan. The three of us pull together atop our horses beneath the low canopy of a copse of trees.

"How far away is Sterlington?" I ask.

"A couple miles." He pats the horse. "If Jack here was fresh, eight minutes tops, but—"

"How long then?"

"Another fifteen minutes, and that's if I'm lucky. Push more than that, I might not make it at all." Bill keeps one ear perked in the direction from which we came, as do I. "You sure this is the right thing?"

I offer a solemn nod. "It's the only thing."

Graham laughs. "The fine folks of Silverton, Nevada are going to be none too pleased with this little plan of ours."

"That's the only part of any of this I'm sure of." Bill meets my gaze and any hint of a smile melts into earnest concern. "You sure you can buy me enough time?"

"If you'll stop jawing and get up the road." I try to play the jab off as a joke. I fail.

Graham leans in, the previous mirth in his voice replaced with grim acceptance. "We'll hold him as long as it takes, Sheriff."

"Right." Bill studies us both for a second. "Be careful, you two. Graham, watch after her." He tips his hat to me. "Rhiannon."

I lower my head in answer. "Bill."

And with that, he takes off at as fast a gallop as his poor injured horse can manage, leaving me alone with Father Graham. Before I can say a word, the priest rests a timid hand on my shoulder.

"The way I see it, Miss Rhiannon, there's no chance in a million years that your theology and mine are going to start lining up any time soon—"

I brush his hand off none too gently and glare across my shoulder at the man. "You can stop right there, Padre. You've made it more than clear how you feel about people like me."

"Wait," he insists with a sigh. "I just wanted you to know that despite our differences, I respect your willingness to lay your life on the line for a town full of people you've never met when all we've done is string you up and leave you out in the cold."

"Why, Father Graham," I turn in the saddle and place my hand coquettishly over my heart, "that sounds an awful lot like an apology."

His cheeks grow a shade pinker. "Let's just save my flock, shall we?"

"No one is saving anyone today, Padre."

Graham and I, both still atop our horse, jerk our heads in the direction of the guttural voice. Rounding the corner atop Adam's horse, Solomon studies us as a child at the Thanksgiving table deciding whether he wants light meat or dark. The horse appears varying shades of frantic, exhausted, and haunted while Solomon smiles at us calmly with what was likely once a kindly grin from a man named Wilbur Driscoll.

One thing is certain. The adjective "kindly" no longer applies.

"Go," I whisper as I dismount, leaving the saddle empty for Father Graham. "Get out of here. Gather the town as we discussed."

With but a moment's hesitation, he nods and gallops away, leaving me alone with a monster who would feast upon my soul without a second thought.

"So, Solomon, it comes down to just you and me."

"You say my name so freely." His grin widens. "Are you truly so eager to die?"

"Only one of us shall suffer such a fate today, demon." I reach into my bag and grasp an herb that I've kept in reserve for just such an eventuality. "For now, though, allow me to release at least one innocent from your clutches."

I hold aloft the sprig of jasmine and whisper words that evaporate on the wind as they leave my lips. A rich fragrance fills the air, and before Solomon can react, his horse lowers itself to the ground, the lids of its soulful eyes sliding shut as it drifts into a deep slumber.

The subtleties of calming a frantic animal in the midst of battle may have posed a bit of a challenge, but simply rendering one unconscious? Child's play.

"Too little, too late, witch." Solomon rises from the sleeping horse and strides in my direction. "The beast has already carried me for the lion's share of the journey. The memories of this husk I wear put me in the center of town in minutes were I to keep even a leisurely pace."

"Minutes..." I whisper to myself. "A quarter hour, if we're lucky..."

"And now," he says, his voice like gravel, "you shall serve as the appetizer for my long-awaited meal."

"You'll have to catch me first." Having seen how fast Solomon can move, I dodge beneath his clawing hands and into the woods where at least the roots and brambles give me some sort of advantage. For all his power and immortality, Solomon still wears a human form with all the frailty that entails.

"You put off the inevitable, witch," he grumbles as he crashes through the underbrush after me. "And all I'm doing is working up an appetite."

There are those who believe that witches can fly, control the thoughts of others, cast balls of fire from their hands, even raise the dead, among other claims. Over the years, while it may be true that I've encountered those who can perform such wondrous feats, my skills revolve mainly around the natural world: the plants of the ground, the beasts of the earth, the skies above.

Goddess, be with me, I will need them all.

I release a pinch of pungent powder into the air and whisper words my mother taught me years ago, asking for the forest undergrowth to slow my pursuer. In answer, I hear a loud crash and a curse from far closer behind me than I would like to imagine.

Next, as I leap across a rocky creek bed, I stretch my senses outward and find in the branches above a resting flock of songbirds. At my whispered urging, they descend as a feathered deluge and fly at the demon, leaving the form of Wilbur Driscoll hidden beneath a dark carpet of wing and feather.

A gentle buzzing echoes in my mind, a nearby bee hive more than ready to defend their queen—and me—from any interloper. A pulverized herb thrown into the air and another whispered phrase I committed to memory when I was but a child and the buzzing in my mind moves to my ears. As the swarm flies around and past me, I almost feel sorry for the monster wearing Wilbur Driscoll's form.

On the other hand, we all have to learn about the birds and the bees at some point.

Carefully, I circle back to the road, doing everything in my power not to leave any evidence of my passing, and find Vasquez's horse just returning to its feet from its forced slumber.

"Good boy," I murmur, rubbing the horse's forehead. "What say we head back to town."

"You'll die, witch," comes a strained voice from the edge of the woods.

Goddess, he's fast.

"With as much pain and suffering as I can muster." He steps

from the woods, his stolen body cloaked in both stinging swarm and fluttering flock. "I swear it."

"Again," I taunt as I race away atop Vasquez's still-waking stallion, "only if you can catch me."

§

I race the last few hundred feet to the edge of town and, as I round the last corner, come upon Graham who has just finished hitching up his horse.

"What now?" he asks.

"Gather all the men." I meet eyes with a gaggle of boys across the street that don't look nearly scared enough. "You four, go to the general store. Bring all the salt they have."

"Salt?" asks the oldest.

"All of it." I turn back to Graham. "Guns are fine, but now that I've seen what Solomon can do, I'm thinking the men may actually fare better with whatever farming implements they can bring that can keep a man at bay."

Or, at least, something wearing the form of a man.

Graham eyes me curiously. "You mean, shovels and the like?"

"Pitchforks, scythes, mattocks. Whatever they've got. Just do it fast."

In minutes, every man and boy in town is gathered on the edge of town at the edge of the narrow channel that once was home to a river and now barely boasts a trickle of water. Silver may be what motivates people to come to this part of the world, but water is the lifeblood of the west. Today, the goddess willing, I will prove that beyond all shadow of a doubt.

"All of you," I shout at the top of my lungs. "Form a circle."

At the men's hesitation, Father Graham shouts, "Do as Miss Rhiannon says, or none of us will see tomorrow morning." At the good priest's words, the men begin to comply, albeit slower than I'd like.

"You three," I gesture to a collection of particularly surly looking fellows who are moving like molasses, "over there." I direct them to the far bank before locking eyes with a tall drink of water across the way. "You, take those four and stand over there."

Painstakingly, I try to convince two-hundred men to listen to a—what did Vasquez call me as they were stringing me up—little *bruja*? In the end, though, their fear of the unknown overpowers their collective natural inclination to ignore anything and everything that comes out of a woman's mouth and they do what I say, however begrudgingly.

Who knows? At this rate, maybe men will even hand over the right to vote in a decade or two...

The gang of young boys returns with half a dozen large sacks stamped with a blue "Morton" logo and start distributing the bags to their fathers, brothers, uncles. They've barely made it halfway around the enormous circle when an explosion in the east shatters the late morning quiet.

We're on the clock.

No sooner has my heart stopped racing from the faraway blast than a piercing voice sends slivers of ice straight through to my core.

"Thank you, witch, for gathering my afternoon repast." A recovered Solomon, his skin the color of night, approaches from the center of the little town, his voice sounding in my mind as much as in my ears. "You've saved me the trouble of tracking down the many men who will serve as my dinner while my pretty desserts, no doubt, await me locked away in their cellars like little boxed candies."

Goddess, does nothing slow down this monster? The body he possesses doesn't seem even the least bit winded. An exhausted groan escapes my lips. For all my skills and learning, what I know and understand about demonic possession still would barely fill a thimble. Not to mention, if I don't get the timing of the next few minutes just right, we're all dead.

Our task is quite simple, really. I and the men and boys of this tiny town need only lure Solomon to the designated spot and ensure he remains there for the next ten minutes.

The rest is up to the lessons of Alfred Nobel and Sir Isaac Newton.

"If you wish to eat, Solomon, then come and get your meal," I shout, "though the men of Dry Creek don't intend to go down without a fight."

"I wouldn't have it any other way." He licks his lips greedily. "Nothing like the flush of battle to give meat a certain...zest."

"No one will be eating anyone today." Graham signals and several dozen men with various firearms all step forward and level their weapons at the form of a man many of them have likely broken bread with a hundred times. "Fire."

The air fills with thunder and smoke as three score rifles, shotguns, and pistols fire in unison. Solomon, wearing the ever darkening form of Wilbur Driscoll, strides ever forward, his form pocked with bullet hole after bullet hole. Flesh and bone torn away reveal char and brimstone, but still, the demon's inexorable stride brings him ever closer.

"The salt," I whisper across my shoulder. "As we discussed."

His face aghast at the unstoppable monster coming for him and his flock, Father Graham retreats with the mob of men and boys. Within seconds, all have disappeared into the shallow gorge to my rear, leaving me to face Solomon alone, yet again. The demon looks on, a hint of confusion in his/its features.

"These men and boys have never faced your like." I open the pouch at my side. "And with the goddess as my witness, they'll never have to."

"Stupid witch, you should have run when you had the chance." He continues his slow walk toward me. "All you've done is bought these helpless mortals a few extra minutes and ensured yours is the first heart I eat today." His gaze passes down his own form before meeting mine again. "Other than that of poor Wilbur's son, of course."

"Bastard," I intone under my breath as I pull a pair of the iron railroad spikes from my pouch. "Maybe hot lead won't stop you but cold iron has already stopped you dead in your tracks this day."

Even as I drop into a low fighting stance taught me by an old friend from the Orient, my mind and senses stretch out in the direction of Sterlington. Tracing the empty river bed along its winding course, I determine that I have at most six minutes to enact my plan.

One minute too early or, worse, too late will spell doom for every man, woman, and child in this town.

Solomon, his transformation into a hulking mass of dark smoking flesh nearly complete, drops into a lope as he comes for me. I fling one of the railroad spikes at him even as I bring the other before me like a fencer's blade. He dodges my hurled attack easily, but the requisite lunge to one side sends him off balance. Recalling another lesson from Master Kawa, I center myself and let fly a high kick. The heel of my boot catches Solomon just above his Adam's apple and sends the chin that was once Wilbur Driscoll's flying skyward.

It's a move that would drop a man twice this size. Solomon laughs, my attack doing little more damage than a playful swat.

"This body I've possessed may be nearly consumed, but you face me now, witch. Driscoll's body left me weak, but this form feels no pain." He grabs my upper arm with his smoldering hand and hurls me to the ground with strength far beyond any this body likely ever knew. "Unlike yours."

"Solomon, dear." I bite my lip to keep myself from screaming in pain at the burns on my arm. "I may be a glutton for punishment, but I must ask." I force my lips into a smirk. "Is that the best you've got?"

He smiles, his teeth like glowing embers. "Despite everything, witch, I was going to show mercy and slay you before feasting on your heart, but now I think I shall dine upon your entrails while you still breathe. I want to see the light dim in your eyes as you watch me consume you, body and soul."

"Nothing I haven't heard before." I roll backwards to get out of range of those smoking claws of his and shoot to my feet. "Another round, perhaps."

He's on me in an instant, his form again a blur as he ducks beneath the iron railroad spike and encircles my neck with an arm like a vise of hot coal.

"I'm going to enjoy this," he whispers into my ear. "Prepare to meet your—"

Neck on fire and lungs burning for air, I jab backwards with the railroad spike and catch Solomon mid-thigh. He howls in agony, ironic after his statement of invincibility moments before, and releases me. Breathless, my neck and chest still burning from his assault, I fall to the ground. Despite the agony, I somehow keep my senses attuned to the world around me.

Four minutes, if that. No time at all, and simultaneously, an eternity.

"You are far more formidable than I gave you credit." Braving the inevitable pain, he reaches down and pulls the cold iron from his leg and hurls it to the ground. "Still, struggle all you want. The outcome will remain the same."

Without the wind to respond, I kick away from him and force myself back to my feet as Solomon continues his unstoppable march. I stumble for the edge of the miniature gorge, a new pain in my ankle threatening to send me sprawling with every step. With a silent prayer to the goddess, I drop to the ground, scoot down the incline on my denim-covered backside, and return to my feet once I reach bottom.

Three minutes.

I make my way to the 10 foot circle of salt at the riverbed's center, ensuring that I disturb one small section of the circumference.

Now, to get him to follow.

As the demon steps to the edge of the bank and looks down on me, I hold aloft my lone remaining railroad spike and motion for him to join me.

"Come, Solomon. Let us finish this."

"You put such weight in your little circles, witch," he taunts. "Surely you know that such obstacles are merely to give you dwellers of the world above a semblance of control over that which you have none."

"You speak boldly, demon. If you are so confident in your claims, come forward and face me."

"So the mighty river you and the sheriff have set free can wash me away? I think not."

My heart drops. He knows.

I stretch out with my senses. A minute remains. Maybe two.

"I shall very much, however, enjoy watching you fall prey to the fate you planned for—"

A shotgun blast from behind cuts Solomon's taunt short, his body thrown forward by the blow and into the gorge. His body rolls to the bottom of the empty river bed and lands a good ten feet away from the salt circle I've prepared to hold him. For a moment he doesn't move, and I chance a look up to find a teenage girl peering down from the spot where Solomon stood moments before—the girl who came to me first thing this morning, fresh tears running down both her cheeks. Though her dark brown curls hang in her face, I finally make the connection. Her features, her skin, her wide eyes at the mention of the deputy's name.

She's Vasquez's daughter.

And the goddess willing, I'm going to make sure she avenges her father's death.

A rumble in the distance lets me know that it's less than a minute till showtime.

Solomon shoots to his feet, forgetting me for a moment, and lumbers across the dry riverbank to the wall and begins to climb, the point blank shotgun blast having damaged his form more than I'm sure he'd care to admit. Her scream punctuated by the ever-crescen-doing sound of rushing water in the distance leaves me with mere seconds to save both the girl and this town.

I rush at Solomon from behind, scrabbling up the riverbank as fast as my legs and free hand will take me, keeping my last iron railroad spike firmly in hand. Solomon has nearly reached the petrified girl when I catch up to him. I leap at him, spike held before me, but this time I've underestimated the demon. As if he had eyes in the back of his head, he shoots out an arm like a striking serpent and catches me by the neck, his smoking fingers like hot coals.

"Perfect," he hisses as he pulls the both of us back up to level ground where the terrified girl awaits. "Now you can watch as I take her body and then the feeding will begin anew."

The sound of galloping hooves returns hope to my heart. Girl, demon, and I all jerk our heads around to find Sheriff William Blatt racing from the center of town straight at us atop a different horse, this one brilliantly white from head to hoof.

The girl leaps to one side and Solomon to the other, but the horse homes in on the demon like a hawk descending upon a scared rabbit. Bill's gaze meets mine and I offer as much of a nod as the ring of coal-like fingers about my neck will allow. From the corner of my eye, I witness the vanguard of the flash flood caused by the destruction of Sterlington's dam, an unstoppable mass of logs, rock, and water.

It's all come down to this. If I leave this world having helped rid it of something so foul as Solomon, then so be it.

"Hey, mister." The girl, forgotten for the moment, pulls the shotgun up and buries its business end in Solomon's armpit, just below the arm that holds me aloft. "My papi always taught me to load both barrels."

And with that, she pulls the trigger. The arm of the man known as Wilbur Driscoll explodes from its shoulder in a shower of coal and bone and gore. The girl spins and shoves me to the ground even as Bill's horse rears before the demon, the stallion's flailing hooves sending the one-armed form flying back into the deep trench even as tons of wood and stone pushed by millions of gallons of water rush by. My eyes track the fiend's upraised hand for all of two seconds before it disappears downstream beneath the unstoppable deluge.

I have little doubt the immortal evil that calls itself Solomon will someday walk the earth again, but Wilbur Driscoll's body and soul has hopefully found peace. And should Solomon ever deign to return, regardless of the form he chooses, he will have to deal with me.

My every muscle aching and the skin of my neck and arm still burning from Solomon's touch, I look up into the eyes of my two rescuers.

"You...you saved me." Tears well at the corners of my eyes. "Both of you."

"You risked everything to save us first, Rhiannon." Bill dismounts and leans over me, offering a gloved hand. "Even when we pushed you away."

As Bill pulls me to my feet, I return my gaze to the girl. "Your father is, was Señor Vasquez. I'm so sorry."

"That thing killed my papi." Her accent thick like her father's, her meaning comes through crystal clear. "I have returned it to hell."

"You're just a girl." I offer her a pained smile. "So brave. What's your name?"

She smiles wistfully. "My mother died in childbirth. All my papi had was me and hope for a better future. He named me after the month in spring when the flowers return so that I would always remind him that there was hope." Her downcast eyes meet mine. "I am Abril."

"Abril. A beautiful name." My mind runs through a thousand scenarios. "But you've lost both your mother and now your father. Who will care for you now?"

"I will." Bill drops to one knee. "Vasquez, this morning's unfortunate misunderstanding aside, was a good man." He squeezes Abril's shoulder. "As of this moment, I will care for his daughter as if she were my own."

"You won't be alone." I rest a hand atop Bill's and bring Abril's eyes to mine. "I owe you my life, Abril. I'd like to stay and be a part of yours, if that's what you'd like."

"But neither of you know me." Abril, so brave before, breaks down in tears. "Why would you do this."

"I've seen all I need to see." I lock gazes with Bill. "From both of you." I motion to the rushing river where only an empty crack in the earth existed before. "And now that Dry Creek is anything but dry, it's a whole new world, wouldn't you agree?"

A Devil to Help

Paige L. Christie

San stepped out the back door of the country club into the afternoon sun, stripped off her uniform shirt and tossed it over the seat of the bike. She opened the tail pack on the package rack and fished out her jersey to change. One day, she'd be caught half-naked in the rear lot, and be fired for shocking the polo guests. And though hope sprang eternal in the face of that possibility, today did not appear to be that day.

A glance at the Garmin on her wrist confirmed that if she left now, she'd just make the studio in time for dance class.

Two months in Tucson and she'd decided that the city's true name was Splits, Squiggles, and Exceptions. North-South the streets divided at Broadway. East-West at the crossing of Stone — except where Oracle got involved. Though that didn't surprise her, oracles being what they were.

So much longing and old disruption dwelt beneath the streets and dried up riverbeds, that sometimes the only way for San's full attention to be called to any one aspect of it was for need to smack her repeatedly in the metaphorical face.

The third-in-three-days saguaro needle buried in the rear tire of her bicycle was just such a cry for help. She crouched for a closer look. The fierce, pronged spine of a saguaro protruded from the tire's sidewall, buried so deep that only part of the areole still showed through the rubber.

Shit and damn.

"Josh," she said, her voice hoarse with exasperation. "When are you going to learn to just pick up the phone and call?" But no. Six cell phones she had purchased him over the years. And sometimes he answered when she called. But he never called her. Just left messages on her bicycle: maple copters in her chain in New England, and honeysuckle vines in her rear sprocket in the southeast, and lodgepole pine needles gumming up her brake rotors in the northwest. Always the same pattern. Once was a fluke, twice a pain, three times and she had to go track down her own personal Jersey Devil.

And in all the years she had known him, that never been an easy task. Josh possessed a unique nose for trouble — regarding himself and other mythical creatures and items. So, what kind of trouble now? And where should she start looking for him?

She sighed. First things first. She reopened the tailbag and dug out her tire levers and patch kit. If he needed her quickly, he should have chosen a less damaging calling card. She paused, hands on the rear wheel quick release. Shit. Josh only turned destructive when something was really wrong. What the hells was he into now?

§

Patching the tire took long enough to irritate her. Finding a space on the edge of the club property far enough from prying eyes for her to work a solid tracking spell took even longer. But she managed, and after scrubbing the remains of her casting pattern carefully into the sand, she snapped the old pine twigs she tagged for tracking, and placed them in the clear-topped handlebar bag that usually housed her cellphone with its GPS map. This evening, though, the sticks offered her better directions. And the fact that she'd broken them meant they'd now only work for her.

The mile ride to the main road allowed entirely too many worried thoughts to fill her mind. They hadn't been here long enough for anyone to take sightings of Josh seriously. So, the trouble was more likely something he'd found rather than something that'd found him. She turned right at the stop sign, and heavy traffic forced her to concentrate on riding rather than a growing worry for Josh, though old experience brought no surprise — that a focused head and a nervous stomach could easily coexist.

The sticks wiggled and wiggled and wiggled in the bag. For the entire ride, wrongness vibrated up from the ancient flow lines buried beneath the concrete. That had to be related to whatever Josh was into. Damn. At last, a tickle in the back of her mind told her that she was close and that the Kino Sports Complex was her destination. Well, that made sense. Josh liked to perch atop the stadium and watch the traffic on the I-10. And if he had to hide quickly, the Restoration Project to the north was an easy flight for him.

Four hundred years her family had watched over Josh, kept him company and safe in his exile from his Pine Barrens home. The least they could do considering the risk he had taken for the sake of her many-greats-gone-back grandmother. And even though San had inherited her role as his guardian, she couldn't find it in herself to resent it. Because of Josh, she knew not only her family's magic, but so many secrets of the native creatures of the whole continent. And she'd seen more of the land — and more of the strange and wonderful of the land — than most people could even imagine existed.

The Lee's curse wasn't much of one as far as she was concerned. Though how Josh felt about the whole thing, even after all these years — well, he never said. And she'd stopped asking years ago.

Darkness was nearly ready to claim the city by the time she rolled up at Kino. Across the entrance road, the last rays of the sun painted the west wall of the stadium in burnished light. Josh wouldn't show himself until darkness fell, no matter how urgent his need.

"Creature of the night," she murmured, "No more flats." Then frowned. Why so many cars here at this time of night? Shit. The Gem Show. Only the biggest event of its kind that she'd ever heard of — taking up venues all over the city, including big chunks of the Kino Sports Complex. Gem show...oh shit. That could only mean one thing, and how in the hells, without total disaster back east, could it mean that?

§

San locked the bike to a tree and sat down beside it, leaned back. Lifting off her helmet, she shook loose her hair and closed her eyes to wait. Beside her, the sticks in the bag quieted with a final click, click, clack. But the dull thrum of the land increased. San sat for a few quiet moments, just listening, unease growing as a stiffness between her shoulder blades. The vibration held steady, hot and unrelenting as Tucson's sun. But it was far stronger in its disquiet than it had been in all the months since she'd come to the city.

San shifted, then shook her head, slipped a hand into the slim travel wallet that never left her waist. Her hand closed around the body-warmed metal of the Mother Ring, and she pulled it out, slipped it onto the middle finger of her left hand.

A simple band, metal welded to conceal a series of gem stones laid side by side by side around the entire circumference, it looked as worthless as it was powerful. The only thing Josh could possibly be interested in at a gem show, was the Sssguilssan, the sacred stone from which his people drew power to protect their homeland. Though it had been years since she required more than the ring for either battle or defense, if the stone were here, she might need to retrieve her matching bracelet and choker from her safe deposit box. The sun slipped lower as she twisted the ring back and forth.

"Spheeeeeeeene..."

San jumped and jerked her gaze upward. Above her, in the crook of the two widest branches, a pair of purple-tinted eyes gazed down at her. Josh had stuffed himself into an impossible position, long talons wrapped around one branch, and jewel-like leather wings folded tight among limbs and leaves, heavy muzzle resting one cheek against the trunk. As always, he reminded her of a cross between an angry chicken, a spray-painted bat, and a Celtic dragon, though the dragons from other continents were considerably larger. Josh's head barely reached the top of her shoulder.

"Titanite, nor Sphene," she said, looking up at him. "Have you been up there the whole time?" She raised a hand. "Don't answer that."

"Spheeeene," he responded. Well, she couldn't blame him for preferring the name original name of the gem. Centuries of practice had given him the ability to speak a certain broken version of her human language, but 'Ts' where hard for him, while the long version of the letter 'E' seemed to give him extra delight to produce.

"Sssguilssan." The word came hard to her lips, as badly pronounced as the worst of Josh's muddled enunciations.

A tremor went through Josh, shaking the whole tree. Seconds later, he clattered beside to the ground beside her. "Heeeere," he said, spreading his wings as wide as they would go and fluttering them for emphasis.

For him to make such a display in a very public space, meant one of two things — they were completely alone with no chance of anyone spotting him, or he was so focused on the Titanite that he didn't care if he was seen. If that were the case, they were in endless trouble.

"Heeeere," he said again.

San pushed to her feet and looked right back at him, moving her chin in a widdershins circle, what passed in Josh-sign as a nod. "All right. Yes. Tell me what you found."

"Olssstone Olssstone Olssstone...home." Every bit of him shivered and trembled, and something almost a hiccup escaped him at the end of the last word. "Wa-ching. So many many ssssshiny come come. Ssssmell ssstone. God. In—in-inside. Many Many...so ONE! OLSSSTONE!"

"You were watching the Gem Show load in and you smelled the Sssquilssan among all these other stones?"

Josh hopped foot to foot, his horsey chin moving in response, so excited now that he resorted to flexing his wings and pawing at the dry earth. Then he opened his mouth and shrieked, his eyes flaring blazing red and turning his appearance fierce and threatening.

Shit and damn. He was furious. And after nearly three hundred years in exile from his home, to now find its most sacred object up for sale, who could blame him?

San met his gaze, letting his hot breath and fury wash over her, opening herself to the passion and desperation behind it, seeking to understand what Josh had seen and sensed, and what it meant to him. Images washed through her mind, scraps and flashes of tall pines on flat ground, cars moving up the access road into Kino — a white hot scent of pine and power filling the air like scorched meat — then the scent of wilderness and slow wind hanging on the breeze — washed away by the hot desert sun beating strange and unwelcome overhead. Josh hated sunlight. Only something as important as the Sssguilssan could drag him out in daytime, especially in a city this busy.

Josh hissed, then shrieked again, and this time her mind filled with aggressive foreboding, determined as fate and heavy as anger. Not Josh. Something he sensed as he watched the carts rolling into the event venue. Whoever had the Sssguilssan had no intention of doing good with it.

"All right, Josh," she said, pressing firm intention to act into her words and his mind. "I'll get it back. And we'll see it gets back to where it belongs."

Her first stop in the morning needed to be the bank.

§

Stopping at the bank for the jewelry, a high-limit credit card, and one of her business licenses to give her access to all parts of the show, meant San's arrival at Kino was later than she wanted. Plus, she'd been up half the night making phone calls, arguing and convincing. But at least now she had back up – if of an absurd sort.

With the full range of her senses opened by contact with the complete Mother Earth jewelry set, Josh's anxiety beat a frantic tempo in the back of San's mind.

"I'm here. I'll find it," she said, hoping the determination behind the thought cut through Josh's anger. A chill awareness washed through her mind in response.

"Stay hidden." San stepped into line to enter the show. "I'll need you to let me know when I'm close to the Sssguilssan."

The response that flooded her mind nearly staggered her. Only pulling a deep breath straight from the pit of her belly, one backed by the years of training, allowed her to respond normally to the registration clerk's questions and fill out the needed forms. In all the long years her family had helped keep Josh safe, she'd never felt need like this. Ever since an Elder Dragon saved Mamma Lee from a witch hunt through the great piney woods, Mamma's family had been charged with returning the favor. Keeping the dragons safe in an area with an ever-growing population of humans wasn't easy. Preventing too many people from entering the woods required a clever plan. Mamma Lee used all her power to fake a pregnancy, and when the 'baby' was born, her oldest daughter presented a baby dragon to the community as the child — and used it to create a legend that would scare people out of the Pine Barrens for literally centuries. Within a few years no one believed in dragons, but they certainly believed the woods harbored danger — and devils.

Unfortunately for Josh, he'd been that baby dragon — and years spent playing the role of The Jersey Devil, had finally exhausted him —

and put such a mark of human affiliation on him that functioning among the other dragons finally became more difficult than any of them could bear. Everyone agreed he'd carried enough of the burden for the forest's safety, and Mamma Lee's eldest descendent, keeper of the family knowledge, took the role of his guardian. She and Josh left to explore the wider world. Exile, no less hurtful for being chosen. No less a commitment for the generations of Lee women who followed that brave daughter.

San smiled at the man behind the registration desk as he handed her an entire sheet of terrible stick-on name tags. She filled out what she needed, then made her way into the show.

As she stepped into the space, she braced herself. Energy — a hundred thousand stones radiating power from all angles, pulsed at irregular intervals, humming, buzzing, singing, and generally overwhelming her. She gave her bracelet a firm twist. The assault faded to a steady pressure in the back of her skull — side by side with her connection to Josh — and she lifted her chin to scan the space.

Row after row, aisle after aisle, tables and fancy booths of glass, and banners and bright lights filled the event space. Everything sparkled and glittered and gleamed, and the hundreds of people already milling among the tables added a myriad of human voices to the hum and rumble beating at her senses. Shit and damn, it was going to take serious focus to find the sacred gem in all this. What could have happened that allowed the Sssguilssan to end up in a place like this? Last night, for the first time in years, she'd sent a message to the old family — and received no response. Whatever had gone wrong back east, she owned the problem now.

She glanced around, up, into corners. Yes. Plenty of security cameras, hidden among the speakers playing gentle music into the space. And guards stationed throughout. No surprise there. Energy and arbitrary value didn't always go together, but, in this place, the connection seemed a given.

Josh's angry need flared in her mind. She sent an equally determined response of assurance, then flexed her hand and let the Mother Ring guide her first step. She turned left, moving slowly, stopping often to admire the shiny wares available at each table, and to let her senses filter through each vendor's offerings. Step by step, display by display, she wound through the venue.

If they were lucky, whoever had the stone was here to sell it. And if San could find it, she had the wherewithal to buy it. Unless the dealer had already sold the crystal and was just awaiting a buyer. In which case, who knew how many people she might have to face down to get the thing back? Be ready, Josh, she thought hard to him. The contingency plan she'd come up with was nothing short of ridiculous, but some situations called for just that. With luck, she wouldn't have to go that far.

Eventually, the booth setups grew fancier — glass cases with spotlights, and wide banners strung overhead proclaiming business names in gold lettering and elegant script. Gladwell's Gems, Haldon Fine Minerals, Jennifer Hancock Design, Wood-Stone & Company, Su Lin Inc, K. Wells Jewelry and Gems, Bandalari.

San stopped, both the Mother Set and Josh's instinct shivering through her. She turned in a slow circle, trying to pick up any vibration that might tell her which booth held what she sought. A step this way, then that, a pivot, and internal reach. Subtle response narrowed the possibility to either Jennifer Hancock Designs, or Wood-Stone & Company. Side by side, both trade displays were shiny with glass fronted cases and sharp lighting, brilliantly cut stones flashed against velvet lining, contrasted with silver and copper and gold. San stepped into the space that separated the two booths. The feeling of connection, of specific power, increased, but the exact where of it came no clearer.

"Looking for something particular, are you?" a female voice asked.

San looked to the booth to her right, at the sharp dressed woman standing behind the counter wearing a dark polo shirt with JHD embroidered in bright thread over the left breast. "Yes." San glanced at the other booth where another woman in a slim fitting green dress smiled expectantly. Flicking her gaze between the two, San said, "I'm looking for a Titanite crystal. Or Sphene. I'm not sure yet."

"Not sure if you want cut or uncut gem?" the first woman asked.

San shook her head. "No. I'm looking for a gift for a friend. Not for jewelry, just for display. He mentioned Titanite, but I'm not sure that whether it's cut, or even polished, matters."

The woman in green smoothed her expression to carefully blank —the look of a hopeful shopkeeper losing all interest in someone who a moment before had been a potential customer, expressing without direct statement, her lack of interest in someone looking for a "new-age vanity rock." But the first woman's smile widened, and she beckoned San closer. "I have several pieces that might interest you."

San stepped up. "Are you *the* Jennifer Hancock?" she asked with a glance at the banner.

"I am," the designer slid open the rear door of the case and drew out a tray. Three large Sphene stones lay gleaming on the dark surface, light dispersed stunningly though each stone, a turning each into a kaleidoscope of color and fire.

"These are beautiful." San leaned close to examine the stones, then asked "May I?" The woman in the polo shirt nodded. San passed the hand wearing the Mother Ring over each one. While the metal band warmed at the proximity, nothing about any of them triggered a response from Josh. "Hmmm...do you have any uncut?" She met the vendor's eyes.

The woman shook her head, "No. I have these large stones, and dozens of smaller. But those are too small for a display piece." She gestured toward the other booth. "I know Casslin has a beautiful crystal."

San smiled, offered a thank you, even as she thinned her mental protections enough to get a sense of the woman in green's reaction to Jennifer's comments.

Nothing.

And that was everything San needed to know.

$

San dropped her chin until it touched the widest park of the necklace where it rested in the hollow of her throat, activating the full power of the jewelry. Then she pivoted, stepping left as she brought her arm up in a sweeping arc, bracelet aligned with the Mother Ring, just in time to ward off the mental bolt of power that rippled from the woman in green. Shit and damn, but this Casslin was strong! And the intention San sensed behind the sending marked neither curiosity nor fearful defense. This woman's energy signature, unmasked, screamed predator. So much for buying back the gem without a fight.

No time for subtlety. Now, Josh, she sent through their connection, hoping he was better with electronics than his refusal to use a cell phone indicated.

The room filled with a rising shriek, like blistering static — then the venue speakers erupted at full volume, and Foo Fighters "Learn to Fly" blasted through the space with enough force to shatter eardrums. Like a pinata on a rope, Josh dropped straight down from the rafters, every bit of his natural iridescence flaring in the too-bright lights, as though he was a pinata-cum-disco-ball meant to highlight the raging music. And throughout the site, in every aisle and doorway, dozens of like-dressed people burst into an ecstatic, coordinated dance.

San met Casslin's stunned eyes as the calculated chaos erupted, and, under the ruse of the flash mob, their battle engaged, looking, San hoped, like a mad dance-off. Just part of the show.

In almost slow motion, Casslin raised both hands, flinging power, blazing, just below the visible spectrum. San countered, moving fast, and responding to one violently tossed spell after another. Around her, every stone in the place began to vibrate, the music and magic bounced and rebounding through every crystal and faceted mineral. Gads — in a place as thirsty and ancient as Tucson's paved-over desert, what might awaken if the contained energy enclosed here in all these stones fully roused? Not something San wanted to discover.

She stepped and wove and dodged while Josh swooped, making himself a second target, taking hits that San likely could not have survived.

Strike followed counterstrike. Casslin sidestepped. Josh's shrieks were barely audible above the crash of drums and swelling guitars, but they signed clearly to San that he was out of patience. He'd just tear this thief limb from limb if this continued. Best to win this quickly, claim the stone, and be gone as part of the 'entertainment.'

Another spelled bolt of power. Another block. A flare of light into the visible that spoke of limits of control reached. She had to end this before the song finished or who knew what would happen. With a whirling leap, timed uncannily with a wild beat in the music, San landed atop the Wood-Stone's main display case. The stones inside leaped and rattled, and she let the Mother Set cushion and comfort their distress, at the same time absorbing the influx of unsettled power. San flung out her arm and drove every sliver of that power, backed by her bloodline's knowledge, into a focused bolt of pure energy. Casslin's mouth formed a soundless 'O' of surprise, and she toppled, the casting that had half-formed between her fingers dissipating harmlessly just as the music faded.

§

"Do you think she'll be okay?" Jennifer asked, concern weighting her words with uncertainty. She rubbed her hands up and down the outsides of her crossed arms. The paramedics lifted the stretcher with a metal 'clank,' and rolled Casslin toward the exit.

San, standing beside the designer, nodded. "She hit her head when she tripped, I think. But they said she'll be fine. Nothing broken. I'd wager on a heck of a headache though." That statement came only from experience. Her skull was already pounding. Gads she needed to lie down. But not yet.

Frowning, Jennifer nodded. "What a wild start to this show. I've never seen anything like it. That music and those special effects! I'm surprised the organizers allowed it!"

"I don't think they did," San said. "Looks to me like a prank."

"Well, a nasty one, then." Jennifer looked the Wood-Stone & Company booth. "I suppose I'll shut down her booth for the day. At least cover things up..."

Exactly what San had hoped for. "Do you think she'd mind you showing me that Sphene crystal you mentioned? If I like it — well — at least she'll get a sale out of this mess. If you can work her Point of Sale."

"We do that all the time for each other," Jennifer said. "Lunch breaks. Hmmm. I don't think she'll mind. It would be a nice surprise for her when she's feeling better. Let me find it..."

Moments later, San held in her hands a stunning crystal cluster dominated by a fist sized spire of Titanite. Fierce and brilliant as a dragon's tooth, the vivid green crystal danced in waves of light reflecting across its surface. From wherever Josh had escaped into hiding came a wave of relief and longing so strong that only the adrenaline still coursing San's blood kept her upright. She had it. They had it. "It's just what I was looking for," San said. "I'll take it. And the middle crystal of the ones you showed me as well."

Jennifer nodded, all polished professionalism in the face of a major sale. "Yes ma'am." She smiled. "I appreciate that."

"They're beautiful pieces." Nothing but the truth. And money spent for good will was worth a lot — especially since Casslin — if she returned to this front of a business at all — was likely going to be furious. And purchasing something from Jennifer would make a connection, let San keep track of the designer. Just in case. One thing the Lee women tried to prepare for was the fallout from their magical interventions.

Moments later, San signed her name across the cellphone screen, handed it back to the other woman, and accepted the heavily wrapped cluster and the boxed Titanite gem. Both went into San's shoulder bag, and she made her way outside.

The weight of the cluster both reassured and unnerved her as she stepped into the sunlight. Across the parking lot, her dance classmates waited. They cheered and clustered around her as she approached, laughing and chattering. San returned hugs and shook hands, congratulating their performance. Convincing her teacher of the brilliance of relocating the planned flash mob from the Mall at the university to the gem show had taken half the night. But the promise of better local news coverage and social media mayhem had enticed her in the end. And thank the goodness. Without the distraction... The ugly possibilities hardly bore dwelling on.

Like what to do about the dozens of cell phones that had captured not only the dance students, but also San's 'dance-off' with Casslin, and, most dangerously, clear video of Josh. With luck, the improbability of reality having any part in the ridiculous performance would relegate the entire incident to the bowels of the Internet archives. At worst, to the feeds and channels of the conspiracy nuts. Either way, it was time for her and Josh to get out of Tucson. And finally, after all these centuries away, to return Josh to Jersey.

She projected the thought with pure intention. Josh, we're going home. And the fluttering joy and terror of his reaction bloomed through her. It mirrored her own emotions. Because the Sphene was here, and no response had come from the old home place. What they hell where they going to find when they got back there?

From overhead came a high, savage cry. She looked up. One of her dance mates, Glenn, pointed to the glittering shape winging its way northeast toward Mount Lemmon. "There's that drone again. Wild! Who hired that thing anyway?"

San laughed, as she watched Josh cut through the sky. "I did," she said. "Pretty cool, huh? They promised me it looked just like the Jersey Devil."

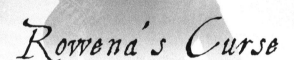

Rowena's Curse

Rebecca Wynick

"Look at those dolts! Scrambling about as if anything they do matters. Buffoons, all of them." Magnus squinted out over the city street, cocking his head to get a better view.

"Nice attitude," Rowena said and sighed.

"Take it or leave it, but that is what I think." Magnus glanced back at her, but Rowena remained turned away, watching the crowd below from her seat on the ledge.

"How can you stomach sitting here, day after day, watching these cabbage heads? Look at that one, that joe over there by the tree." He pointed. "That genius doesn't know where his next meal is coming from, and the fool splits his sandwich with his dog without fail."

"His name is Lou," Rowena muttered.

"The man or the dog?" He waited, but she didn't answer. Undeterred by her silence, Magnus barreled on. "Frankly, I'd be more inclined to spend time with the mutt. I mean, he, at least, knows how to take advantage of an opportunity."

Magnus's voice faded into white noise for Rowena. She leaned into the wind, especially strong at this height, that buffeted the building. Eyes closed, she lifted her face to let the morning sun warm her cheeks. The temperate spring thawed the ache in her bones. She smiled slowly, widely, as if to a pleasant memory or a secret of which she was the sole keeper.

Rowena's eyes blinked open. She shook her shoulders and the past several days' tension away. She glanced to where Magnus sat, still rambling.

"...I say, if you are going to be 'wrong' you might as well be 'really wrong'. But midget Elvis? Seriously, who pays to see that?" Magnus paused, hopping up and down for a better view, neck outstretched. "Ro, Ro!" He wildly gestured now. "Take a look at the gams on that one! The broad in the hot pink spandex. God, I love women with hips."

Rowena narrowed her eyes as if straining to see to whom he referenced, leaned further forward still, and dropped from the ledge.

The pavement raced toward her. Rowena fought to hold her elbows tightly to her sides for a long as she could. Magnus could be heard screeching after her. Wind muffled her ears, garbled his voice. But Rowena knew she daren't turn her head at this speed. The air pressure pummeled her face with a force that brooked no challenge. Rowena, determined, focused on the pavement, and watched it shift from a long, bland, gray strip, to segmented panels, to distinctive stone. Magnus shrieked madly now from above.

With a swift shift, Rowena unlocked the elbows she'd wrestled tightly to her sides and unfurled her wings. The air resistance fought her for control. Clenching her mouth, Rowena counted one, two, three, and held her wings taut. Hold it, just a second more, she muttered internally. For a moment she thought she'd miscalculated, but she muscled through the pain and quickly made a banked turn. The few tourists already standing in line at the French Broad Chocolate Lounge scrambled across Pack Square to get out of her way. When Rowena cleared the corner she breathed a quick sigh, released the tension in her sinews, and coasted to a running stop. Her feathers shifting like louvers, slowed her pace.

Magnus landed shortly thereafter, clearly furious, his neck feathers ruffled and standing at attention. He marched a frustrated circle around her, each step pronounced and echoing his anger.

"What was that stunt about? Trying to gum up the works?"

Rowena took a few wobbly steps before settling in on the stone wall. Ignoring him for the moment, she began to preen, working swiftly to sort and assess the condition of her feathers.

"Ro, what the hell?"

"Oh, please, Magnus. It was nothing. Just something to try. No big deal."

"No big deal? No big deal, you say!" He flapped about madly. "You could've killed yourself!"

"Could I?" Rowena cocked her head to the side. "I'm not so sure— at least not until I've paid my debt. I'm sure the Elderwood would think that an easy way out."

"Oh, I can guaran-freakin-tee you can die! And it ain't pretty. What, are you... depressed?"

"Nope. Just tired of it all." She sighed, the feathers around her middle splayed out briefly before settling.

"Sheesh, is that all? Talk about drama!" He waved a wing angrily. "Remember, I was here long before you, doll-face. You haven't begun to see everything I've seen."

"Yeah, like that is a selling point for staying with the status quo. Look how you turned out."

Magnus began a strutting march, ducking and jutting his chin and beak. "And what is wrong with me? What, I ask you? I'm just fine. F.I.N.E.—fine."

"You don't even try."

"Oh, that?" He paused and shrugged. "I have that under control. I don't care about that."

Rowena peeked out from under her wing where she'd been sorting her feathers. "Not at all?"

"Nope." Magnus shimmied his shoulders making his tail feathers fan out.

"Come on, you can't mean it?"

"Look, we get twelve hours a day in human form—and the worst twelve I might add." Magnus punctuated each point with the tip of a wing, "No bars, no night life, no...*gasp* late night sex. Just the part of the day when we get to sit in traffic and go to work."

"But you don't work."

"Living is work!" Magnus's neck feathers bristled as he glared at her. "Do you know how difficult it is to talk a woman into bed, and drag her across town to your tiny apartment in the middle of the day?"

"My apartment, that I work for I might add."

"Your choice." Magnus squawked.

"But what about your debt?"

"What's the rush?"

"What's the...?" Rowena trailed off.

"Think about it. You would have never been able to pull off the stunt you just did in your human form." Magnus waved a wing in the direction of the building from which Rowena had dropped.

"You are ridiculous." Rowena huffed. "I wouldn't have been bored enough to try it. In fact, I'd still be cozy in bed at this hour or just having my first cup of coffee instead of waiting and watching. Always waiting and watching."

"Your problem is that you are trying to be helpful. You genuinely feel guilty. Such a waste of time, guilt."

"But our debt?" Rowena said and sighed.

"Yeah, and then what? You've paid your blood debt. Ta-da! And now you are back in human form full time again. So what? Have some fun with this while you have it. Think about it. Wouldn't you rather be the hand of karmic retribution, dishing out punishments rather than rewards? Oh, the fun we could have in this form! It'd be so satisfying." A wicked grin spread across Magnus's face.

"You're sick."

"No. You didn't give it any real thought. I've had longer, much longer, to think on it. Retribution is where it is at."

"You'll never pay your debt that way."

"Exactly!" Magnus smiled.

Rowen gave her feathers a quick flick, and each settled back into streamlined formation.

"I don't have time for this. I have to get over to Lexington, and I'd rather not have to walk." Rowena primly replied.

"The kid will open up for you. Come on, doll. Let's quick dive bomb the tourists before you have to get back to the grind. Although, I don't know why you bother." Magnus gave his most winsome look.

Rowena whipped her beak around and jabbed at him.

"Because I want my life back!"

"I got news for you, honey—that life is gone. You flushed that away when you poisoned lover boy's family."

"I didn't mean to..." She gave a quick, involuntary shudder.

"Yeah, sure, doesn't matter that you only meant to punish him. That's intent. Sugarcoat it all you want. You used your power to kill. Sure, the others were collateral damage, I'll give you that, but you did the crime."

"You're an ass."

"But an honest ass." He paused, taken with a thought, "Now THAT would've kiboshed the works...being a literal ass. Crow is so much better. Actually lucky, now that I think about it." Without waiting for a reply, Magnus hunched down and sprang into flight. He called back over his shoulder, "Don't come home for lunch. I'm feeling lucky."

$

Sarah unlocked the double door panels and secured them to mounted wall hooks on either side of the opening to allow fresh air and light to flood the shop. She must've heard Rowena coming and stepped aside to let her fly right in. Rowena landed on the polished concrete floor with a squawk and quickly strutted behind the curtain dividing the shop from the storeroom.

It took only a moment for Rowena to shift into human form. She slid the large, golden hoops into her earlobes, tens of bangles up each wrist, and fluffed her long, layered skirt before entering the shop proper. Sarah, already busy with a customer, gave her a quick nod in greeting.

Once the initial rush dispersed, Sarah commented, "Cut it close this morning. Everything okay?"

"Yeah, just got tied up in a philosophical debate with Magnus."

Sarah laughed, "Oh, lord. You're lucky you got here at all today."

"Yes, well, let's get to it and get ready before the next wave."

Rowena folded back the accordion-shuttered window coverings, creating a large opening in the wall. With Sarah's help, she slid to the forefront the display of glass mobiles and whirligigs to better catch the wind and the attention of the shoppers.

Rowena looked down the street and saw people lounging on benches, plenty of Bermuda-short-clad seniors, and a passel of tourists waiting at the streetlight for the walk sign to change in their favor. She gave a big sigh.

Rowena hated this part the most, the waiting, the waiting to spot the person who needed her to salvage his or her ill-fated path, and to in turn, pay her blood debt to the parliament of elders. Furtively looked around to assess where Sarah was, and seeing her busy, Rowena took the opportunity for action. It really wasn't a violation of her parole, to hurry the process along, wasn't it?

With a flick of a wrist and a quick, circular twirl of an index finger, a gentle wind began to swirl around the shop, setting the chimes off in succession. The glass and stone mobiles tinkled prettily, and the suspended, silver birds spun about their anchoring axis. The noise drew a few glances, but Rowena needed more. She clapped her hands once firmly. Each hand grasped the other. Then she began to rub them. Eyes narrowed, she called to the sky for storm clouds to form. Rowena swayed with her entreaty, and her eyes rolled back in her head. She was as far removed from this place and awareness as possible.

At the first clap of thunder, Rowena jolted and began to topple backwards, and were it not for Sarah, she might have fallen to the floor. But the girl had slid up behind, dragging a cushioned-backed stool with her. Rowena stumbled into the chair, grateful for the save, but also unnerved that the girl had anticipated her.

Rowena turned as tourists, drenched by the unexpected squall, ran into the shop for shelter. "We will talk about this later."

They remained busy for the next two hours, after which Rowena allowed the steady rain to recede and the clouds to thin and waft away. Rowena slumped onto the stool.

"Well, that was quite a rush. I think we made record sales this morning. You might need to order more glass drops soon." Sarah smiled.

Rowena grunted. "We'll see."

Used to her boss's moods, Sarah pulled out the polishing cloth and began to remove rain spots from the metallic mobiles at the front of the shop before the sun dried them.

"Earlier, you anticipated I'd need the chair. Why?" Rowena tone was even, but her eyes narrowed to slits.

Sarah hemmed. "I'm—I'm not sure what you mean?"

"What made you bring me the chair?"

"I just...I saw that you were...concentrating. When I focus deeply sometimes it's hard to...shift that focus."

"Hmmm. Fair enough." Rowena rose to stretch her legs.

"A very good morning, all in all," Sarah said.

"Depends on how you measure that."

"Well, profitable, then."

Rowena harrumphed. "Profitable, no, not so much. Nothing more than a migraine as far I could tell."

"Oh, I'm sorry." Sarah jumped up. "I can get you some aspirin."

"Not me. One of that lot," Rowena gestured to the group of tourists that lingered across the street. "Nothing for me there." Rowena shuffled slowly. "I'll be in the back room working the wire. Looks like we need more chakra charms, too." Without waiting for a response, Rowena slid behind the curtain and into the darkness. She wanted the darkness. It matched her mood.

Rowena spent the better part of the next hour twisting metal around stones and forming leaflike designs for the framing of her mobiles. But her senses would pick up as each patron entered the shop. She would pause, mentally reaching and assessing their thoughts and mood. Upon finding none to rescue, she would continue with her work. When she finally tired, Rowena rose and stretched the kink in her back that had formed from sitting hunched over her tools.

"I'm off to fetch lunch. I'll bring you back something." Rowena called to Sarah as she brushed past.

"I can get lunch," Sarah began to say, but Rowena was already out the door.

§

Rowena walked to clear her thoughts and stretch her tired muscles. Without realizing she was doing so, Rowena made her way to where she knew Magnus preferred to perform and "Swindle the rubes" as he'd say. Despite his earlier boasts, Magnus wasn't entertaining a guest in their shared apartment, but rather doing his stock and trade magic routine to a horseshoe crowd of tourists. Standing before the "Jack of the Wood" pub, his back to the open picture window, he charmed with his flourishes. A mug of Guinness sat propped on the ledge behind him. Rowena watched him dazzle and befuddle the crowd, shaking hands and removing bracelets, rings, and the stray wallet in the process, amazed at his daring.

When the crowd dispersed into the onslaught of yet more people making their way down the crowded pavement, Magnus darted around the corner with his booty. His head bobbed, eyes scanning the crowd. Taking another route, Rowena arrived at their apartment just before him.

"Dangerous moves, don't you think?"

"Ahem," Magnus said and coughed. "I didn't think to find you here midday."

"I'm sure you didn't."

"I just came back to get ready for—"

"For jail if you keep pocketing trinkets on the street, or worse yet, a meeting with the Elderwood Parliament."

Magnus sputtered. "I have no idea to what you refer." Magnus strutted around the small studio.

Rowena wondered if he had any idea how many of his movements mimicked those he made when in crow form. Then the thought extended in her mind. Panicked, she raced to face herself in the long, warbled mirror over the bathroom door. She turned her head this way and that for any tell-tale sign that she, too, was appearing more crow-like. Relieved when she saw no such indicators, she returned to face him.

"Oh, don't take that offended tone with me. Dicey business lifting wallets in broad daylight when they already know you to be a trickster."

"Trickster!" Magnus's chest swelled. "I assure you there is no trick in—"

"Just because the magic is real doesn't mean you should entertain with it. To demean it into a form of a mere charlatan is—" Rowena reached for a word, "disgraceful."

"You're one to talk. I saw that little trick of yours earlier. Spontaneous, and might I mention, unexpected, thunder storm ring a bell?"

"That's different. I am trying to fulfill my penance. You cannot claim the same."

"True, I concede the point, but you have no idea how to have fun, how to live."

Rowena's eyes narrowed. "Silly me, not enjoying the thought of someone tracing you and your stolen swag to my apartment."

"Our apartment."

"My apartment," she reiterated. "You are a squatter at best. I pay the rent."

"That, my dear, is what I was trying to do, you see. All this," Magnus fanned his hands open to reveal the morning's haul, "is for you, to pay my way."

Magnus smiled the slow, languorous smile of a cat who has had its cream. He tilted his head to present his most winsome look. When he saw she was having none of it, he snapped his fingers and the jewels were stowed away somewhere in the magician's tux he affected to wear when panhandling.

"Oh, give me a break." He huffed and twisted his neck from side to side in an agitated manner. "What is the use of eternity if you can't have any fun? And those people certainly don't need all the stuff they have or they wouldn't be shopping for more."

"Your logic is truly amazing." Rowena shook her head.

He made a sweeping, theatrical bow. "Why, thank you."

"You could justify stealing a bottle out of a baby's mouth."

"Actually, I think I might have at one point." Magnus scratched his head as if trying to remember.

"I do not intend to be living like this for an eternity. I've two more lives to save and then I am done. Finito. Out of here. Back to my life."

"Your life?" Magnus choked back a hard laugh. "Honey, your life passed half a century ago. You can go back, but it won't be to your life. The people you knew are either dead or have long forgotten you."

"I know that!" Rowena said curtly. "But I can start over, live the rest of this life out. Maybe even—"

"Don't say it."

"What? Just because you can't stand the thought of marriage and a family doesn't mean everyone is against the practice."

"Romance didn't work out so well last time. Your jealousy—"

"Yes, I know, got me into this mess. But people can change."

Magnus laughed. "Yes, yes, we can." Magnus quickly affected his bird face with a sweep of one hand over his face.

"Idiot!" Rowena turned to storm out, but stopped with one hand on the doorknob. "Just make sure you get rid of that stuff ASAP. I am not adding time to my sentence because you got greedy and bored. Oh, and by the way, all the time you've spent in crow form is starting to show in your mannerisms. Be careful or you could be stuck like that forever."

Before Magnus could make a pithy retort, Rowena slammed the door shut.

§

Rowena sensed the woman long before she entered the shop. It came like a ripple upon the air, the desperation—the stench and resignation that death was the only way out. Rowena dropped her pen onto the ledger and hurried into the showroom.

The woman's entrance set the door chimes ringing. Sarah moved to assist her. Rowena intercepted the girl's path and redirected Sarah to the pair of shoppers.

The old woman Rowena had sensed stood close to the window opening. Her eyes bobbed from item to item, frustration evident in her sigh. A bead of sweat ran along her hairline, and her spotted hands trembled.

"May I help you?"

The woman startled, jarred from her thoughts.

"I need something for my granddaughter. Something to help her understand—" Her voice broke as she choked back a sob.

Rowena stepped closer, drew out a tissue from her waist pocket, waved it under the woman's nose while she hunched over in despair.

The woman jerked upright. Her pale eyes were tear-rimmed and reddening.

"Most people don't carry tissues anymore." Her voice rasped, raw with emotion.

"My grandmother taught me otherwise. She said a lady should always be prepared."

"I agree, but not many do these days." The woman pulled her own handkerchief out of her sleeve and wiped her eyes.

"Now, tell me about your granddaughter," Rowena said, prodding.

Fresh tears began to form. "I need gift. Something she will see and think of me. Remember that I love...loved her best."

Rowena patted the woman's hand. "We'll look together and find just the right thing."

As she slid an arm around the woman, turning her towards the boldly-hued sun catchers and mobiles, Rowena felt the jolt of recognition.

Death was near. Both by choice and by Fate. Rowena sought to draw out the cause, shutting out outside stimulus, and mentally reached. While the woman chatted animatedly about the girl, Rowena focused on the sensations running down her arm and across the woman's back. When the truth became clear, she removed her touch—stung as if by an adder. She had cancer. Ravaged with it and beyond hope, her body was rapidly failing. And over it all Rowena felt her own anger—anger that she'd been deceived. This was not one to pay her debt. The woman had a plan, the pills ready, and only two tasks left—a gift and a letter stood in the way of the her eminent departure.

Encouraged by Rowena's attentions, the woman rambled. Rowena brusquely interrupted her. "I think perhaps Sarah would better be able to find what would suit. I believe she's of a similar age with your granddaughter." Without awaiting a response, she called to the girl.

Sarah hurried over as Rowena brushed past with a low growl. "I'll be in my office. I do not wish to be disturbed."

The woman startled at the abrupt shift in attention. And with the quick flash of Rowena's temper, the winds lashed at the shutters, causing the whirligigs to turn madly.

Sarah stepped in and had the woman convinced she'd found 'just the right thing' in almost no time at all. Sarah carefully wrapped her purchase, tucking in a gift card for good measure, and sent the woman off.

Eventually, the wind died down. Sarah took that as a sign that it was safe to make her way back to the workroom. She gently tapped her fingers against the doorframe.

"Go away."

"I just wondered—"

"Can't help you." Rowena said harshly.

"It's a quarter of—" Sarah began again.

"Fine. Close up." Rowena yanked the curtain back.

With a curt nod, Rowena was out the door and off towards home.

§

Rowena opened the apartment door to find Magnus already on the couch for the evening, bag of tortilla chips on his lap, in one hand the remote, beer in the other.

"Home early."

Rowena grunted in response and took the beer out of his hand to gulp down herself. She went over to the small alcove at the far side of the room to sit on her bed, kicked off her shoes, and slid off her bangles. She made a mental note to have Sarah come by tomorrow and pick up these shoes, and others, that lay tossed to the side. She'd need to restock her clothing options at the shop soon.

"Rough day at the office, dear?" Magnus prodded.

"I found the next one."

Magnus tossed the chips to the side and sat up straighter. "Then why aren't you celebrating? Did I lose count or wouldn't that be the next to the last one of your final ten-fold debt?"

"I didn't save her. No point. I'm not going to save her. She's already dying."

"What are you talking about?"

"It wouldn't matter. She's only got days, maybe weeks left."

"Ah."

"Yeah, just my luck."

§

The moon was just breaking over the ridge at Beaucatcher Mountain. Rowena sat in wait. She nervously pecked at the feathers under her wing. She hadn't slept since the summons.

Slowly the tide of moonlight relieved the shadows from their post before the grand hall at Overlook Castle. Rowena watched the light overtake the darkness. She shook with a sigh as the glow crossed to where she perched.

Magnus leaned in. "There now. Almost time. Pull yourself together. The Elderwood should be along shortly."

With a sudden chill, clouds shifted and blocked the moon, drowning them both back into shadow. A thick and unnatural fog rolled across the grounds, broken only by the red glow near the base of the castle.

"Dramatic entrance. Nice." Magnus bobbed his head in appreciation.

"Shut up, you idiot." Rowena jabbed him in the ribs.

Rowena shivered, splaying her feathers briefly, and exposing herself further to the chill.

Magnus wrapped a wing over her shoulders and made a low cooing sound. "Keep it together, Ro. It'll be fine."

The cloud cover began to shift, accompanied by the sound of wings beating in unison. The Elderwood Parliament swooped in and landed. Each arrived in the shape of a majestic, great horned owl, oversized, and fitting to their post. They landed in succession of rank. Most cocked his or her head, turning an eye to scrutinize those gathered. And one by one their eyes lit upon Rowena and narrowed. They snapped their beaks closed in a sign of disapproval.

As the members of the council took their places, they assumed their human forms. Billowing cloaks replaced feathers. Most of the parliament were silver haired, made all the more regal by the light of the moon.

Torches, previously unnoticed, lit in succession to form a half circle, effectively separating the parliament from the others who had arrived to act as witness. Trees were filled with crows, hawks, and visiting ravens who flapped in anticipation before quieting and settling.

"Rowena Witch, step forward!" a voice boomed.

Magnus gave her a nudge. Rowena dropped from her perch and moved forward. When she stepped into the circle of the torches' glow she, too, shifted into human form, sky clad.

One of the council, a woman, stepped forward, and with a snap of her fingers, dropped a crimson cloak around Rowena's shoulders, covering her nakedness.

Rowena thanked her with a low bow. The parliament member grunted in response and returned to her position to the right of the grand-master.

§

"You made a choice."

"She was dying." Rowena pleaded.

"We all die. But who gave you the right to decide when?" The grand-master challenged.

"But—"

"No buts. You saw someone desperate, and you did nothing. That makes you party to her death." At the elder's words the others nodded in unison.

"She would've been dead in days anyway."

"True. But you denied her another visit with her granddaughter by not interfering with her suicide plans. She didn't get to speak to her brother when he called for advice. And she never received the grateful letter from a former student that was making its way through the post. You let her die."

"She was riddled with cancer." Rowena whispered.

"You could've saved her."

"Saved her? Only to let her die days later."

The grand-master raged. "You could've provided comfort! Instead you ignored your duty. Your mission. You still believe you can decide who lives and dies, who is worthy. How dare you?" His voice boomed, echoing in the trees.

There was a general titter among those observing. Wings snapped open and shut like umbrellas against the storm.

"The question the council must now determine is whether to hold this death on your account. Do you owe yet another tenfold payment for your selfish lapse of humanity?"

Rowena paled further in the moonlight, her face frozen as if she were another chiseled sculpture upon the lawn. She looked away to shake off their scrutinizing glares and to calm the panic she felt in her breast. Rowena's gaze focused on three windows close to the ground, aglow with a pulsing red light through their cross-shaped panes. She swallowed a deep, dry gasp as she awaited judgment.

Several minutes later the woman again spoke and announced, "We will reconvene in a fortnight's time. It shall give you time to think of the folly of your actions and for us to deem what is just."

Rowena blanched as if slapped to attention, stiff in the cooling night air.

Magnus flew to her side and nudged her. "Let's get out of here."

§

Rowena restlessly perched next to a gargoyle overlooking the square. She watched while people paired off for the night. Some headed off to tent city, others to the burbs—most couldn't tell at a glance who was homeless or hipster. But she was getting better at it. She'd had nothing but time to watch and observe.

"I thought this is where I'd find you." Magnus alighted on the other side of the gargoyle. "Fantastic view of the late night rubes. I have spent many a fine time here back in the day."

"I don't want to hear it."

"Well, that's a fine attitude."

Rowena sighed, "I really don't want to hear how you duped those people."

Magnus rose, puffed out his chest, and shook his feathers to ready to leave. Then he settled down again, sliding his plump middle to fully cover his legs and feet.

But the insult he'd felt could be heard in his voice as he began, "I didn't always steal. Sometimes I got tips, generous ones, and other times a meal. It was nice." He paused, pensive. "People were more trusting when I started. Now it's all me, me, me. Everyone trying to be 'special,' and if they haven't 'got it', they try to buy it."

Magnus waited for a response. Getting none, he tried one last time. "Come on, Ro. Let's go home."

She turned so that one eye could scan him. But there was no warmth there. She sighed, and turned back away.

Magnus rose on his toes and launched off the building.

$

Magnus didn't come home that night. Rowena knew that he often didn't. But she checked his basket filled with silk scarves just in case. She tugged at the bedding with her talons and found her first assumption to be correct; he'd not returned. She'd apologize to him later.

Rowena looked around the snug, studio apartment, far more than enough room for two who spent their sleeping hours in crow form. Magnus had often called her a fool for paying rent when she could sleep in her shop if she just dodged the night security guard. How hard could it be when she was so small in her crow shape? But Rowena had wanted to have a place ready for "after."

"After what?"

"Okay then, for sick days when I am off of work." Rowena sighed, exasperated.

"You don't take sick days."

"But I could."

"You haven't ever been this healthy. It's a kicker, isn't it? We're cursed, so they want us healthy to feel the full impact of what we lost." Magnus looked down at his torso in disgust. "Black, always dressed in black."

"It's classic."

"It's boring."

"It's elegant—like a tuxedo."

Lost in her thoughts, Rowena didn't sleep. She worried about and missed her friend. He was either still angry or hanging out with the likewise cursed ravens and crows having philosophical conversations. It would be so like him to stay out to punish her.

§

When the parliament reconvened, Rowena and Magnus faced only one council member. Gone were the torches and the onlookers. The only light this night was cast by the waning moon and the ominous glow of the crosses cut into the castle's base. Nothing was as Rowena expected. The councilwoman did not shift from her owl form nor allowed Rowena to shift either.

Magnus reached out a wing to hold Rowena. It appeared judgment would be hasty. Magnus's touch helped quell Rowena's shaking.

The woman cleared her throat and began. "I am here to report the decision of the parliament. No time shall be added to your penance at this juncture. We, the council, concede how you might have thought the woman's despair to be the logical culmination of her illness, and incontrovertible."

Rowena jutted out her beak to speak, but was quickly cut off.

"But you erred in judgment." The owl paused, cocked one eye, and held Rowena in her gaze, weighing the impact of her words. "However, your failing was not malicious or purposeful. It is for that reason, and that reason alone, that you have been spared further retribution."

When again Rowena made move to speak, she was cut off.

"That is all. Good night to you." She pushed off, aloft and away before either Rowena or Magnus was granted leave to utter a word.

Magnus sighed. "So, lucky break there."

Rowena gave in to her exhaustion and nerves and leaned into his shoulder. She'd never figure Magnus out. He was both the most frustrating and genuinely kind man she knew. Cynical but deep inside lived a gentleness.

§

Rowena had nothing to gain by interfering.

Lou shared what he had with his friends, his dog, and strangers. And when he didn't have anything, he never stopped looking for something to eat so that at least his dog didn't go hungry. She'd seen him take off his raincoat when the rain turned icy, to drape it over his four-legged pal. And she'd watched the dog shake—from age, his thinness, and at the cold. He, surely, didn't have much time left, but Lou was set on keeping the dog with him for as long, and as comfortably, as he could.

And she'd seen that momentary panic when it looked like he'd be unsuccessful in finding a meal. On those days Lou's eyes took on a hollowed out emptiness, like a candle flickering out. And then someone would round the corner. Lou would smile brightly, just happy being in the company of another. It was enough it seemed. She didn't understand how he did it. Ever optimistic, Lou was everything Rowena wasn't. She had no faith—in mankind or herself. And she seldom trusted anyone.

She was watching one night when Lou, who had nothing, had been rolled while he slept. His pockets searched, the remnant of a sandwich tossed aside carelessly. A sandwich for a rainy day, literally, tossed aside, without a thought of his need.

Rowena swooped down, tried to draw the hoodlums away. She'd chased them two blocks, squawking and displaying her displeasure and only narrowly missed being hit by the pipe the one thief pulled from his boot and swung wildly at her.

But when Rowena returned to where she had last seen Lou, he'd moved on in search of a new place to sleep. And she felt a pang of guilt when she thought about her empty apartment.

§

The days in the shop blurred with the passage of time. Rowena grew restless and left the shop to Sarah while she holed up in the back, busy with one task or another. She'd grown tired of the inane banter a storekeep needed to maintain; the feigned interest in other people exhausted her. And day after day, her hopes were dashed of ever paying her debt.

Some days, she went in search of Magnus. She could count on him to keep things interesting. Today, she found him at the edge of a park, sitting on a bench, a new favorite haunt of his.

Rowena chose a seat near Magnus, but said not a word for a few minutes as his attention was elsewhere, watching a crow being chased by a pack of tiny starlings.

"Why do they do that?"

"Do what?" He responded without taking his eyes off the chase.

"Why do they gang up and bully the bigger bird?"

"You don't recognize him?" Magnus cast her a side glare.

"No, should I?" Rowena squinted, tried to keep up with the mad chase unraveling before her.

"He's the new guy. The one who's stuck twenty-four seven in crow form. Sorry bastard."

"Well then, why don't you help him?"

Magnus snorted, "And why, pray tell, should I do that?"

"Well, it was just a thought."

"Not my problem. Contradicts my motto. Look out for Numbero Uno."

Rowena shifted. "Yeah, you're a real prince, a bleeding heart. Still doesn't explain why they are chasing him. What'd he do?"

"He didn't have to 'do' anything. He's one of us, an imposter, if you will. And they know it and want him gone."

"Really?" Rowena watched the chase a few minutes longer. "Is it always one of us, the doomed, that's being chased?"

"Nah, sometimes birds are just assholes." Magnus smiled.

"Some more than others," she muttered under her breath.

When the birds circled near them once again Rowena abruptly stood, extended her arms out to each side and then quickly lowered them, causing the chasing birds to plummet to the earth like pebbles tossed in the air. The crow paused midair to acknowledge her with a brisk nod before darting away. She strode purposely to stand within the circle of dazed but otherwise unharmed birds.

"Next time, none of this bullying nonsense, or I'll knock you out of the sky forever." She towered over them, scowling.

Magnus nodded like a bobblehead with a loose spring.

"What are you grinning at, you loon?"

"Karmic retribution. I knew you'd prefer that."

Rowena glared. "You are unbelievable."

§

Rowena had watched them both so long that she wasn't surprised when the dog Lou travelled with, Cosmo, began to go blind, and was a hazard to himself. Lou often kept him on a rope tether, but sometimes Lou lost track of Cosmo—especially when they were at the drum circle. He'd wanted the dog to get his groove on, too—or so he'd say. It seemed cruel to keep him tied when he loved the crowds so. And sometimes the locals or tourists brought dog treats, or human treats, on those summer, Friday nights in Pritchard Park. Lou foolishly trusted in karma and the glorious beat to keep the dog safe. And while Rowena admired Lou, even envied him his freedom, she'd never understand his logic.

§

Midsummer night, Magnus found Rowena, as expected, at the edge of the park hosting the drum circle. She was in one of her moods. She nodded to acknowledge him when he settled in on the branch just to her left.

"Anything noteworthy?"

"Hmm, not really. The usual locals and a horde of tourists. Although that kid, Sean, is making a mint pick-pocketing tonight. He's gotten much faster. They do grow up so quickly." She sighed.

"Then why do you bother coming? There's nothing for you but that incessant beat. Back in my day they knew how to play music. Not all this thump, thump, hippie-voodoo stuff, arms flailing around like they are tangled in seaweed," Magnus grumbled.

"Then why are you here?"

"Same as you, hon', watching the crowd."

Rowena turned in surprise. "Don't tell me you've decided to work down your debt?"

"Don't be silly, doll. Just watching the marks."

"You really are something else, you know that?" She gave him a glare.

Magnus laughed. "Look after Numero Uno, baby, and the world will take care of you."

"You don't really believe that, do you? You couldn't possibly. I remember all the stories you told me. You were never like that."

"Yeah, well, time hardens people." He closed his beak to form a grim, straight line.

"All the more reason to pay my penance so that that doesn't happen to me." Rowena said.

"You're too soft." He shook a wing at her. "And that's dangerous. Mark my words, girlie, no good will come of that." Magnus flitted up to a higher branch and pouted. But from his vantage point he could still watch Rowena and the crowd clearly.

Magnus saw Rowena's face light up. He turned to see what had broken her mood. Lou had just rounded the corner, chasing after his over-zealous and overwhelmed dog. Cosmo was easily confused and disoriented from all the sights and smells of the crowd. He bumped and jostled into pedestrians.

A woman, shoved by Cosmos accidentally, spilled her latte, and swung the huge bag she had nestled into the crook of her elbow in retaliation, knocking Cosmos into the street. Lou lunged after the dog.

Rowena released a high-pitched squeal, and the sound sent Cosmos to find cover. Rowena dive-bombed the street. She beelined towards Lou, knowing something he couldn't. She'd sensed it before she saw it—a late-night delivery truck barreling around the corner. She slammed into Lou's shoulder with all the force and gravity behind her, knocking him onto the curb and into safety. But the force with which she hit him thrust her back and into the path of the truck.

§

Magnus heard the thud. Rowena lay broken upon the pavement. One wing sickly twisted and snapped. A rivulet of blood leaked from her mouth. Her eyes stared, frozen in horror. Cosmos emerged unscathed, sniffed, and prodded her inert form with his nose, and whimpered.

And from his vantage point Magnus had seen everything. At first he'd been motionless, crippled with fear. Magnus swooped down now, squawking madly. He violently flapped his wings at anyone that came near her broken body. He slashed his wings at bystanders standing too closely. He bit the shopkeeper that moved in to clear the road.

Magnus didn't see the broom head that came from behind, knocking him into a tailspin, slamming him to the pavement, to ultimately roll into the darkening alley. When his head cleared moments later he saw that someone had dug out of storage a snow shovel, and Rowena lay in its basin. Still dizzy from his fall, he wobbled after the man who carried her and watched in horror as he lifted the dumpster lid and dumped her inert body into the bin. Magnus screeched his rage and attacked, but was soon silenced by the blunt end of the shovel.

He awoke just before dawn. Remembering how and why he came to be in the alley, Magnus quickly flapped his way to the edge of the dumpster. With several grunts and thrusts of his remaining strength he opened the lid to reveal its contents. Rowena lay nestled in the trash, but otherwise much as he'd remembered last seeing her. Her left eye accusingly stared up at him, and his heart broke, shattered in a million pieces. With several frantic flaps and a quick leap, he was aloft.

Magnus returned within the quarter hour, a large, silk scarf in his beak. He hopped down into the dumpster. His first order of business was carefully nudging and closing her eyes; once done, he breathed his first sigh of relief.

"Oh, Ro, what have you done now? And for what?" Magnus swung his head from side to side sadly. But he allowed himself only a moment to wallow. Dawn would rise soon, and soon after, the bewitching hour of transformation. He couldn't be sure if Rowena would remain as a crow or take her human form.

Magnus worked quickly to wrap the silk around her broken body, securing her within its folds with several tugs and hard-earned knots. Cursing under his breath, Magnus wished he could access magic in this form to move her. Instead, he began the slow work of dragging her home.

After what seemed like days, Magnus sighed, catching his breath, and looked upon Rowena's inert form as she lay in the middle of the rug upon their apartment floor. Gently he shifted the silk to reveal her face and waited to see what the morning would bring and prayed for a miracle.

Bleary-eyed, Magnus sat in watch as the hours passed. Dawn came, and with it, sunshine that filled the apartment, but he felt none of its warm. He sat cross-legged and barefoot in his human form, wearing sweatpants topped with a Pittsburgh Steelers' jersey. He came to the realization that she wouldn't transform back into her human form, and he wept now for the one he'd loved most.

§

"Don't get attached, that's my motto. Look after Numero Uno and you won't get hurt."

Magnus strutted around the studio apartment, his bill jutted and retreated with each marching step. His basket of scarves were notably placed on the center of Rowena's empty daybed.

"You can stay as long as you pull your end of the rent and pick up after yourself. But I'm not your nursemaid or your friend. Waste of time that. I won't be here long enough for that to matter. Just do as you're told and pay down your karmic debt. Understood?"

A scrawny crow looked back at him, shivered, and stood silent.

"Well?" Magnus prodded.

"Y—yes, sir."

"Good. I will see you when I see you."

The new penitent watched as Magnus flew through the open window and mourned that he had such a cold and unfeeling companion. He would never know where Magnus went until the wee hours of the morning. Had he ventured out he might have seen him perch where he did every night, at the unmarked grave of his last friend.

Unbroken

Alexandra Christian

That stink comin' from the mash barrel don't do much to hide the smell of Caroline's body. Them devils that took her left her a-layin' out till she was plumb green in the face. Even now while Mama and Aunt Sadie are scrubbin' her down with lye and rosewater, I can smell it.

I 'member this one time Daddy and me was walkin' down yonder by the river and we got to smellin' the awfulest smell. It started kinda sweet like the late-summer honeysuckle right before it falls off the vine, but when we got closer the sweet turned to sour milk, sulfur, and copper all rolled up together. When we come 'round the bend, we could see an old coon dog layin' in the grass, kinda half in the river and half on the bank. Its body was all bloated and rank, its tongue swole up and lolling. I asked Daddy why the dog's fur was blowin' around when there w'ant no wind. When we got closer, I could see that it w'ant no fur, those was maggots crawlin' and a-writhin all over the belly. I 'member I jus' threw up right there.

Caroline smells like that old coon dog.

"Steer up that mash good, Betts. Granny Jude gon' need that 'shine ready to run tonight."

"Yes'm."

I pass the time with the turns of the stir stick. I can hear it scrapin' along the bottom of the pot. *One...draaaag... two... draaaag... three... draaaag...*I'm hopin' I can get so lost in the stirrin' that I can forget that my sissy's body, all bloated and blue is layin' by the fire on a bed of mountain laurel. Even in the shadows I can see the slashes and the hate they left all over her body. Places where the dried up blood is streaked all over her arms and legs still glisten in the moonlight.

I can feel the tears wellin' up in my eyes, makin' 'em burn. I don't want to cry no more. Seems like my whole face is tight and crackly like I been out on the mountain in January, but I jus' cain't stop 'em. My brothers, Bishop and Josh, they ain't cried this whole time, and they was the ones found Caroline up on the ridge. I asked Bishop if he was scared when he saw her and he jus' shook his head. "No Betsy-girl. I ain't scared." He had a funny look on his face when he said that.

There's a buncha shoutin' on the other side of the clearing and when I look up I can see 'em leadin' old Granny Jude down the path. Ain't no tellin' how old she is. She was at least a hunnert when she delivered me, and I'm eighteen nowadays. She uses a gnarled cane to pick her way through the rocks and roots breakin' up the ground. Bishop and his friend Timbo are standin' on either side of her, but she's steady as an old mare. She's strong like this old mountain a-holdin' us up, but I don't know if'n she's strong enough to work some evil. When she gets close, I can see that glassy, dead eye sparklin'. It makes me shudder and I have to look away. Bishop always tole me that if you look too close in that eye, you gon' see how you die. I ain' sure I b'lieve that, but I ain't gon' take no chances.

"Keep a'stirrin', Betsy-girl," Granny Jude says as she passes. She clasps my arm with those craggy fingers of hers. Her hand was cold as ice even though the fire under the pot was hot and the sweat's pourin' off my brow. "It's gon' make a fine spirit."

"Yes'm," I murmur with a nod. She offers a small, toothless smile and gives my arm another gentle squeeze. Her skin feels like moldy paper, but I don't pull away. Mama always says we gotta treat all our elders with respect, but especially the old Grannies. *One sligh' and they'll a-curse you good,"* she always said. I guess I'm lucky 'cuz Granny Jude always shined to me. Said I had the gift, whatever that means. There is one question burnin' in my brain, though, and 'fore I could stop myself I caught Granny Jude before she shuffled away.

"Granny Jude?"

She turned, smilin' like she knew what I was gon' say already. "Yes, chile?"

"Did... did Caroline... did she get cursed?"

That milky eye twitches, but Granny's face is kind. She takes my hand betwixt hers and leans in close. "A-course not, Betts. Our sweet Caroline was a good girl. She never crossed nobody. Them boys was jus' devils."

A sob come out before I knew what was gon' happen and I have to lean on the stir stick to keep from fallin' down. The tears is rollin' down my face, mixin' up with the sugar and the rye as they fall in the pot.

Granny Jude takes me by the shoulders and turns me 'round to face her. That glassy eye gleams in the dark, but the other eye is full of fire. "And devils always get their due."

Timbo leads her away and for just a second she keeps her gaze on me. It makes me feel some kinda way and the hairs on the back of my neck stand up. Bishop pulls up a chair right beside Caroline. I watch as Granny's old bones seem to groan and grind while she lowers herself gingerly to the wooden seat of the old-timey rockin' chair. For a few minutes she jus' rocks, the creaking of the old joints matchin' time with my stirrin'. It's the only sound in the holler, which I cain't help a-thinkin' is spooky. Usually, there's always birds a-squawkin' and the whisperin' hiss of the wind in them old pine trees, but to-night it's jus' as silent as the grave. It gives me a chill and I find myself steppin' closer to the fire under the mash pot.

"All right, Betsy-girl." I jump when Bishop's hand falls down on my shoulder. "Let's get that mash ready to run."

"There are loved ones, in the glory. Whose dear forms you of'n miss."

Granny Jude's voice is like dead leaves underfoot when she starts to sing. It's a song she always sung to us when we was jus' tee-taw-ncey. She said her great-granny used to sing it to her. It's such a sad song, but the gentle rhythm of it is a comfort tonight.

"When you close your earthly story, will you join them in their bliss?"

She ain't got no guitar and Bishop's old fiddle don't have all its strings, but Granny Jude don' need none of that. Her voice and the creakin' of that old rockin' chair keepin' time is all she's got to lull us into tonight's work.

My brothers come over and take the stirrin' stick from me. I step back to watch as they begin pouring the pungent mash into the cop-per still pot. Now more people are a-comin' down the path. My mama and Aunt Jessamine hold hands while Meemaw and Miss Grace lead the way into the grove. Cousin Sarah, Miss June, and the Owens sis-ters follow behind. One by one the women of the holler join the shod-dy circle, taking up the song until their voices rise over the trees and reverberate off the mountain face.

"Will the circle be unbroken, by and by; by and by."

Mama and Meemaw kneel down beside Caroline. They smile at her with all the love they got left in their hearts. Mama touches her face, brushing the fiery strands of her hair away. She sings the song in a sweet voice like a lullaby while Meemaw takes a rag from the washtub at her side. The women gather 'round and begin to wash the blood and muck from Caroline's arms and legs.

Granny Jude sees me still standin' on the edge of the grove. Her one good eye rolls over and while she don' say a word, I can feel that blind gaze boring into me. Slowly, I start walking to where they're bathin' Caroline. I ain't looked at her this whole time, afraid my poor heart would jus' break if'n I seen her. I can hear Mama n' Meemaw singin' to her so sweet when I get close, like she was just layin' there sleepin'.

"Is a better home awaitin' in the sky, in the sky?" Mama whispered as she brushed the soppin' wet sponge acrost Caroline's brow. I can smell the soap, made special jus' for tonight. Its strong scent burns my nose, but it helps. Meemaw takes my hand without missing a beat and pulls me down on the mossy ground beside her. The twigs of mountain laurel tear at my knees, but I don't dare say a word.

In the light of the fire, I can see Caroline. Her mouth is split from cheek to cheek in a bloody line. Her lips that was once so plump and pink are shriveled and torn, peeled back over broken teeth. Grisly black jewelry encircles her neck and wrists where they held her. When Mama picks up her hand, I can see little marks in the heels under her thumb.

"In the joyous days of childhood, oft they told of wondrous love."

The moonlight makes her eyelids sparkle and I can see slashes of blue paint. Mama said that when she went off to town that only vipers would be there waitin'. She warned Caroline about paintin' herself like a whore and wearin' high-heeled shoes. She said it would be nothin' but a heartache. That family was the only thin' we got on this earth and she better cling to what she got, but Caroline wan't the home-lovin' kind. She had big dreams and she meant to follow 'em. Caroline was my hero like that. She always said, "Betts, you got to go out there and take what's yours if'n you don't want to be stuck here, scroungin' for scraps."

I can barely see her face through the haze of tears in my eyes. "Look what leavin' got you, Sis."

"Pointin' to the dyin' Savior."

The sound of the wooden paddle scrapin' the last of the mash out of the pot is loud and I suck in the cool air. It turns to ice in my throat and I start chokin' and coughin' till the tears start a-runnin' down my cheeks. Such a little thing, but now I cain't stop. I bend down over Caroline, layin' my head against her cold, still chest. The rotten stink of her makes me gag, but I don't care. I can only cry harder for my poor, broken sis.

"Now they dwell with Him above."

There's a slight warmth on my back, gently patting me in time with the music. It ain't Mama or Aunt Jessamine or Meemaw, but Granny Jude that tries to comfort me. She comes down from her old rockin' chair and kneels right b'side me. I'm snifflin' and snottin', but she takes my hand and gives it a squeeze. "There now, Betsy-girl. You got ta be strong now."

I shake my head, wanting to block out her words. When she tries to put the old butcher knife in my hand, I shrink back, like it might be a snake. "No, Granny Jude. I cain't do it."

"You can," she said, placing the knife in my palm and closing my fingers around the hilt. "You will. For Caroline."

The song got louder as ever'one in the holler joined. Even the wind through the trees and the chattering of squirrels started to chant the revenant ritual. The orchestra of our voices rose over the mountain. It was a deafening roar and it hurt my ears.

"Will the circle be unbroken? By and by, by and by."

Bishop and Timbo light the still with a hollow whoosh. Blue flame lights up the grove and I can smell the gas heating up under the heavy copper pot. It's now or never, I'm thinkin'. My hands shake as my fist tightens around the knife. As soon as the fires are lit, Bishop and the other men back away. They know their part is done. As Granny says, the power of men don' hold no sway in the veil between this world and the next. Only women, God's own vessels of creation, can pull back the cobwebs and walk with the dead. Only women will be able to pull Caroline back from the shadow-land to take her revenge.

Granny Jude whispers gentle prayers in my ear as the blade comes down. First through the thin fabric of Caroline's favorite dress. The one Mama bought her for church when Sarah got married. Smart blue cotton with little pink roses and the lace around the collar. Daddy told 'em that dress was too much, but once Caroline saw it in the winder of the store in town, nothin' would do but she had to have it. Mama took in sewin' from the town ladies to pay for that dress and cuttin' the buttons off now is 'bout more than I can stand. I try not to notice the splatters of blood that stain the lace from where they cut her. Or the gashes on her neck and chest when I lay the dress open. The cuts look glossy and black in the moonlight next to the pearl skin of her belly.

"Granny, I cain't," I whine again, almost collapsing against the old woman. "They already sliced her up so bad. How can I cut her agin'?"

"Is a better home awaitin' in the sky, in the sky?"

She don't say a word, but guides my hand, pushing the blade through the hollow just under Caroline's throat. The blade is sharp, but the flesh is unforgiving. It takes more strength than I thought to push through. I expected there to be more blood, but I reckon Caroline's plumb dry. When the skin opens up, there's more of that rotten smell. I almost gagged, but I bit the inside of my cheek hard. I wan't gon' throw up on my beloved Sissy. Granny Jude never looked away as I drawed the blade down Caroline's chest, pushing hard through muscle and sinew. The knife catches on bone and I cain't get it to move. I look back at Granny Jude and she nods and takes the blade from me. I watch, fascinated as she saws at it. As the bone give way I can see the bright white of it against the dark blood that sat still in Caroline's veins. It's so peculiar. The more I cut, the more my sister looks like an old broken china doll.

"You remember songs of Heaven which you sang with childish voice."

The circle draws nearer. So close I can feel the gentle breath as they sing. Some spirit takes ahold'a me and I'm singin', too. Granny Jude puts the knife aside and dips her hand in the slimy, black death that oozes from Caroline's chest. She stands up easy as a she-cat and holds her hands above, swaying with the rhythmic voices. "Do you love the hymns they taught you?" Her voice is a shriek into the wind, like she was shoutin' to Lord Hisself. "Or are songs of earth your choice?"

"*Will the circle be unbroken*," the women sing, on their knees and crawling toward Caroline. Granny Jude draws the old symbols on her cheeks and forehead, then kneels down and does the same to me. I can smell the coppery, rotten bile that drips down my face and wets the collar of my dress.

"The circle is unbroken!" Granny Jude cries. "By and by. By and by."

The women begin to dip their hands into the wound and paint their own faces and arms. "The circle is unbroken," they chant. The wind rises with the sound and I can hear thunder in the distance. My eyes is so wide, watchin' the frenzy as the women writhe together. I can't look away, don't want to look away. We move together as one body, drawin' the power of Mother Earth into ourselves. The men just stand back and watch, transfixed by the strange magick that's drippin' from our lips and flesh.

In the midst of the ritual, Granny Jude grabs my shoulders and pulls me close. "We got to run this 'shine now, Betts." She points to the moon high above the trees. It busts through the gathering storm clouds, its beams creeping to the center of the grove.

"It must be close to midnight, Granny."

She nodded. "Yes, child. The witchin' hour its close at hand. We got to hurry before Caroline sours." It's a curious thing to say, but I know what she means. Caroline is a vessel, but the heathen spirit we've conjured is fickle.

Granny Jude says no more, but kneels beside the body, pullin' me down with her. I know what I have to do, but I don't think I can stand it. Ever'thing I ever learnt from Mama tells me that I'm gonna burn in the deepest fires of Hell for the desecration we've already done. I can't do what she wants. I'm cryin' so hard that I feel that bile a-risin' in my throat. "Quick now, girl."

"Granny... the devil gon' git us," I cry, shakin' my head. "Raisin' up Caroline, we'll be damned for sure!"

"Take the heart, child! Now, or the devil *will* git us!"

An empty vessel lyin' open invites evil. Granny Jude knows an uninvited comes quick. I bite my lip, steeling myself for what's to come. "Is a better home awaitin', in the sky? In the sky." I take up the song softly as I go about my work, slipping my hand into the ragged wound in my dead sister's chest. I closed my eyes, feeling my way through the rancid meat and stringy sinew.

"That's it, girl. You gots to feel your way."

"You can picture family gath'rins, round the fireside long ago."

My hand closed around the squishy cold muscle. I have to pull it out slowly, careful not to break apart the membranes that hold it fast to Caroline. The blood is congealed around it in a black, mucky ooze that sticks to my hands. Granny Jude uses the knife to clip the veins away so that I can lift it free of the corpse. The blood that drips from the heart is slow. It looks like the chocolate syrup on those hot fudge sundaes you get in town.

As Granny Jude cuts away the ganglia, I lift the heart carefully. Such an intricate thing should be handled with care. When I stare at it, it don't look the way I thought. Bishop and Timbo had found Caroline two days ago, so the blood inside was cold and still. The veins and branches were shriveled and black. When I walk with it over to the still site, I notice how much heavier it is than I expected. It isn't hard to imagine this muscular thing pumping blood through Caroline's body. How it must have gone faster and harder as her terror grew while they were hurting her. I closed my eyes, trying to block out the visions of her last moments on this Earth.

Then suddenly, without warning, I can feel this burning feeling in the pit of my stomach. It feels like the first horn of Bishop's apple rye shine a-boilin' and rumblin' 'round in my belly. I don't know what it is, and I start to say something to Granny Jude. Then I realize that it must be all that rage that's been buildin' inside me like the steam

in Daddy's still. When I look down at the broken heart in my hands,
I don't feel anymore sadness, just this burnin' rage. My sorrow had
been pluggin' up my soul like that goopy oatmeal paste around the
copper cap, but now nothin' but vengeance was startin' to ooze out.

Bishop come to me with his hands held out. I could see my reflection in his stormy blue eyes. I didn't look like myself anymore.
Not sweet baby Betsy-girl. All that innocence is gone now and only
bitterness ias left behind. It must scare Bishop 'cause his hands is
shakin' and he cain't look at me.

"And you think of tearful partings when they left you here below."
The fire is high under the copper still pot and the blue flames lick
and leap out from under it. Timbo takes my hand and pulls me back
a little. "Careful you don' get yer dress in the fire, Betts." I look down
at his hand, still holdin' mine like he's 'fraid to let go. His hand is
sweaty, but I keep it. I need somethin' to hold to while I watch Bishop
drop the heart into the pot with the rest of the mash.

"Will the circle be unbroken? By and by, by and by." My voice
sounds like it belongs to someone else. A voice from long ago. I've
sung the song a million times in church, but the words never meant
so much before. Their gentle rhythm is drivin' the magick and as our
voices rise, I can feel the spirits abidin' there in the grove.

Once the heart feeds the mash, all we can do is wait. Bishop and
Timbo take turns stirrin'   until it starts to boil. The steam rises and
I can smell the alcohol fumes, the wood fire, and the copper burnin'.
They put the cap on and start to paste up all the holes. We don't want
any of it to escape. The Revenant is greedy.

Behind us, the other women rush in and start to prepare Caroline. I can't help smilin' when all the little girls big enough to walk
come forward carryin' baskets. They don't seem to be bothered by
Caroline's body lyin' there. Seems like death is an old friend in the
holler and it's really just a game to them. Granny Jude sent 'em into
the woods to gather up as much foxglove and witch hazel as they
could find, along with wildflowers, bergamot, and mint. As the wom-

en cleaned Caroline's wounds, they stuffed the herbs into her chest, pushing them down so that her body was plump once more. When it was done, Granny Jude and I stitched her up with an old darning needle and Mama came with a new, blue dress.

In the end, Caroline was beautiful on her bed of mountain laurel. Her red hair brushed into the curls she loved, her lips stained with wild berries. Granny Jude squeezed my hand and I knew that Caroline was ready.

"One by one their seats were emptied. One by one they went away."

The singing is low now, as if we're all waitin' on the edge of a storm. Granny Jude sits back in her chair and begins to rock. She motions for me to come to her, but I want to stay with Caroline. For hours it seems, I sit down beside her, singing along to the dark melody. I take her hand. It's so cold, but I try to warm it between mine. I rock back and forth on the dewy moss. "Now the family, is all parted. Will it be complete one day?"

I hope so, Caroline.

"It's a-comin' out, Bishop!" The boys spring to action to catch the sacred 'shine as it starts to dribble out the worm. Bishop takes his trusty pecker bone out of his pocket and sticks it into the copper tube so the stream runs into the glass jar. He lets it run for a little while, then throws the liquid into the dirt behind the still. I asked Daddy once why they did that, and he said it was the death's head. If you drink it, it's poison. I don't think it'd make much difference to Caroline either way, but Bishop threw 'em out just the same.

When the first jar is full, Bishop brings it to Granny Jude for inspection. I stand beside her, watchin' as she holds the jar up to the moon, turning it in her gnarled fist and shakin' it a little. Again, I'm surprised by the look of it. Usually, Bishop's 'shine is clear as a bell, but this ain't right. The liquid looks thicker than water and there's a thin wisp of black that swirls around, lookin' almost alive. It don't mix with the rest, just moves unnaturally around inside.

"What's wrong with it, Granny?" I whisper.

"Nothin', child," she says, handing it back to Bishop. "The spirits is with us tonight."

Bishop collects the rest of the run and each jar seems to be...infected with this blackness. When the fire is out, the menfolk begin to drift away, leavin' us out here with Caroline. Most would say they'd rather not know about female magick. It's both fascinating and scary. I always thought that men was the strong ones, holdin' up the whole world, but the older I get the more I come to know that ain't true. Granny Jude says that men are of the earth, but women are pure fire. And I guess that's true. Women bring babies into the world and that's magick if I ever seen it.

Granny Jude pushes the jar of 'shine into my hand and everyone draws close until we form a circle around Caroline. "Come children," Granny says. Her voice is so strong even though we've been out in the cold for hours. "Our circle is broken tonight with the loss of Sister Caroline, gone too soon. Lord, tonight we ask that you make it right." She nods to me and I open the jar of 'shine. The sharp smell of the alcohol burns my nose and my eyes immediately start to water. Staring down into it, I would swear that I could see the faces of the family that's gone before starin' back. Maybe just a trick of the light and shadow, but I can see all of them there with fierce eyes that burn with vengeance.

"One by one their seats were emptied. One by one they went away." Granny Jude sings. "Now our family, reunited." She kneels down and I follow. Her withered old hand slides under Caroline's back and lifts her up a little. When she does this, Caroline's head falls forward, snapping her neck with an audible crack that makes my belly roll over. Granny Jude presses her lips to Caroline's cheek, whispering gentle words of comfort before easing her head back. Caroline's mouth flops open and it makes the gashes at either side gape making her look like one of those clown heads that pops out of a child's toy.

"By and by. By and by." Granny Jude whispers as I pour the 'shine into Caroline's throat. I can hear the liquid gurgling as it slides down the narrow path and into her belly. She sounds like an old sink drain half-blocked with muck and dead hair. My hands shake and I try to pull back, but Granny Jude shakes her head. "No, child. She's got to drink it all down. Ever' drop."

I bite the inside of my cheek, trying not to gag at the sound as I pour more of the drink into the lifeless corpse. Finally, just as the first mockingbirds begin to whistle for the dawn, the jar is empty.

Everyone is holding their breath, not sure of what's gon' happen next. We wait, watchin' Caroline's body. Our eyes are keen for any sign of life, but it doesn't come. The tears start to burn behind my eyes as I turn to gaze at Granny Jude. "I...I didn't do it right," I stammer. "It didn't work."

Granny Jude's thin, hard line of a mouth splits into a wide, toothless grin that was as grotesque as it was beautiful. "You give up too easy, girl. Our work's just begun."

She pats me on the arm and Bishop appears back at her side. She takes his arm and lets him lead her away from the circle. She leans heavy on his side, once more an addled old woman. I look around as the rest of the women, even Mama and Aunt Jessamine, start to make their way back home. I want to shout at them to stop. Who was gon' stay the night with Caroline? I din' think I could leave her in the dark alone again. But one by one they was gone.

"Come on, Betts." Josh stands beside me, stock still. The overalls he wears are stained with sweat and soot from the still, and the ends of his hair are curly and wet. My big brother Josh ain't scared of nothin', but I can see a wild look in his eyes that tells a different story. "Let's go to bed, now. Quick."

He pulls at my arm again, and this time I let him lead me back home.

Josh is one of those boys that can talk the horns off a brass billy-goat, but the whole way down the path he din' say a word. He had me by the hand, practically draggin' my exhausted self across the dead leaves and twisted roots. I want to slow down, and I start to whine, but Josh just shushes me and keeps going.

By the time we reached the house, Mama was already sawin' logs beside Daddy. Josh leaves me at the door of mine and Caroline's room and disappears to the other end of the house. I want to talk. My mind and heart is racin' and I don't think I'll ever get to sleep.

I pull off my clothes and leave them piled in the corner. They smell like woodfire and Lord help me, Caroline. I don't think I'll ever get that smell out. I lay down in the bed and pull the covers up to my chin. The wind outside picks up as that storm finally gets over the mountain. The howling in the trees sounds like the wailing of the banshee from the old stories Mama used to tell. I want to close my eyes, but every time I do I can see Caroline's horrible smile as I pour the jar of 'shine down her gullet. My heart is beatin' so fast I can almost see it pushin' against Meemaw's quilt.

The first clap of thunder draws a small shriek. I slap my hand over my mouth, hopin' I din' wake Mama. I wait for the sound of her angry feet on the creaky floor, but there's just silence. The thunder crashes again and I pull the quilt over my head. My breath is hot and suffocating, but I don't care. I don't want to see the lightnin' for fear her shadow might show itself outside my window.

The storm don't last too long. Mostly just a gentle rumble off the rock face. Maybe the storm was already there, or maybe we brung it with our ritual. Maybe it was like Gabriel's horn heralding the arrival of the Revenant spirit.

When I'm sure that the worst is over, I push the covers down, happy to breathe again. Out of the corner of my eye I can see there's a little glass of water on the bedside table. A little habit Mama had since Caroline and me was jus' babies. Leavin' a glass by the bed so we didn't have to get up. I sit up in the bed and take the glass. The first swallow is like Heaven, cooling me down from the top of my head to the tips of my toes. I drink deeply, gulping the water like I've been wanderin' the desert with Moses and the Israelites.

When I'm finished, I put the glass down and lie back against the pillows. My body is tired, but I don't want to sleep. I notice that it's still pitch dark, but the sky outside my window is startin' to go purple with little streaks of fire. When it gets like that, you can see everything in the room, but it looks like it's made of shadow. The dresser by the door, the closet with its rusty doorknob, Caroline's hope chest—I can see them, but they ain't quite there. The little figures that dance behind your eyelids swirl, distorting everything.

A shadow in the corner moves and suddenly my mouth runs dry. My breath hitches deep in my chest and I'm squinting my eyes, willing them to adjust. At first, I think it's just Mama's old dress dummy where she'd been mendin' my dress for Caroline's funeral. Then I see the wisps of red hair that fall in loose waves over one shoulder.

That fetid stench of mold permeates my room. The thing moves in a slow shuffle. Its arms are stiff at its sides and its hands look like claws. I know it's Caroline before it steps into the predawn light. It turns with a heavy groan and stares at me with a milky dead eye. The long, jagged gash where I cut her was still there, stitched up with Granny's thick, black thread. The edges glistened and black blood still seeped from it. I should be happy to see her, but this ain't my sister. This is the demon we summoned. Its gaze is so cold. The warmth and mischief is noticeably absent in those eyes. I want to call out to her, but my mouth is so dry and the words come out like a crackle of dry leaves.

"Will the circle..." The Revenant rasps. "Be unbroken. By and by..." I can hear tears in the voice. Such sorrow and confusion. It wanders around the room, running gnarled hands over the dresser and knocking perfume bottles and makeup cases to the floor. It stops for just a second and stares at itself. Bloody fingers slide over its cheeks and lips, leaving a dark smudge of color. The thing stands there, swaying to a silent rhythm as it strokes its hair and face. I'm holdin' my breath and prayin' to God it don't come near.

It makes an anguished cry as if suddenly it knows its purpose. It pulls at the straggly hair, crying and screaming as it starts to understand. How is it Mama don't hear? Why don't nobody come? I glance at the door, wonderin' if I can get away, but then it stops. It goes silent again, once more fascinated by the reflection in the mirror.

"Will the circle be unbroken, in the sky...in the sky."

The words to that old time hymn that are s'posed to be comfortin', now they just make my blood run cold. I can see the smoky breath risin' from my mouth as I try to keep breathin'. What we done tonight was evil, and someday we might have to pay for it. The Lord Almighty never forgets our sins, but like Granny always says: sometimes you got to fight the devil with the devil.

Caroline turns back, her blind eyes lookin' straight at me. I should be scared. I should scream, but some kinda peace settles over me like Mama's warm quilt. She presses a bony finger to her lips as she comes closer. I sit up in the bed, watching. Her slack jaw opens and closes, as if she's tryin' to talk, but nothin' comes but a sickening scrape like rusty hinges. She raises her hand and I can see the silver nail file. The one Caroline always kept in the dresser. She hid it from Mama, just like all her other makeup and hairbows. Mama said that stuff was 'ginst God. I guess she must have been right. At first, I think Caroline means to come at me with it, and I cower behind the pillows. But then she turns and stumbles out the door and into the hallway.

"There's a better... world a'waitin'... in the sky."

Contributors

Jody Lynn Nye

Jody Lynn Nye lists her main career activity as "spoiling cats." She lives northwest of Atlanta with three feline overlords, Athena, Minx, and Marmalade, and her husband, author and packager Bill Fawcett. She has written over fifty books, most of them with a humorous bent, and over 170 short stories. Jody has been fortunate enough to have collaborated with some of the greats in the field of science fiction and fantasy. She wrote several books with Anne McCaffrey or set in Anne's many worlds, including *The Death of Sleep*, *The Ship Who Won*, *Crisis on Doona* (a New York Times and USA Today bestseller), and *The Dragonlover's Guide to Pern*. She wrote eight books with Robert Asprin and has since his death continued two of his series, the Myth-Adventures and Dragons. She edited a humorous anthology about mothers, *Don't Forget Your Spacesuit, Dear!*, Her latest books are Rhythm of the Imperium (Baen Books), Moon Tracks (with Travis S. Taylor, Baen Books) and Myth-Fits (Ace). She is one of the judges for the Writers of the Future fiction contest, the largest speculative fiction contest in the world. Jody also teaches the intensive two-day writers' workshop at DragonCon. You can find her online on Facebook, Twitter, and her website, Jody Lynn Nye |

Gail Z. Martin

Gail Z. Martin writes epic fantasy, urban fantasy and steampunk for Solaris Books, Orbit Books, SOL Publishing, Darkwind Press, and Falstaff Books. Recent books include *Witch of the Woods*, *Sellsword's Oath*, *Inheritance*, and *Night Moves*. With Larry N. Martin, she is the co-author of the Spells Salt & Steel, Wasteland Marshals, Joe Mack and Jake Desmet series. As Morgan Brice, she writes urban fantasy MM paranormal romance including the Witchbane, Badlands, Treasure Trail, Kings of the Mountain, and the upcoming Fox Hollow series.

Find her at www.GailZMartin.com, on Twitter @GailZMartin, on Facebook.com/WinterKingdoms, at DisquietingVisions.com blog and on Goodreads https://www.goodreads.com/GailZMartin. Never miss out on the news and new releases—newsletter signup link http://eepurl.com/dd5XLj Follow her Amazon author page here: https://www.amazon.com/Gail-Z-Martin/e/B002BM8XSQ On Bookbub: https://www.bookbub.com/profile/gail-z-martin On Instagram: https://www.instagram.com/morganbriceauthor/

And get a free complete short story, Catspaw, here: https://claims.prolificworks.com/free/UAjd6

Join her Facebook group, the Shadow Alliance https://www.facebook.com/groups/435812789942761

Janet Walden-West

Janet Walden-West lives in the southeast with a pack of show dogs, a couple of kids, and a husband who didn't read the fine print. A member of the East Tennessee Creative Writers Alliance, she is also a founding member of The Million Words craft blog. She pens diverse Urban Fantasy and inclusive Contemporary and Paranormal Romance.

A 2X PitchWars alum, 2019 Pitch Wars Mentor, and Golden Heart® finalist, her debut multicultural Contemporary Romance, *SALT+STILETTOS*, released in April 2020 from City Owl Press. She is represented by Eva Scalzo of Speilburg Literary Agency.

Find her at:

Website: https://janetwaldenwest.weebly.com/

Facebook: https://www.facebook.com/janetwaldenwestauthor/

Twitter: @JanetWaldenWest

Instagram: https://www.instagram.com/janetwaldenwest/

Amazon: https://www.amazon.com/Janet-Walden-West/e/B07DD9FNQ5/ref=dp_byline_cont_ebooks_1

Bookbub: https://www.bookbub.com/authors/janet-walden-west

Goodreads: https://www.goodreads.com/author/show/18062729.Janet_Walden_West

Michele Tracy Berger

Michele Tracy Berger is a professor, a creative writer, a creativity coach and a pug-lover.

Her short fiction, poetry and creative nonfiction has appeared, or is forthcoming in 100word story, Glint, Thing, FIYAH: Magazine of Black Speculative Fiction, Flying South, Oracle: Fine Arts Review, Carolina Woman, Trivia: Voices of Feminism, Ms., The Feminist Wire,

Western North Carolina Woman, various zines and anthologies.

Her science fiction novella, *Reenu You* was recently published by Falstaff Books. Much of her work explores psychological horror, especially through issues of race and gender.

Nicole Givens

Nicole Givens Kurtz's short stories have appeared in over 30 anthologies of science fiction, fantasy, and horror. Her novels have been finalists for the EPPIEs, Dream Realm, and Fresh Voices in science fiction awards. Her work has appeared in Stoker Finalist, Sycorax's Daughters, and in such professional anthologies as Baen's Straight Outta Tombstone and Onyx Path's The Endless Ages Anthology. Visit Nicole's other worlds online at Other Worlds Pulp, www.nicolegivenskurtz.net

J. D. Blackrose

J. D. Blackrose loves all things storytelling and celebrates great writing by posting about it on her website, www.slipperywords.com. She has published The Soul Wars series and the Monster Hunter Mom series, both through Falstaff Books, as well as numerous short stories. Follow her on Facebook and Twitter. When not writing, Blackrose lives with three children, her husband and a full-time job in Corporate Communications. She's fearful that so-called normal people will discover exactly how often she thinks about wicked fairies, nasty wizards, and homicidal elevators, even when she is supposed to be having coffee with a friend or paying something called "bills." As a survival tactic, she has mastered the art of looking interested. She credits her parents for teaching her to ask questions, and in lieu of facts, how to make up answers.

Darin Kennedy

Darin Kennedy, born and raised in Winston-Salem, North Carolina, is a graduate of Wake Forest University and Bowman Gray School of Medicine. After completing family medicine residency in the mountains of Virginia, he served eight years as a United States Army physician and wrote his first novel in the sands of northern Iraq.

His novel, The Mussorgsky Riddle, was born from a fusion of two of his lifelong loves: classical music and world mythology. The Stravinsky Intrigue continues those same themes, and his Fugue & Fable series culminates in The Tchaikovsky Finale. His The Pawn Stratagem contemporary fantasy series, Pawn's Gambit and Queen's Peril, combines contemporary fantasy with the ancient game of chess. His short stories can be found in numerous anthologies and magazines, while those about a certain Necromancer for Hire are collected and available for your reading pleasure.

Doctor by day and novelist by night, he writes and practices medicine in Charlotte, NC. Find him online at darinkennedy.com.

Paige L. Christie

Raised in Maine, Paige L. Christie became obsessed with books after falling in love with the movie, *The Black Stallion*. When her mother presented her with a copy of the book the movie was based on, worlds opened up. It had never occurred to Paige that there was more to a story than what a movie showed. Imagine her joy at learning that novels had more to say than movies.

What followed was a revelation that stories could not only be read, but *written*. This led to decades filling notebooks with stories.

Two random Degrees later (in English and in Web Technology), the gentle prodding of a friend urged Paige into an experiment that broke loose Paige's writing in completed-novel-form for the first time. (No she was not bitten by a radioactive anything.)

Along the road to authorship, Paige had adventures in everything from weatherstick making to cross-country ski racing, white water raft guiding, wedding photography, website design, and the dreaded 'retail'. (Lots and lots and lots of retail.)

Her current obsessions include the study of Middle Eastern and North African folk dances, costume design, and dreaming up new ways to torture...err...*explore* her characters.

Paige resides in the mountains of North Carolina where she runs a small art gallery and wine shop. She spends her evenings writing speculative fiction, walking her dog, and being ignored by her herd of 3-legged cats.

A believer in the power of words, Paige tries to tell stories that are both entertaining and thoughtful. She enjoys stories with intense impact, and strives in her writing to evoke an emotional response in her readers. Especially of interest are tales that speak to women, and open a space where adventure and fantasy are not all about romance and happy endings.

Rebecca Wynick

Born Rebecca Sánchez, Wynick was raised in the Hudson Valley of upstate New York. She often reflects on the people and places of her youth in her writing. Of the first generation on both sides of her family to speak English as a first language, she was taught early on the importance of words—the right words. However, like many, she had to leave home to realize what she needed in a college was in her (metaphorical) backyard at her beloved SUNY New Paltz. There, she continued her education and received both her Bachelors and Masters degrees in English. Wynick later traded the Shawangunk Mountains of New York for those surrounding Asheville, North Carolina where she spends her day largely in the past—teaching about dead British writers. On weekends, she likes to treasure hunt with her husband, rummaging through estate sales, and collecting pottery and blown glass from local artists. She is enslaved by two cats that frequently let her know her services are lacking. However, her grown children seem to tolerate her better as she makes a mean cheesecake.

Alexandra Christian

Alexandra Christian is an author of paranormal and contemporary romance with an occasional foray into horror. Her love of Stephen King and sweet tea has flavored her fiction with a Southern Gothic sensibility that reeks of Spanish moss and deep-fried eccentricity. Her guiding principle as a romance novelist has always been to write romantic adventures for people who think they hate romances. After all, love itself is life's greatest adventure.

A self-proclaimed "Southern Belle from Hell," Lexx is a native South Carolinian who lives with an epileptic wiener dog and her husband, author Tally Johnson, in a small town in South Carolina. In addition to her writing, she also has unhealthy obsessions with supervillains, Sherlock Holmes and Star Wars. Her long-term aspirations are to one day be a best-selling authoress and part-time pinup girl. Questions, comments and complaints are most welcome at her website: http://lexxxchristian.wixsite.com/alexandrachristian

Backers

In late 2019, these generous backers supported the *Witches, Warriors, and Wise Women* campaign on Kickstarter. Prospective Press thanks them for helping to bring the Dream to life!

Stephanie A.

Robin Sturgeon Abess

Cadence Alvarez

Anonymous

Anonymous

Anonymous

Anonymous

Anonymous

Anonymous

Anonymous

Anonymous

Anonymous H.

Veronica Baker

Wil Bastion

Judy Black

Kari Blocker

Michelle Botwinick

Nyla Bright

Brynn

Thomas Bull

Laura Burns

Brookie Butler

Susan Carlson

Roselyne Caron

Mark Carter

A.Y. Chao

Stuart Chaplin

Allie Charlesworth

Brandi Clark

Georgina M Coates

Cyn Covert

Antoinette Cudney

Trevor Curtis

Deborah Davis

Shelby Dickinson

Jett Dixon

Viannah E. Duncan

Brandon Eaker

Moscabianca Edizioni

El

Lynn Emery

Jessica Enfante
Pierce A Erickson
Dori Etter
Mark Featherston
Judi Fleming
Deborah A. Flores
Thea Flurry
Todd Gee
CJ Gibson
Abi Godsell
Les & Kristen Gould
Cathy Green
Lynn K. Grimmedian
Sebastian H.
Eleri Hamilton
Jennifer Hancock
Benjamin Hausman
Julia Henken
Robin Hill
Cynthia Huscroft
Lilly Ibelo
Amelia Ikeda
Ludmilla J.
Jinx
Erik T Johnson
Kim Jonasson
Michael M. Jones
PJK
Kayliealien
Connie Somerville Kotkin
Nabia Libélula
Daniel Lin
Bernd Linke

Kaytlin Llwyd
Beth Byrne Lobdell
Spryte Long
James Lucas
Mark Lukens
Ajuan Mance
Alex Matsuo
Meesmar
Matt McBride
J. W. McCain
Ashley McConnell
Michael the horologist
Emily K Miller
Eben Mishkin
Sharon Moore
Tristin Magpie Morgan
Myrweleen
Jared Nelson
Linda Nesko
James Newman
Anaïs Noa
Bishop O'Connell
Amy O'Neal
Chance Parker
Erin Penn
Ben Pick
Mary E. R. Pulley
Catie & Matt Putnam
Scout Raven
Thomas C. Raymond
Jenny Reed
Rem
Leann Rettell

Jessica Robin

Heather E. Robyn

Scott Roche

L. Rolon

Dale A Russell

Laura S

Shell S.

Susan S.

Crystal Sarakas

Seleweleboo

Sofia Serrano

Christa Sheffield

Patti Short

Jason Sickmeier

Susan Simko

Crystal Smalling

Dedren Snead

Vicky Staubly

Alana M T

Andromeda Taylor-Wallace

The Selkie Delegation

Cartier Tiggs

Jose Tovany

Arlene Valencia

Benjamin Verdouw-Olges

Susan J. Voss

Victoria W

Rebecca Wagoner

Meghan Watts

Bill Walter

Jean Marie Ward

Evelyn Weidig

Steph Wetch

Michelle Wierenga

Jessa Willson

Sharon Wood

Christy Yow